HIDDEN QUEEN

LAS VEGAS MAFIA SERIES

AMBER ALLEE

Cover Design: Graphics by Stacy
Editing: Kristen Portillo @ Your Editing Lounge
Formatting: Stacey Blake @ Champagne Book Design

Trigger Warnings:
This is a mafia book. If you are not one who likes action, murder, or violence then this novel is not for you. This book is meant for audiences that are 18+ years old.

To the man who came into my life over nineteen years ago.
There is no one I'd want to do this life with but you.
Thank you for doing this journey with me. ♥

HIDDEN QUEEN

LAS VEGAS MAFIA SERIES

CHAPTER ONE

I'M AWAKENED IN MY PINK PRINCESS BEDROOM TO THE SOUND of yelling and screaming from the hallway. My door flies open with a bang against the wall startling me, and I see my nanny, Sarah, running over to me.

"Come, little one, we need to leave now!" she tells me in a frantic tone that has me frozen in place. What's happening?

Sarah rushes over to the corner of the room and grabs my backpack from the chair next to my vanity. She starts collecting clothing and anything else she can grab within arm's reach. I'm still in my mermaid nightgown sitting on my bed watching her in a daze. Why is she packing my things? Gunshots ring out down the hall pulling my eyes from her busy work.

"NOW, Lexi!" she screams, and it's enough to move me into gear. "Only take what you can fit into this backpack."

I nod and reach on my bed for my sandy-brown teddy bear named Xander. I move over to my vanity grabbing for my jewelry that Mommy and Daddy have given me. I can tell something bad is happening and tears are starting to form in my eyes. Why are we doing this?

"Lexi, put your shoes on, we have to exit out the window. Quickly, we don't have much time!" That's when more gunshots echo down the hallway and the yelling gets closer.

Sarah covers my mouth and moves me to the window. I'm scared, and my body starts to shake violently. What about my family? Are they getting out too? Who is shooting in the house? The smell of gasoline has reached my nose and I know we don't have much time. Sarah now has the window open and is throwing our things out. She grabs my hands and pulls my arms around her neck.

"Lexi, I need you to hold on to me and don't let go. Can you do that?" Something flashy catches my eye and I see fire and smoke coming from the bottom of the door. "Lexi!" she yells bringing my attention back to her. I nod and squeeze her tight around her neck.

It is still dark outside with the moon and stars still high in the sky as Sarah climbs down the lattice on the side of the house. We huddle in the dirt and bushes as men with guns walk by screaming orders at each other. Some have masks on and they're all dressed in black. Sarah has her hand covering my mouth still and the other is rubbing up and down my arm for comfort. We can hear one man bossing everyone around.

"The boss said to leave no survivors. Make sure they're all dead then light this place up!" he commands to the man in black and into a radio.

Once the area is clear, Sarah grabs me tight and we take off in a sprint across the lawn towards the wooded area at the back of the house. We finally make it to the wooded area only to stop to catch our breath. Looking back at my home, I can see the entire house engulfed in flames before explosions shatter the windows and the roof caves in. The sound of branches breaking behind us makes us turn quickly to see what may have caused the commotion. A man in black grabs for Sarah but is tackled to the ground by another man before he reaches her. Sarah is shielding me from the fight that has ensued, but I chance a peek through her arms. That is when I see Liam, my daddy's right-hand man, snap the other man's neck. Then he comes closer and pulls us into his arms.

Off in the distance, we watch as men are lined up in a straight row only to have a round of gunfire go off, making the men fall to the ground. I let out a small cry seeing the men being killed and Liam clamps a hand over my mouth to muzzle the noise. One man in black snaps his head

*up and lifts his mask as he turns toward the woods in our direction—
as if he can see us. I can almost see his face…*

My body bolts up from my sleeping position on the bed covered
in sweat. My breathing is erratic and heavy. *Not again!* I haven't had
one of these dreams in almost a year. This is the longest I've gone
without it resurfacing. Usually, something triggers it, and I realize
it must be because of the decision I made a week ago.

The dream is always the same with a little girl named Lexi who
is in a fire. My aunt and uncle say it's just my imagination. Maybe I
watched a movie once and a few memories from my childhood all
molded into this horrible dream that keeps reoccurring.

I glance over at the clock and see it is 5:48 a.m. Well, I might
as well get my day started. I doubt sleep is going to find me at this
point. After one of these episodes, it's a losing battle with my brain.
Throwing the covers back, I swing my legs off the side of the bed
and stand. My arms reach up toward the ceiling, stretching out my
muscles. My body goes on autopilot as I walk into the closet for my
running gear and make my way to the bathroom. Doing my morning routine, I pull up my hair, brush my teeth, and tie my laces, not
even bothering to look at myself in the mirror. In the kitchen, I grab
a pen and pad to write a note to my roommate, letting her know
I'm going to work out in the gym downstairs. I know Harper won't
be up at this hour but we always promised to let each other know
where we are since freshman year in college.

Harper Benson is a one-of-a-kind person. She's been my
roommate, best friend, and soul sister since freshman year at Texas
Christian University. We met at Frog Camp—an extended orienta-
tion for incoming students to TCU—the summer before we started
and have been attached at the hip ever since. We've been through
heaven and hell together over the years with boys, parties, finals,
and stalkers. Harper is five-nine with red hair, hazel eyes, and flaw-
less skin. She is beautiful and never worked out a day in her life.
She can pack food away like a chipmunk, and where it goes, I have

no idea. Her family lives in Florida and we make frequent trips out there for mini vacations. I love her family and they treat me as one of their own.

Toward the end of our freshman year at TCU, Harper went out on a few dates with a guy from our brother fraternity. Chad Hopkins was always a strange bird in my book, but if he made Harper happy, who was I to get in the way of that? After a few weeks, Harper didn't want to continue their relationship and called things off, but he continued to act as though they were still together. He called a hundred times a day or showed up at the dorms and would wait for her outside on the steps. We finally went to campus security to get some help and see what our options were. We also spoke to the President of his fraternity who promised he would handle it. Two weeks later shit hit the fan; he tried to kidnap her as she was walking home from class. Thank goodness some other students happened to be there to stop him. The police were called and he was arrested. Harper's parents flew in from Florida and stayed until the end of the semester to help ensure her safety. We didn't hear another word from Chad after that.

That summer we decided to leave TCU and the horrifying incident behind. After a substantial donation from the Benson family, we both transferred to Stanford University in California. Harper became a guarded person and had a hard time socializing at our new school. Gone was the carefree girl who would make friends everywhere she went, but this past year she has started coming out of her shell, even though she is still very cautious.

Besides my Aunt Sarah and Uncle Liam, Harper is the only family I have. When her family suggested a change in college, I hopped on that train not wanting to be away from my best friend. Aunt Sarah and Uncle Liam understood the trauma she went through and helped make it a smooth transition. We spent the next three years at Stanford, and Harper is slowly starting to come back to her usual self. When she locked herself away from the world, she turned to video games and now is an expert on just about every game out there. Finally, after giving her the time and space she needed, I stepped in and forced her back into the land of the living. I am a social person by nature and drag her out everywhere with me.

We just graduated two weeks ago and as far as my aunt and uncle know, we are traveling to as many big cities as we can for the summer before we start classes to gain our master's degrees. Little do they know, I received a letter in the mail from a Victor Slater who runs a mega empire in Las Vegas, and I'm to be his intern for the entire summer. My duties are to shadow him and see how a big business is managed, which is my dream job, but Las Vegas is the battleground of all the arguments I have had with my aunt and uncle over the years. Every time a vacation comes up with my friends they are constantly telling me that Las Vegas is off limits.

The most recent argument with Sarah and Liam about Las Vegas replays in my mind when I mentioned Sin City over this past spring break.

"No, Kendall. We have talked about this and Las Vegas wouldn't be good for you," Uncle Liam argues placing the dishes in the sink.

"Why not? Everyone my age wants to go and experience it," I argue.

"Kendall, we told you about how your father had a horrible gambling problem and never recovered from it. He got into some trouble out there with several unsavory guys. Your mother took a liking to alcohol and drugs and started to develop a dependency. We just don't want you to struggle with the same demons they did. Vegas is a very influential place and we don't want you to get sucked into the flashing lights and glamour of it all."

"Going once won't cause me to develop a gambling problem or become an alcoholic, Uncle Liam. I just want to go and have some fun with some friends, that's all."

"You have your whole life ahead of you and I won't let you throw it away to that awful place. The answer is no. I'm not going to say it again." He storms out of the room ending the discussion.

"AH! You're being so unreasonable! I can make my own choices, you know. I am an adult now," I whine, petulantly at his retreating back.

"Kendall, we only want what is best for you and for you not to make the same mistakes that your parents did," Aunt Sarah chimes in to smooth things over like she always does.

I think they're worried the gambling and risqué nightlife will corrupt me. If they only knew the things college has to offer. Regardless, here I am for the next twelve weeks in a once-in-a-lifetime opportunity in hot as hell Las Vegas, Nevada.

In the gym, I stretch my muscles and head over to the treadmill to start my five-mile run. Once my earbuds are in place, I set a good pace on my hamster wheel and get after it. It's more than I normally do, but after having this nightmare I usually beef it up, as if I'm trying to run away from something or someone. After making good time, I wipe the sweat off and gulp down the bottle of water from the mini-fridge against the far wall. Once my heart rate is back to normal, I start a circuit on the weightlifting machines in front of the mirrors.

Leaving the gym, I walk over to the concierge in the front lobby and see Cynthia working behind the desk. I give her a warm smile as I approach her. "Good morning, Cynthia!" I say cheerfully. "I was wondering if you got my email about needing to use the spa for a massage, manicure, and pedicure for myself and Harper?"

"Yes, of course, Kendall! I have you both booked for an hour-and-a-half massage at two. The pedicures and manicures are scheduled for three forty-five. Light refreshments will also be available," Cynthia recites checking over the computer screen. "I have Sandra for you and Connie for Harper. Is there anything else I can help you with?"

"Not at all. Thank you so much for doing this. I know how hard it is getting in with only a two-day notice." I give her my sincere thanks.

"That is what they pay me the big bucks for!" She giggles at her own joke, and we say our goodbyes before I head back up to shower.

The darkness under Harper's bedroom door tells me that she's still not up, so I grab the note off the counter, trash it, and walk to my bathroom to rinse off my sweat. The hot shower is just what I need to wash away all my tension. Throwing on my plush robe, I grab my laptop and jump on my bed to get a little research done on Mr. Victor Slater and all his businesses. I want to make the best impression because I know this opportunity is going to change my life.

"Shit!" I mutter after just poking myself in the eye with mascara. "I can't believe we agreed to do this, Harper. This is the last bet I ever make with Gracie. I swear she had some kind of inside tip to those fights."

I hate being set up on dates, especially when it's to a wedding where I don't know anyone. I love to have fun, but it helps when I know more than two people in a room. We've only been living in Vegas for a little over a week, and on the first day, we met Gracie Dawson, who lives across the hall from us, the only other occupant on the top floor of this complex.

"Come on, Kendall, it can't be that horrible. At least you get her hot brother, Wyatt. I got stuck with the brother's friend, Gabe. I spotted a picture of Wyatt in Gracie's apartment and he is one fine piece of—"

"Harper!" I shout cutting her off. "Why do you always have to be so crude? First off, we don't even know these guys, they could be creeps. Secondly, we're going to a wedding where we don't know anyone but each other. And finally, I have an internship that starts Monday and I need to prepare for it. I should be focusing on that and not worrying about this stupid blind date," I huff out. At least if it were at a public place and things went south we'd be able to slip out and grab a cab, but a wedding means we're stuck until everyone is ready to go.

"Kendall, tonight is about fun and letting loose. We just graduated; this will give us a chance to meet new people. Who knows you might be able to network at the wedding and land an awesome job after this internship is over. This is a fresh start for us to get out there and start our adulthood!" Harper says more to herself than me. She is getting really good at giving pep talks lately. She has made such great strides, and for her to want to do this is huge. I need to suck it up and pull on my big girl panties. A bet is a bet.

When we hear knocking on the front door of our apartment, Harper tosses the makeup brush on my bathroom counter and bolts out the door.

"I got it! Must be Gracie," Harper yells over her shoulder.

A few moments later Harper comes into my bathroom with Gracie, who is carrying several clothing bags and a makeup case.

"What up, bitches! Ready to pay up on your lost bet!" Gracie boasts. She places the bags on the hook behind the door and plops herself down next to us while pulling out makeup. Gracie is in her final year here at UNLV and a total social butterfly who doesn't know the word no. From the moment we met her, she's been a giant ball of energy; her personality is the size of Texas and it makes it hard not to like her.

One by one we finish up with the makeup—Gracie is a natural beauty and doesn't require much to make herself presentable—before taking turns styling the others' hair. Once I am finished, I head out and grab three glasses and a bottle of *Dom Perignon* from our fully stocked wine cooler and head back into the bathroom. I pour the champagne for each of us and sit back to watch them curl and spray their hair.

Thinking back to a week ago, I remember exactly what got me into this situation. Harper and I had met Gracie as we were moving our things into our apartment, and we all decided to go out to a nightclub called 1 OAK to celebrate our coming to Las Vegas. Drinks were flowing, and some of Gracie's guy friends from college noticed her and came over to sit with us. The conversation turned to sports and before the end of the night, Gracie and I had a 'friendly' bet over who was going to win in an upcoming UFC fighting match. The loser had to fulfill any request by the winner for one night with no complaints. She has the hottest Porsche 718 Cayman sports car and I was planning on driving it around for a few days. Thinking I watched enough Mixed Martial Arts to accurately predict the winner, I thought it would be a fun bet. Now, one week later I'm here fulfilling my loss by accompanying her brother to their cousin's wedding. Harper just got pulled into this because Wyatt's friend, Gabe, didn't have a 'suitable' date to bring with him. I bet these guys are total douchebags if they can't find a suitable date on their own to take to a family event.

"Are you guys ready to see our outfits for tonight!" Gracie jumps up from the chair after spraying a last puff of hairspray. She bounces over to the clothing bags and unzips them.

She pulls out three of the most gorgeous dresses I've ever seen. The first is Armani, a beautiful ultra-blue one-shoulder bow gown. The second is a La Petite Robe di Chiara Boni, an elegant black one-shoulder ruffle gown. Lastly, Gracie pulls out a fitted one-shoulder St. John in the color Tanzanite. 'Perfect' is the only word to describe this beauty. Each of these dresses must have cost a fortune and Gracie is standing here with three of them, tags still attached.

"Here, Harper, I think you'll look best in this one." Gracie hands Harper the La Petite Robe di Chiara Boni. "You and Gabe should match perfectly."

Harper takes the dress and heads to the bedroom to change out of her robe.

"Kendall, I think Wyatt is going to flip his lid when he sees you in this one." She passes me the St. John and I almost pass out when I glance at the price tag.

Harper and I come from money. Her family owns a few large shipping companies at several ports in Florida, and I have a large trust fund from my deceased parents that I received when I turned eighteen. Not to mention my aunt and uncle do very well with an automotive repair chain back in Texas. Regardless, I was never one to go crazy and spend *this much* on a dress.

"Thank you, Gracie, this is a beautiful dress. I hope it fits."

Gracie smiles at me and we head out of the bathroom and into my bedroom to get changed. Once we're all zipped up, we take turns observing ourselves in the mirror. I'm pretty sure this is the nicest wedding I'll ever go to in my life, and it's certainly grander than any sorority formal we went to in college.

"Here put these on. The limo will be here any minute to take us to my parents' house to pick the guys up." Gracie hands us each a box.

When we open them we see matching silver crystal-studded red-bottom high heels. Holy cow, I am going to be walking around in almost $4000 worth of clothing and shoes.

"Gracie, this is too much. I feel like we're going to be over-dressed for a wedding," I say as I twirl around in front of my mirror like a little girl playing dress up.

"Kendall, we're not overdressed. Trust me. I know my family, and we only do over-the-top events. You'll see that you and Harper will fit right in," she assures me.

Gracie heads back to her place to get her accessories and Harper goes to her room to find jewelry to match her dress. I walk over to my own jewelry box and peek through my jewels. I pull out the chandelier diamond earrings my aunt and uncle gave me for graduating college and put them on before opening the next drawer where I find my diamond cuff and place it on my left wrist. I look at myself one last time in the mirror and head out into the living room to wait for the girls to finish up.

The condo we're renting is in the *Park Towers* at Hughes Center. We have three bedrooms and three and a half bathrooms with over thirty-five hundred square feet. The view alone is spectacular, especially at night when all the brilliant lights of the Las Vegas Strip and the grand hotels come to life. The condo was already furnished when we moved in, but Harper's parents bought little things in blues, browns, and cream colors to make it our own for the next three months, and the amenities are the best Vegas has to offer. We have a full spa downstairs along with a gym and a restaurant. We also have a doorman along with a security company in the building because feeling safe was a prerequisite for Harper's parents when we moved here from Stanford.

I take a seat on our chocolate leather sofa and try to calm my nerves that are slowly starting to fray at the thought of meeting the guys. Sure, I can hang out with a group of them and have a good time, but being set up gives me a little anxiety. Harper finally joins me and after a few minutes, Gracie knocks, letting us know it's time to head out. We both grab our clutches and make our way to the elevator and then to the black limo that is waiting out in front of the lobby. Security greets Gracie and holds the door open for us as we exit.

After only being in the limo for a few minutes, Gracie grabs a chilled bottle of champagne and pours each of us a glass. I need to pace myself with all of the champagne we've been drinking.

"To a fun night with family and new friends!" she says bouncing in her seat.

We all clink glasses and take a drink as we head north on Highway 15. About ten minutes later we're turning west onto Summerlin Parkway. Harper and I are taking in the scenery when Gracie receives a phone call and gets into a deep discussion with whoever is on the other line.

"Hey, girls, that was my mom. She said the boys had to deal with an issue at work and are running a little behind. Not to worry though; I can give you the grand tour while we wait," she explains putting her phone back in her clutch.

The limo pulls past a gated golfing community and the houses are enormous. We turn down the last street and encounter another gate with heavy security. After being allowed to enter, we pull up to an exceptional two-story massive Mediterranean-style estate. It more resembles a private resort on a tropical island. The landscaping alone probably costs as much as our condo just for the upkeep. We exit the limo and step onto the brick-laid driveway when the black front door opens. A middle-aged woman steps out with dark hair and piercing blue eyes. She's wearing a lilac-colored gown shaped perfectly for her tiny body.

"Hello, girls! I'm Gracie's mother, Mary Dawson. Welcome to our home, come on inside out of this heat and I'll get you something to drink while we wait for our men," she offers and stops in her tracks when she takes me in. It looks as though she's seen a ghost and I quickly glance behind me to see if maybe someone else has arrived. When I turn back, Gracie's mother has her hand over her chest and is scanning me from head to toe. Weird, if I wasn't feeling insecure before, I am now. Does she not like what I'm wearing?

"That would be lovely. Thank you, Mrs. Dawson," Harper speaks up to break this awkwardness, and Mary seems to shake herself out of whatever just happened.

"None of that Mrs. Dawson business; call me Mary, please. Mrs. Dawson is my mother-in-law."

We both nod as we continue into the house. Once in the foyer, I notice the walls are marble along with the floors and lead to a grand staircase towards the back of the room. The center has a circular table with freshly cut flowers, no doubt from her plethora of bushes and landscaping along the outside of the house. Everything is spotless, not an object out of place. To my left, I see the dining room that could fit about fifteen people. One entire wall is covered with floor-to-ceiling windows overlooking a garden. To my right, is a formal living room with a marble fireplace and FOUR different sitting areas. Who do they entertain that would need this many?

Mary walks us down past the staircase and to the left where the kitchen and another living area are located. The kitchen has dark cherry wood cabinets with a marble backsplash and marble countertops. There is a woman dressed in a knee-length black skirt and white blouse rinsing off a plate at the sink when we enter.

They say everything in Texas is bigger but I'm starting to think everything in Nevada is over-the-top extravagant.

"Linda, these are Gracie's friends who live across from her apartment. Could you please get us some drinks while we wait for the men to get here?" Mary asks.

"Yes, Mrs. Dawson, right away." Linda wipes her hands with a dishrag and walks over to a small counter to retrieve glasses and a bottle of champagne.

"Thank you, Linda," I say, and offer her a smile when she hands us our glasses. I feel so out of place here, but at the same time, I feel like something is so familiar about Mary. She seems so motherly like I've known her for years.

"Would you girls like to go to the sitting room for a little while and enjoy some fruit and chat with one another? I'm just dying to know how Gracie is behaving these days and to get to know you two a little better. Gracie has spoken very highly of you both."

"Mother! You are not going to interrogate my friends. You promised," Gracie whines and crosses her arms over her chest.

Mary just waves her daughter off as we grab our glasses and make our way out of the kitchen and into a room that looks out over the backyard. The sun is almost down and the backyard and patio are overly lit. *Their electric bill must be through the roof.*

"So, Kendall, where are you from?" Mary asks before taking a sip of her drink and leaning back in her chair. I notice Harper and Gracie are talking about our plans for the Fourth of July, which is still a month away.

"Well, I grew up in Fort Worth, Texas with my aunt and uncle. After high school, I was accepted to Texas Christian University, where I met Harper. We transferred our sophomore year to Stanford University and we got our undergraduate degrees in business a few weeks ago. We've decided to come here to Las Vegas because I got an offer for a summer internship," I explain as she inspects every inch of me. I feel like I'm being strip-searched just from her gaze. *Do I have something in my teeth or on my face?*

"That's lovely, dear. Where are your parents?" she asks never breaking eye contact.

"Mom! Stop with the fifty questions. When are Dad, Gabe, and Wyatt getting back? We're going to be late and you know I hate being late for anything."

I'm grateful for Gracie's interjection. Talking about my family is always hard for me, even after all these years.

"Soon honey, calm down. You know they won't start without us." Mary waves her off and focuses back on me.

"May I use your restroom?" I ask feeling too nervous with all of these personal questions. Sure, give me a crowd and I can have them eating out of the palm of my hand, but focusing on my parents makes me sweat bullets. She must be trying to get a feel for if I am good enough to hang out with her daughter. Or maybe her son?

"Of course. Go past the kitchen and hook a right down the hallway. It's the second door on the left."

I thank her and make my way to my destination. After using the facilities and washing my hands, I survey my appearance in the mirror. Everything looks to be in place and nothing is on my face or teeth, so why was Mary staring at me like that?

I'm brought out of my thoughts when loud voices echo in the hall. I can tell they're a little farther away from the bathroom but I can still make out some of the conversation.

"I don't care, Wyatt! This is not how we handle business! If you ever want to take over, you need to learn how to control your temper. There are certain relationships we must maintain to keep the peace! Get yourself in check or else!" a man's voice booms.

"He shouldn't have disrespected us like that! He had it coming anyway from the last time we did a pickup. We can't allow people to show us disrespect!" another voice yells.

"I don't care! I'm in charge until my body is cold in the ground. The next time you go off like this, you'll see the consequences. Do you hear me?!"

"Yes, sir." I hear a man's voice, but it is almost a whisper.

"Now go and get cleaned up, we have to leave soon." It's quiet for a beat before a door slams, making me jump.

Wow! What was that about? I wait a few moments before exiting, hoping they've had plenty of time to pass the bathroom. I turn the knob slowly, open the door, and hurriedly rush out to get back to the girls before anyone knows I've heard their conversation. Only I bump into a human wall. My body bounces off rock-hard muscle, and my feet falter as I reach out to latch onto anything that will stop me from falling. My hands find purchase on the shirt of this person and in turn, the person grabs my upper arms tightly to keep me upright.

"Sorry," I say and gape at the person I crashed into.

In front of me is a guy who jumped straight out of a GQ mag-azine. He has short dark-brown hair, spiked in the front, and pierc-ing blue eyes. His lips are full and cover a perfect set of white teeth, and his five-o'clock shadow makes him even sexier. He stands about six feet tall maybe more and built from what I can tell by hold-ing onto him. The feel of him this close to me does things to my body. He exudes power and sex. The smell of his cologne is doing my head in. Please be my date tonight. *Good God, Kendall, breathe before you pass out.*

"Can I let go now or are you still going to fall?" he chides in an annoyed tone. Man, I wish he would have kept his mouth shut. *Way to ruin a moment, dude.*

Remembering myself, I let go of his crumpled shirt and take a step back even though my body wants to mold to his again. "Yeah, sorry. I didn't expect anyone to be outside the door."

"Well, maybe try looking both ways next time."

Asshole.

"Thanks for the advice. I'll remember this house has bathroom monitors next time," I snap back. I take another step away from him and get a better glance at the man in front of me who has caused my panties to dampen. He's wearing a black pinstriped suit, with a white button-down that has the top two buttons undone. Very stylish and very expensive attire for someone his age. I would say he's probably a few years older than me.

"You do that," and without another word, he stalks down the hall before disappearing around the corner.

Once he is out of sight, I try to calm my breathing, feeling my blood pressure rise after having to deal with such a hot arrogant prick. I retrace my steps the way I came towards the sitting room to meet back up with the girls and I can't help but wonder, *were those blood droplets on the collar of his shirt?*

CHAPTER TWO

I SHAKE OFF THE FOUL MOOD BROUGHT ON BY THE handsomely rude stranger in the hallway and make my way back to the ladies, who have now moved into the kitchen. Harper and Gracie are sitting on barstools and I try to gracefully walk over and sit beside them.

"Did you find the bathroom alright, honey?" Mary asks.

"Yes ma'am, I did."

"Good, good. I was just telling Harper since we all are going to be getting home pretty late from the wedding, you girls can just stay the night and join us for brunch and a swim tomorrow," Mary suggests from across the kitchen counter.

I am about to respond when a tall older gentleman struts into the room like he owns the place. He has salt and pepper hair and is wearing a black tux. He appears to be in his early fifties and very well-built.

He's greeted passionately by Mary. "Oh, you're home, honey!" She hugs him tightly and kisses him eagerly on the lips in front of us, and it almost feels like we're intruding on a private moment.

"Don't worry you'll get used to it. This is how they always are when they see each other," Gracie whispers to Harper and me as she rolls her eyes and makes a gagging noise. I'm used to the shows of affection though, as my aunt and uncle are the same.

"Come, I want to introduce you to Gracie's friends who live across from her," Mary says and leads the man over to us.

"Dad, this is Harper Benson. Harper, this is my dad, Bobby Dawson"

He shakes her hand as we stand to greet her father. "Pleasure to meet you, Harper. I know some Benson's on the East Coast. Any relation?" he asks.

"Yes, I'm from Florida. Doug and Jennifer Benson are my parents. They own a few shipping companies at several ports along the coast." She smiles at the same time Mr. Dawson does in recognition.

"Of course, I've done business with Doug for years. I didn't realize his daughter had grown up so quickly. What brings you over to this side of the country?" he asks.

"Oh, well, we went to college at Stanford and graduated a few weeks back. We're starting our masters in the fall," she informs him.

"That's fantastic! I am sure your parents are very proud," he says warmly and then turns to me. I see his eyes widen and his smile falters a bit. A small gasp leaves his mouth when he takes me in. Mary clutches his arm and he quickly recovers. *What is up with her parents?*

"Dad, this is Kendall Drake. She and Harper are roommates," Gracie explains.

"Kendall, it's lovely to meet you. Gracie raves about how wonderful her neighbors are. It's a pleasure to finally place a face with a name. Are you from Florida also?" he asks as if trying to subtly see if I also come from a well-to-do family.

"Nice to meet you too, sir. No, I grew up in Texas and attended both TCU and Stanford with Harper. We both have the same degrees and are working towards our master's degree."

"None of this sir business. Call me Bobby. Only people I do business with call me sir, and if you are a friend of Gracie's then you're family."

At the sound of footsteps entering the kitchen area, we turn to see who they belong to, and two guys arrive to stand at the end of the kitchen counter. One is tall, blond-haired, muscular build with a sexy smile and hazel eyes. The other is the sexy, arrogant prick from the hallway. They both look exceptionally handsome in their tuxes. Mary moves to greet them both with hugs and light kisses on their cheeks before leading them over to where we're all standing to make the introductions.

"Boys, these are your dates, Harper Benson and Kendall Drake. Girls, this is Wyatt, our son, and his best friend, Gabe."

Why do I feel like we're in high school going to prom? This is so uncomfortable. *Why did I agree to this?*

"Well, since a bet is a bet, Wyatt and Kendall are paired up, which leaves Gabe and Harper." The little matchmaker rubs her hands together and bounces on her feet. As if the night couldn't get any worse. Of course, I get the arrogant one who has a chip on his shoulder. I should've known he was Wyatt with the way he and Gracie look so similar.

When Gabe reaches to take Harper's hand and kisses the back of it, she lets out a small giggle. Oh boy, she's a goner. Wyatt makes no move to greet me other than a nod and I am perfectly fine with that. I come across arrogant men all the time in my business classes who I've had to suck it up and be pleasant to; he's no different. I can only hope the evening ends quickly. I should probably continue to drink to make the time pass faster.

"Okay, well since you kids like to stay out at all hours of the night, your mother and I will be taking a separate car. That way we can leave early if need be. Come, let's go." Bobby commands the last part with such authority I almost expect him to snap his fingers.

Everyone moves quickly to keep up with him when he turns on his heels and heads for the front of the house. We make our way to the limo while Bobby and Mary get in the back of a dark-colored Bentley. There are also two extra SUVs in the driveway, one in front of the Bentley and one behind our limo like a motorcade. I swear this family must be as important as the president. *Why do they need escorts?* I need to get Harper alone and speak to her about this. Who are these people?

In the limo, Gracie is the only one rambling on about nothing in general. *This is so painful and unpleasant.* My date hasn't even glanced up from his phone since we entered the car.

"Gracie, where is your date tonight? You do have one, right?" Harper asks when Gracie pauses for a fraction of a second.

"Oh yes! He is one of the groomsmen." Gracie swoons with a glint in her eye. "Jackson is so dreamy!"

I roll my eyes and let a giggle slip out. Sometimes, I think she's still in high school crushing on a celebrity.

"So, Kendall, what is it you do?" Wyatt surprises me when he pockets his phone in his jacket and turns his attention to me.

"Harper and I are students at Stanford getting our master's degrees," I state.

"In what?" Gabe jumps in.

"EMBAs, Executive Master of Business Administration. I want to be a CEO of a Fortune 500 company one day," I comment proudly. "What about you, Wyatt?" *See I can be pleasant and engaging.*

"I'm Dad's right-hand man in the family business. I—"

He's cut off by Gracie. "We own restaurants, hotels, and a bunch of other places and things. Dad has his hands in a lot of different pies." She lets out a nervous laugh.

We all fall silent, not sure what else there is to say until Harper pipes up. "Kendall has an awesome internship she's starting soon!" she says, trying to make small talk and clearly not picking up on the tension in the car. "It's the reason we came to Vegas."

"Really? Where at?" Gracie's voice sounds a little sad. "Why didn't you say anything?"

"I'm sorry, Gracie. I thought I'd mentioned it when we were moving in. I received something in the mail offering me an internship shadowing the boss a few hours a week for the rest of the summer," I share hoping to lighten the blow.

"It's fine, no big deal. Where at? Some place cool I hope!" And like flipping a coin, Gracie is back to her normal self.

"Well, it's the CEO of Slater Industries. I'll be shadowing Mr. Victor Slater for the duration of the internship."

I see Wyatt tense beside me and notice Gracie's mouth has gone slack. Gabe rubs his palms up and down his thighs and closes his eyes. Did I say something wrong? I peek over at Harper and she has the same inquisitive facial expression I feel I must be wearing.

"You can't be friends with Gracie and work for that bastard!" Wyatt says, raising his voice.

What?

"I'm sorry, what did you say?" I snap before I can stop myself. Maybe I heard him wrong. I focus my gaze on Gracie and she still has her mouth open, glaring at Wyatt, but not saying anything.

"I. Said. You will not hang out with Gracie or have anything to do with her if you go to work for that lowlife, bottom feeder, BASTARD!" he grits through his teeth, and I shift in my seat to move away from him. His expression is tight and he flexes his fingers into fists.

"Kendall, our family has bad blood with Slater and those he surrounds himself with. We don't associate with anyone who has ties with him," Gracie finally explains. I can only stare at her not knowing what to say. This is going to be awkward since I start on Monday. The following silence in the limo is unbearable as we all just stare at one another.

Thankfully, we arrive at the church and stand together waiting for Bobby and Mary to get out of their car to join us, but before they can, Wyatt takes me by the elbow and leads me away from the group. Harper sees this and is about to say something but is distracted when Gabe blocks her way.

"What now, Wyatt?" I hiss. "My dress is not the right color or I'm too tall to be your date?" I yank my arm out of his grasp refusing to acknowledge the tingling I feel when he touches me.

"Listen, I'm sorry about being so abrupt in the car. You

surprised me by saying Slater's name. I don't do well hearing it. Can we just get through this evening with a smile on our faces for my family and Gracie? We can discuss this internship business later." Is he for real? I want to hail the next cab home and never see him again! He must see my reluctant expression because he adds, "I promise to be on my best behavior the rest of the evening. Cross my heart." He says it mockingly and holds up the Boy Scout hand sign. I'd bet my trust fund he has never been a Boy Scout.

"Fine, but another tantrum like that and I'm leaving." My aunt and uncle have always made sure I stood up for myself, and would never allow anyone to disrespect me in any type of way, which is why I add, "And if you ever raise your voice to me again, I will break your nose!" I shoulder-check him as I walk back to the group that is now waiting for us to walk in.

"Is everything okay?" Mary asks looking between Wyatt and me.

"Everything is perfect, Mom." I flinch when Wyatt puts an arm around my waist, and Mary raises an eyebrow but doesn't say anymore. We fall in line with the rest of the group who are walking in the church. "You look amazing by the way," he whispers in my ear provoking goosebumps to erupt down my body. *Not now Kendall! He's an asshole that deserves an ass-whooping.* When I chance a quick look up at him, however, his eyes are different, almost soft and lustful. I whisper a thank you and his hold on me tightens. He looks as if he wants to say more but we're ushered through the doors of the church.

The sanctuary is packed and everyone turns their bodies to where we're walking to our seats. Wyatt has my arm intertwined with his now and his head is held high as we are guided to the front of the room. As we approach the third row from the pulpit, I notice all the men give Bobby a nod as he struts by. Bobby and Mary let us into the pew first so that they are seated on the end, closest to the center aisle. It isn't long after we take our seats that the music begins. *Were they waiting for us to start?*

The ceremony is elegant and beautiful and short, thankfully. Now and then I catch Wyatt looking over at me, especially during the vows, and after, we take a quiet ride in the limo to a magnificent banquet hall. The place is classy with high-end decorations and a cream and light purple color scheme the same shade as the bridesmaids' dresses. The chandeliers are marvelous with dangling crystals above the circular tables that boast large vases with pale roses as their centerpieces and dozens of candles. The room is gigantic with plenty of space to dance, a designated gift area, a bar, and a stage. On the far side of the room, there is a kitchen where the food will be brought from.

Once again, we're sat up front next to the bridal party but to the left side of the room. Men, every so often, make their way over to shake Bobby's and Wyatt's hands. I also notice some of the men try to hand Bobby envelopes but another man comes over to retrieve them. Trying not to be nosy I focus back on our table as our waiter comes to ask what main course we would like, fish or steak. After asking Bobby and Mary, the waiter turns his attention to Wyatt and me.

"What can I get for you, sir?" the waiter asks Wyatt.

"We will both have the fish—"

Oh no he doesn't! Who does he think he is?

"Excuse me, I'll actually have the steak, medium well. Thank you!" I smile sweetly at the waiter as he marks through what he had originally written and writes *my* correct selection on his notepad.

Once the waiter moves on to Gabe and Harper, Wyatt puts his arm around the back of my chair and leans in close to my ear so his warm breath tickles me.

"Do not ever disrespect me again in public," he seethes, trying to whisper, but it comes out loud enough for others at the table to hear him. *The nerve of him.* I whip my head toward him and will my temper to a calm.

"Calm down. I didn't disrespect you. You're just being sensitive." My teeth clamp together but my smile doesn't falter. "I don't like fish and I will not be made to eat something I don't like." I shrug one shoulder and pick up my glass of water while taking a sip to cool down. "You shouldn't assume to know what I'll eat when we only met an hour ago. I can make my own decisions, especially when it comes to food." I make a mental note to ask the waiter for something stronger if I am forced to stay the entire time.

"Wyatt, leave the poor girl alone. I would choose steak over fish any day too," Bobby points out to his son and gives a wink in my direction. How can this prick be related to such admirable people? Tension leaves Wyatt's body after being chastised by his father and he starts to run his fingers along my shoulder. I think he likes to torture me as he continues to keep a hand on me over the next while.

The meal is delicious and very filling. I even share some of my steak with Wyatt, who moans in appreciation. I mentally pat myself on the back for playing nice. Once the alcohol starts flowing, we all relax a bit more. The conversation turns to Mary telling embarrassing stories of when Gracie and Wyatt were younger. Both groan and mumble things under their breaths, and as the night wears on, we all have an enjoyable time and a good laugh.

After dinner, Wyatt receives a phone call and leaves to take it outside, so Gracie, Harper, and I hit the dance floor. There are a lot of bodies on the floor, so we're dancing pretty close to one another, but the music is too loud to carry a conversation. Of course, the songs turn into a slow one and everyone is paired with their date except me. I glance around, hoping Wyatt has come back, but no such luck. I'm about to leave when I feel a hand on my shoulder. Turning to see who it might be, I shift my eyes upward due to how tall this man is and see a blond-haired, hazel-eyed man with a smile admiring me.

"May I have this dance?" he asks holding his hand up for me to take.

I look around one more time for Wyatt, but I still don't see him. Not wanting to feel like a fool in the middle of the dance floor without a partner, I nod. He puts an arm around my waist and his free hand in mine, yet despite how alluring he is or how close we're dancing all I can think about is when Wyatt is coming back.

"I'm Charlie by the way. Are you with the bride or groom's side?" he asks.

"It's nice to meet you, Charlie, I'm Kendall. Umm, I guess you can say the bride's side. My date is part of her family."

"A gorgeous name for an exquisite woman with the most mesmerizing green eyes. If I were your date, I'd never let you out of my sight for the vultures to descend upon."

"Not only are you a good dancer, but you're charming as ever." I give him a shy smile and he returns the favor.

"Are you from around here?" he asks as he twirls me around the dance floor. "We should hang out before I have to fly back out East."

"My roommate and I are visiting here for the summer; we're going for our master's degrees in a few months at Stanford. What about you?"

Before he can reply, he's snatched out of my arms by a furious-looking Wyatt who drags him away from me by his suit collar.

Splendid. That's all we need, a scene that could ruin the reception. *He really could use some anger management.*

"Dude, what's your problem?" Charlie straightens to his full height and stands toe to toe with Wyatt.

"My problem is that you're dancing with my girl," Wyatt announces. His girl? Not his date, but his girl. Like we're in some kind of relationship. I'm starting to think Wyatt didn't share his toys with others growing up. "Do you know who I am?"

"Should I care?" Charlie questions. "Maybe you shouldn't leave her unattended—"

Just when they're about to come to blows, the groom grabs Charlie by the arm and pulls him over to the side of the dance floor where he talks to him in his ear. Charlie's body tenses before he shrugs out of the groom's hold and walks away shaking his head as he makes his way to the bar. Wyatt comes to stand in front of me and I'm still in shock he almost had an actual fight right here in front of everyone. He puts both arms around my waist and tugs me in tight to his rock-hard body. My arms automatically go around his neck and we start to sway with the music. Glancing around at the people on the dance floor, it's like the altercation never happened. Not even Harper is paying attention over here. Then I feel Wyatt's lips on my ear and when it sends a shiver down my spine, I want to scream at my body for betraying me.

"Possessive much?" I can't stop my lips from moving as we sway to the song.

"If you wanted to dance, all you had to do was ask, Kendall," Wyatt purrs.

"Not that I owe you an explanation, but I looked for you, and you were off outside on the phone. The music turned to a slow song and I was left out here without a partner. Charlie was here and asked for a dance. I didn't realize it was going to set off World War III," I respond trying to explain even though I know I don't have to.

I feel him exhale a lengthy breath that prickles my skin. "Kendall, you are a very challenging woman, you know that?" he says with a chuckle.

I giggle because I know this to be a true statement.

Not wanting to ruin the night for everyone I decide right then to let everything before this moment go and try to have a decent night. I'll never see him or any of these people again, so I'm going to enjoy this fancy dress with my rockstar shoes and top-shelf beverages.

"You might be onto something, Mr. Dawson! My aunt and uncle used to say it all the time growing up," I claim, and a fit of giggle escapes me. "Although, the same could be said about you!" I point out not letting him off the hook.

"You don't know the half of it."

The rest of the evening goes by without a hitch and we all have a blast dancing and drinking.

"You're a pretty good dancer," Wyatt compliments as we wait for the bartender to pour our drinks.

"Yeah, Harper's parents thought we should take lessons during our junior year."

"What'd you think of the wedding so far?" He takes a drink of his whiskey as I bring my lemon drop up to my lips.

"It's beautiful. The bride's dream, I'm sure."

"Not yours?"

"I think every girl is different; some want the over-the-top, grand wedding where others like a small, simple more intimate wedding."

"Which are you though?"

"Give me a handful of white roses and I'll meet you at the courthouse."

"Most women I know would want their event to be splashed all over the internet with outrageous costs."

"Maybe you're hanging out with the wrong women then," I say as I finish off another drink.

"I'm starting to think so." Wyatt's face has softened a lot as the night progressed and with more drinks in his system.

The song changes to a slow one and the lights dim slightly.

"Are you up for another one?" Wyatt points back at the dance floor.

"Why not?" I slip my hand into his and he leads me out to the center of the crowded dance floor.

After the song, the DJ calls for all the single women to gather around for the bouquet toss and for the single men to stay close by for the garter toss. I unexpectedly catch the bride's bouquet much to my displeasure and Wyatt catches the garter. They make us dance in front of everyone and as awkward as it is being stared at by a room full of strangers, Wyatt makes it comical by twirling and dipping me. It's enjoyable to see him laugh and be so carefree instead of the brooding prick he was earlier. *Note to self: keep him supplied with alcohol if you want to have a good and fun night!*

"We are going to have to stop meeting like this or the gossip pages will start to get curious," Wyatt jokes as we continue to dance. His arms are now more comfortable around my body as the night goes on and he's holding me so close not one inch of space separates us.

"After tonight I'm sure they'll never see us like this again," I say with my head resting on his chest.

His body tenses and his hold on me tightens. "I'm pretty sure they're going to be seeing a lot of us together in the near future."

My head is a little fuzzy from the dancing and drinking so I chalk up his words to the alcohol streaming through our bodies.

Before the bride and groom leave for their honeymoon, Wyatt introduces me to several big-name businessmen here in Las Vegas. Some are owners of hotels and casinos; others are in retail or the entertainment business. When he mentions that I'm looking for an internship, they all offer to have me shadow them if I'd like. My mind is blown by all of the doors opening for me just from being Wyatt's date. I take their cards and promise to give them a call sometime next week. Maybe I can split my time and do several internships over the summer; I'd just need to manage my time wisely.

After the happily married couple exits in a white vintage Rolls Royce, we gather up our belongings and make our way to the limo. I can't believe I actually had a good time after the way the night started. Once Wyatt loosened up, we got along fabulously. Bobby and Mary left a while ago, and now we're waiting for Gracie to say her goodbyes to Jackson, who has his tongue down her throat. Gabe and Harper seemed to have hit it off also, as they're snuggling together in their seats. Wyatt made sure to interlock our fingers as we traveled out with the crowd to the parking lot. All night I noticed he wouldn't stop touching me. Any opportunity he got, we were either holding hands or he had an arm around me.

Quietly, Wyatt nudges me and leans his body into mine filling my airspace with his manly scent. "I had a really good time tonight, Kendall. Sorry, I was such an asshole at the beginning." I smell the whiskey on his breath, and I think the driver must have turned on the heat, or the alcohol is getting to me because my cheeks start to simmer.

"The first step is always admitting you have a problem," I joke to get a rise out of him and it works as his eyes widen. He proceeds to tickle my sides as payback. When he stops and I've got my fits of giggles under control, I add, "I had a lovely time too! Who knew you could be such a gentleman?" I jab him with my elbow in the ribs and smile. He snorts and leans his body into me. I think he's going to kiss me, but the door opens and Gracie gets in next to me, breaking up our moment.

"Whew! What a night! I invited Jackson to brunch tomorrow and a swim afterward." She wags her eyebrows. "So, did everyone have a good night? I thought you held up your part of the bet pretty well seeing as everyone is still in one piece and no one at the party left in a body bag." She giggles. "You are now cleared of all debts!" She waves her hand around.

The limo ride back to Bobby and Mary's house is a quiet one. I think all the alcohol has taken its toll on us. Wyatt has an arm around my back so my head and body are held tight to his side, and his other hand is tracing circles on my exposed thigh. He's also resting his head on top of mine and I'm not sure if he's fallen asleep or if this is how he gets when drinking to excess, but my mind is racing as fast as my heart. It's such a tender and intimate gesture I'm not sure what to think of all this. Harper is already asleep with her head on Gabe's lap as he brushes his fingers through her hair.

When the limo pulls up to the house, Gabe carries Harper up to a guest room and the rest of us go to the kitchen to grab some water before bed. As we approach, we hear raised voices. "Did you see her? The resemblance to her mother is uncanny! And those eyes, I thought I was looking right at my best friend again," we hear Mary say. I wonder who she's talking about.

"We don't know who her mother is!" He lets out a long sigh. "They are gone Mary and you need to accept that. We can't bring them back, no one can and the faster you understand the sooner you can heal after all these years. Yes, she has her eyes, but she can't be alive. We saw the house and the pictures of the bodies, Mary. Please don't do this to yourself; we've come so far for you to back-slide now," Bobby pleads with her.

"Will you at least consider doing a background check for me? I need some kind of peace of mind."

"NO! I will not, and that is final! Get yourself together or I'll call Doctor Brinkman and make you an appointment," he fumes.

Feeling like we shouldn't be listening in on this conversation, I go to turn around to head back to where Gabe took Harper but am stopped by Gracie's hand on my arm. "Mom, Dad, we're home!" Gracie yells like she is across the house when she's really on the other side of the door.

We walk in and see Mary trying to wipe her eyes and get herself under control. Bobby is on the other side of the counter shooting back the last of the liquid in his tumbler.

"Hey guys, I'm glad you made it home safely. Do you need anything? Food? Drink?" Mary offers. I notice she is looking everywhere but at me, which I find weird because not just a few hours ago she couldn't stop watching my every move.

"We came for some water before we head up to bed, Mom," Gracie informs her, grabbing three bottles of water from the fridge.

"Okay, well, goodnight. We'll see you all in the morning for brunch. Try not to stay up too late."

"Mom, we're adults, not kids!" Wyatt remarks and I almost burst out in a giggle at his reaction.

Mary kisses them both on the head then comes over to me and engulfs me in an airtight hug. My arms automatically wrap around her and give her a light squeeze. The hug seems to last a little longer than socially acceptable for people who have just met and it's Bobby who finally breaks it up.

"Come, sweetheart. Let's get you to bed." He takes her by the hand and leads her out of the kitchen with his arms around her.

I regard both Wyatt and Gracie as they give me a sympathetic look.

"Sorry about Mom. She has had a hard time lately. Let's go to bed," Gracie says sadly.

We make our way up the stairs winding towards the back of the house. Gracie walks through a door I assume is her bedroom, but I am stopped by a familiar hand on my elbow. "I had an exceptional time tonight, Kendall. Thanks for being a lively date and not some crazy psycho," Wyatt jokes.

"Me too, although I was worried when I bumped into you in front of the bathroom downstairs." I giggle and stare into his deep blue eyes. "Goodnight, Wyatt."

With that, I move towards the bedroom only to be stopped again, but this time I'm twirled around, and then two hands are on both of my cheeks and soft lips are on mine. It only takes a few seconds for my brain to catch up and I kiss him back. We part too soon, and I'm confused by what just happened. I couldn't stand this man hours earlier and now I'm kissing him? What was in the drinks tonight?

"Come with me somewhere," Wyatt says. He still hasn't let me go.

I must be out of my mind because I nod. Wyatt leads me back down the stairs and through the kitchen. He grabs a few containers from the fridge and hands me two more water bottles. We walk out the patio doors and down a path past the pool. We finally stop at a set of chairs surrounding a firepit. As I settle in one of the chairs, Wyatt starts the fire and pulls one of the chairs right up next to mine.

"What are we doing out here, Wyatt?" I ask as he takes the tops off the containers revealing small sandwiches and fruit.

"I didn't want our night to end."

"Well, this is not how I saw the night going earlier," I laugh as I pop a grape in my mouth.

"Yeah, sorry about that."

I wave my hand out, "We've moved on from that hopefully."

"We have. Now, tell me more about you."

"Well, I'm from Texas, I'm an only child, and I want to run a big business as my dream job."

"I already know that. What else?"

"Are we doing the twenty-question game here?" I wink then melt as he places his hand on my exposed knee.

"As long as I learn more about you I don't care how many questions we play." His voice has turned sultry as the blaze grows higher in the pit.

"Okay, well, I love most sports and cars. I'm super picky about food and I'd love to have a dog, but until I get my career going and I'm financially stable I don't have the right amount of time to spend with one, and I think it's unfair."

"What about cats?" His finger twirls a lock of my blonde hair.

"Are you a cat lover?"

"I don't have the time for animals. Why?"

"Cats are a deal breaker for me. I have the worst allergy to them."

"Good to know, babe."

"What about you? Did you always want to be a part of your dad's businesses?"

Wyatt brings up our joined hands that I didn't even realize were interlocked and grazes his lips against my knuckles. "With my family, we are born to take over when our father steps down or dies. It's ingrained in us from the moment we're able to understand."

"So you didn't go to college?"

"No, we are taught on the job training. I think I was eight when I first started to shadow my dad. I didn't understand until later the actual responsibilities but I knew the general concept."

"Eight! Wow, seems a little early to have you start working, but I kinda did the same with my uncle. He owns several auto repair shops and I'd go and be there with him. I knew how to change oil and tire by ten."

"I don't think we're so different."

His eyes focus in on my lips and I can't stop my brain from wanting him to kiss me.

"I'm going to kiss you, if you don't want me to, now is the time to speak up," Wyatt says as he leans over slightly.

We're only inches from each other. If the wooden armrest wasn't attached to the chair we'd be in each other's laps with how close our bodies are to one another. When I don't answer, he continues the last two inches and seals our lips together. My body ignites as I move closer and my hand lands on his firm chest. His hand cups my neck as our mouths open and our tongues caress.

A howl off in the distance breaks our moment and gives us a second to collect ourselves, though, we don't separate much.

"You have the most alluring set of eyes, babe," he says of my emerald-colored eyes.

"Thank you," I say then the sound of twigs breaking startles me.

I turn to the noise and see a man off in the distance walking around. I gasp and pull away at the sight of the intruder.

"He's part of security here on the property. You don't need to worry about anything happening here or at my place."

"Why do y'all need so much security?"

"We are a very prominent family here in Las Vegas and on the west coast. Over time you won't even notice them."

"I'm not so sure about that," I mumble and try to focus back on Wyatt but my eyes follow the man as he loops around the wall and then the corner.

Wyatt stands bringing my attention back to him. "Let's head to bed. Mom and Gracie will be pounding on our doors in a few hours for brunch."

We gather up the containers and waters and make our way back up to the house. Once we've put everything away we find ourselves back at the doors we started at earlier. This time it's not as awkward.

"Goodnight, babe. I can't wait to see you at the pool tomorrow in your sexy bikini." He winks before walking through another door ten feet away.

"Only in your dreams," I retort with a smile.

The night started a bit rocky but I think we made some major progress as it moved on. Maybe he's not as big of an asshole as I thought? Shaking my head to try and clear my jumbled thoughts, I realize I need to get Harper alone at some point to ask about who this family is. Her family has done business with them in the past and something is off. Maybe she can call her dad and he'll tell us all about them.

CHAPTER THREE

THE DELICIOUS SMELL OF FOOD WAKES ME FROM MY Wyatt-filled dream. I take in the dim room, and note on the edge of the bed is a stack of clothing laid out for Harper and me. Among the articles of clothing, I spot swimsuits and cover-ups. Something moves beside me and Harper rolls onto her back. Knowing Harper hates mornings, I give her a nudge and lightly tickle her upper lip. She groans and swats my hand away.

"Harper…wakey wakey!" I sing. She kicks her feet out and throws her arms above her head. She's really not a morning person. "Come on girl, I need to talk with you before we head down."

"Okay, I'm listening," she mumbles sleepily never opening her eyes.

"What do you think of Gracie's family? Do you find them as strange as I do? What kind of business do they do to have to have security around them?" I ask.

Harper opens one eye and exhales, "Well, I find them to be your typical royal elite rich family. I saw a lot of this in Florida growing up, so they seem pretty normal to me. My family isn't quite as rich as the Dawson's, but they run in the same circles, I imagine. As far as business goes, I have no idea. My father never discusses business or associates around us. He separates it when the family is around.

As far as what business they have, I'm sure it's goods from China or somewhere else to get their supplies shipped over at a cheaper rate than American-made," she explains. "Why? What are you picking up on?"

"I'm not sure, I just feel out of sorts I guess. The way they watched me so intensely all night made me feel a little uncomfortable. Like I was going to tell a secret or something. I don't know." I shrug, something is definitely not right. "Do you think Wyatt is bipolar? He goes from hot to cold at the snap of a finger."

Harper lets out a laugh and sits up in bed stretching out her arms. "No, I think he is a serious guy who seems like he's having a hard time getting to know new people and letting loose. Maybe even a bad boy who is very intimidating. We were thrown together at the last minute by Gracie, so maybe he was happy about that. But I do want you to be careful. He seems to be a really intense guy. Don't let him raise his voice to you again. That's not cool. Remember, we are keeping a watch for red flags." She reminds me of our promise to each other after the Chad situation a few years back. "If I remember correctly you two were getting pretty cozy on the dance floor." She smirks.

"I noticed you and Gabe were hitting it off too." I smirk back trying to take the heat off of me. The last part of the evening was really fun once the alcohol was flowing and everyone relaxed a bit.

"I know, right! He has this whole hot guy vibe just like Wyatt, and he says some of the sweetest things. I know once we're back at Stanford this won't work, so I'm just going to have some summer fun while I can." She winks. "Just relax, Kendall, and go with it. Don't overthink it. Have a fun summer fling for the next few months. You never know how it could turn out. For god's sake, we are in Sin City, act your age for a change and let loose! I know you have an inner bad girl in there somewhere!" We both burst out laughing at that. "Don't let this internship engulf all your time here. We only get to enjoy our early twenties for such a short time so let's make the most of it. Plus we have many more summers you can intern before you find the right company."

She's right, maybe I am thinking too much about this.

We take turns in the bathroom, showering and changing into the clothes that were set out on the bed before heading down to the kitchen. I'm wearing mid-length white shorts and a black chiffon shirt with lace straps. Harper has on khaki shorts with a blue chiffon shirt. We're both sporting rhinestone flip-flops with our hair up off our shoulders.

As we turn the corner to the kitchen, we find the entire family, along with Gabe, sitting on the couches drinking out of coffee mugs. Wyatt is the only one missing but can be seen pacing the patio just outside the French doors on his phone. *Geez, I think the thing is surgically glued to his ear.*

"Morning, girls! How did you both sleep?" Mary pops up from her seat and makes her way over to us.

"Very well, thank you," I answer kindly as we retreat to the empty sofa before we greet the others.

"What would you like this morning for drinks? Coffee? Espresso? Juice?" Mary offers and signals for Linda to come over.

"Umm, orange juice if you have it, please," I say. Harper asks for a coffee with cream and sugar.

The TV is on the local news channel; Bobby is flipping through the newspaper; Gracie is on her phone texting; Mary rejoins us, picking up a book that was keeping her seat occupied, and Wyatt's strained voice is getting louder from the patio. Bobby whistles loudly, getting everyone's attention. Wyatt yells one more time, hangs up, then makes his way into the room. Plopping down opposite me, he gives a firm nod to Bobby. Some unspoken conversation passes between them before Bobby turns back to me.

"So, Kendall, Wyatt tells me you're here to intern for Victor Slater's company this summer."

"Yes, that is correct." I shift a little in my seat. *Not this topic again!* "I received a letter about two weeks before graduation informing me I'd been selected to intern for his company here in Vegas. To be honest, I don't really remember applying, but I did fill out stacks of applications to a lot of different companies."

"Well, I have an offer that might reflect better on your resume. Justice Williams, who runs my day-to-day operations, would be willing to have you shadow him for the summer if you'd like. I'm not sure if you know but Victor Slater is a shady underhanded businessman in our community. Not something you would want Fortune 500 companies to associate you with, if you know what I mean." The room is quiet while everyone waits for me to answer Bobby. "He's been under surveillance with the State of Nevada for several years. Of course, he has the money to make certain charges and allegations go away."

I have no idea what I've gotten myself into. I don't want to hitch my wagon to a shady businessman; it could taint my reputation before I even get out of the gate. On the other hand, I have no idea what the Dawson's do. They obviously make good money going off the way they dress, their cars, and this enormous house. But what are they into?

"Please forgive me, Bobby, but what exactly is it you do?" I ask.

"Well, we own hotels, casinos, most of the transportation here in Vegas, restaurants, clubs, real estate, and a few other businesses here and along the West Coast. You'll get a great deal of experience in all business ventures if you'd like. If there is a specific area you'd like to focus on, Justice can make it happen."

Well, I was not expecting this.

I'm sure the shock is evident on my face.

"Oh! Wow! I…thank you…sure…I mean, yes, I would love the opportunity to work alongside a well-established company." This could be the foot in the door I'm looking for. But then reality sets in. "I'm sorry but I've already committed to Mr. Slater. I'm sure it wouldn't be very professional to rescind my offer the day before I'm supposed to start."

"Kendall, believe me when I say it's in your best interest to steer clear of Victor Slater." I know he can see my reluctance, so he continues, "I've known him for three decades and will clear this up for you. No one will be the wiser," he assures.

After giving it a lot of thought, I go with my gut. "How soon would I start? I'll still need to inform Mr. Slater in person that I'll be declining his offer—" I share but am cut off by Wyatt.

"No need, I will take care of informing Vic. There are some things I need to drop off for him anyway," Wyatt announces in a firm voice.

"I appreciate that, but I need to do this. He offered me a position and I need to be the one to decline it."

I see a tick in Wyatt's jaw and I know he is trying to bite his tongue right now.

"Kendall, I think Wyatt might be right on this one. Victor Slater is a man who doesn't take no for an answer. Wyatt and I have had many dealings with him and we know how he works. Let us deliver this for you. If you really want to, you can send an official email declining his offer so you'd have everything in writing if that'd make you feel more comfortable."

I think about what he says and take it all in. "I'll send an email as soon as I get home," I agree.

"How about you start this Wednesday and it'll give you some more time to settle in before Justice puts you through your paces." Bobby leaves no room for argument so I nod but what I really want to do is vocalize that I can handle myself. How am I ever going to run a company if I can't take the reins on my own life?

"Harper, are you in need of an internship also?" Bobby offers ending our conversation.

"Oh, no! I only came along to lay out, drink, and go clubbing all summer!" she says in the flippant way only rich kids can get away with. She and Gracie make the perfect pair. I always wonder if she'll ever get a job or if going to college was just a social experience for her. The look both Harper and Gabe give each other tells me he'll soon be on our approved visitors list at the apartment building.

Linda, the housekeeper, informs us that brunch is now served out on the patio, so we all make our way out to eat. The glass table is spread with every type of breakfast and lunch food. I notice how everyone waits until Bobby has his plate before diving in to get their own. Then, once again, they wait until he takes the first bite before they start to eat. It was the same last night at the wedding. Not really understanding their home rules, I follow along with what Gracie or Mary do and start to eat after I see them pick up their forks. It has a very *Godfather* feel to it, but the conversation flows nicely. Bobby, who sits to my left at the head of the table, asks about what I plan to do after graduate school.

"Well, ever since I can remember, I've wanted to take something and help build or grow it. When I was younger, my uncle owned several auto shops. I would come home after school and help out wherever he'd let me. I did the books, detailed the cars, or changed the oil. When I hit my teens I did some marketing and brought more work in that year than the last five years. I've got this knack for finding ways to build and expand companies to reach their highest potential," I remark on my accomplishments. "During my time at Stanford, I did the same with a local grocery store and a few retail businesses."

"Well, I think that is something to be proud of. I can't wait to hear from Justice how you're working out for my company," Bobby says.

Once we've finished brunch, we change into our swimming suits. Bobby and Mary leave to run some errands, so they say their goodbyes as we're coming down the stairs. The guys are already in the pool and Gracie suggests we lay out for a bit. I'm still trying to get my mind around working for Bobby and turning down Mr. Slater when Wyatt pulls himself up from the water and stalks over to the lounge chairs. He's got several tattoos I wouldn't even know were there if he had a shirt on. I spy the name, Avery, on the inside of his left bicep, the words 'My Angel' over his heart with the initials LC just below them, and the name Dawson with what can only be described as a family crest on his back. I've seen the same symbol throughout the house in several rooms.

Never slowing his pace, Wyatt makes it over to me in five strides. Before I can blink, I'm picked up bridal style and plunged into the pool, still cradled in his arms. After the shock of the chilled water wears off, I dunk him under the water and then splash him when he comes up for air. Gabe follows Wyatt's lead and grabs Harper cannon-balling into the pool after us. Jackson finally arrives and is seated next to Gracie's chair chatting about god knows what. After losing horribly at volleyball, we decide to play a few rounds of chicken, which Wyatt and I dominate.

Wyatt now has me cornered in the furthest spot of the pool in the deep end, away from everyone else. My body is boxed in by his massive form and he's hooked my legs around his waist to keep me upright. With his arms on either side of my head on the ledge of the pool, we float in place as his phone rings right beside his hand.

"Yeah?" Wyatt answers without taking his eyes off of me. "Tonight?"

I can only hear his side of the conversation.

"On the glass for sure, man," Wyatt responds again. "Send me the info."

"Everything okay?" I ask when Wyatt tosses his phone onto the chair a few feet away.

"I've got a surprise for you."

"For me?" I ask surprised. "What if I don't like surprises?" I taunt playfully.

"I think you'll like this one."

"I guess we'll see," I say trying to come off unimpressed.

Wyatt playfully wiggles his fingers on my sides like he did last night making me laugh out loud.

"I envisioned what you'd look like in a bikini, but this by far surpasses any image my brain could conjure," he says, changing the subject. His voice is low and seductive as a finger traces the string from my neck towards the triangle patch that covers one of my boobs.

"I'm glad it doesn't disappoint." I'm trying to be flirty but my words come out breathy. *Get a grip, Kendall! You're not a hussy.* "I definitely didn't expect you to have all this artwork on your body."

"It's just one of the many surprises I have in store for you, babe."

He presses me up against his body and his lips crash into mine. Not caring that others are around, we start making out like teenagers. His hands explore my upper body and I can't stop the moan that leaves my throat. It's been far too long since I've had any sexual pleasure and I'm starting to think my libido is taking over my brain. All too soon, we're interrupted by his and Gabe's phones going off. With a grunt, Wyatt reluctantly pulls his mouth from mine.

"It's work," he offers as an explanation, like I'm supposed to know what that means.

With one last peck, he pulls away and exits the pool.

Wyatt has his back to me and his shoulders tense when he reads whatever is on his phone. Retracing his steps, he walks back over and squats down. "Hey babe, I have to go take care of some business. I'll call you later about the surprise," he informs me. "You'll want to wear jeans and a thin long-sleeve top."

"Sure," is all I can get out. With a peck on the cheek, he stands to his full height and leaves the pool area making his way into the house.

The rest of the day is relaxing. We stay outside for a few more hours, tanning our bodies at the house, then get driven back to our apartment by one of Bobby's security guys. Once we're back, Harper and I go our separate ways, both of us saying goodnight and love you to each other. I take a quick shower wanting to wash the chlorine and tanning oil from my body before getting changed into my favorite pair of denim that makes my butt look good. After going through my routine of shaving, scrubbing, and putting on lotion, I crawl onto the bed and reach over to the nightstand to retrieve my laptop.

When I finish going through my social media, I check my email and find I have two new ones. The first is from Aunt Sarah asking how our travels are going and giving me updates on how life is back home in Texas. She and Uncle Liam are thinking about taking a small vacation at the end of the summer but haven't made up their minds on where to go. I remember when I was younger, we would open a map of the U.S. then close our eyes and point to where we would start our vacation. Aunt Sarah signs off, telling us to be careful, to have a good time, and to call when I can. I send her a quick email letting her know Harper and I are having a fantastic time and will call her sometime this week letting her know all about our adventures so far. I hate lying to her, so I keep it short and sweet.

The next email is from a Leah Nelson who is the Secretary for Victor Slater. My heart immediately shoots up to my throat when I click on the unopened email.

To: Kendall Drake
From: Leah Nelson
Subject: Internship with Victor Slater

Dear Kendall Drake,
I hope this email finds you well. We are looking forward to having you work with us this summer and hopefully in the future. Please arrive at least 30 minutes early so that we can have you fill out the correct paperwork and receive your badge. If you have any questions, please don't hesitate to call the number listed below in the attachment. Again we look forward to you working with us.

Leah Nelson
Secretary to Victor Slater

Crap! I check to see the time it was sent and notice it came through this morning. I know I agreed to let Bobby and Wyatt handle this, but they didn't say when they would. I reach over to my phone and text Wyatt.

> **Me:** Hey, did you get a chance to inform Mr. Slater about declining the internship?

I put my phone back in my lap, not sure when he will respond, but before the screen light dims I hear a ping.

>Wyatt: Yes, he was informed around 3 hours ago in person. Message was received personally.
>
>Me: Thank you!
>
>Wyatt: You're welcome, are we still on for me to get you in an hour?
>
>Me: Not sure. I was never asked. I might be washing my hair.
>
>Wyatt: Don't make me put you over my shoulder and drag you from your apartment in only a towel 😉
>
>Me: I'd like to see you try mister!
>
>Wyatt: I've done a lot worse, babe. Test me, please! 😏
>
>Me: I bet you have. See you then.

I smirk at his endearment towards me as I set my phone down beside me and glance back at my laptop. I still feel terrible I wasn't the one to deliver the message since it was my internship. I read over the email from Leah Nelson one more time and decide to reply to her email like Bobby had suggested.

To: Leah Nelson
From: Kendall Drake
Subject: Re: Internship for Victor Slater

Ms. Nelson,
Thank you for emailing me, but unfortunately, I will be declining the offer to be an intern for Mr. Slater. I realize this is last minute, and I am sorry for it being such short notice. I appreciate the opportunity, but at this time I cannot accept the offer. Mr. Slater was informed earlier of this change in person.

Warm regards,
Kendall Drake

I press the send button and then close the laptop. Closing my eyes, I can't keep the smile off my face. I definitely didn't expect the weekend to go as well as it did. Who would have thought making a bet on a fight could lead to meeting a handsome guy and landing an awesome internship?

An hour later I'm tossing my empty water bottle in the recycle bin when a knock on my door grabs my attention. Checking my watch I grab my crossbody purse and open the door. Wyatt stands in the hallway looking delicious in his dark jeans and tight-fitted black long-sleeve shirt. I'm matching him except for my shirt is white. He's holding a bouquet of white roses.

"I can't believe you remembered my favorite flower," I say as he hands them over.

"I remember everything about last night." He places a hand on my hip and my body breaks out into goosebumps.

"Let me put them in some water and then we can go."

Wyatt waits in the doorway while I find a vase and pour some water into it.

"You could come in," I say as I take the roses and place them in the vase.

"We'd be late if I did." He winks at me when I look up.

"You sure are cocky, Mr. Dawson."

I approach the front door where he is stationed and his smile lights up the closer I get.

"You'll get used to it."

We both chuckle as I lock the front door. Wyatt ever so gently places his hand on the small of my back as we walk down the hall to wait for the elevator. Once inside, his cologne surrounds me, making me lightheaded as we descend to the lobby. When we walk out of the building, I'm given a chance to catch my breath from being in such close quarters, and when we reach the car, Wyatt quickly opens my door for me, giving me his hand as I step in.

Whoever said chivalry was dead?

"Where are we going?" I ask as we pull out onto the street in his sleek black Corvette. We drive for a few minutes before a stadium comes into view.

"A friend had some tickets available and I thought we'd go to a game. You mentioned you like sports."

"Look at you trying to collect all these brownie points!"

"I have a lot to make up for."

I thought we were going to see a baseball game but it turns out it's a hockey playoff game.

His friend must be a VIP because Wyatt flashes an employee a badge and has us pull into a private parking garage attached to the stadium. We're directed to a reserved spot next to the elevators and Wyatt quickly jumps out of his side and over to mine before I can open my door. He guides me over to the bank of elevators and scans the badge making the doors open immediately.

"Your friend must have really good passes," I mention as the elevator brings us to ground level.

"When it comes to sports, Bishop, only gets the best."

When we walk off the elevator, Wyatt scans our badges one more time with security and they grant us entrance to the stadium. The crowd and atmosphere are charged with excitement, and die-hard fans are decked out from head to toe.

"Let's get some gear." Wyatt ushers us over to a stand with jerseys, hats, and scarves.

"I've never been to a hockey game before," I admit as we wait our turn in line.

"Really? What sports are your favorite then?"

"Football and baseball mostly.

"Well, hockey is in a league of its own. You either love it or hate it."

We pick out our items and then head over to the food lines.

"Thanks for my jersey and scarf, I thought you were crazy when you mentioned wearing a long-sleeve top for tonight."

"It gets super cold in the arena even with this on," he holds up my arm and points to the long-sleeve top.

After getting our food and beers we make our way to our seats which happen to be dead center and on the glass. The buzzer starts and within the first five minutes of the game, the players have had a total of three fights. Gloves are thrown off and fists fly. The crowd loves it and it is exhilarating to watch. These guys don't give a flip about getting caught or what penalties they incur. I think I even see a player's tooth shoot across the ice.

"You want another beer?" Wyatt asks when the buzzer ends the first period and people are on their feet heading up the stairs for either the bathroom or more food.

"Sure."

A man comes around and Wyatt gets our drinks and a bag of peanuts. "What do you think so far?"

"Is it always this exciting at every game?"

"Pretty much."

"Tell me more about you, Wyatt," I say as I crack a shell and pop the peanuts in my mouth.

"There isn't much to tell. I've lived here my entire life and worked for the family business since I was eight."

"How long have you and Gabe been friends?"

A slight smirk tugs at the corner of his mouth. "We've been best friends forever. The things we've gotten into, it's a wonder we survived our teen years." He laughs and it makes me smile. "Dad says we're the reason he started getting gray hair."

By the middle of the second period, I'm on my feet screaming and hitting the glass along with everyone else as our team is ahead and trying to score again. After banging on the glass as three players slam into the wall right in front of us, I impulsively yell out, "Knock his fucking head off!"

As soon as the words come out I look over at Wyatt. I was so wrapped up in the game I almost forgot he was there. I quickly look around hoping I'm not embarrassing myself or him.

"I'm so sorry," I say.

"Babe, this is the most fun I've had in a long time just watching you and not the game. The fact that you're enjoying them beat the shit out of each other is icing on the cake."

"I didn't think I'd like it either, but it's so fun to watch it happen."

We won in overtime and by the time we're walking to the car my adrenaline is starting to wane. This is why I love sports. Wyatt has a protective arm around me, and I'm tucked in close to his body as the crowd moves toward the parking garage.

"Thanks for bringing me to the game. I had the best time," I say as he pulls out onto the road.

"I'm glad you liked it. If they make it to the next round I'll get Bishop, to get us more tickets."

"I'd love that," I gush.

He pulls my hand over to the gear shift and interlocks our fingers. It's becoming a normal thing for us to do since the wedding.

The drive back to the apartment is a slow one with all the traffic letting out. Wyatt parks his car at the front of the lobby and then comes around to open my door. He tells our doorman to keep an eye on it for him as we walk through the lobby to the waiting elevator. When the elevator door dings we move to my apartment door as I dig out my keys.

"Have lunch with me tomorrow," Wyatt states when I open the door.

"Aren't you tired of me yet?" I ask, shocked he'd want to go out again so soon.

"Not even close." He gives me the sweetest kiss before nudging me lightly through the door.

"Go inside since I'm trying to be a gentleman for you."

"Is it a hard feat?" I tease.

"Only for you, babe."

Arriving at the restaurant a few minutes before noon, I take a last-minute look in the mirror at my makeup. Wyatt had texted me earlier saying he was running a few minutes behind. Something about a meeting running late and spilling something on his clothes, so he needed to run home and change. I, myself, had changed my clothes about fifteen times before settling on a black polka-dotted white blouse, a just-above-knee-length black skirt, and bold red heels to give me some height since Wyatt is so tall. I exit my arctic-blue black-top convertible Chevy Camaro and hand my keys to the valet before walking into the three-story restaurant on the Strip. Harper and I decided to only bring my car here for the summer and left hers at our place in California.

As I approach the hostess, I give her mine and Wyatt's names, noticing how she straightens her back a little when I mention the last name *Dawson*. She finally remembers herself and gives a polite smile before walking us through the bottom floor. She stops in front of a velvet rope leading upstairs, unhooks it, and motions for me to go up. The décor of the building reminds me so much of home back in Texas. I really should tell Aunt Sarah and Uncle Liam where I'm at. They'd be devastated if they found out I kept a whole summer of being here from them. The hostess guides me to a private corner booth that already has a bottle of wine on ice. I roll my eyes. Isn't it a little early in the day to be drinking? I mean I just got up a few hours ago.

I text Wyatt I've arrived and sip the water the waiter brought me. To pass the time until Wyatt gets here I open the menu to see what is offered when I hear a throat being cleared. Startled, my eyes dart up and see two massive, bulky men dressed in black suits with black undershirts and sunglasses. They're intimidating and I think maybe the hostess sat me at the wrong table. I try to peer around the two beasts and notice we're the only ones on this floor.

"Excuse me, ma'am, but we need you to come with us," Beast Number One demands and gestures with his hand to follow Beast Number Two.

"Uh, I think you've got the wrong person. I'm here meeting a friend for lunch." I slide my purse a little closer to me in the booth.

Did I remember to transfer the pepper spray from my other purse? Would pepper spray even affect these hulky guys?

"You're Kendall Drake, correct?" he asserts.

"Yes, that's me." I'm suddenly confused. "But I don't know you and how did you know where I would be?" *Have I done something wrong?* "Did Wyatt send you?"

"Mr. Slater would like a word with you. So, if you'd please follow me this way." He gestures again, a little too impatiently this time. I can tell he's trying not to be harsh with his words as his jaw is flexing as if he's grinding his teeth. His large hand reaches down and gently wraps around my left wrist, pulling me from the booth when I don't make any attempt to move.

I try to steady my wobbly legs but this man isn't giving me much time to get my balance. My heart is beating so fast that the cardio workout I did this morning pales in comparison. Bobby was correct about Mr. Slater not taking *no* for an answer, and now he's sent two goons to retrieve me. I'm terrified. We're almost to the stairs when Beast Number Two stops, making me bump right into the back of him. I feel something hard against his back where his belt and pants meet. Oh shit! Does he have a gun on him? Holy shit! I need to get away from them. I cannot get in a car that'll go God knows where with these men. A hand goes around my upper arm and I hear a voice I've never been so glad to hear.

"Well, well, well! Hey, Tony, I see Vic still has you on grunt work after the Reno job barreled south," Wyatt taunts in a cocky tone and I hear snickering coming from a few others. I still can't see over the beast in front of me, so I'm not sure who it is or how many there are.

"Wyatt—" I plead but am cut off, and I whimper when the hand on my arm crushes me in a death grip.

The sound of metal clicks erupts through the room and when I peek around the beast holding me, I see guns being pointed at everyone in the room. As if they are all synced, each man cocks the hammer back on their handpieces. Oh my god, I feel like I've been thrown into some gang turf war movie. Wyatt and three other guys, one being Gabe, each have guns pointed at Tony and Beast Number Two. They in return, have their guns pointed at Wyatt and his friends. I'm a shaky mess and regret my choice of shoes. I think I might pass out. The room feels like all the oxygen has been sucked out. Uncle Liam showed me how to use a gun properly growing up, but that didn't prepare me to be in the middle of the action.

"Now boys, I don't think you want to die today, so why don't you let her go and we can all go our merry little way without any bloodshed? What do you say?" Wyatt placates tauntingly. I'm watching him, and his demeanor is cool as a cucumber. Like he's done this a million times.

"No can do, Dawson! We have strict orders to bring her back with us. Boss wants to have a word with her, so that's what's going to happen," Tony declares and tugs my arm making me wince.

Wyatt grips his gun tighter and narrows his eyes. "She's mine, Tony, let her go now."

"Last chance to walk out with your lives," Gabe broadcasts from across the room by the staircase. My heart can't take any more pounding against my ribcage and it feels like everyone is now miles away.

I decide if I'm going to be caught in the crossfire I might as well go down swinging. My right leg kicks out to the back of Tony's knee jolting him off balance. He shifts to regain his stance but suddenly the back of my head explodes with pain like something crashed into me. My head starts to pound and I'm light-headed. The next moments pass in a blur. My legs immediately give out and my knees hit the wood floors as gunshots ring out. I'm in a crouching position with my hand over my head as liquid coats my fingers. My vision starts to narrow when two hands sweep me up. I can hear a voice, but the darkness takes me under before I can register who it belongs to.

CHAPTER FOUR

SOMETHING COOL IS ON MY FOREHEAD, BUT MY EYES REFUSE to open. I can hear voices in the distance, but everything seems a little foggy.

"Did you have to make such a scene in front of her? How are we going to hide what happened from her?" I hear a familiar woman's voice. Mary, maybe?

"I wasn't thinking at the time, Mom. They were going to take her, and I couldn't let it happen." Wyatt sounds annoyed. "Don't worry, the restaurant has already been cleaned up, and no one is going to say anything about the incident. I'll talk with Kendall and explain." He lets out a long sigh before continuing. "Look, Mom, I really like her. She's…" There's a pause and another sigh before he continues, "She's different and I want to see where this could lead." Thank God it was his arms that grabbed me from the floor of the restaurant. My head is pounding with a steady annoying thump.

"Dude, if you need to get laid, get one of your usual girls from the club to service you." I think that might be Gabe.

"Shut up, Gabe! Kendall is different, and I want to try with her," Wyatt growls. "OUCH!"

"Sorry, Mr. Dawson, but if you'll sit still I'll be done with the stitches faster," a man whose voice I don't recognize says. He sounds older, with a heavy accent I'm not sure from where.

"Honey, I hear what you're saying, but I just want you to be careful. She's only here for the summer. I just want you to be happy and not heartbroken is all," Mary whispers. "Now, your father is on his way, and I think you need to have some sort of plan of what you're going to tell her. It's too soon to let her in, Wyatt. I know your father is going to agree with me, but I'll support you in whatever it is you want."

Thinking now is a good time for some answers, I try to sit up. The cool rag falls off my forehead and lands on the comforter covering my lap. My eyes adjust and take in my surroundings. I'm in a large bedroom with light gray walls and oversized furniture. The bed I'm currently occupying is a four-poster bed with a blue and black comforter. The room has a very masculine feel to it, along with the dark hardwood flooring. Mary, Wyatt, Gabe, and another man with gloves are in a sitting area over by a group of large windows. Wyatt is the first to notice me. He jumps up from his seat startling the man with gloves and makes his way over to me.

"Hey, how are you feeling?" he asks as his hand cups my cheek. I lean into his touch for some much-needed comfort.

"I'm fine, I think." I clear my throat which has gone dry. I gaze at him and see he's wearing black sweatpants with a plain white shirt. A string and needle are hanging off his right arm. "Oh God, Wyatt, are you okay? Did you get shot?"

He inspects his arm, shrugs, and turns back at me. "It's just a scratch, nothing to worry about. Are you feeling okay?"

"Yes, I—what happened back there and where are we?" I ask. How long have I been out?

"My house right outside the city. As far as what happened, Dad and I tried to tell you Victor Slater was a shady guy who didn't take no for an answer. I'm just glad we arrived when we did or they would've overpowered you to get you into their car. It would have taken a while before we knew what happened to you. Did those two guys say anything to you before we arrived?"

I shake my head and regret it immediately when the ache intensifies. I can't believe Mr. Slater wanted to force me into a car. *Isn't that kidnapping? Oh my gosh, I was almost taken!* This can't be happening. It was the middle of the day with a restaurant full of people.

"No, they just insisted I come with them, that Mr. Slater wanted a word with me. What would he want with me? I'm just a college graduate declining an internship from his company?" My mind is going in a thousand different directions at the moment, trying to figure out what Mr. Slater could possibly want with me.

"Honey, this is the reason Bobby and Wyatt wanted to get you away from him and his business." Mary has now come over from the large chairs and is running her hand through my hair, careful to not touch my tender spot. "You'll be safe with us." She looks between Wyatt and me, then continues. "I would suggest staying here with Wyatt for a little while until we can find out Victor's true reason for wanting to speak with you," she says and then turns to nod at Wyatt. She moves to leave the room and motions for Gabe to follow her.

The man with gloves makes his way over to the bed and tries to finish with the last of Wyatt's stitches. "Ms. Drake, I'm Dr. Kennedy, one of the Dawsons' family doctors. How are you feeling right now? Any pain anywhere? How's the bump on your head?"

"No, I must've fainted, but physically I think I'm fine other than my head."

He nods while cutting and tying the last stitch. "Good, I'll call and check up on you tomorrow morning. You don't seem to have a concussion but we'll keep an eye on it for now. Continue with the pain meds and ice it every few hours. If something changes alert me immediately. Wyatt has my number if anything should arise."

I thank the doctor as he heads out of the room closing the door behind him. Turning my attention back to Wyatt, I see he hasn't taken his eyes off of me this entire time and is now holding both of my hands in his. I'm not sure how many minutes pass before one of us talks, but we've got some pressing matters that need to be discussed.

"Wyatt, what happened at the restaurant?" I ask just above a whisper. "Why were you and the others carrying guns?"

Do I really want to know or should I just let it be?

"Kendall, for your own safety, I can't go into detail about it. I can only give you a short version of the incident." He waits for my confirmation, so I nod. "Okay. The reason I carry a gun is because my family is very powerful here in Nevada, mainly Las Vegas. We own a huge chunk of this city and our businesses run most of the economy. There are others who want to take our businesses from us and will go to extraordinary measures to make it happen. There's always someone who wants a piece of what we have. Victor Slater is one of our biggest business rivals, who would love to have a fraction of what we have." He pauses for a moment and I dare not interrupt him, fearing he won't tell me anymore.

"Two years ago my older sister, Avery, was gunned down while shopping with her friends. We could never prove who did it, but we know it was a rival." He has a vacant look in his eyes full of pain. His hand comes across and rubs the inside of his bicep where her name is tattooed.

Is he saying Mr. Slater gunned his sister down for a business deal? What kind of business deals go on with casinos and hotels and restaurants? Does that mean I'm now a target?

"Wyatt, I'm so sorry about your sister, that's horrible." I reach out and squeeze his hand. Now I know why he has her name tattooed across his body. "Am I in danger?" I hate to bring myself up when he just opened up about a painful event in his life but my head is bogged down with the what-ifs right now. "How did they know I'd be at the restaurant?"

This is why my aunt and uncle wanted me to steer clear of this place. I'm starting to realize I should've listened to them.

"I'm pretty sure when I told Vic about you not working for him and working for us it set this entire situation in motion. I'm sorry we've dragged you into this. I'm sure Vic wanted to send us a message today and wasn't anticipating us being there. I'd like for you to stay here at my house for a few days to make sure though." He leans in and kisses my temple. It's so tender compared to all the chaos we experienced earlier.

"Okay." What other option do I have? I try to wrap my head around today, but this conversation is making my headache start to throb more. As Wyatt opens his mouth again to say something my stomach growls, interrupting him.

"Let's go and get the monster fed, shall we?" He places a hand on my stomach. "Then we can relax for the rest of the evening." Wyatt stands, pulling me out of bed. My eyes catch the mirror on the wall and I notice my apparel. I'm no longer in my blouse and skirt but in tight cheerleading shorts and a matching spaghetti-strap shirt.

"Wyatt, where are my clothes?" I squeak out.

I must look horrified because he starts to rub the back of his neck.

"Oh, I umm, had to change you when we got here. Gracie has some clothes in the guestroom, so I put those on you," he admits looking a little sheepish.

"You changed me!" I'm shocked and almost cover myself even though I'm fully clothed.

"Yes, of course I did. I couldn't very well leave you in blood-stained clothing, could I? Plus, I didn't want to ruin my bedding, so I did what I had to do. By the way, your clothes are trashed. Those types of stains never really come out, especially from white." He continues to pull me towards the door of his bedroom and I follow still bewildered by his actions.

We make our way down a long hallway and into an open area with a living room and kitchen. The house is grand, not like Mary and Bobby's house, but still grand in a smaller version. Mary and Gabe are seated on the couches and Bobby is in the kitchen on his phone talking in a hushed tone. Wyatt clears his throat to announce our presence and they all snap their heads in our direction. Bobby hangs up and makes his way over to us as does Gabe and Mary.

"Kendall, dear, I'm so glad to see you up and unharmed." Bobby gives me a side hug. I feel so uncomfortable in the clothing I'm wearing in front of these people right now. "I would like you to stay here for a few days or you can come and stay with Mary and me?" he proposes.

"She'll be staying with me," Wyatt asserts with finality in his tone and grabs for my hand. Both Mary and Bobby exchange an expression and I wonder what they must be thinking. We've literally only just met and all of a sudden Wyatt is being all possessive and caveman.

"Wyatt, I need a word." Bobby motions with his head toward a hallway on the other side of the kitchen.

Wyatt pulls me into his body and kisses the top of my head. "Make yourself at home. I'll be right back. Then we can eat."

"Kendall, why don't I take you to the room where Gracie leaves her clothes? We can find you some sweats to put on," Mary suggests. She must sense my distress in trying to cover myself the best I can. If I pull the bottom of this shirt down any farther my boobs will pop out the top.

I nod and follow her down a different hallway from the master suite. Mary and I pass several closed doors until we come to the last one at the end of the long hallway. She opens it, and if I didn't already know this was Gracie's room, I would just by how it's decorated. High-end furniture—a vanity and mirror opposite a king-sized bed—with bling throughout the entire space. Mary walks over to one of the three closed doors and opens one to reveal a closet the size of my actual bedroom stocked with clothes, shoes, and purses.

"Wow! Does Gracie stay here a lot?" I ask wondering if they share the house or if she uses Wyatt's house as a storage for the overflow of clothes that don't fit into her apartment.

"Oh no, Gracie and Wyatt would kill each other if they lived under the same roof for any amount of time. You know Gracie. She likes to have choices when it comes to outfits." Mary chuckles as she waves her hand at the rows of clothing. "Help yourself to whatever you like, and I'll meet you back in the living room." She rubs her hand up and down my back in a loving gesture, then retreats out of the room.

If Gracie doesn't live here, then why does she have so many clothes here? Shaking my head, I start to circle the room looking over the clothes that might cover a little more than what I'm wearing right now. Will Gracie ever wear all these clothes? There's an island with drawers in the center of the room and I discover her panty and bra drawers with tags still attached. I open the bottom one to find an entire drawer with sweats—of course, all high-end. I grab a pair of baby blue bottoms, pull the tag off, and slip them on. Then I open the bra drawer and get a white lacy one out and put it on along with a plain white T-shirt.

Inspecting my appearance in the mirror, I see my makeup has been wiped off. Wyatt must've cleaned me up before putting me to bed. I shrug still thinking this must be a dream and I'll wake up soon and be back at my apartment with Harper.

Harper.

Is she okay? Will Mr. Slater try and kidnap her too? My thoughts are running wild and I need to get to her or at least speak with her to make sure she's okay. Hightailing it to the hallway back towards the living room, I find Mary sitting on the couch reading over something on her phone. When she hears my frantic footsteps coming she snaps her head up and must see the panic in my face.

"What is it, honey? Are you okay? Did something happen?" she asks rising to her feet.

"I need my phone…I need to make a call…It's important," I blurt in choppy sentences. If something happens to Harper it will be all my fault, and I'd never live with myself. I feel my body start to shake.

Mary comes around the couch and starts to rub my arms up

and down to try and stop the shaking. "Honey, calm down and I'll find your phone. Who do you need to speak with?"

I shake my head because I am having a hard time trying to speak at the moment. Harper is the most important person in my life, besides my aunt and uncle.

"Wyatt!" Mary yells as she covers my ears.

I'm not sure when it happens but the next thing I know I'm wrapped in Wyatt's arms being cradled against his chest. I wrap my arms around his neck and press my body to his like he is my lifeline. My face nestles in the crook of his neck. "Babe, what's wrong? Did something happen?" Wyatt tries to pull back to scan my face. "I need you to breathe, in your nose out your mouth, just like me."

I follow his instructions and feel my body relax enough to finally find my voice. "I need my phone to call Harper. What if Mr. Slater went to my apartment and she's there? I need to talk with her."

"Gabe has already spoken with her. She's with Gracie at Mom and Dad's house. You can speak with her, but you need to calm down first, okay?"

I nod and continue breathing in through my nose and out my mouth. Wyatt reaches into the pocket of his sweatpants and pulls out his phone. I watch him call Gracie's number and then hand the phone over to me. She picks up on the second ring.

"Hey, Wyatt, how is everything going?" Gracie asks, and I clear my throat to help swallow the lump.

"Gracie, is Harper there; I need to speak with her."

"Of course, Kendall, she's sitting next to me." I hear Gracie pass the phone.

"Hello?" I sigh hearing Harper's voice. Relief floods my body, if only for a brief moment.

"Harper, are you okay?" I try not to let the panic into my voice.

"Yes, of course! Now tell me how your date with Wyatt went or is it still going? I know it's been a long time since you got some but remember to play a little hard to get," she jokes, and I can almost see her wagging her eyebrows. She is something else, and she obviously doesn't know what went down earlier. It's probably best not to say anything that would upset her; there's no reason to involve her.

"Uh, well I think it is still going." I turn my head and see Wyatt with a huge grin on his face listening in on our conversation. I lightly smack him on his good shoulder and lean away to keep him from eavesdropping anymore.

"That's great, Kendall. Listen, I know you're about to start your new internship and will be really busy the next few days, so Gracie has invited me to go on a little trip. We're going to go to a resort in Arizona for a week. If you want me to stay, then I will, but I really hope you don't mind."

"No, Harper, I think it's a perfect idea. I don't mind at all. This is your vacation too and I want you to have as much fun as possible. I'll be busy getting into the groove of my internship and you won't see me for a while. You go and have fun with Gracie, but make sure to check in every day, okay?" This is a perfect way to get Harper out of the way so Mr. Slater can't try anything. Did Bobby and Mary plan this trip or is it coincidental?

"Yes, Mother!" Harper giggles. "I love you, Kendall. I'll see you in a few days."

"Love you too!" I end the call and hand the phone back to Wyatt, who's still close by.

Wyatt embraces me after pocketing his phone, then drags me to the couch where everyone is sitting. I go to sit in the middle to give him some room, but he plants me on his lap. He places an arm around my waist with his other hand rubbing my thigh. I try moving off his lap again to take the seat next to him but he just holds me there and tightens his arm around my waist. I feel so much more relaxed now, and having his hands rubbing against my body has a calming effect.

"Kendall," Bobby, who is seated across from us, says my name tearing my attention from Wyatt, "I know today must have been frightening, but we need to know a few things so we can better protect you from Victor."

I nod wanting him to continue his questioning so that I can have my turn when this is all over.

"How do you know Victor Slater?" Bobby asks.

"I don't know him at all. Like I said, I received a letter in the mail at Stanford saying I'd gotten an internship for the summer at his company. I've never even met him and only glanced at his picture when I googled him after accepting the position. It was the only paying internship and it was in Vegas, so Harper and I jumped on it."

"Tell me about your family, Kendall," he digs.

"Well, I grew up in Fort Worth, Texas. My parents and brother died when I was five and I was raised by my Aunt Sarah and Uncle Liam." Something passes over Bobby's face, but it's only there for a split second.

"What happened to your parents and brother?" he asks and I feel like this has turned into an interrogation.

Thinking about them brings back so many emotions it's hard to keep them in check. Tears well up in my eyes and I try to wipe them away before they drop to my cheeks. Wyatt rubs my back in circles trying his best to comfort me. I don't have too many memories of them but it still hurts to talk about.

"We…our house caught on fire due to some electrical wiring or something. They got trapped on one side of the house and weren't able to get out in time. Aunt Sarah was able to get me out through a window while Uncle Liam tried to go back for my brother and parents. I don't remember much, just bits and pieces of that night, and what my aunt and uncle have told me over the years."

"Are you close with your aunt and uncle?" Bobby pushes.

"Yes, I have a phenomenal relationship with them since they're all I have left. Except…" I trail off.

"Except what, Kendall?" Wyatt questions, encouraging me to continue.

"I…they don't know that Harper and I are here in Vegas. They think we're traveling around the U.S. this summer before we start our master's program." I see everyone's eyebrows shoot up and feel like I'm about to be grounded. "They never approved of Vegas and were always very adamant about staying away from it, but when this opportunity arose, I felt like I couldn't pass it up."

"So, they have no idea you're here in this city," Mary chimes in. "Kendall, as a mother I would be devastated to learn that one of my children ventured behind my back and didn't tell me where they were. It's a parent's worst nightmare."

I know she's right and I need to come clean with Sarah and Liam. I nod my understanding. "We send each other emails and texts all the time and talk once a week to check in with each other but you're right I need to tell them."

I let out a long breath after being chastised, but now it's my turn to get some answers about today. "Are Mr. Slater and his goons going to come after me again?" I stare directly at Bobby for answers.

"I don't know at this point. I thought maybe you were holding something back from us about your history, but I can tell you're speaking the truth. I don't know what Victor wants from you, but I can assure you we'll get to the bottom of this and keep you safe. My family will make sure no harm will come to you or Harper."

"Do I still have an internship with your company?" I hope this doesn't ruin my shot at getting some great experiences.

Bobby chuckles and shakes his head. "After everything, you still want to work?"

"Of course! I really want the opportunity to work and be challenged, unless you think it'd be too dangerous," I say thinking about how it would work with me in the office always wondering if I'm going to be taken.

"The job is still yours if you want it. Wyatt and I will secure arrangements to make sure you're safe, but I don't see any problem with you starting in a day or so." Bobby checks his phone. "Well, it's getting late and I think we should leave the kids to it. Come, Mary, let's go home and have some dinner."

They both stand, as do Wyatt and I. We give them parting hugs and walk them out as if it's the most natural thing. Gabe speaks with

Wyatt for a few minutes off to the side and then takes his leave. I'm left standing in the foyer not knowing what to do with myself or where to go.

When Wyatt comes back, he closes the door, locks it, and sets an alarm. He reaches for me and pulls me into a big bear hug, squeezing me tight. He starts kissing the top of my head, then my temple, and keeps going south until he reaches my lips. It starts soft and gentle but as I part my lips to grant him entrance, the kiss becomes passionate. I let a small moan escape my throat then feel my back being pressed up against a wall. All too soon, Wyatt pulls back from me and looks deep into my eyes.

"I thought I was going to lose my mind when I heard you say my name earlier at the restaurant. Then to see the prick with his hands on you…" He reaches up with one hand to cup my cheek.

"I was so scared, Wyatt. I didn't know what was going on or what was happening."

"I know, babe." He presses me tightly to his chest and I breathe in the smell of him. "Let's get you fed and then some sleep, okay?"

Wyatt takes me by the hand and leads us to the kitchen where two plates are laid out on the counter. *Who put that there?*

"I have a housekeeper that cleans and makes my meals for me," Wyatt answers my unspoken question.

We sit at the barstools and eat spaghetti and meatballs with a side salad and garlic bread in comfortable silence, stealing small touches. When we finish, Wyatt picks up our plates, rinses them off, and places them in the dishwasher. My expression must throw him off.

"Why are you looking at me like that?"

"I just didn't think you were so domesticated," I tease. Wyatt gives me a playful smirk. "I mean if you want, I've got some dirty clothes that need to be washed and ironed and a fabulous car that needs to be detailed."

Wyatt comes around the counter and before I can even jump

off the stool, I'm captured as he wraps himself around me, causing me to let out a squeal.

"Is that right? Well, I think I've got a dirty girl in my arms that needs to be cleaned first before I start my other chores, don't you?" he says and playfully smacks my ass.

Oh god, he wants to shower together. I've never done that before with a man. Shit, I'm not that experienced with men at all. Guys were put on the back burner for both of us when Harper was almost taken by crazy Chad. I've had sex before but the last time was during freshman year. They were all boys compared to Wyatt. Now, I kind of wish we'd had little romps because I'm so out of my league with this guy. Wyatt is the first man I've wanted and been attracted to in a long time. But can I jump into bed with him after only knowing him for such a short time? He seems very experienced and from the conversation I overheard with Gabe when I woke up, he seems to get 'serviced' from a club.

"Babe?" Wyatt pulls me out of my thoughts.

Nervously, I look around and see we're already in a bathroom and I'm sitting on the vanity counter. "I'm sorry…I was… this… we…"

Wyatt puts a finger up to my lips, silencing me. "It's okay. We don't have to do anything you aren't comfortable with. Why don't you shower in here and I'll take one in the guestroom down the hall, okay?"

"Thank you."

Wyatt gives me a sweet kiss on the lips and makes his way out of the bathroom, closing the door behind him. I exhale and move over to the massive shower in the corner. Steam starts to fill the room quickly as I undress and jump in. I wash myself with Wyatt's shampoo and body wash; I love the smell of him on me and I'm relieved there's not a woman's shower kit here. Maybe he doesn't bring other women here? When I'm done I towel dry my body and open a few drawers to find some lotion. Something moves out of the corner of my eye and I lose it.

My screams echo against the bathroom walls before my brain can register. Moments later Wyatt charges into the room with his gun in hand and his finger on the trigger. He surveys the room and then looks at me. "What is it? What happened?" he asks approaching me a little out of breath.

"I…I saw a man outside the window with a gun strapped to his chest." My arms circle his waist.

"Okay, here put this around you and come with me." Wyatt hands me my towel from the floor as his eyes roam over me like I am his last meal, and I realize I'm completely naked in front of him. My nerves are shot and my head that was feeling better starts to ache again.

Wyatt leads me out of the bathroom and into his closet. It's the same size as the one Gracie has, but not nearly as full of clothing.

"When I walk out of here lock this door and latch it up here. Only open the door if you hear *my* voice. Understood?" He kisses the top of my head before leaving the closet. Once I hear the clicking sound, I rush over to lock and latch the door.

I press my ear to the door to see if I can hear anything, but I don't hear a thing. After opening Wyatt's dresser drawers, I pull on a pair of his boxers and a T-shirt. Turning my back to rest up against the dresser, I notice the full-length mirror is slightly opened from the wall. *Umm, that's strange.* I walk over and pull the mirror open a little more and see it's another room but hidden behind the mirror. Letting curiosity get the better of me, I step into the hidden room and an automatic light turns on revealing what this room is for.

"Holy shit!"

CHAPTER FIVE

"Holy Shit!" I whisper, looking around the hidden room at the four walls. Wyatt has a lot of explaining to do.

As I'm about to step further in, there's a knock on the closet door and Wyatt's voice comes from the other side. "Kendall, it's me open the door."

Turning, I walk to the door, unlock it, and swing the door open wide. He comes in and sweeps me up in his arms and hugs me tight.

"Who was out there?" I ask once we pull apart. "Was it more of Mr. Slater's men?"

"It was just one of my men, babe. I have some guys watching the house in case Vic tries anything, but you're safe with me."

"Oh. I'm sorry, I just saw him and thought…" My voice trails off after I realize I overreacted to the situation. I'm really on edge after the day I've had.

"Don't worry about it. I told the guys to not be so close to the house. I should've told you about them so you wouldn't have been so scared when you saw him," Wyatt says.

"Wyatt, can I ask you something and you'll be totally honest with me?"

"Sure, you can ask me anything," he says with slight hesitation.

"Why do you have a hidden room behind your mirror?"

From his shocked expression, wide eyes, and tensed body, that wasn't what he was expecting. He peers over my shoulder and sees the mirror open wide. "Oh shit," he murmurs under his breath.

I pull back, waiting to hear his response, but he just stands there, like if he doesn't move then he won't have to have this conversation. Finally, after a few more moments he speaks. "Kendall, I don't normally have people over. Usually, I'm more careful, but I can explain."

I nod waiting for him to continue. Time passes as neither of us moves or speaks, and I can tell he is trying to find the best way to tell me about this room. He is definitely having an internal battle with himself. I decide to help tip him a little and walk over to the hidden room. He's by my side within seconds of me entering.

"I…it…"

I hold my hand up to stop him from stuttering more. I don't want him to tell me a lie or hide anything from me. "Wyatt, are you waiting for the zombie apocalypse? Is that why you have your own gun store located in a hidden room in your house?" I joke, hoping to break some of the tension that's built up in the confines of the room.

Walking more into the hidden room, I look at the guns and ammo he has on all four walls. There are at least two of every type of gun on the market, plus a few that might not be legal. There are also grenades and other devices lined on the wall along with knives, gloves, masks, and goggles.

"I love guns," he blurts out and I almost burst out laughing. I've never seen a more confident man stumble so much over his words.

I keep walking around the room, tracing my fingers over several guns, and my eyes venture to the other side of the room to a table with stacks and stacks of bundled cash piled up. I swear this room is straight out of a doomsday show.

"Kendall, say something."

"Well, this is not what I expected, but I can't fault you for owning guns unless it's used to rob banks," I say with a nervous laugh.

"Do you rob banks, Wyatt?" I add to make sure he knows I'm serious despite my joking tone.

The corner of his mouth lifts slightly. I can tell he's trying not to chuckle. "I don't rob banks. Bishop would torture the shit out of me."

"Bishop?"

"He's my friend who gave us the hockey tickets. He also owns and funds almost all the banks here in Las Vegas."

I nod and continue to gaze around the room. "At least it's not a room full of torture devices or cages keeping people in. I guess there are worse things people could have in their homes."

His shoulders relax a bit.

"So you are okay with me having a room full of weapons?" He gestures around the room.

"Sure. I'd be a hypocrite if I didn't. I have a few guns of my own."

That seems to get his attention, and when I turn to face him, Wyatt is already in front of me placing his hands on my shoulders to hold me there. "What do you mean by that? Do you carry a weapon on you?" he asks.

"Not on me right now, but yes, I have a few guns of my own. I have two in my apartment and one hidden in my car." He studies my face. "As soon as I found out I was heading to Las Vegas, I filed the necessary paperwork to obtain my concealed carry permit."

"Kendall, guns are very dangerous. It's not a good idea to carry without the proper training."

"Honey, I'm from Texas. I've been handling guns since I was ten years old. My uncle was a soldier back in the day; he trained me in guns and knives from the very beginning. I bet I can outshoot you." I give him a playful wink and he smirks.

"I'd like to see you try!" He gives me a chaste kiss on the lips. "And for the record, I like it when you call me honey." He reaches around my waist with his large arms and pulls me to him while kissing the sensitive spot under my ear. I love how playful he can be.

"I feel a challenge coming on and I never back down when I know I can win. I'm also good in hand-to-hand combat if you want to try and take me down too!" Wyatt raises an eyebrow. "I might appear small and sweet, but I can kick some serious butt when I need to." I throw my arms around his neck. "Those guys at the restaurant caught me off guard is all."

"Babe, I am not in the business of harming women, but I'd love to see you shoot. Maybe after breakfast tomorrow I can take you to the shooting range and see what you're made of with these so-called skills you have."

"Sure, but don't I need to start my internship soon with the company? I don't want any special treatment or being coddled because we are…" I trail off, trying to find a word that best describes our relationship since it is only a few days old. *Is it even a relationship?*

"Since you're dating the boss' son." Wyatt finishes my sentence for me.

Are we dating?

"Technically, we haven't had one date since the other was interrupted by Mr. Slater." I point out.

"We've been on multiple dates," he says and the confusion on my face must prompt him to continue. "We went to the wedding, then we had brunch and swimming, then we went to the hockey game." He pauses for a second, thinking about something before he speaks. "And now you're living with me so doesn't it bump you up to girlfriend status or something?"

I almost choke as I swallow at him calling me his girlfriend.

"Umm…" I really don't know how to respond to that so I just stare at him.

He shrugs and tugs on my arm to leave the closet and his artillery behind. "Let's go to bed. You've had an exhausting day and I know some sleep will do you some good. Plus, if we're going shooting tomorrow I want you well rested so there aren't any excuses for me beating you at the range."

He walks us over to his bed, pulls the covers back, and motions for me to hop in first. Are we sleeping in the same bed? Wyatt must sense my hesitation.

"We're only going to sleep, Kendall. I promise we won't do any-thing unless you make it happen."

Climbing into the center of the bed, I snuggle under the covers. It's almost as comfy as mine. Wyatt follows in behind me and grabs his phone off the nightstand. He presses a few buttons and all the lights in the house go off, then a faint beeping noise sounds, like an alarm is being set. He places the phone back on the nightstand and pulls me so I'm using his chest as my pillow. His bare strong body has me wrapped around him in a tight hold. I still have so many questions about those men at the restaurant today but will have to wait until tomorrow because the soothing motion Wyatt is mak-ing with his hand on my back is making my eyelids even heavier.

Right before sleep claims me, I hear Wyatt's voice. "Goodnight, my angel."

There's a buzzing sound in the distance and I try to swat at it. I feel movement under my head, so I squint my eyes open and realize I'm still using Wyatt's chest as my pillow. Wyatt reaches over with his long arms and grabs for the buzzing noise, which happens to be his phone, and answers the annoying thing.

"Yeah!" He all but yells into it. "No, I told you in the text last night I wasn't coming in today. You are more than capable of han-dling the run." He follows that up with a series of negative and affir-mative grunts and then, "Listen, Gabe, I told you I'm not coming. If you can't handle this for today then maybe I should start research-ing for another right-hand man…keep her out of this…look if you have a problem you know how to reach me, but we will have a con-versation face to face about this later."

He hangs up, tossing the phone back on the nightstand, and lets out a long breath. I guess Gabe must not approve of Wyatt spending the day with me and not going to work. The last thing I want to do is come between him and his business.

"Wyatt, if you need to go to work I can go back to my apartment and hang out until you're finished," I offer, my voice sounding rough with sleep.

"What? No! Gabe is just acting crazy right now. We have a shipment coming in and he's more than capable of handling it." He stops abruptly like he gave a secret away then shakes his head. "Besides, I never take off and I really want to see these mad skills you've been bragging about." He crushes me back into his chest and we lay there for a few more minutes.

The rhythm of his heartbeat and the smell of his skin could lull me back to sleep within seconds. If we don't start our day soon, I'll never leave this bed. Rising up so I'm hovering over his face, he still looks just as handsome as he did last night.

He reaches up with his hand and cups my cheek. "I think you're the most beautiful woman I've ever seen. I've only ever seen one other pair of emerald green eyes like yours. They set you apart from everyone else in this world."

It amazes me how this big brooding guy can say some of the sweetest things. I can feel the heat in my cheeks from his words, and I lean into his hand and kiss his palm.

"Thank you, Wyatt. You're not so despicable yourself."

He brings my face so it's hovering over his and plants the softest kiss on my lips. The kissing turns more passionate and he's pressing me against himself with his hand on my butt. I hear a moan, not sure which one of us it is from, and feel his impressive member growing against my belly. I know we need to stop or we're about to head down a road I'm not sure I'm ready for yet. Thankfully, his phone goes off to the sound of Elvis Presley blaring throughout the room. I raise a questioning eyebrow when I pull back from our heated exchange. Wyatt growls and slams his hand over to his phone.

"Yeah!" he greets the person on the other line. "Yes, Dad, I know all about it…no, I'm sending Gabe…because I have other matters to attend to today…yes, she is right here and safe. Apparently, we have our own gunslinger right here in the mix, and I want to make sure she knows what she's doing with firearms before she ends up hurting herself or someone else…yeah just call if you need anything…I will. Thanks, Dad."

"So, Elvis Presley is your Dad's ringtone?" I tease after he hangs up.

"Uh-huh." He mimics Elvis and it makes me laugh. "Who better to represent my father than the King! My buddy Luca and I have this ringtone for both our fathers as a joke," he says. "Now, where were we?" Wyatt leans in again to pick up where we left off but I put my hands on his chest and push off to lay back on my side.

"We need to get up and going if you want to see this shooting champion work her magic," I say. Wyatt pouts, and just when I didn't think he could get sexier, he surprises me. "Tell you what, if you outshoot me today then I'll be at your mercy for the rest of the evening, but if I win then you have to be at mine." I love making deals I know I'll win. Although Gracie just recently caught me off guard, I ended up meeting Wyatt so I can't complain.

I see the wheels turning in his head and then an arrogant smirk tilts his lips. I can only imagine what he's thinking. "I like the idea of you being at my mercy. Deal, babe!"

I stick my hand out to shake on it, but he grabs my wrist and yanks me forward so our bodies collide. "I'd rather kiss on it than shake!" he states and locks his lips to mine.

After sealing the deal, we go our separate ways to get changed for our outing. Walking into Gracie's room, I pick out an outfit that will be appropriate to wear to the gun range. Twenty minutes later I'm in black skinny jeans, a fitted white T-shirt, and a pair of black lace-up boots. All of which still had tags on them. Thank goodness Gracie and I are the same size in shoes and clothing. In her bathroom, I find some basic makeup and a brush to comb my wild hair since I went to bed with it wet last night. After brushing my teeth, I apply some powder, eyeliner, and lip gloss, then I pull my hair into a side French braid making it run down past my shoulder, and secure it with a hair tie. I give myself a once over in the full-length mirror then set out to find Wyatt.

I hear him before I see him. Wyatt is in the kitchen with an older woman who is working over the stove. From the smell of it, I think it could be eggs and bacon, maybe even pancakes. Rounding the island Wyatt sees me as he's pulling juice from the fridge.

"Wow, Kendall you look enticing and badass all in one." He looks me up and down like I'm his meal instead of the heaping plate in front of him. "Are you trying to distract me from winning our bet? Because it just might work."

"Who me?" I try to play innocently and place a hand on my chest. "Never." I prop a foot up and pretend to adjust my shoelaces, giving him a view of my backside. And for good measure, I give my butt a little shake.

I hear Wyatt growl as he wraps an arm around me. He kisses right below my ear sending a shiver down my spine. I take a step back and give him a once-over. He's wearing a black polo shirt with dark blue jeans, making him look edible as ever.

"Come. I want you to meet, Carmen, my housekeeper," he says then smacks me on the butt hard. "Behave."

After meeting Carmen, who is the nicest woman ever, Wyatt takes me back to his hidden gun room. He places a black bag on one of the tables and starts collecting guns and ammo to take with us to shoot.

"Do you see any in particular you want to shoot?" he asks me.

"No, you grabbed all the ones I practice with." I wink and he shakes his head.

Wyatt zips the bag up, slings it over his shoulder, and we walk through the house to the garage. There are a handful of cars and trucks in front of different bays. I see an SUV, three different sports cars, a truck, and on the very end next to a few motorcycles is my Camaro.

"I thought we could take your car. I had one of my guys pick it up last night from the restaurant and bring it here," Wyatt says as he opens the passenger-side door for me to get in. I had completely forgotten about my car.

Once on the road, Wyatt talks about growing up around the area and he points out several places he loves to visit and where his old schools are at. He seems so carefree, as if he wasn't in a shootout yesterday.

"Wyatt?" I interrupt. "Did you kill those two men at the restaurant yesterday?"

He pauses for a moment and rubs the back of his neck. "Do you really want to know, Kendall? Sometimes ignorance is bliss."

I pause for a brief moment to consider. "Yes, please tell me."

"We shot and killed both men. It was either them or us and I wasn't about to let them take you out of there." He glances at me and interlocks our fingers over the center console.

Growing up, Uncle Liam always drilled it into my head that I need to stand my ground when put in a dangerous situation. "Never back down and if they keep coming at you, finish the clip until they stop. You have the right to defend yourself," he'd always say.

"Aren't you worried about the police? I mean shouldn't we be at an attorney's office pleading our case or something or making a report?" It all happened so fast and then was treated as if it never happened.

He brings our joined hands up to his mouth and places a gentle kiss on the top of my hand.

"No, babe, we don't have to worry about the police. It was settled yesterday and you don't need to worry about any of that. I would tell you if it was a concern." He glances over at my face giving me a reassuring smile, then looks back at the road. "I won't let anything happen to you, I promise."

"Okay," I say, even though I'm not so sure, but the discussion ends as we pull up to a warehouse. Wyatt parks my car and gets out. Stepping out of the car, I adjust my clothing as he comes around to the trunk, grabs his bag of guns and ammo, and we walk up to the building.

The inside looks nothing like the gun ranges back home in Texas. This place is more like a five-star hotel. When we first walk in we're met with a large oak counter and a uniformed person standing behind it waiting to help us.

"Hello, Mr. Dawson. How can we help you today?" the man with a name badge that reads Thomas asks.

"Hello, Thomas. I need two private lanes today with an instructor on standby."

"Of course, sir. Please follow me and we'll get you both set up in a room before going to your lanes." Thomas makes his way around the counter and toward one of the open archways.

We follow behind him, and I realize Wyatt is standing taller and more dominant; his shoulders are squared, and his voice sounds very deep and commanding. The softness he shows around me is gone. Back is the man I ran into coming out of the bathroom before we left for the wedding.

As we continue to walk through each room, I notice it resembles a high-end gentleman's club, with lots of leather chairs and couches and wood end tables. The only thing missing is a fireplace, cigars, and decanters of brandy. Although, alcohol and guns don't mix so I guess that is why I don't see a full bar anywhere. We walk through a door into a private room with three big screen TVs, leather couches, and a mini kitchen off in the far corner. The back wall is a large window that looks out at the indoor gun range.

"Please put your bag down and have a seat. Jerry will be with you shortly," Thomas says then exits the room closing the door behind him.

"Wow! This seems VIP just to shoot some holes in a piece of paper."

"Only the best for my girl!" he says with a wink as he places the bag down with a clank on the table.

We hear a throat being cleared and turn to see another man standing in the doorway. He's in the same uniform as Thomas but his name tag reads Jerry.

"Mr. Dawson, it's a pleasure to see you again." Jerry puts his hand out to shake Wyatt's hand.

"Jerry, good to see you too. This is Kendall Drake." He motions at me.

I walk from the window over to the man and shake Jerry's hand.

"Hello, Jerry."

"Hello, Ms. Drake."

"Please call me Kendall!"

"So, Kendall, I'll be assisting you today, is that right?" Jerry looks at me.

"Actually, I don't need the assistance, but you're more than welcome to make sure this guy doesn't cheat." I point my thumb at Wyatt.

Jerry seems at a loss for words and his eyes ping-pong back and forth from me and Wyatt.

"Jerry, you'll be on standby in case we need you, but please by all accounts make sure this is a fair shoot for the two of us. I would hate for Kendall to claim cheating," Wyatt says watching me with a smirk.

"Yes, sir. Do you have the guns and ammo with you or do you want to use our supplies?"

"We have our own."

Jerry nods and we walk out into the indoor range to our lanes. We have glasses, earplugs, and gloves waiting for us. Wyatt places the bag on the table set to the side and starts to lay out the guns and ammo. I see he's got a Glock 9mm, Sig Sauer, Desert Eagle, and a Beretta lined up on the table. He double-checks the safety on all of the guns before turning to me.

"Babe, which one do you want to start with?"

"I have my own," I say and pull my custom-made 9mm Smith and Wesson M&P 9 out from the back of my waistband and set it down on the bench at my lane with the magazine clip next to it. I see Wyatt's eyes go wide as he comes over to check out the diamond-studded beauty I just set down. He checks the safety and clip before turning to me.

"Where'd this come from?" he demands. Ever since we came here his entire demeanor has changed and a little bit of the asshole from the other night has crept in with the way he speaks. One thing is for sure, I don't like it.

"I told you, I have a secret place in my car I keep it. I got it out when you were getting your bag from the trunk." I see him huff. "And I'd watch your tone when you speak to me. There's no need to be mad or so snippy with me."

He seems to check himself for a moment and a slight softness emerges from him. "No, I just want you to be safe, that's all." He bends down and kisses the top of my head.

"I'm safe with my weapons, Wyatt, I promise," I reiterate and Wyatt nods. "Now are you ready to get your butt whipped by a woman or what?" I nudge his shoulder.

Wyatt laughs and it echoes throughout the room. Wanting to remember this moment, I pull out my phone from my back pocket and hand it over to Jerry. "Jerry, can you please take pictures and record some of this? I want to be able to have it later for bragging rights!" I see him look over to Wyatt for confirmation and with a nod he agrees.

"Of course, Ms. Drake. Just let me know if you need any help while shooting." He takes my phone and I see our targets are hung up, ready to be used in the back of our lane.

I lean over to Wyatt and plant a chaste kiss on his lips. "May the best outlaw win!"

We both take our places putting on our glasses, earplugs, and gloves. I haven't been to the range in a while but it usually doesn't take long before I get in my groove. We agree to see who has the best score after three clips, so I take my stance. My feet are shoulder width apart with my left foot slightly in front of the right and I gaze down the barrel of the gun with my arms straight. I zone in on nothing but my target in front of me, take a deep breath, press the safety off, and fire away, vaguely hearing Wyatt's gunshots over mine. In a matter of seconds, I've popped out the clip from the bottom of my gun and reloaded, snapping the new clip into place. I continue my assault on my target and when the last bullet shoots out of the gun, I repeat the process of unloading and reloading the gun before taking my last set of rounds. I'd forgotten what a stress reliever this was when I used to practice with Uncle Liam at the gun range in Texas. Feeling the last shot race out of my gun, I stand still for a few seconds before placing the safety back into place and putting the gun down on the bench. I step back from my lane just as Wyatt finishes his last few rounds. Moving to stand next to Jerry, I wait for Wyatt to safely secure his weapon before, he walks over to us and Jerry leaves to determine who the better shooter is. We both remove our glasses and earplugs and set them down on the table where Wyatt's gun bag is.

"You surprise me at every turn, Kendall. I think you're definitely a pro at handling a gun."

"I told you. Now let's see if I shot better than the skillful, Wyatt Dawson!" I place my arms around his waist and hug him. "Oh, and you know if I do beat your butt I'll never let you live it down, right? Speaking of, do you own any aprons?"

"Babe, I play to win so there is no way you beat me." He smiles and kisses the top of my head. I find Wyatt likes to keep constant contact with me when I'm within arm's reach.

Jerry walks back over to us with our targets in his hands. He's boasting a slight smirk on his face. Wyatt and I have both trash-talked so much about being better that the anticipation is killing me.

"Well, it was a very close match. Two points are what set you two apart, but the better shooter today and who has bragging rights is…" I feel both Wyatt and I lean in closer, waiting for the name. "Kendall."

I think the expression of shock and disbelief on Wyatt's face is one for the memory books. My sense of pride can't be held back in this moment and the words spew out before I can swallow them down. "Told ya!"

CHAPTER SIX

WAKING THE NEXT MORNING, I FIND MYSELF COVERED in sweat. I had the same nightmare of my house catching fire, being attacked, and my family being killed. It's always the same from beginning to end like it's on a movie reel. I know Aunt Sarah says most of my nightmares aren't true, but it's too detailed to be my imagination. It feels so real, and at the end of each one, I feel like I'm closer and closer to seeing the face of the man who's in charge. Although I'm still not sure who Lexi is.

I shake off the nightmare and fling the comforter and sheets away from me to let the cold air cool my heated body. Stretching out in Wyatt's warm, comfortable bed, I can't keep the smile off my face remembering yesterday's events. I kicked Wyatt's butt at the gun range and have been on cloud nine ever since. *Kendall for the win!* Wyatt was stunned and asked Jerry to recount the score again. Wyatt even suggested maybe Jerry switched the targets by mistake. *Talk about a sore loser!* Jerry came back again with the same score and my victory lap continued. After a few sulking minutes Wyatt was able to swallow his pride and congratulated me on my *'beginners luck'* win.

As we were leaving the gun range, his phone started blowing up. Apparently, one of his father's businesses had a large shipment coming in today and it was stolen or never made it. Wyatt had to drop me off at his house before heading over to the job site. Not having any of my stuff with me, I hung around the house and visited with Carmen, the housekeeper, for most of the day. Some of that time I laid out by his pool since he made it clear he'd probably be working through the night to fix the problem and that if I needed anything to call but otherwise, make myself at home.

Today starts my internship with Justice Williams, the man who runs the Dawson fortune. I hope I can do a good job and prove to be an asset to their company. With a huge selection from Gracie's closet, I walk out in a black pencil skirt and an emerald green shirt that matches my eyes, along with a pair of black sling-back heels. My makeup is light and my hair is curled. I feel like a million bucks; now I just need to get my nerves to calm down.

Carmen is in the kitchen with my breakfast already fixed and a note next to my plate of eggs, bacon, and fruit. I flip the envelope open and pull it out.

Kendall,

Sorry I wasn't able to see you off for your first day at the business, but I hope you have a wonderful day. The address listed below is to our main office where Justice will be waiting for you. Call me if you need _anything._ *Frankie will be tailing you to make sure you're safe and secure. Hopefully, I'll see you tonight and we can have a quiet dinner while you tell me all about your day. Don't worry I haven't forgotten about our little bet at the gun range and will be at your mercy soon!*

—Wyatt

I can't help the smile on my face when I put the note back into its envelope. Carmen gives me a wink as she finishes rinsing the dirty dishes and places them in the dishwasher. After eating breakfast, I grab my purse and keys from the counter and make my way to the garage where Wyatt parked my Camaro yesterday. A man is leaning against my car with his eyes on his phone, but his head snaps up immediately at the sound of my heels clicking against the concrete, and he stands taller as he moves away from my car.

"Hello, Ms. Drake. I'm Frankie." He puts his hand out to shake mine.

"Hi, Frankie. Please call me, Kendall." I shake his hand. "Will you be escorting me to work?"

"Yes, but I'll be in a car behind you. Wyatt doesn't want you to feel suffocated by the men guarding you."

Thank god!

"Thank you. Shall we?" I make to open the car door but Frankie being the gentleman he is, opens it for me to get in.

I love the rumble my car makes in the garage as I turn the key in the ignition. I put the address to Bonneville Street into the navigation and pull out of the garage. Peeking in the rearview mirror, I see Frankie in a black SUV following me out of the driveway. After getting through some light traffic, I pull into the four-story glass office building that is next to one of their hotel and casinos. Their offices are in the downtown area, which surprises me. I thought with all the money Bobby seems to have, it would be on the Strip and not in the older part. Frankie parks next to me and we walk together silently into the building. The lobby is professionally done and has a masculine feel to it. Frankie guides me over to a bank of elevators, presses the top floor, and we ascend.

I step off the elevator and expect the office to be the same as the rest of downtown but am surprised once again. We're met with a colossal foyer and an equally enormous reception area. Three receptionist are hustling around answering phones or typing swiftly on their computers. Frankie guides me past the desk and through swinging glass doors into the office area. The room has an open concept with cubicles in the middle of the room and glass along the outer walls with closed-in offices lining the entire length of the top floor. We head straight towards the back of the room through another set of swinging glass doors and are met with a matching foyer and reception area like the one by the elevator. I notice there is only one receptionist here and she is currently speaking on the phone. Frankie leans on the reception desk, swiping a mint from the bowl while I get a good view of the receptionist. She's an older woman with gray hair pulled tight in a French twist and she's dressed like she could give the Princess of Wales a run for her money. She ends her call and types a few things on her computer before acknowledging us.

"Good morning, Mrs. Bowen," Frankie greets her after pocketing the wrapper from the mint.

"Frankie, how many times have I told you to call me, Molly? You make me sound so old when you do that!" She chuckles and winks at him. "And who do we have here?" She nods over at me.

"This is Ms. Kendall Drake, the intern to help you guys out for the summer. I believe Mr. Dawson set it up with Mr. Williams."

"Oh yes, I remember now." She looks over her calendar probably thinking she made a mistake.

"It's nice to meet you, Mrs. Bowen," I say excitedly and she gives me a warm smile.

"Well, no time like the present. Let me buzz Mr. Williams and let him know you're here to start. Come have a seat behind the desk while you wait."

I thank Frankie for escorting me up and make my way around the desk as he exits out the glass doors. Sitting down, I hear Molly on the phone.

"Mr. Williams, I have Kendall Drake here at reception…yes, I know…okay…okay…okay I'll send her in." She hangs up and turns towards me with a sympathetic expression.

"Mr. Williams will meet you in fifteen minutes in his office to go over your job assignments," she states as she stands. "Come, dear, I will show you where the breakroom is and how Mr. Williams likes his coffee. It seems to always make his moods more bearable."

Molly shows me where everything is located and just how much cream and sugar to add to Mr. Williams' mug. We both make ourselves one and then she tells me to make him one before going into the meeting. "Trust me, dear, a little mug of coffee will go a long way with Mr. Williams," she jokes and then pushes me toward the two large oak doors.

I try to steady my hands so I don't spill his coffee when I knock on the door. Why do I feel like I'm standing outside the principal's office? *Oh, that's right because this is your first real adult-paying job and you don't want to ruin it.* After hearing a muffled reply to come in, I slowly open the heavy door and walk into a floor to ceiling glass office. Over in one of the corners is a seating area with leather couches and a coffee table. The other side of the room is set up with a long glass conference table with the capacity to seat ten people. Mr. Williams' desk is in the center of the room; a large oak desk with two leather chairs sitting on the other side.

He snaps up from the papers he has in his hands and then stands. Mr. Williams is a tall dark-skinned man and very attractive for his age; I'm guessing mid-forties. He looks like he played football in college with his broad shoulders. When my eyes meet his, I can see a hint of annoyance in them.

"Ms. Drake, welcome." He puts his hand out for me to shake, but when I reach out to shake it, I end up shoving his coffee at him instead and almost spill it. *Fantastic! Way to look incompetent.*

"Thank you, Mr. Williams," I stammer and notice he's switched the coffee to the other hand and still has his hand out to shake. Taking a deep breath, I calm my nerves and give him a firm handshake.

"Thank you." It's like pulling teeth to be polite. "Now, I was told you're here to intern for the summer. Is that correct?" I nod as he sits back down. "Good. Now, I have a busy schedule and Mrs. Bowen will help you with anything you might need," he says dismissively. My body turns automatically to head towards the door.

"Wait, I thought I was working alongside you during the duration of the internship?" I ask confused as my hand touches the door knob.

"Ms. Drake, I'm far too busy to have a sidekick nipping at my heels. Mrs. Bowen will help with any questions you may have. That is all for now and tell Mrs. Bowen to call out for Italian for lunch." With the dismissal, he picks up his papers again to continue looking them over.

What an ass! This isn't the internship experience I had in mind. I could've been a receptionist anywhere. I stalk out the door and march back behind the desk where Molly is typing away. She stops when she hears me slump down beside her.

"Well?" she asks.

"He's a charmer," I announce, and then under my breath, I add, "I believe he thinks, he's God's gift to this Earth."

She laughs out loud and it echoes throughout the foyer. It takes her several moments before she composes herself and my face flames from the embarrassment of being heard.

"Most men in his position and in this business usually do. Give it some time and you'll make a name for yourself here, don't worry. He can be tough as nails sometimes. Just keep supplying him with coffee and a few chocolate bars from time to time and you'll survive." Molly pats my knee.

"He said to call out for Italian for lunch," I remember to tell her. The last thing I need is to screw up the first task he gave me.

"We'll go and have lunch there, and I'll tell you some stories about this place. We can bring him some food on our way back."

The rest of the day Molly shows me around the office, introduces me to people, and gets me acquainted with the computer and phone system. We have lunch together at a family-owned restaurant down the street with Frankie and make sure to bring back Mr. Williams something. *Maybe they spit in it!* At five-twenty Molly sends me into his office to see if there is anything else he needs before we leave for the day, but he just waves me off like some fly buzzing around his head.

While driving home I decide to be more assertive in my approach. Starting tomorrow, I plan to get the list of all the companies Bobby owns and see if my skills can really help out.

The next morning, I walk into the building with a new purpose and goal to reach. Much to my disappointment, I find out Molly has called in sick due to her husband taking a fall and injuring himself. She'll be out of the office until next week, which leaves me to handle all of Mr. Williams' schedule and the busy phone lines. My plans might be on the back burner until then unless I can work it in.

At lunch, I have a few minutes to call over to Debra in accounting to ask for the documents I need: a list of all companies and vendors and anything else that would help me save money and explode profits.

"Ugh Kendall, that may take me a while to compile. Does Mr. Williams not already have those available to him?" I knew this was a possibility when asking for the information.

"Debra, he just wants a hard copy of the updated list. How long do you think this will take to have at my desk?"

"Well, I can have it to you by the end of day tomorrow at the earliest."

"Awesome, I look forward to having it then." Hanging up, I feel giddy at the prospect of helping more than just answering the phone and making coffee this entire summer. This might be my big break.

The rest of the day is spent answering phone calls and booking meetings for Mr. Williams. HR sent up a random person to check on me throughout the day in case I needed help but I was on top of my game and managed to handle the entire calendar and phone system without any help.

It's now Friday afternoon. I want to strangle Mr. Williams and maybe pour laxatives into his coffee. He really could be more pleasant if he tried, but he's only been short and clipped with me and I'm ready to throw in the towel. How does Molly put up with this? She's been here forever tolerating his moody butt and I'm at my wit's end after only a few days.

At five Debra makes her way into the foyer and has a stack of papers and a flash drive in hand. "Hey Kendall, I wanted to drop this off before I left. The flash drive shows the products we use and the amount it costs from each vendor." I hope they pay this woman a fortune for her overachiever attention to detail. "I had to pull in a few people to help."

"Thank you, Debra, I'm sure this is exactly what was needed," I say.

She wishes me a wonderful weekend and heads back out the same way she came.

Now, I'll have the entire weekend to work on this since Wyatt is in a totally different state at the moment. He received a call early this morning about needing to head to the port in California to welcome a shipment and meet with a few new vendors. He's hoping to be back by midday Sunday, so we'll have some time by ourselves before Gracie and Harper return from Arizona.

At five-twenty, I do my usual knock at the door asking Mr. Williams if he needs anything, and like every other time I've gone in there, he waves me away while on the phone. I barely make it until the door is closed before rolling my eyes. Gathering up all my belongings along with the stack of folders and flash drive, I make my way to my car.

In the parking lot, Frankie approaches me carrying my bag of goodies. I'd asked him about stopping by my place so I could get my laptop, but he said he'd take care of it. After handing me my brown leather bag, I get in the car and we drive back to Wyatt's house. I'm so ready to dive right into working on this project and show my worth, but I know I can't right now. Mary asked if I wanted to have dinner tonight with her since Bobby went with Wyatt to meet up with the potential vendors. Of course, I agreed.

At six-thirty, I climb into my car and make my way to *Doña Maria Tamales Restaurant* on Las Vegas Boulevard, near downtown. Frankie has been commendable at keeping his distance and I hardly ever know he's there. Pulling up to a yellow stucco building trimmed in green with a flower on the double doors to the entrance, I circle the building and park in the back. It feels cozy and makes me miss Texas and family so much. I really need to call Aunt Sarah and let her know I'm in Las Vegas.

After entering, I walk in and can tell right away this is a family-owned restaurant. The booths are white and green with tables in the middle throughout the rooms. Each room is decorated differently. One room is dedicated to boxing with posters of fighters and fights. Another is painted with a family in a kitchen cooking together. The feel is family-oriented and I love it, and the aromas of food make my mouth water. I see Mary in the far corner booth seated by a set of boxing gloves hanging from the wall. She's reading over the menu and when she glances up she waves me over. As I approach the table she stands and gives me the biggest hug.

"Thank you for meeting for dinner tonight, Kendall. I always hate when everyone but me is out of town. Eating alone really sucks, don't you think?" Mary says as the waitress brings us water and chips and salsa.

"I was thinking the same when you called and invited me out." Mary smiles and we scan over our menus. "Any time you want to have a meal and some girl time let me know. Harper and I don't really know anyone here other than Gracie, so it'll be nice to hang out."

"Of course!"

I bet she was a cool mom to have growing up.

The waitress comes back to take our order; Mary orders the carnitas plate and I order chicken nachos. I wonder if Frankie will eat. Turning to find him in the restaurant, I see he's seated with three other men and they're in a deep discussion. The other men must be here to watch over Mary. I wonder why she needs three.

"So, how are you and my son getting along?" Mary asks breaking me from my thoughts.

"Beautifully, I think! He had a few late nights, but other than that we've been getting to know each other pretty well. I never would've thought he'd have such a soft side to him after our first encounter."

Mary laughs at my comment. "Well, he seems completely smitten with you. I've only ever seen him like this once before when he was much younger and I love the effect you're having on him." I blush at her words. "How are things working out for you at the business? Justice treating you okay?"

Oh boy, now this is a loaded question. "Ugh, well, things are going okay, I guess. I thought I was going to be working side by side with Mr. Williams, but apparently, I'm only good at taking calls or getting coffee." I look down at the tabletop to try to hide the frown forming on my face and the bitterness in my tone.

"Don't worry, dear, your time to shine will come. The business you're in is a man's world. I know I sound ancient, but they haven't realized it's the twenty-first century yet!" We both giggle. "I'm sure you'll prove your worth in no time. For now, just keep doing what you're doing."

I nod knowing this weekend is going to be spent researching and proving my worth. I'm not willing to accept the man's world excuse.

The rest of the evening we keep the conversation light and she tells me all about herself growing up and meeting Bobby. They had a brief courtship before they married six weeks later. She talks about all her children including Avery, who was killed two years ago. We both tear up and hold hands as she tells the story. She also talks about her best friend who was killed in a house fire similar to mine. It feels too close to home as she describes the incident, but I know house fires happen all the time. She also talks about another friend, Adele Falcone, who she's very close to and wants me to meet. They have a new grandbaby that just arrived and I can hear the envy in her tone. She thinks I'd love Adele's new daughter-in-law, Gemma, and makes plans for us to all go out and have a girls' night.

When we finish our meals, we share the fried ice cream and I tell her about our little adventure to the gun range. She is so surprised someone was able to best Wyatt because he has always been a very competitive person, even when he was a small boy. She then goes on to tell me more embarrassing stories of Wyatt and Gracie growing up, and we laugh until our sides hurt. When it's time to leave we embrace each other like we've been friends forever. She really makes me feel like a part of their family.

"Thank you for coming tonight, Kendall. I really needed to get out of the house and have some chatty conversation with someone other than Bobby!" Mary giggles.

"Well, thank you for inviting me. I had a great time and we can do it again anytime you want," I say before allowing Frankie to escort me to my car as Mary walks with her men to theirs.

By the time I get home, it's after ten but feels much later. I text Wyatt just like I have every night this week if he is not home when I'm there.

> Me: Hey, I'm home and heading to bed. Can't wait to see you Sunday night! How are things going with the new vendors?

It doesn't take long for him to respond.

> Wyatt: Glad you made it safely. Hope you and Mom had a great time and behaved yourselves! Vendors are being difficult and holding out for more money. Sunday night can't come soon enough! I miss your face and it's only been a few hours.

> Me: I miss you too, especially in this big bed! Who will I cuddle with now? Your mom wants me to meet her friend's daughter-in-law, Gemma. She thinks we'd be great friends.

> Wyatt: Don't worry I'll be there before you know it. I know Gemma's husband, Luca. We grew up together. I'll give him a call and set up a double date if you're interested.

> Me: That sounds like fun if you want to get together.

> Wyatt: I'll make the call later. How is working with Justice? Learning a lot?

Crap! I'm not sure what to tell him.

> Me: Things are overwhelming! After this weekend I'll hopefully be able to pull my weight around the office better!

> Wyatt: That's great! Keep up the good work!

Me: Thanks. Going to bed now, will talk tomorrow.

Wyatt: Night Babe!

Me: Night

I put on some pajamas and slip into bed. I want to get up early tomorrow and start my work so I can have the majority of it done by the time Wyatt gets back on Sunday and we can focus on hanging out.

As soon as my head hits the pillow, my eyes close, my body relaxes, and sleep takes over from a long week at my new internship.

CHAPTER SEVEN

THE NEXT MORNING, I POP UP WITH A SURGE OF ENERGY. Quickly showering, I pull on some comfortable sweats, since I will be on the sofa using my computer most of the day. Carmen has made me my favorite breakfast of eggs, bacon, and pancakes, which I scarf down. After telling her thank you, I make my way with my brown leather bag with all my papers, flash drive, and laptop to a room next to Gracie's. Wyatt is letting me use his office, and he had Carmen add a desk, chair, printer/scanner, and computer to the room for me. She also added a few girly touches to the masculine decor. He really went overboard but I smile at how he seems to always take care of my needs, even before I need them.

Dropping my bag on the desk, I pull out all the papers I'll need along with the flash drive. I plan on organizing the paperwork by business categories so I can keep similar ones grouped together. It takes almost two hours but I've sorted through each business and have every one of them grouped. Starting with the transportation section, I dive into the vendors and how each company handles vehicles along with gas and employees. I look on my laptop over some of the files I've used in the past for Uncle Liam's business plan and start with employees. Bobby employs over three hundred people between the trucking business, towing company, and all the taxis and buses here in Las Vegas. He uses a different health and benefit plan for each company and this is where I work my magic. I know for a fact if he uses the same health and benefit company to supply all his employees and companies across the board he'll likely save an enormous amount of money. These healthcare providers will cut him a deal for bringing so many people all at once. I search several health and benefit companies, send them an email requesting a proposal providing my personal email and phone number, and then move on to the next recommendation I can find.

After spending some time reviewing the actual vehicles and the shape they are in, I think instead of trashing all of them after five years he should keep the ones that are in top shape and donate the others to local charities around the city. This way Bobby will have some significant tax write-offs when tax time comes. Another option would be to auction off the used cars in good condition or give them away to high-performing employees in need. Nothing builds morale more than giving away cars! After typing up my recommendation for this section I move on.

I scan over the amount of gas being used for all transportation and the amount is astounding. I think instead of the employees finding the nearest gas station, Bobby should take two of the empty lots he owns on opposite sides of the city and convert them into fill-up stations for all company vehicles. He would have to contact a fuel company and work out the details but in the long run, the price of gas at a regular station will eventually be an end to his fleet.

After all is said and done I feel pretty confident about the estimated money I'll be saving Bobby and move on to the next business category. A knock on the door brings me out of my thoughts. Carmen brings me a sandwich along with some white roses and a bag of gummy bears Wyatt had sent over. I try to call him to thank him for being so thoughtful, but the calls go to voicemail so I send him a picture and text saying thank you instead.

When I finish lunch, I start on the restaurant portion of the companies. This one seems to need a lot of attention. I break down every restaurant by Cuisine because he seems to have a lot of differ-ent restaurants, and right away I take note that each restaurant uses a different vendor for supplies. If they would use the same vendor for all cutlery or glasses in each business that would save a bundle. Also, I think using the same place to buy all your meat and vege-tables is good business, and I recommend making each restaurant donate the end of day leftovers to the nearest shelter to help out the homeless. Another noteworthy tax write-off and he will look good in the community's eyes. I compile my recommendations for this section and then print them off to place in a binder under the 'Restaurants' section.

Hours have slipped by, and when I sit up to stretch out my stiff joints I see the sun has already set. Glancing at my watch it's after eight in the evening. I blow out a breath and look around my office; I have papers with post-it notes everywhere, all organized in per-fect chaos just how I like it. What would help is a large corkboard to pin all my ideas on so that organizing would be easier instead of trying to find where I put certain papers. I then call it a night and relax my brain and body until tomorrow morning. One last smell of the white roses Wyatt sent me today and I exit the room.

I shut the office door and make my way down the hall towards the kitchen. The smell of something good hits my nose and makes my stomach grumble. I expect to see Carmen when I round the corner, but I'm met with silence. I look for her but find the kitchen is empty. There's a note on the counter with my name on it next to a bottle of wine and corkscrew. Opening the note, I can't help but appreciate the beautiful handwriting.

Kendall,

I left you barbeque chicken with potato salad in the oven warmer. The salad is in the refrigerator along with a slice of lemon pie. Call me if you need anything. If not, I will see you Monday morning before you head to work.

Carmen

Putting the note down and making my way over to the warmer, I pull out the plate. Everything smells delightful and I can't wait to sink my teeth into this meal. After gathering my salad and drink, I forgo the kitchen counter and move to the couch. I've spent the entire day on the floor or office chair and I need some cushions right now. I grab the TV remote, switch on the movie channel, and flip through the hundreds of options. After finding a murder mystery, I settle in and relax as I enjoy the meal Carmen made.

At some point during the movie, I fell asleep only to be woken up by a loud blast coming from the TV. Spying the digital clock, it reads after midnight. I stand on shaky legs and move to Wyatt's bedroom.

The next morning, I wake to the buzz of my phone alerting me to a text message. Focusing on the screen, I see it's from Wyatt.

> Wyatt: Good morning beautiful. I just wanted to let you know we should be home around 6. I have a special night planned out so be ready to go around 6:30.

> Me: Morning stud! Sounds good, can't wait to see you. How should I dress?

> Wyatt: Stud, huh!! Dress casual. Jeans, shirt, and sneakers.

> Me: Okay! See you soon!

I place the phone back on the nightstand and stretch out in bed. Things with Wyatt seem so easy and we fit together like we have been with each other for a long time instead of over a week. I definitely think I could get used to this, but unfortunately when the summer is over I have to return to California to attend my graduate program at Stanford. Maybe we'll be able to have a long-distance relationship and travel back and forth for visits. It's over an eight-hour drive, but only an hour and thirty minutes flight. I can't worry about that right now though and put the idea on the back burner, intent on enjoying the time I have with him here in Las Vegas.

After swiping some juice out of the fridge, I sit behind the desk and start working on the casino and hotel category. My thought was that this section was going to be my biggest task to conquer, so I saved it for last and I'm glad I did. There are so many different types of hotels and real estate throughout the city, that I find it hard to group them. Finally, I leave everything that isn't within the Las Vegas City Limits alone until I can get a better idea of how to manage all of these companies and make them as functional as the other categories I have already finished.

Once again each company uses a different vendor so I already know using one vendor for all the businesses will save money. I make some recommendations that will use the same linens along with big companies who sell mattresses and bulk furniture so each hotel or motel can be styled almost the same. I know the higher priced hotels will need to have higher end furniture but Bobby has a lot of lower end ones they tend to cater to.

I check out the websites for the hotels and motels and find them to be basic. I think sprucing them up will help the traffic to each website. Maybe adding a few pictures of the rooms or the pools might help also. The website could also offer a discount to the restaurants he owns if a person stays there. Everyone always likes a good deal or at least when they think they're getting one.

The next task is tackling the casinos. I have no experience with gambling or even where to begin with this type of business so I place a post-it note on the stack of papers and leave them for after Mr. Williams sees my work. I'm hoping to save Bobby a lot of money with my initial assessment. Hopefully then I'll earn some respect from Mr. Williams and show him I can be a superb asset to the team.

I continue to polish my proposal and check emails regarding group discounts for the rest of the day. I want my presentation to be spot on without an error to undermine all my hard work over this weekend.

I wrap everything up in a big fat bow before putting it away in my brown leather bag. I straighten the office and bring the dirty dishes to the kitchen. The clock on the oven says it's almost five.

Wyatt should be home in an hour, so I need to start getting ready for our date.

Walking to Gracie's room, I pull out a black lace bra and panties set along with a pair of dark denim jeans with a plum V-neck shirt. I find a box of new black Converse sneakers from the bottom of the shoe closet and make my way to Wyatt's bathroom. Eyeing the deep soaking tub, I throw my hair up in a clip, start music from my phone, grab the razor, body wash, sponge, and shaving cream, and step into the hot water. I feel my muscles relax as I sit there with my head laid back against the tub and let the tension from working this weekend slip away.

As the water starts to cool, I step out of the bath after making sure I'm completely hairless in all the right places and smell wonderful. I find one of Wyatt's white plush robes hanging from a hook on the wall and slip it on.

I wonder if he has ever used this or if it is more of a decoration. Shrugging the thought off, I brush my teeth and then hear the most exciting sound!

"Babe, I'm home!"

I spit the mouthwash out in the sink and make a break toward the front door. I barrel through the hallway and see him walking into the kitchen holding some mail in his hands. He sees me just in time to catch me as I launch myself at him. Lifting me in his strong arms, he swings me around kissing me deeply. This is what I have been missing for the last few days. Wyatt places me on the kitchen counter never breaking contact. My hands move to his hair returning his kiss with just as much enthusiasm. We break away only to catch our breaths and Wyatt leans his forehead up against mine.

"Well, if I knew this was the type of homecoming I'd be getting then maybe I should go away every weekend!"

"Absolutely not!" I say, my breathing almost back to normal.

Wyatt's eyes leave mine and travel down my body. I follow his blazing eyes down and I realize I'm still in his robe and it has come loose exposing me and all my glory to him. He makes no move to look away and I watch him lick his lips. I quickly grab the robe and close it, trying to restore some of what is left of my modesty. Wyatt takes a step back from the kitchen counter, groans, and closes his eyes. When he opens them back up I see him smirking with lustful eyes.

"I really could get used to a homecoming like this!" He winks at me. "I'm going to go have a very cold shower before we go." Wyatt turns on his heels and walks towards his bedroom.

I can't believe that just happened. Oh my gosh, it was hot! I remove myself from the counter and make my way into Wyatt's room to finish dressing for our date. As I enter the bedroom the shower turns off so I sit on the bed and wait for Wyatt to exit the bathroom so I can get my clothes that are hung up on a hook behind the bathroom door. He exits two minutes later with nothing but a towel around his waist and drops of water littered across his mesmerizing body.

"Would you like a little show? I think it's only fair since I got one in the kitchen," Wyatt says and he holds the edge of his towel in a gesture to let it fall to his feet.

My body is still as a statue ogling his physique and all rationale has left the building. Wyatt must take my silence as approval and drops the towel making a slow walk to me.

"See anything you like, Kendall?" Seduction drips from his voice.

I nod raking over his nicely sculpted body and his hard dick. He stops in front of me never breaking eye contact once I tear my eyes upward.

"Wyatt," I whisper so low I don't even know if he heard me. "I've only had a handful of sexual encounters almost four years ago and it was nothing like what is about to happen here. My experience is probably non-existent compared to yours," I say looking into his eyes, embarrassed.

"Kendall, I told you we'll take this slow. You have no idea how grateful I am to hear you have almost no experience. I can't wait to show you all the ways I am going to pleasure you," Wyatt says as he cups both of my cheeks with his large hands. I nod because I don't trust my voice.

"Babe, lay back and let me give you a preview of how extraordinary we're going to be together. I need to feel your tight little body against mine."

I lay back on the bed at his command and Wyatt slowly unties my robe, exposing me. My hands automatically try to cover my most intimate parts but he holds my arms at my sides.

"Don't try to cover yourself from me, babe. You have the sexiest body and I want to enjoy the sight in front of me."

My entire body trembles and flushes and I feel it from my cheeks to my toes. I nod once again as he leans his naked body over mine and presses his lips to me. The tension in me starts to slowly relax the more he kisses me. I feel his hard member against my core and the tension that had left returns. Wyatt must feel it because he pulls his mouth away from mine and stares into my eyes.

"Babe, relax; I won't do anything you're not ready for. Let me explore this perfect body." He continues kissing me to my ear, giving it a small bite making a moan release from my mouth. "Besides, he's only saying hello to your hot little pussy." His shaft bumps my clit sending a shockwave through my insides.

"Wyatt!" I gasp at hearing him say *that* word. He makes it sound so dirty, yet very arousing at the same time.

Wyatt descends to my neck leaving wet open mouth kisses in his wake as he moves to my breast. He nips and sucks on both giving them the same amount of attention before continuing down to my navel and then to the top of my pelvic bone. It feels like my body is on fire and I'm writhing underneath him, fisting the sheets while he plants light kisses down my pelvic bone before feeling his hot breath right above my core. I sneak a peek and see him inhale through his nose.

"Oh, babe, you smell delicious. Watch me taste you."

He places his tongue flat against me and takes the longest lick. I almost convulse on the spot. The sight is so erotic, I feel a tingle in the pit of my stomach. My head falls back on the mattress suc-cumbing to this feeling. Wyatt never lets up on his attack. He even adds his finger into my core and I don't know how much more I can handle.

"Wyatt!" I moan as my fingers find their way into his hair, pressing him closer to me.

"Just feel it, Kendall." He flicks his electric tongue against my clit in a side to side motion, and I feel my body quake. Then he wraps his lips around it applying pressure and my head shakes back and forth. "Come for me, babe. Come now!" he growls, and the vibra-tion is too much.

My body follows his command and I spasm in the most heav-enly way. I swear I see stars. When I finally come back to my senses, Wyatt is lying beside me with a shit-eating grin on his face. I'm mir-roring him and lean in to kiss his lips, tasting myself at the same time.

"Welcome back, what'd you think?"

"I…well…it was incredible!" I praise because I'm not sure how one thanks another for the most heavenly experience of their life.

"You don't have to thank me. I plan on doing this as much as you'll let me. Let's get dressed and head out on our date." Wyatt gives me a peck on the lips and moves to get off the bed.

"Wait, what about you?" I ask gesturing to his engorged dick.

"I'm good, babe. This was all about you right now," he says and helps me stand. He leans down to my ear and whispers, "If you're a good girl, then I'll let you suck me off when we get home later."

Wyatt heads towards his closet as he pushes me to the bath-room. I take a look in the mirror before getting dressed and can't stop the smile that has permanently taken up residence on my face. Just five minutes ago I let a man explore my body and it was the best experience of my life. Harper is going to flip when she hears about this! I still have the flushed look going on and I don't care. This man is going to do many other naughty things to me and there is no reason to be embarrassed about it.

I get dressed, fix my hair and makeup, then head out to find

Wyatt. I find him sitting on the sofa in the living room gazing at his phone. His back is to me so I wrap my arms around his neck and give him a hug while hiding his eyes with my hands.

"Guess who?"

"Hmm…I'd know that scent from anywhere!" I giggle and he pulls me over the back of the sofa and into his lap. "How do you feel right now, Kendall? About what we did?" Wyatt is scanning my face with his curious eyes.

"Wonderful! I've never done anything like this before, and now I see why Harper was always trying to get me to date or have a friend with benefits."

He growls as he tucks a strand of hair behind my ear. "You won't be needing any of them, so tell Harper you're good. You need something, you come to me for it," he says with a firm voice.

I nod. Who would have thought his possessiveness could be so hot?

"Good, I want you to feel comfortable with me and I want you to tell me if you don't like something we do. I like you a lot Kendall and don't want to mess this up because I got a little carried away or went too fast."

"I like you too Wyatt, but I just worry my inexperience will put you off. I'm sure you've had many women who are far more… advanced than me and maybe you might get bored." I can't even look at him when I say this.

Wyatt hooks a finger under my chin and makes me look in his eyes. "Yes, Kendall, I've had many women in the past, but they don't even hold a candle to you. I've never had a single connection to any of them emotionally. I know this is going to sound harsh but they were just there for me to get my rocks off. A release and nothing more. With you, everything's changed for me. It doesn't matter what your experience level is, I will never get bored."

His confirmation of having many women is like a punch to the gut. I know I was the one who brought it up, but man, it stings. I start to wonder how many have laid in the same bed I've slept in for the past week or how many have used the same bathtub or shower. Wyatt must sense my internal struggle.

"Babe, look at me. You are so special to me. I can't put words on it but there is something about you that draws me in. I never thought I'd feel this way about someone. You're the first woman besides my family or Carmen to enter my home. The first one to ever sleep in my bed or use my towels or wear my clothes. I knew the moment we bumped into one another you were something special. I hope you feel the same about me." Wyatt lightly brushes his fingertips against my cheek. He looks so sincere and so far, I have no reason to not believe his words.

"I do. You have this pull on me that seems like we've known each other far longer than just a week. I trust you and that in itself is huge for me. I don't normally trust men so easily, but I know you're different."

"Good. Now let's get this date started!" Wyatt helps me stand and we make our way towards the garage and into one of his many sports cars.

We head to the downtown area and grab a bite to eat at one of the restaurants his family owns.

"This burger is so good," I moan as juices run down the side of my mouth.

Wyatt takes his napkin and wipes up the mess as my hands are covered in ketchup, mayo, and the delicious burger.

"I thought you'd like this place. Glad you approve," Wyatt says then takes a big bite out of his own.

His legs are wedged on the outside of mine under the table making sure we're constantly touching.

"How was California? Did y'all get your supplies from the vendor?"

Wyatt wipes his hands with a new napkin, having finished his burger, and reaches for our shared pile of fries.

"Yeah, we did but it seems these guys are starting to give us the run around. We'll probably start looking for new ones if they don't get their act together." He offers me a bite of his fry.

Once we finish eating Wyatt takes me to Fremont Street.

"How adventurous would you say you are?" Wyatt asks as we walk under a large canopy with a ton of people around. Even for a Sunday night the area is packed.

"I'm up for most things, why?" I say cautiously because I have no idea what he has in mind.

"Do you trust me?" He looks down into my eyes. He has his arm around my shoulders and our hips are joined as we walk.

"May-be?" I drag out teasingly. "What'd you have in mind?"

Wyatt takes me over to the other side of the street on the opposite side of where we came in. The lights and music are blasting and everyone is having such a good time here. We walk up a set of stairs and I see exactly what he has planned. Out in front of us is a zipline scaling the entire length of Freemont Street to the entrance where we came in.

"We're ziplining!" I say with excitement.

"I thought you might like it."

"It's a good choice." I lean up on my tippy toes and kiss the shit out of him.

How fun of a date! People are gathered below to watch the light show on the world's largest video screen.

"Race you to the end!" I yell over the noise as we wait for the workers to make sure we're strapped in and do the final check.

"Is everything always a competition with you?" Wyatt retorts, turning his head to the side to look over at me.

"Life would be boring if it wasn't."

"I'm starting to see life with you will never be boring," he comments but before I can reply we shoot down the wire over the crowd.

The entire night is a blast and a unique welcome back date for Wyatt and me. We talk and drink until two in the morning. Later that night as we crawl into bed, we kiss and hold each other tight before falling asleep.

How did I get so lucky to catch such a wonderful man?

CHAPTER EIGHT

HE NEXT MORNING, I TAKE IN THE VIEW BESIDE ME. Wyatt is sleeping quietly on his back with his arms above his head looking so peaceful. I check the clock on the nightstand and see our alarm goes off in ten minutes. Hmmm, that is plenty of time for a little fun. I slowly pull the sheet down until it reveals black boxers. His skin immediately produces goosebumps from losing the warmth. Ever so lightly I lift his waistband, slide my hand in, and connect with my destination. He's already hard. Gripping his dick I give it a testing squeeze which earns a deep moan from Wyatt. Taking it as encouragement I continue to squeeze and slide my hand up and down his shaft. After three pumps I feel fingers tangle in my hair and look up.

"I could get used to this wake-up call every morning," his voice is deep and sexy, laced with sleep.

With his other hand, he lifts his hip and pushes down his boxers to give me better access. Not wasting any time I start to work his shaft as drops of clear liquid leak from the tip. My hand spreads it along his hard rod that grows with every pump.

"Put your mouth on me," Wyatt encourages.

I lean in licking my lips and encircle the bulbous head of his erection with my mouth. The skin is soft yet firm. The noises he's making are giving me the confidence to speed up my assault.

"God, Kendall, that's it."

My head bobs as I take more in my mouth. His fingers tighten in my hair and it spurs me on. My tongue is working the underside and when I come to the top I swipe the tip earning me praise I didn't realize I needed.

"I'm there, babe," Wyatt announces as I continue to bob, going deeper with every descent. "Jump off if you don't want to swallow," he grunts but doesn't remove his hand from my hair. He keeps a firm hold in place and helps the movements along.

I stay in place loving the feel of power that can make a man like Wyatt become putty with my actions. I feel him pulse in my mouth and with careful attention, I bare my teeth and lightly graze them up then down his shaft, humming.

"Oh shit!" Wyatt moans.

With both hands, he shoves my head down on his dick and the feel of thick liquid hits the back of my throat. Wyatt grunts as each spurt of cum rushes out. After three more pumps, his fingers let go of my hair. His heavy breathing starts to calm as I ease back and look up at him lying on the bed.

"Good morning," I say as I wipe the corner of my mouth.

"Hell yeah, it is." Wyatt wastes no time bending down and flipping me on my back in the middle of the bed. His lips crash to mine as his fingers find their way under his T-shirt I'm wearing to squeeze my boobs. "You naughty little minx," Wyatt says as he runs his lips down my cheek and neck, touching the sensitive spot just below my ear. His hand finds its way into my panties and he groans at the wetness. "You're going to be late for work."

An hour later we're showered, dressed, and sitting at the table in the kitchen eating our breakfast. Wyatt refuses to keep his hands to himself after my little morning surprise. He had originally wanted me to eat while seated on his lap, but I didn't want us to spill our coffee or food on our clothes, so we compromised on setting our chairs next to each other so that they touch.

"What does your day look like?" Wyatt asks while sipping his coffee and leaning back in his seat. He's making circles on my upper thigh, driving me nuts.

"Well, I have work until five, but then nothing. I need to call Harper and Gracie to see if they're back from Arizona."

"They're still at the spa. Gracie convinced Mom and Dad to let them stay another week." He shrugs like it's no big deal. I'm sure she didn't have to try too hard. Gracie could convince a woman wearing white gloves to buy a ketchup popsicle.

"Oh, okay. Well, that means I only have work for today. What about you? What do you have going on?"

"I have to make a few drop-ins on some of the businesses but I wanted to take you out for lunch if you're free around one."

"Really! I would love that!" I kiss his cheek after placing my napkin down on the table.

"Cool. How about I drive you in today and pick you up from work? I should be in the area around five and then we can ride home together."

"Like my own personal chauffeur? Careful I might get used to this kind of treatment!"

I gather my leather bag with all the proposal folders and we head out in one of his prized cars. It still seems so surreal that I have a boyfriend and he's taking me to work.

"Where's Frankie?" I ask just remembering I didn't see him this morning.

"He'll meet us at the office. I don't need him to follow you when I'm around. I'm all the protection you need," he says flippantly.

"Oh really? You sound pretty sure of yourself. After our shooting match, I should be the one following you around for protection. I did outshoot you!" I poke my finger in his chest and stick my tongue out at him.

"I am never going to live that down am I?"

"Nope! Not a chance!" I grab his hand and intertwine our fingers. "Better get used to losing bets."

He lets out a big sigh as the light changes to green and then kisses the back of my hand. The rest of the car ride is spent trying to agree on a radio station we both like. When we pull up to the glass building, I see Frankie waiting by his SUV smoking a cigarette. He quickly drops the lung-killer to the ground and twists his shoe to extinguish the stick.

"Morning, Boss," Frankie greets Wyatt with a handshake. "Morning, Kendall," He nods my way.

"Morning Frankie. Thanks for keeping my girl safe," Wyatt says to him.

"No problem, easiest assignment to date."

"Good. Let me walk her in and then I need to address some business with you." Frankie nods and walks back over to his SUV.

Wyatt walks me into the building and over to the elevators holding my hand. I notice several women glancing at him swooning. Some aren't even trying to hide it, and most are very vocal with the, "Good morning, Mr. Dawson." I wonder if he slept with any of them. God I hope not, it could get very ugly at the workplace.

Speaking of the workplace…

"Wyatt, why don't you have an office here in the building?" I ask as the elevators ascend to the top floor.

He stares at the numbers above the door and then quickly pushes the red stop button on the panel. Wyatt turns to me and pulls me into a tight hug with his large arms around me. He has his face nestled against the side of my neck. It's sending shivers down my spine, and I feel his breath on my ear.

"I hate to be boxed in all day long and prefer to be out in the field. Now that you're working here every day I might need to rethink the position. Although, I don't think I'd get much done if you worked down the hall from me." He places a sensual kiss on my neck.

Yeah, we definitely would not get any work done.

His phone buzzes and he stops his assault on me after getting me all worked up. Wyatt takes a step back never taking his eyes off of me and reaches blindly for his phone. He cuts his eyes to the phone and sighs.

"Alright, babe, stop trying to seduce me in the elevator. I need to get to work and you need to go before you're late." He says it like I'm the one who is keeping him here against his will.

"Right, because I'm the one who just accosted you," I say and roll my eyes at him. "I'll need to work on that, *Mr. Dawson*." He chuckles as he presses the red stop button again and wraps his arm around my waist as the elevator starts to rise.

When the doors open to my floor, we walk side by side through the office to the reception desk where Molly is seated.

"Good morning, Mr. Dawson, Kendall," Molly greets us.

"Good morning, Molly. How is the old ball and chain doing after his fall?" Wyatt asks jokingly.

"Much better, thank you, dear. We all know when men are sick or hurt it's like the world is ending." Molly laughs. "I didn't know you had an appointment this morning with Mr. Williams. He won't be here for another thirty minutes or so."

"No, it's quite alright, I was just dropping my girlfriend off before heading out."

I see Molly raise an eyebrow when she turns to me. I'm already behind the desk sizing up today's calendar.

"Well, isn't that lovely of you, dear. I think you two make an extremely cute couple." Molly sounds dreamy when she says it. No malice or judgment behind her words.

"Thank you, Molly. Can you make sure she has lunch around one so I can take her out to eat?" Wyatt asks in a whisper like he's telling a secret and I'm not standing right beside them.

"Of course, dear, anything for you." I watch her wink at him. Dear Lord, is there anyone who is immune to this man!

"Perfect! I have to go but will be back to pick you up, so be ready," he says to me. He leans over the desk and puckers his lips to mine. "Have a great day, babe!"

"You too," I say as he turns and heads out towards the elevators.

I put my purse and leather bag down under the desk, turn on my computer, and notice Molly staring at me. Her reading glasses have slid down her nose and she's eyeing me up and down waiting for me to start gossiping. *Not a chance!*

"So…how is it you and Mr. Dawson know each other?" she asks crossing her arms over her chest.

"Oh, we were set up on a blind date by Gracie. We both lost a bet to her and ended up going to a wedding as each other's date. I hope my dating Wyatt isn't a problem. I just want to learn the ropes of running a big business. I had an internship with Mr. Victor Slater, but after meeting Wyatt, he and Bobby made sure that I interned here instead."

"Oh dear, thank goodness Mr. Dawson saved you from working with Slater. I have heard he is absolutely horrible to his employees," Molly states.

"Really? What have you heard?"

"The main consensus is that he is truly a tyrant. His turnover is the highest in the business around here. Can't keep administrative staff for longer than six months."

We finish gossiping just as Mr. Williams walks through the reception door with his briefcase in hand and passes us with only a nod and a mumble of, "Good morning."

I offer to make his coffee so that I can speak with him about my research. Knocking on the door I wait for an answer from the other side. When I hear a grunt, I take that as the green light to enter. He has papers scattered all over his desk, mostly spreadsheets and reports of some kind. He really should have a better organizing system.

"Here you are, Mr. Williams." I offer him his coffee and he points to the usual spot at the corner of his desk. I really want just an hour of his time and I know he will be blown away if only he'll give me a chance, so I wait to be acknowledged.

"Is there something else, Ms. Drake?" he asks still not looking at me.

I muster up all the confidence, square my shoulders, and breathe out a subtle breath. Why am I so intimidated by this man? *Because you want to impress him with your ideas!*

"Yes, I would like to have you look over some proposals I've worked on over the weekend to see if there are any ideas that might help save the company money."

He is still working on his computer and not paying any attention to me. "Sure…sure just leave it on the desk and I will get to it later," he says dismissively.

I roll my eyes knowing he can't see me. He refuses to acknowledge me or anyone else so I make my way back to the desk where Molly is answering the phones. I pull out all the folders from my bag and walk back to place them on Mr. William's desk.

I swear, working for the tyrant, Mr. Slater, is looking better each day.

The rest of the morning flows like last week: scheduling appointments, answering phones, and making coffee. Molly tells me a few stories about young Wyatt who would run through the halls and create a shitstorm as he went. We both snicker and carry on with our morning duties. By twelve-fifty Molly has returned from taking her lunch, and when the phone rings Molly answers it and quickly hangs up.

"Dear, your sweetie pie is downstairs waiting for you," she says with a smile that could light up Vegas at night.

My heart flutters at hearing this, and I quickly clean up my area, grab my purse, and make my way down through the lobby to the parking lot. Wyatt is leaning up against his car at the curb with white roses in his hands. He looks edible in his tailored suit and sunglasses against the car. He meets me halfway and crushes his lips to mine right in front of the office building. When we finally break apart and stop giving the workers a show, he says, "I got these for you. I couldn't pass them up on the way here."

"Thank you, Wyatt. They're beautiful and very thoughtful of you." I place my hand on his chest and lean up for another quick peck. As I glance down at where my hand is placed I notice a few spots on his shirt.

"Is that blood?" I ask.

Wyatt takes a step back and peers down at his shirt. He tries to wipe at his shirt with his hand but the stain is already set in.

"Umm…yeah I guess it's from a nosebleed I had earlier." He shakes his head and curses under his breath as if chastising himself for something. "Yeah, you know with all this dry heat in the desert and all—let's get you to lunch, shall we?" He takes my hand and leads me to the passenger side before opening my door for me. *Whoever said chivalry was dead!*

"It's okay, I used to get nosebleeds all the time growing up. Although, I don't know if you'll be able to get the stains out. I guess it's a good thing your family owns a few dry cleaners," I joke, trying to lighten the mood.

Wyatt takes me to a restaurant called *The Capital Grille* located in the Fashion Mall towards the end of the Strip. Lunch is delicious and the service is outstanding. Even though the place is packed we're served immediately with no wait on our food and drinks. On our way back, we have to make a detour away from Las Vegas Boulevard due to some construction. We pass through some of the outer communities away from the downtown area but as we're stopped at a red light at a busy intersection, I notice several strip malls. Something is very familiar with them and at first, I can't quite put my finger on it, but then it strikes me.

"Wyatt, doesn't your family own these three strip malls here on the three corners?"

"Yeah, we do. Why?" He looks over at me and raises his sunglasses, squinting at each building.

"Oh nothing, just spotted them and remembered it from my

research from this weekend is all. I think there was a laundromat, a dry cleaners, and a convenience store in one of the buildings, but I don't see them," I say more to myself than anything. "I could have my streets mixed up though. Your family owns so many businesses it's hard to keep track of them all."

I look back over at Wyatt and see him swallow making his Adam's apple bob. He doesn't say anything, only replaces his glasses over his eyes and guns it when the light turns green. We make it back to work in no time and I know our little bubble is getting popped to head back to real life.

Wyatt pulls up to the curb and turns in his seat so he's now facing me. "Alright, babe, got you back safe and sound."

"Thank you, Wyatt, for the incredible lunch date and roses. You know we could have gone and had fast food and I would have been okay with that, right? I don't want you to think that you always have to spoil me and eat at such fancy places."

"Kendall, I plan on spoiling you every day if you'll let me, so get used to it."

"Okay," I say timidly.

Wyatt gets out of the car and comes around to open my door to help me out. "Listen if for some reason I'm not here at five to pick you up then I want you to ride home with Frankie." He completely changes the subject and says in a stern voice. "Only Frankie, okay?"

"Yes, sir!" I mock salute him.

We say our goodbyes with a kiss, and as I turn to head back in to work, Wyatt playfully swats my ass.

"Hey, what was that for?" I say rubbing my ass as if it hurt.

Wyatt can be so playful sometimes!

"You know how I feel about being disrespected." He tries to give me a stern expression, but the smile on his face gives him away. I make a show of rolling my eyes and with a wink, he pulls his sunglasses back down, gets in his car, and drives away.

Making my way to the elevators, I notice the glares from the other employees. I guess the word is out that I'm dating the boss' son. I spend the rest of the day helping Molly out and once again, not really getting a peek into what it's really like to run a big business.

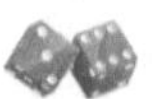

Mr. Williams never comes out of his office once or calls me in about my reports. I chalk it up to him being busy the rest of the day, but now it's the end of the next day, and I'm starting to think he forgot or doesn't care. I would've thought he threw them away except they're still sitting in the same spot on his desk where I placed them on Monday.

I check his calendar and it shows he's free from meetings and calls for the rest of the day so I decide to bite the bullet and ask him. Following Molly's advice, I make my way over to the breakroom and make his coffee just how he likes it. I need all the points I can get at this rate. Knocking on the door, I hear the usual grunt from the other side. Mr. Williams is in the same position he was in two hours ago when I had to have him sign some documents for accounting. I feel my steps falter slightly as I take a few breaths to steel myself for this conversation.

"Mr. Williams," I begin setting his fresh mug of coffee on his desk and removing the empty one. The man usually goes through at least four to six mugs a day. "I was wondering if you had the chance to review some of the reports I left you on Monday?"

He finally stops whatever it is he is doing on his computer and gives me a scowl that could turn me into stone.

"Ms. Drake, does it look like I have any free time to go over your reports? I'm a very busy man trying to run an entire business. I don't have time to critique some college paper telling me how to run the business I've been in charge of for almost a decade," he snubs me.

Wow, I wasn't expecting that response. I channel my Texas confidence to respond. "Mr. Williams, I can assure you that this isn't some type of college paper. I did a lot of research and found several ways to save this company loads of money. I—" I start to plead my case but he rudely interrupts me.

"Ms. Drake, I get it. You are trying to make a name for yourself here, but I don't have the time to babysit or coddle the new girl who is only going to be here a couple of months. I don't have the luxury of making mistakes. I run an empire for Mr. Dawson and my job is to make sure his assets are in good hands. You, Ms. Drake, have been here for less than a week and you're already trying to make waves. I think it's best if you stick with Molly and keep out of my way. Just because you're sleeping with the boss's son doesn't give you any special treatment here under my watch. Are we clear?"

I feel my heart rate accelerate and I think I might faint. I always thought he was rude but this is an entirely different level. How dare he say those things to me? He doesn't even know me, much less have the right to judge me like this. I need to calm down before doing something that will land me a night in jail. I know if my eyes could shoot daggers I would have him pinned against the glass windows right now.

And sleeping with the boss's son to get special treatment! Do not punch him in the face. Do not punch him in the face. I close my eyes and start counting to ten to try and regulate my breathing. Once I have myself somewhat under control, I open my eyes.

"Mr. Williams," I almost spit, "I would never expect special treatment under any circumstances and I'm completely offended you'd suggest otherwise. I was only trying to help this company out by doing those reports. A fresh set of eyes never hurts. I passed up another internship to come work here and learn from the best, but all I have learned from you is what an arrogant prick you are and how unwilling you can be to try different things or hear other opinions when it comes to business. As far as the boss' son goes I would watch your tone. You know nothing about our situation. I have never asked for special treatment since starting here and I suggest you get yourself in check before you become a liability for Human Resources," I state firmly never budging or breaking eye contact.

I grab the folders on his desk and hold them up.

"If you aren't interested in saving this company money then so be it." I toss them in the trash next to his desk, turn on my high heels, and march out of the room slamming the door on the way out.

The nerve of this man. How is he in charge of a big business anyway?

I notice Molly staring at me with her mouth open and I realize I must have left the office door open. She probably heard every word of our conversation.

"Dear, are you alright?" Molly gently asks patting my knee.

"Oh, Molly, how can you work for a man like this all these years? He is truly a nightmare. I wonder if he treats his wife or family like this." I place my hands over my face. "I think I just got myself fired," I whisper as realization settles in.

"Don't worry, Kendall. Everything will work out fine. I don't think anyone has ever stood up to him like you just did. It was kind of refreshing," she giggles, which in turn makes me giggle.

We have about thirty minutes left of our day so we start organizing and getting everything ready for tomorrow. Shutting down my computer, I gather my things, wish Molly an enjoyable evening, and make my way down. I really need a good stress reliever right now. I wonder if Wyatt would be up for running and working out. I know he has his own gym down the hall from the office I work out of. Plus, with all the fancy food he keeps feeding me, I need to frequent it a lot more. Or alcohol. Definitely lots of alcohol.

I saddle up in my car and let her purr for a minute as I watch Frankie start his car and we drive out of the parking lot before making our way onto the highway to head home.

On the car ride home, I decide not to tell Wyatt about what happened with Mr. Williams. I would be proving Mr. Williams right if I had Wyatt fight my battles for me. I'm a big girl now and can stand on my own, even against a prick like Justice Williams. I'll have to make the most of my time here over the next few months and maybe go to each department on my own to try and learn about each one of them.

The next morning, I'm working alongside Molly trying to ignore everything and anything that has to do with Mr. Williams. She must realize the tension between us, so she offers to take his coffee to him. When Mr. Williams leaves to go to a meeting across town for the next few hours the coast is clear. Debra from accounting stops by to get a few signatures for payroll and I tell her that I'll place them on his desk to sign first thing when he returns.

Once again, his messy desk is littered with papers. How someone who is in charge of running a big business can be so messy and unorganized is beyond me. I move some files around so he'll see the payroll documents when I knock over a file labeled 'Quarterly Reports,' making the papers go scattering all over the floor. Frustrated I'm so clumsy, I don't even notice the first couple of pages I pick up. It's not until I am on my knees that I see the next report and something catches my eye.

On the paper, I see a list of businesses and their quarterly profits. Not a big deal except the laundromat and dry cleaners that are listed are the same ones we drove by earlier in the week and they don't exist. *What in the world?* It states they each made over a hundred thousand dollars this past quarter. That is impossible because they don't even have their doors open for business. There must be a mistake. I look through the rest of the pages and since I don't know about any of the other ones I decide to investigate. I need to get to the bottom of this. I might be blowing this out of proportion *or* I might find out Mr. Williams is running some kind of scam that could hurt Bobby or Wyatt in the long run.

Gathering the entire file, I rush out of the office to the copy room and start making a copy of the papers. Thank goodness each business has the address included next to the name. This will make it easy for me to find and see if the business is actively open or empty. When I finish, I briskly walk back to Mr. Williams' desk and place the folder where it was before I knocked it over. I tuck my copy under my arm and move to the reception desk, placing them in my leather bag. I feel sick to my stomach at the thought that someone is being underhanded. But what really makes me mad is the thought of an arrogant prick like Mr. Williams doing something underhanded after the way he treated me yesterday. I need to find the truth and I need to do this now.

"Molly, do you think it would be alright if I left for the day? I'm not feeling well right now," I say.

"Of course, dear, go and rest up. If you need tomorrow off just call me on my cellphone."

"Thank you, Molly." I gather up my things and practically run to the elevators.

Once I'm in the lobby I see Frankie enter through the door and realize he'll be following me if I leave work. *Crap!* I place myself behind a column next to the elevator and watch him walk into the men's bathroom. I couldn't have planned it any better. Now is my chance. As soon as the door closes I race out the front door to my car. I turn her on and gas it out of the parking lot before he even comes out of the bathroom. Taking a deep breath, feeling like I'm escaping from the cops, I put the address to the laundromat into my phone. It's three minutes away according to the screen, so I sit here at a red light and scan over all the pages to try to figure out how the best way to map each business.

I pull into the parking lot that's supposed to house a laundromat and dry cleaners and see the two businesses are empty. Getting out, I walk up to the glass window and peek in. Nothing. Empty space. I see the other side is a cellphone provider and walk in to ask some questions. Maybe they recently shut down.

"Excuse me," I ask the male sales clerk. "I was wondering if you know how long the two spaces next door have been vacant?"

"Well, we've been here for about three years and those two spots have been vacant since we started renting this space," the young man who is wearing a red polo and khakis answers.

Holy shit! They have been vacant for at least three years. I wonder how long Mr. Williams has been reporting a profit? I need to give him the benefit of the doubt. Maybe someone from accounting put the numbers in the wrong space. I'll just continue with the list and see if there are any other discrepancies.

As my car door closes my phone rings. Wyatt comes across the screen and I know I've been reported gone from work by Frankie. I just need to uncover a few more before I can turn this over to Wyatt and Bobby. I need facts and to do that I need to keep going. Pressing the silent button on the side of the phone, I toss it over to the passenger seat. The next address says I'm four minutes away.

Forty-five minutes later my mind is blown. I'm back in my car after finding out that this location is also vacant and has been for two years, but the profit shows to be a little more than two hundred thousand dollars for this quarterly report. I gaze down at my pages and I can't believe what I am staring at. Out of the twelve businesses I've been to, nine have been vacant and could not have produced the profits being represented on these reports. We are talking about several MILLIONS of dollars that are showing up. How am I going to tell Bobby and Wyatt? This is going to hurt their family and they're going to take a huge hit. No wonder Mr. Williams didn't want anyone working close alongside him. They would have found out his deceit.

Just as I'm about to start my car four vehicles pull into the lot and block me in so I can't back out. One by one they all exit their vehicles and lean against them. *Shit, why did I have to give Frankie the slip.* I take a few calming breaths never removing my eyes from the rearview mirror to keep each one in view. *Think Kendall.* Slowly I press the hidden button on my door panel and reach for my gun. I try to keep my movements to a minimum to not alert the men. My phone goes off again and I reach for it.

"KENDALL! What the fuck do you think you are doing?" Wyatt yells through the phone.

"Wyatt four men have me surrounded. Please…" I whisper frantically but a knock on my window startles a scream from me and I drop the phone between the seat and the console. Wyatt is yelling but I can't make out what he is saying.

The door to my Camaro swings open and one of the men motions for me to step out. I slowly get out of my car and shield my gun from the men. The man grabs my upper arm in a tight hold that I'm sure will leave finger bruises, and starts leading me towards the other men who are now standing behind my car.

"Ms. Drake we were told to hold you until the boss gets here," the man states.

Holy Shit! What have I gotten myself into this time? How does this keep happening to me?

I have two choices: wait until his 'boss' shows or I can fight.

CHAPTER NINE

WITH MY MIND MADE UP, THERE IS NO WAY IN HELL I'm waiting for his boss to show up. I feel like déjà vu all over again from back at the last restaurant. I need to get the hell out of here. I tug my arm free from the man and brandish my gun. The others all produce theirs and I feel like I'm in the Wild West. I have mine up against the neck of the man who had my arm in a vice and the others are all pointing their guns at me.

"No one is holding me. I suggest you all put your weapons down and let me go or someone is going to die today," I boom my voice trying to keep my heart from beating out of my chest. *Just stay calm*, I hear my Uncle's voice.

"Shit, where did she get a gun from?" I hear one of the men.

"No one is going to die today, Princess. Put your weapon down and we can talk about this. We don't want to hurt you. We have strict orders to—" One of the other guys says but is interrupted by a car screeching to a halt.

I don't take my eyes off the three guys holding their guns still pointed at me, so I'm not sure if the *'Boss'* has arrived. The door slams and I hear yelling.

"What the fuck is going on. Put your fucking guns down

NOW or I'll shoot every one of you in the fucking head," a familiar voice yells.

I watch the guys slowly holster their guns but I keep mine snug against the man in front of me.

"Babe. It's okay, you can put your gun down these guys aren't going to hurt you. I promise," Wyatt says in a calming voice.

Wyatt.

Finally, I cut my eyes over to him and see that my ears weren't playing tricks on me. He really is here and walking slowly towards me with his hands up. I feel myself blink a few times still taking him in and realize I still have a gun pointed at someone. I ease my grip and push the man forward and away from me. I must look like a cornered animal because all of them now have their hands up.

"Wyatt," I whisper.

"It's me, Kendall. They won't hurt you. They work for me. We've been trying to find you for the last hour. I told them if they found you to hold you until I could get there. I'm sorry if they scared you."

I nod, trying to wrap my mind around what just happened. The adrenaline that was pumping through my veins earlier is now receding from my body and I feel like I'm about to crash. I lower my gun and take a shaky step toward Wyatt as he reaches out and catches me. My body is now shaking and tears are wetting my face. So much has happened in the last few days it's catching up to me.

"Shhh, babe, it's okay. I got you," he coos, holding me tight. "Thank god you're safe," he whispers rubbing my back trying to soothe my shaking body.

"I…I…I thought they were going to…to t-take me like those guys from the restaurant, Wyatt. And when the man grabbed my arm like the other guy did I…I…" I feel Wyatt's body tense then his body leaves mine as he steps back still holding on to me.

"He grabbed you?" His tone is harsh. I show him my arm which now has five red circles where the man's fingers dug in.

I nod, not realizing the storm I've just caused. The next few moments happen in a blur. Wyatt pounces on the man who had grabbed me out of the car. Punch after punch Wyatt keeps throwing them as the guy falls to the pavement. The other three men just stand back and watch, not bothering to stop the assault.

"Did I say to touch my woman?" It's a rhetorical question. Not that the poor guy could answer him anyway.

"Wyatt!" I find my voice finally.

He looks up from the man who is semi-conscious and sees me as if he forgot I was there. He must realize how this must look because he straightens up, fixes his clothes, and turns to the other guys.

"Get this piece of shit out of my sight. He knows better than to touch another man's wife," Wyatt seethes as I stand there in shock. This day continues to get crazier as the minutes pass.

"Yes, sir. We'll take care of it," one man says as the other two pick the beaten man off the ground.

"Clean this up and get my car back to my house. Call Frankie and let him know I've got her."

"Yes, sir."

Wyatt walks away from them and back to me. He reaches for me in a few strides and engulfs me in his arms. "Kendall, I need you to hand me your gun?" He speaks softly to me.

I completely forgot I was still holding it. I nod checking the safety before turning it over to him. He takes the gun and guides me over to the passenger side of my car. He helps me in and buckles me up. He climbs into the driver's side and places my gun in the center console.

"Not right now, but when we get home you and I are going to have a serious conversation about you giving Frankie the slip today. Then about how the hell you ended up all the way over here."

I nod again.

"Okay. I have something I need to tell you and Bobby also. It's really important too. Life changing even," I say in a gloomy voice.

"I'll call Dad and have him meet us at home. Then we can take a long soaking bath afterward and relax." He grabs my hand as we pull out and onto the streets to head back to the house.

The car ride is quiet the whole way but Wyatt never lets go of my hand. I can see his knuckles are red from where he punched that guy over and over again. He did that for me because the guy touched me. I don't think I've ever had a guy defend me like that. In some weird way, I feel cherished and loved that he's willing to go to such lengths for me. *Love?* Do I feel love from him? I mean he's been an amazing boyfriend. Is this love? Surely not, we've only been together for two weeks. There's no way I could love someone in this short amount of time. Although, Uncle Liam and Aunt Sarah both claim from the moment they saw each other that they knew. Aunt Sarah also told me my parents married each other almost right after meeting, so I guess it could be possible. Earlier, when Wyatt was punching that guy's face in, he called me his wife and it did sound good rolling off his tongue.

"You called me your wife earlier," I blurt out.

"Oh, you caught that," Wyatt says not looking at me, but he's wearing a smile that could split his face in two and I'm sure if I looked in the mirror we'd look identical right now.

We don't say another word until the car pulls into the driveway and we see Bobby getting out of his car as well. Wyatt puts my car in park and turns to me. "Please don't run off like that again. I was going crazy trying to locate you because I thought something horrific had happened." He kisses my hand and then exits the car.

I watch Wyatt greet his dad and I know the information I'm about to give them is going to change everyone's world. Reaching into the back seat, I gather up all my papers and my bag.

Placing my bag down on the kitchen counter, I walk over to the fridge. I open up the freezer, grab a bag of peas, and walk over to Wyatt who is watching me. I place the bag on his hurt hand and then look up at him. I see something in his eyes that hasn't been there before. A throat being cleared reminds us that we aren't alone.

Turning away from Wyatt, I walk over to my bag and get out the necessary documents. *Here goes nothing.*

"Bobby, there is something I think you should know and I don't really know how to say it, but here goes. I think Mr. Williams is doing some shady and illegal work with your company. That's what I was doing this afternoon."

I proceed to tell them everything I know starting with my reports I researched all weekend to everything that happened today. I also show them the paperwork to back up my accusation. They both listen intently but I can tell Wyatt is getting upset. His forehead is glistening with sweat, his jaw ticks many times, and he keeps glancing over at Bobby for some kind of reaction. Once I'm done, I feel like the weight of the world has been lifted off my chest, but Bobby and Wyatt are a little too quiet after just hearing that someone is cooking their books.

"Kendall, sweetheart, how did you come about this information again?" Bobby asks me calmly. A little too calm if you ask me.

"I was putting some documents on Mr. Williams' desk and knocked over a folder. The papers went scattering to the floor."

"I would like to see the research you presented to Justice. He obviously needs a refresher on how to speak not only with women but with employees too."

I feel like Bobby is missing the point here. Mr. Williams has created millions of imaginary dollars for businesses that don't exist, and Bobby wants to see my research on saving money.

"Shouldn't we call the police or the FBI? I mean this has to be a crime, right? He's the person who runs your entire empire and he is doing some illegal things," I insist coming back to what I think is the most important point.

I notice Wyatt's eyes widen when he looks at Bobby, who is still watching my every move.

"No, Kendall, we aren't going to call the police. We usually handle things in-house when we've been wronged," Bobby says.

I must look so confused right now because that is definitely how I feel.

"Dad."

"In-house?" I raise an eyebrow. What is that supposed to mean?

"Dad. Don't," I hear Wyatt say but I'm still watching Bobby.

"Kendall, it means that we take care of the problems ourselves and we *never* involve the police."

"I don't…understand what that means." Do they have their own cops who deal with criminal activity? Maybe the rich elite have their own sector of government.

"It means we—" Bobby goes on to say.

"DAD! Don't do this now," Wyatt yells and makes a move from his position to come over to Bobby.

Bobby finally turns his eyes away from me and pins Wyatt where he stands with just a look. The tension in the room is so thick it's suffocating.

"Is she it, Wyatt?" Bobby asks.

It?

"Dad, please not yet," Wyatt begs. His body is so tense it's shaking. "She's not ready."

"IS she it?" he demands again, his voice deadly.

I see Wyatt give a small nod still looking at Bobby.

"Do you love her?"

"Please, Dad," Wyatt is speaking barely above a whisper now. "Don't do this."

"Answer me," Bobby says through gritted teeth.

There is a short pause and then Wyatt gazes over in my directions and into my eyes. He looks pained and tormented. "You know I can't," he admits and rubs his upper chest on the left side.

My heart beats out of my chest. I can't believe this is happening. I have so many emotions consuming me right now and I want to express how I feel, but Bobby moves himself into my line of sight blocking Wyatt.

"Kendall, the reason we don't involve the police is because *our people* can't ever be associated with them. We aren't rats."

"Our people?" What is that supposed to mean? Where is this conversation going?

"We are the Las Vegas Mafia."

CHAPTER TEN

MAFIA?

Is he saying that they are a part of the mob? Like the Five Families in New York or Chicago. That mafia? This has to be a joke surely. They're not mafia…but from the serious look Bobby is giving me, this is no joke. What have I gotten myself in to? I was just supposed to be interning for a summer job and now I'm standing in front of a Mob Boss having a come to Jesus moment. I should've listened to Aunt Sarah and Uncle Liam about staying away from Las Vegas. *How could I be so stupid?* Everyone knows about the mob, but not everyone is actually aware of it still going on in today's society.

Holy shit! The Dawson's are well to do people too. They truly own more than half the town.

My fingers dig into my temples trying to stop the throbbing in my head. The room has gone quiet for what seems like hours but only a few minutes have passed. When I look around the room I see neither Bobby nor Wyatt have moved from their previous spot. Unknowingly, I take a step back at their intense stares. I need some space; the room feels like the oxygen has been sucked out causing my breathing to become uneven. My hand goes to my chest to help regulate it as much as possible. *I'm too young to die from a heart attack, right?*

Wyatt makes a move towards me but Bobby holds up his hand stopping him in his tracks. The threatening glare Wyatt shoots Bobby would bring a normal person to their knees, but Bobby doesn't even blink an eye.

"Kendall, do you understand what I've just told you?" Bobby speaks in a controlled manner.

"Y…yes," I stutter nodding.

"Then you understand going to the cops about…anything is not in your best interest. Ever."

I totally get the underlying threat. Loud and clear. "Mmhmm." I jerk my head up and down.

"Not good enough, sweetheart. I need to hear the words."

"Yes," I say a little firmer. "I won't say a word."

"Good. Welcome to the Family. Mary and I will see you both Sunday for family brunch." He turns, and with the clap of his hands, he nods to Wyatt, and leaves the house.

And I'm left blowing in the wind, not knowing which way is up. How can he go from threatening Mafia Boss to Super Dad next door in a split second? The room doesn't seem so suffocating anymore now that he's left though, and I'm able to breathe a little better now.

Wyatt waits for the front door to close before making his way over to me. He stands in front of me but makes a point not to touch me. I'm thankful for that because I'm not sure how I'd handle it right now. I can see in his eyes that he is worried.

"Wyatt, what the hell just happened?" I ask hoping there has been some kind of misunderstanding. That a camera crew is going to pop out of the pantry at any moment and declare this is all a big prank.

"Kendall, this is not how I wanted to tell you. I thought I'd have a little more time. I know this is all happening so fast but at least now it's out in the open and we can move forward." The tension in his body relaxes and I swear I've got whiplash from the Dawson Family.

"Forward?" I choke. He's acting as though a bomb hasn't been set off in my life. "Are you kidding me right now? Your dad just said you all are mafia like it's some casual declaration," I argue.

"Come, let's have a bath and we can talk more." He reaches for my hand but I take a step away from his touch.

"I need to go. I want to go back to my place and think about all this." My mind is racing.

"You can't leave, Kendall." The words sound so final.

"Of course I can. I'm not a prisoner." I pause and bile threatens the back of my throat. "Right? You'll let me go right. I said I wouldn't say anything." I start imagining ways to plead for my life.

"You're not a prisoner, babe, but you can't leave. Vic is still out there causing problems." He steps up and places his large hands gently on my shoulders. "You're safe here with me."

I'm so deep in my head I didn't realize Wyatt had walked me down the hall and into the bathroom. He's stripped me of my clothes and is helping me in the hot water. He has me lying up against his chest and his arms are around my midsection while his face is in the crook of my neck. My body is on autopilot.

"Please talk to me, Kendall. I know this is a lot to take in but say something. Anything."

I'm not even sure where to start. Never in my wildest dreams did I think I'd have a conversation like this. "You kill people, Wyatt." I stare at the tile on the wall unsure of what to say next but the silence is making the bathroom feel smaller.

He hums a non-answer in his throat. "You can ask me anything and I'll always be honest with you. Now that you're in, I'll tell you whatever it is you want."

"In? I don't want to be *in*," I say. "I wasn't even asked if I wanted to be in."

"That's really not an option right now. Things will get easier once you've some time to think about all of this."

I shake my head. This feels like a dream and I'll wake soon to find it's all been a funny prank. The restaurant shootout comes to mind and all the 'bloody noses' Wyatt's claimed to have send a shiver down my spine. The less I know the better.

"What does this mean for us?" I finally ask and I hear him exhale, probably glad I'm still communicating.

"Well, we continue on with our relationship. Then marry and have a bunch of kids to fill this house." I feel him smile against my neck after softly pressing his lips there.

Has he lost his damn mind? How in the hell can he just throw something out there like that? The more time that passes the angrier I get. Talk about misreading the room!

"Wow, seems you already have it wrapped up in a tight perfect red bow. Does it matter what I want or is this how it will always be; you making all the decisions?" Bitterness seeps into my words. I'm not just some little lady to be ordered around. "We don't even know each other and you just told your dad that you don't love me."

He turns me around to face him. My legs go around his waist so that we are now nose to nose. I swear he manhandles me like a ragdoll and any other time it'd make me giggle.

"Babe, what do you want? I will give you anything in my power and lay it at your feet." He holds my chin in place so I can't look away. "You have become my whole world and I want you to be happy," he says. "In such a short time you've worked yourself into my whole being and I can't even picture a life that doesn't have you by my side."

"Except love, right? That is what marriage is. At least that's what I was brought up to believe. And I'm not going to marry someone I've known for two weeks. On top of finding out that he'll never love me."

"Not loving you has nothing to do with you. I gave my heart away a long time ago to someone and I just can't give those feelings to someone else, but that doesn't mean we can't make this work. We care about each other and that's something to build on. We can have a good life together. I'll make sure you want for nothing and that you're happy. We can make this work; our chemistry is like no other and I'll work my ass off to prove that I'm in this with you."

I know he means every word he says because of the way he has made me feel these past two weeks. He would give me things before I even knew I needed or wanted them. Can I be married to someone who can't love me? Is that what I want for the next fifty years? Being second best in someone's heart? Can I live in this world that his family lives in? Does this mean I have to give up my dreams of running an empire to be the little lady with a kid on her hip and a casserole in the oven? I need time to process all of this. Time to wrap my head around everything.

I stare into Wyatt's eyes as he waits for my answer and I hate to be the one to put sadness in those beautiful blue eyes, but I need this for me. I need time. This can't be a spur of the moment decision. I'm too young to be strapped down with these decisions, especially when I've been thrown into this.

"Wyatt, I need some time right now. I need to think about all of what was revealed today. Tomorrow I'd like to go back to my apartment alone."

His muscles tense and his fingers flex into my hips. It's like he's trying to make sure I don't bolt.

"Kendall, I know this can be pretty heavy, but nothing has changed between us. I meant what I told my dad. I think I have from the moment you knocked into me and didn't take any shit from me." He pulls me in tight against his rock-hard body. "I am still me, the same man who loves to sleep next to you and hold you every night and spoil you with fancy dinners. We can have the best life together, I promise you. You'll want for nothing. This doesn't have to change anything between us."

I start to melt when I hear him say such nice and caring things, but is that enough? Can I just bury my head in the sand?

"Wyatt this is all happening so fast. I mean, can't you see how crazy all of this is? Your family is involved in organized crime and I haven't ever even gotten a ticket. What about my dreams of a career? Do I just hang up my degree and grab an apron instead? What about me finishing my master's degree? I want to run a corporation one day."

The water is starting to cool off, but I need to know where his head is on where I fit in. What if we don't work out? Will he let me leave? Can you just walk away from the mafia? All the movies I've watched show the only way out is a body bag.

"I know this is a lot to handle right now, but trust me, I'll shield you from everything. You'll never have to worry about that side of the business if you don't want to." He places his large hands on my shoulders and brushes my hair back. "As far as your career, if you want I'll buy you a business or whatever it is you want and you can run it. *When* we have kids, if you want to stay home you can, or we can hire nannies to help us, or Mom would love to take care of the little ones. I still want your dreams to come true; all I ask is that you let me be a part of the journey with you. As far as school goes, I was hoping maybe you might transfer out here to the UNLV so you'll be close to me. I'd never put you in a cage and keep you from being happy, babe."

He looks so sincere saying all this and it makes my heart expand a little more. Wyatt seems to have put a lot of thought behind this, but how can he mean any of it and not be in love with me?

"The water is getting cold. Let's get out and into bed then talk some more," he says and stands with me still wrapped around him. The fact we're naked and I can feel him pressed against my most intimate parts finally computes with my brain. Any other time it would be such a turn on, but everything that's happened over the last few hours has my head scattered in twenty other directions. We dry off and throw on some clothes from his closet. He has me snuggled up against his chest with his arms wrapped around me before my head can touch the pillow.

"What if we don't work out? Will you let me walk?" I ask because the silence is getting to be too much. He tightens his grip on me.

"We *are* going to work out, you don't have to worry about that. You're it for me, Kendall. I have never wanted something so much in my entire life, but if you want out…then I'll let you go. I would never hold you against your will." I let out a breath I was holding. I believe him. Or at least I want to believe him.

"Are you going to have affairs and be with other women? I won't be in a relationship or marriage for that matter where I'm the laughing stock wife with her head in the sand." I refuse to be like the women in the movies who are married to rich men who have side pieces but come home to tuck in the kids.

Wyatt physically moves my body so I'm lying on top of him, staring into his blue eyes.

"I would never disrespect you that way. Ever since I met you, I haven't even wanted to look at or touch another woman. Yes, I've been with women in the past but ever since I met you something clicked inside of me. I've never considered having a relationship since I was younger. I was raised by both my dad and grandfather to respect the woman I'm committed to. You are it for me. You are my last, Kendall Drake. Please tell me you believe me."

I search his eyes and know he is being truthful so I nod once. This badass man who is rubbing circle on my back just poured his heart out to me and I can't help but think that this might work.

His declaration does things to me. How can I not want to be with this man forever? He is saying everything I want to hear. I lean in and press my lips to his. I pour everything I want to say into this kiss because I'm too afraid to say what I really want to say. Once we break apart to catch our breaths, I lay my head on his chest and close my eyes. I don't move from my position on top of him because right now I need this connection, and I don't want to be anywhere else but in his arms. Who knows what tomorrow holds and if this is my last time with Wyatt then I want it to last as long as possible.

"Wyatt, can you tell me about this tattoo?" I'm tracing my fingers over the cursive letters that read '*My Angel.*'

"When I was younger, my family was close with another one of the Five Families here in Las Vegas called the Chapmans. We were a tight-knit group and together our families pretty much owned Las Vegas and the surrounding areas. The Chapmans had two children, an older son and a younger daughter." I can hear the sadness in his voice. "Our fathers announced when we were of age we'd marry to join our families and keep the businesses going strong and to continue our alliance. I was going to marry her when she turned eighteen and I would have been twenty-two at the time. My father told me when I turned eight what he expected of me and that I was to be her protector until she was old enough to understand. So, everywhere she went I followed her to make sure she was safe. We were inseparable.

"She stole one of my stuffed animals from when I was born and slept with it every night. I made sure to read her a story most nights and check under the bed and closet for monsters before heading home. On her fifth birthday I gave her a heart shaped locket she wore with every outfit. She always looked like an angel every time I saw her, so that became her nickname." He takes a deep breath and I can feel his heart pumping faster.

"Then one night the entire family was murdered. She was only five and it shook our whole family to the roots. I got this tattoo when I was sixteen to always remember her and I hope maybe she's watching over me. It also reminds me not to take people for granted." I peer up at him as he places his hand on my cheek. "You remind me a lot of her with your eyes."

"I'm sorry she's gone." My heart feels like a dagger is piercing it. How can I compete with the death of a small child that he was promised to. If I stay, is that who I'll be compared to in his eyes the rest of my life. Is that something I can deal with? To be compared and second best over a childhood connection that was supposed to be his forever?

"I've learned to deal the best I can. I know you have reservations about my commitment to you but I'll be loyal to you in every way."

Don't I deserve to be loved though? To be someone's first choice and not runner up?

I don't reply and settle against him thinking over everything. He places a tender kiss on my lips and we fall asleep together.

Walking into my apartment the next day, I'm met with utter silence. This is not going to work so I grab for my phone.

"Hello stranger!" Harper answers cheerfully.

"Harper, it's so good to hear your voice. When are you coming home?" I whine.

"We're flying out in the morning. Girl, you should have come to this spa. It has been fantastic," she gushes.

I'm slightly jealous that she doesn't seem to have a care in the world, and I feel like mine is crumbling to the ground. "Really? I really wish I went too," I say somberly. "I miss you."

"What's wrong Kendall? You sound sad," she asks and I hear a door close on the other line.

"It's nothing, I just wish you were here so we could talk. I really need my friend right now." I guess I didn't realize how much Harper and I rely on each other. We've been through so much together over the years, I guess she's become my other half. My security blanket.

"Kendall, talk to me. I don't think I've ever heard you so down before." There's a pause and I hear tapping on the other end. "I can probably get a flight out in a few hours."

"No! Don't do that. Enjoy your last day there. It's nothing really, I just wanted to hear your voice and see you. I think this is the longest we've gone without seeing each other since freshman year."

"I know, right. How's the internship going? Is it everything you thought it would be?" Harper asks.

"Oh, it's everything and more." I can't keep the sarcasm at bay. "I've been the coffee runner for the most part but it definitely is something else." I don't want to have this conversation over the phone. "Listen I have to get going, but I'll see you tomorrow, okay. Love you!"

"Love you too, Kendall!"

I hang up and walk around our apartment. It's been almost two weeks since I've been here. Nothing has really changed. Everything is in the same place we left it before we were uprooted. Before a bomb was set off. Too bad we aren't able to go back in time and get a redo.

Sitting out on our balcony that overlooks the Strip, I think about how my life has changed so much in the last two weeks. I was here for a summer internship and Harper tagged along to celebrate our graduation from college. This was supposed to be a fun and last hooray before having to be out in the real world becoming adults. Crazy how two weeks changed all that. I met a guy, changed internships, guy became my boyfriend who I started living with after only a few days, almost got kidnapped, and found out that his family is part of the mafia. And that he will never love me but wants to get married and have a house full of babies. That about sums up the last two weeks in a nut shell. Oh, and I've been in a shootout where someone died.

I'm brought out of my train of thought when my phone buzzes.

> Wyatt: Hey Babe, I know you need some space but I just want you to know that I'm thinking about you.

> Me: I'm thinking about you too.

And all the other craziness that's going on.

> Wyatt: Remember if you go anywhere make sure Frankie is with you. I know you need space but I still want you safe.

> Me: Aye Aye Captain!

> Wyatt: KENDALL!

I send him a smiley face emoji that is blowing him a kiss and he sends one back with hearts in the eyes.

This is the kind of interaction I've been looking for in a relationship. We can be silly and fun and act our age. If it was just like this then I would have no problem making a decision, but this isn't all that there is. We have this dark cloud that will always be hanging over our heads. Always looking over our shoulders to see if the police are watching or if a rival is wanting more of our territory. Is this a life I want to bring my children up in? I mean, Wyatt and Gracie seem to have turned out okay, but their older sister was gunned down. Was that from being a part of the mafia or was it a random shooting?

I decide to clear my mind for a while and not think any more about my dilemma. I call Molly to inform her I'm not coming into the office today.

"Mr. Williams office, how can I help you?" Molly answers after being transferred to her.

"Hey, Molly, it's, Kendall."

"Oh, hello, dear! How are you today?"

"Fine, but I won't be in the office today. I still feel under the weather," I say, sticking with the reason for my sudden departure yesterday.

"I figured as much. Mr. Dawson has been here since early this morning and made sure to tell me that you might not be able to make it in today. He insinuated after he left the house last night you looked a bit pale."

"Bobby is there right now?" I squeak…or maybe she's referring to Wyatt.

"Oh yes, the big boss is in the building and let me tell you, the yelling coming from the other side of the door has been going on for quite some time. He told me to clear Mr. Williams' schedule for the rest of the day. Wyatt only got here about twenty minutes ago. Something major must have gone down for both of the Dawsons to be here," she gossips.

"Oh," is all I can manage.

"Well, I hope you feel better and have a great weekend. I'll see you on Monday morning, dear."

After saying bye, we hang up.

I can't help but wonder what their meeting with Mr. Williams is about? Surely not me. Right? I push the thought out of my mind and try and relax for the rest of the afternoon.

I call down to the concierge and speak with Cynthia to see if she has anything available today at the spa. I could use a good massage to get some of these knots out of my shoulder. Thank goodness I'm able to schedule a massage, a wax, a mani and pedi, a trim and blow out. The rest of the day I spend sipping on champagne and being pampered.

Throughout the day, Wyatt texts me just like all the other days. We carry on a playful banter and keep everything light. I want to ask him about his meeting with Mr. Williams but refrain. It's none of my business. He asks me if I would still be willing to go to brunch on Sunday and I agree as long as Harper is also invited. I can use some backup. He assures me she is welcome anytime.

The next morning, I get a call from Mary persuading me to have lunch with her. She informs me that Gracie and Harper must have partied too hard last night and missed their flight. They should be returning sometime in the early evening. We have a good laugh and decide on meeting at Crown and Anchor British Pub which is a short drive for me.

After hanging up with Mary my phone shows no texts from Wyatt which is strange.

> Me: Hey, I haven't heard from you and wanted to let you know I'm having lunch with your mother. That's ok right?

The response takes a while to buzz back.

> Wyatt: Morning beautiful! I had an early meeting and wanted to let you sleep in. I told Mom to let you be but she is not one to listen.

> Me: I gathered as much which is why I agreed to lunch.

> Wyatt: Can I see you tonight?

Do I want to see him yet? Have I worked everything out I need to? The answer is a big fat no.

> Me: Harper and Gracie will be back and we're having a girls' night in. Maybe we can hang out after brunch?

Wyatt: Okay. Have fun tonight. Can you call me before you go to bed though?

Me: I'll try

I check the time and decide to head out to meet Mary at the pub. On the way out of the lobby, I remember our mail is probably full by now and stop by the desk to claim it. The guy gathers two stacks worth wrapped in rubberbands and hands them over. I sure hope most of this is junk mail. Harper and I forwarded our mail from our apartment at Stanford so we could pay any bills that got sent there, and in case Aunt Sarah sent me a care package. I notice several magazines and two large manila packets that seem heavy with something in them. I decide to wait until later to open them because I need to get going if I'm going to be on time to meet Mary.

Parking at the restaurant, I make my way in and get us a booth in the back corner. I wave her over when she walks in and notice her security meets up with Frankie at a nearby table.

"How are you, sweetheart?" Mary greets me with a hug and kiss on the cheek.

"As good as can be expected," I answer and we sit down at our booth.

"Oh, sweetheart, I heard all about it from Bobby last night and then from Wyatt this morning. I know you probably have a million questions running through that pretty little head of yours, so I thought maybe I could answer some of them for you. First, let me ask you the most basic question."

"Okay?" I say and wonder what the most basic question could be.

"Do you love my son?"

CHAPTER ELEVEN

I STARE AT MARY WITH MY MOUTH OPENING AND CLOSING like a fish out of water. Definitely wasn't expecting this question to start our conversation. This Dawson Family sure knows how to shock the socks right off someone and put a person on the spot.

"It's a simple question, Kendall. Do you love my son?" Mary asks again when I still haven't mustered a peep.

"It's not that simple at all, Mary. If this was a normal relationship, then I could answer immediately but this is far from normal," I say defensively.

"Oh hog posh! Just because we come from an extremely colorful background and line of work shouldn't deter you from opening your heart to loving someone or letting yourself be loved." She waves her hand around. The waitress approaches, takes our drink order, and leaves. I wish I'd ordered something with a little kick to it. I have a feeling I'm in for a rollercoaster. This family is going to drive me to become an alcoholic with all the stress they cause.

"Kendall, I know this can be unnerving but you couldn't ask for a better family to marry into." *She might be a little biased.* "And I'm not just saying this because I am a part of it. I'm saying it because we look after each other and love fiercely. You'll not find another man who will love and cherish you more than Wyatt. He would lay down his own life for those he loves." She reaches for my hand. It could never be said that she doesn't champion for her children.

"Except he doesn't love me. He told me all about the girl he was supposed to marry and that he could never give his heart to another. I'll be someone he cares for dearly but never his loved one. I deserve to be loved and not someone's second choice."

"He told you that?" She sounds horrified. "Kendall, you have to know that my boy does love you. I can see it on his face when you walk through the room and in how he speaks of you."

"I wish it were true…" I trail off really wishing I could believe her.

"He never got over losing her. She was the cutest little thing but I never realized he felt like he couldn't move on from what had happened," she ponders. "He'll come around though, I know he will. He just doesn't know what to do with what he feels. Guys are completely dumb when it comes to this, you'll see. But he does love you. He just doesn't know how to move away from the past yet. Be patient, dear."

"How do you do it? How are you okay with this…lifestyle?" I ask.

"I wasn't at first, but the more I learned about what Bobby did and how he gave back to the community to balance everything out, I understood that someone has to do it. So, why not him? He's a much better leader than most."

The waitress comes with our drinks and takes our food order. Mary gets the fish and chips and I get the pulled pork sliders with chips even though eating is the farthest thing from my mind.

"Kendall, you need to ask yourself if this is a lifelong commitment you're willing to make. Right now, you have the option to walk away and have a different type of life. But if you say you're in, then it's for life. Do you understand me? I refuse to have my son torn apart years from now because you changed your mind." I nod understanding the underlying threat in her words. "He is a good and faithful man but has also had to deal with some issues growing up."

"You mean with Lexi and Avery."

"The guilt followed him for over a decade. He blamed himself for not protecting her. He couldn't wrap his head around that he was only eight years old and it wasn't his fault. Then Avery was killed and he went back to that dark place again. It really wasn't until the night of the wedding that I saw him acting like himself again. You've really brought him back and I don't think he could take another hit like you leaving. You are a strong woman who won't take his shit and will call him out when he's being an ass. You are the one for Wyatt, I'm sure of it."

I understand everything she's saying but talk about a guilt trip.

"I know he comes off as a real hard ass. Over the years he's built up these walls to protect himself, but then you came along and exploded each one. I've never seen him so tender with someone who wasn't family. He loves you and would do anything for you, like Bobby would for me."

She keeps saying that he loves me but she's not listening. He told me that he will never be able to. "Mary, aren't you worried about always having to look over your shoulder for the police or another mafia family trying to take you or someone you love?"

"Sweetheart, I could walk out of here and be hit by a bus or get a life-threatening illness. When it is my time, it is my time. This is where you need to have faith that Wyatt will protect you at all costs. I know for a fact Bobby has so many people in his back pockets that they sag to the ground. He has safeguards in place if something should ever come up and Wyatt is no different. We protect our family and you're under that umbrella now. As long as Bobby pays his taxes on time and continues to put the right people in place, there will never be any worry from law enforcement or government. As far as the other Families, they all work closely together and each have their own area that they stay in."

She sounds so sure. Could she be naïve or does she know this for a fact? Her being in this life for thirty years is proof of that, I guess.

"Kendall, I think you need to sit down with Wyatt and figure out what type of relationship and marriage you both want." Marriage? This family wastes no time.

"What do you mean?"

"I mean, do you want him to be open about everything? Even the smallest details or do you want to know nothing about the business and play oblivious every time he comes home or has to 'go away' on business."

I sit back in the booth and think on it. I'm not even sure I want to stay but here I am contemplating different scenarios. Do I want to hear him tell me about killing someone or do I just want him to say that his day was busy and make up in my head what he did? Right now, neither sounds appealing.

We eat in silence for a while and let our conversation sink in. I never imagined this way of life for me. How are Aunt Sarah and Uncle Liam going to be a part of my life if I choose to be a part of a mafia family?

"What about my aunt and uncle? Do I have to give them up and walk away? They are the only family I have left." The thought of losing them makes tears well up in my eyes. They are a deal breaker for me if it comes to it.

"Sweetheart, don't worry." Mary reaches across the table again and clasps my hand. "Most people think Bobby is a businessman, and he is. He just happens to have many other illegal businesses too. You wouldn't have to tell them anything related to that part of the lifestyle. If and when Bobby thinks they might be ready to hear the truth, *then* he'll tell them and only then. It's up to Bobby to let people in."

I feel some relief. I don't think I could walk away from my family. Everything Mary is telling me sounds like sunshine and rainbows but I know that there is a downside to being part of a mafia family. There has to be. "So, what's the negative side of being part of this family? I know this pretty picture you've painted has a downside."

"Well, the guys are always having meetings at horrible hours or have to travel to another state for a shipment that went wrong. The violence is never fun. I remember when Bobby would come home bloody and bruised from a deal gone wrong …" She gazes off like she's reliving a memory. "No, it's not all glitz and glam but there are more good moments than bad. The important thing to remember is to be supportive."

"Have you ever been asked to take part or be a part of that side of the business? Like on a deal or shipment?" I wonder if the wives get involved.

Mary shakes her head. "Heavens no, and Wyatt would never want the business to touch you. He would be ecstatic if you worked at the office or stayed at home if you wanted."

I feel somewhat relieved about not having to get involved.

"Speaking of work, Bobby told me about your reports on how to save the company a lot of money. He was very interested in your ideas and wants to talk to you more about it at brunch tomorrow."

"Really?!" I let out a shriek and she laughs. With everything that has happened in the last few days, I've completely forgotten all about those proposals.

"Oh yes. When he met with Justice yesterday you came up in conversation. They spoke about your ideas and reports moving forward on several opinions you offered."

"Wow, I can't believe that. I thought they got thrown away after the confrontation Mr. Williams and I had," I say with wonder. I thought for sure I'd be without a job come Monday morning.

"Well, apparently they didn't and Bobby is thrilled to have an outside voice to ping ideas off of," Mary says and then eyes her watch. "Oh dear, where has the time gone? I must get going. I'm meeting up with Adele. I'll see you for brunch tomorrow and don't be late."

We both stand and hug before she races out with her security hot on her heels. I lean over the booth and pick up my purse before heading towards Frankie and the doors. I let Frankie know I'm heading home and we drive to my apartment.

Walking into the apartment, I hear music coming from the

living room. I rush in and see Harper playing on her gaming system with her earpiece in. Ever since she boarded herself up after the stalking situation, she took on a love for gaming. Her parents make sure she has the newest games before they hit the stores and send them as care packages. I love watching movies so they always throw in the newest movie for me.

It seems Harper didn't hear me come in so I sneak up while she is commanding her team to raid a warehouse and scare her. She screams down the house and turns to me. "Christ, Kendall, I almost shit my pants!" Harper grabs her chest. I'm laughing because she is always so dramatic. She puts her hand up to her headset and glares at me. "Yes…yes, I'm okay. My best friend thought it was a good idea to sneak up on me. I gotta go, I'll meet up sometime tomorrow," she tells her team from the game.

Harper presses some buttons on her controller turning off her system. I go around the couch and sit next to her.

"Well, how was the spa?" I ask.

She seems to be glowing. "It was refreshing and so relaxing. We each had our own suite next to each other and we both got a surprise visitor." Harper is beaming. Not only does she look a little tan but her whole demeanor has changed. She seems…optimistic.

"Who were the visitors?"

"Well, Jackson came about two days after we got there and surprised Gracie and me at the pool, and then Gabe came the next day."

"That sounds like you guys had a world-class time. Did Gabe stay with you?" I pry.

Harper turns as red as her hair and she looks down at her hands in her lap. She is the cutest person when she is embarrassed. She nods and finally looks up at me. "Yes," she says and bites her lip.

"That's it? That's all you're going to give me? Come on, Harp, I want details!"

Harper has always talked a good game, but when it comes time for some action she usually chickens out. I'm the same way. Well, until Wyatt, I guess.

"We shared a bed the entire time and he was so sweet. The things he said and did made me feel real special, Kendall. I know at the end of summer it's going to be hard to walk away."

"Did you guys have sex?" I feel like I have to pull teeth with her.

She blushes again and this time the tops of her ears light up red and the smile across her face tells me everything I need to know. "It was out of this world!" she giggles. "He was so gentle but then would order me around. He did things to me I didn't even know was possible."

Who is this girl? Never has Harper beamed like this.

"Okay, okay. I don't want to hear too much of what you did, but you are being safe, right?"

"Yes, Mom, I am. Remember we both got the shot before we came out here *and* I made him use a condom."

I know I come across as a mother hen, but I've always felt the need to protect her ever since Chad almost kidnapped her. I feel like she is my responsibility.

"What about you? Have you and Wyatt done the nasty? Gracie bragged that you were staying at his place the whole time we were in Arizona."

"Well, Gracie has a big mouth!" I wink at Harper. "No, we haven't done the *deed* yet. We've done other things but not the nasty. I want to but things are a little complicated right now and I want to make sure it's the right decision for me. I think I'd be all in if we did. Heart and everything," I confess and then frown.

"Wow, Kendall, it's kind of soon to be talking hearts and love. That's a big leap, don't you think? What happened while I was gone, and what are you going to do at the end of your internship when we go back to Stanford?"

And there is the million-dollar question.

"I don't know. I thought maybe I'd transfer here to UNLV." I shrug and Harper's jaw drops.

"What?! You would do that? Uproot for a guy. What about

me?" I hear the panic in her voice. We have never been away from each other for too long since freshman year.

"No…yes…maybe. I don't know. This is why I haven't gone all in yet. It could be life-changing." I wish I could tell her about Wyatt's family being in the mafia but I remember Mary explaining only Bobby is allowed to bring others in. Harper and I don't keep secrets from each other and I feel horrible that I can't tell her what my hang-up really is.

"Well, let me know what you decide so that I can tell Mom and Dad. I'm sure they can make a donation and get us in the program here," Harper says, not skipping a beat.

Wait? Does this mean…

"You would come with me? Pack up and move just to be with me?" I ask, stunned.

"Of course, silly. I go wherever you go. We're a package deal, remember?"

And this is why Harper and I will always be family.

"I love you, Harper." I lean over and give her the biggest hug. She has always been my rock and I have been hers.

"I love you too, Kendall. So, what is our plan for tomorrow? Gabe wants to hang out at some point. He asked me to come and stay at his place for a night or two. Maybe you could have Wyatt come and stay here with you while I'm with Gabe?" I roll my eyes as she wags her eyebrows.

"We're having brunch tomorrow at Bobby and Mary's house, but afterward Wyatt wants me to go somewhere with him."

"Cool. I'm heading to bed and will see you in the morning." Harper says and makes her way to her room. "Night! Love you."

I stand from the couch, turn the lights off, make sure the apartment is secure, and head to my bedroom with my phone in hand. I go into the bathroom, brush my teeth, and then wipe off my makeup. Once I am under the comfort of my sheets I call Wyatt.

"Hey, babe, I was just thinking about you," he says on the third ring out of breath.

"Really? Why are you panting?"

"Oh, Gabe and I are working out at the house. He was just telling me all about his fun vacation in Arizona." His breathing is now back to normal.

"Yeah, Harper just told me all about his surprise visit. She confessed she had an awesome time getting to know Gabe," I tell him.

Now I feel like Molly, the office gossip.

"Alright, enough about their little sex-filled vacation. I want to talk about you and your day."

"I had a great day. I had lunch with your Mom and then Harper came home and we sat around and spoke for a while. How about you?"

"What did you and Mom discuss?"

"We talked about you and the business. She answered some questions I had and gave me some insight on being a part of the lifestyle." I try to give a broad answer so I don't have to rehash the entire conversation.

"If you have any questions you know I can answer them for you, right? I'll always be honest with you, Kendall. I want to be the person you go to for questions and who you lean on when you need it."

"I know. I just wanted to get someone's perspective that wasn't on the front line. Mary helped me see things I hadn't seen before. I promise if I have any more questions I'll come to you. Now tell me about your day."

"Well, I got up…alone. Had breakfast, went and dealt with a few issues with the business, and then came home. Gabe showed up a while ago and we hit the gym, now I'm talking to you. What are you wearing right now?" he asks and I burst out laughing.

I swear I'm going to ask Mary if he's bipolar tomorrow.

"Wyatt, you're crazy!"

"Crazy about you. Is Harper coming tomorrow? I invited Gabe only if he promised to stop gossiping while we worked out."

"Yeah, she'll be there. She mentioned Gabe wanted her to spend a few nights over at his place. Then she insinuated it would be a perfect time for you to come here and stay with me."

"I would love that. Is that something you want? Kendall, I know my family can be overwhelming and tomorrow is going to be exhausting at brunch, but I would really like some one on one time with you. You're all I think about and not seeing you for two days is driving me insane."

"You know, they say distance makes the heart grow fonder," I joke then sober when I remember I'll never have his heart.

Wyatt growls. "Distances is overrated."

"I know. Texting and talking is grand but I miss your touch and just being with you. I feel like we've gotten so close over the last two weeks and that our connection has grown so much."

"I feel it too. Are you sure you want to sleep alone tonight? This bed feels awfully big and cold when you aren't here."

"I'm sure," I say and hear him sigh.

"Okay."

"Wyatt?"

"Hmm."

"Thank you for being so patient with me. I'll see you for brunch and then we can hang out the rest of the day if you're free."

"Deal."

"Night, Wyatt."

"Night, babe."

CHAPTER TWELVE

Early the next morning I stare up at the ceiling before the alarm goes off. I guess I'm a little anxious about brunch today. All night I tossed and turned thinking about being in this type of family for the rest of my life. Or if this is something I even want.

I really observed how Bobby was a few days ago. The way he spoke with Wyatt and the authority he exuded, but Bobby also has a soft side when it comes to his family, especially Mary. You can tell he loves her with all his heart and she is his priority.

Mary has been loving since the moment we stepped out of the limo. She's very affectionate and has done everything to make me feel welcome. Having lunch with her yesterday really showed me how much I miss having a mom. Aunt Sarah has been invaluable and given me everything I needed, but I've always felt like I was missing something. Something on a deeper level.

Then there is Gracie. The little over-the-top loud, sometimes annoying sister I always wanted. Growing up I thought Uncle Liam and Aunt Sarah would have a baby and I wouldn't be so lonely but it never happened. Gracie is definitely a handful and spoiled by everyone. She's the baby of the family and I guess with Avery gone, she doesn't hear the word *no* too often. She does have a compassionate and loyal side to her though. She's the type that once she makes up her mind she jumps right into the deep end. I wonder if she's aware of her family's lifestyle or if she is totally oblivious to it.

And finally, Harper. Can I bring her into this type of situation blindly? She's my sister for all intents and purposes. Can I keep a secret this big from her until Bobby deems fit that she know? Will she be a causality because of her association with me? Would she still want to be around me if she finds out I'm a part of a mafia family? How do I pick one family over another?

Ugh! This is so frustrating. I truly feel like I'm standing at a fork in the road trying to decide which path to take. A loveless marriage with unexpected chaos or an unknown future and leaving all this behind. Will I look back on the decision to leave and wish I'd stayed?

I get out of bed and put on my workout gear before heading down to the gym. I need to burn some energy off and get out of my head for a while. I leave a note for Harper on the kitchen counter like always, but I have a feeling she won't be up anytime soon. The gym is empty when I enter which is how I like it. I select the treadmill I want, pop in my earbuds, and set my pace for five miles. Running has always been refreshing for me. I can tune out the entire world and lose myself in some good music. Forty-six minutes later, I'm dripping in sweat and downing the bottle of water from the mini-fridge. I stretch out on the mat and begin to do a circuit of weight training. If I am going to be with Wyatt, I think I might invest in a personal trainer. He's always taking me out and feeding me crazy meals.

The clock on the wall shows it's getting late so I head back upstairs to get ready for our brunch with the Dawsons. Walking back into the apartment, I see Harper is still asleep, so I throw the note in the trash and knock on her door. We have about an hour and a half before we need to leave so this is plenty of time to get her up and ready.

"Harper time to get up. We need to leave in about an hour," I say gently.

She has her blackout curtains covering the windows so no light can disturb her. I always have to give a thirty-minute window because she's never on time.

"Go away." Her whine sounds like a baby kitten.

"Come on, Harp, we need to start getting ready for brunch."

"You go. I think I'll stay here and sleep some more," she grumbles.

"Oh, okay. Well, I'll just tell Gabe you were feeling under the weather."

Harper jolts up from her pillows. I knew that would get attention. "Gabe! He's going to brunch today?" Harper asks rubbing her eyes.

"Yes, Wyatt invited him last night since he knew you'd be there."

"Okay, we better hurry then. I don't want to be late." She jumps out of bed and darts into her bathroom.

She makes this way too easy sometimes!

After my shower, I'm in my closet trying to find the right outfit to wear. I feel like the pressure to be perfect now for this family is going to give me an ulcer. Finally, I decide on a navy silk one-shoulder romper with a pair of nude platform wedge sandals. I apply light makeup with a little lip gloss and curl my hair.

Twenty minutes later Harper emerges in a pair of shorts and a white lace floral shirt with a pair of flat sandals. I check my phone for the time and she made it with five minutes to spare.

"Ready?" I ask as we grab our purses before heading down to the lobby.

On the drive over Harper tells me more about the spa and how she and Gracie met a group of women there for a spiritual retreat to cleanse the soul. The weather was perfect and the drinks kept flowing. It sounds like she and Gracie had a really good time. There was a nightclub they frequented each night with their guys and that was one of the reasons they missed the flight back yesterday morning.

In no time, we pull up to the gates of Bobby and Mary's house and are granted entry. We park next to Wyatt's truck and make our way up to the door. We aren't even able to knock because the door flies open and Gracie is bouncing in front of us hugging me tight.

"Kendall, I missed you!" she says, easing her grip.

"What about me?" Harper says giggling.

"Yeah, yeah you too, Harp!" Gracie hugs Harper.

We walk in the house and I'm immediately swept off my feet and lead in the opposite direction of our group. Gracie and Harper are laughing as I stare up at Wyatt who is holding me bridal style. We go into a room where he closes and locks the door behind him after placing me on my feet. Wyatt turns to me, a predatory hunger in his eyes.

"Wyatt, is everything okay?" I ask unsure as to why he would bring me in here. Did something happen?

He doesn't answer my question; he just devours my lips and pulls my body to his. It only takes a second for my mind to register what's happening before I return his kiss. We are making out heavily while the rest of the family is in the other room waiting for us to start brunch. When our lips pull apart, Wyatt's hands are all over me.

"Wyatt, what's wrong?" I ask again.

"I—I just missed you and felt like you were going to bolt once you got away from me the other day. I never thought I'd feel this way about someone before and I don't want to screw this up." His words are heartwarming and I'm reminded of the conversation with Mary at the restaurant yesterday. Does he love me and not know it? Could we make this work?

"Wyatt, I'm here."

"But for how long, Kendall?" he implores.

I still don't know the answer to that question, but for right now I don't want to be anywhere else. "Can we just take it day by day for now? I'm still wrapping my head around everything. I want to make a choice and not have any regrets. Okay? Let's just enjoy what is in front of us now and worry about long-term later."

"Okay," he agrees and pulls me into another desperate kiss, but the kiss is short lived when there is pounding on the door.

"Hey, we're ready to eat! You two cut it out in there and join us!" Gracie yells from the other side. "You can hump each other later!"

"I guess we better get going before she calls for backup," Wyatt says and leads me out toward the patio hand in hand.

Everyone is standing around the patio when Wyatt and I make our appearance. Both Bobby and Mary embrace me and ask how I am. We make small talk then get our plates and walk down the line of the buffet-style brunch. Of course, Bobby goes first and we all follow his lead. It's the same way as the last time. After everyone is seated with their plates of food Bobby begins eating and then everyone follows. I now understand why.

"Kendall," Bobby starts, "we'd like to meet your aunt and uncle. I think this Friday would be a good time for them to fly in and meet us. We are, after all, going to be family soon and I'd like to meet the people who raised you."

I nearly choke on my mouthful of eggs. He wants to meet my family? I haven't told them about being in Vegas yet, let alone having a boyfriend. Aunt Sarah is going to kill me!

"Dad," Wyatt starts to say but is interrupted.

"What do you mean *going to be family soon?*" Harper pipes up. "Are you getting married? Holy shit, are you pregnant? Is that why you were asking about transferring here to finish your master's degree?"

I literally could die right here, right now. This is why I needed to tell her everything about the Dawson Family.

"She's not pregnant," Wyatt answers Harper for me because I don't think I could form a coherent sentence. He then snaps his head over at his father. "We want to take things at our pace and not have a timeline of when we make that leap yet, Dad."

"This is not up for discussion, Wyatt. Your mother and I have spoken and we would like to meet her family. This is going to happen. I know they don't know she's here but she can make the phone call or I can." Bobby nods over at me giving me the option.

The table has become extremely quiet. Everyone is looking back and forth at Bobby, Wyatt, and me. Harper is giving me pleading eyes wanting to know what the hell is going on.

"I—I will make the call tomorrow," I say, even though I really want to argue. I feel like I'm not in control of my life anymore.

"Great! I will have the jet ready for them Friday morning for pickup. Does your uncle like to golf?" Bobby asks and his tone has softened.

"Yes, he does but doesn't do it as often as he'd like," I offer. The atmosphere that was colder than ice a minute ago is slowly melting back to normal.

"Good. I think Wyatt and I will take him for a few rounds while you girls have a spa day." Bobby turns to Mary. "Set everything up, sweetheart."

Mary nods with a big smile and squeezes his hand.

The rest of brunch is light conversation but I'm on edge about my family meeting the Dawsons. Wyatt keeps a gentle hand on my knee the entire meal trying to calm my bouncing leg, but nothing is working. I should have told Sarah and Liam weeks ago about being in Vegas and now I feel sick to my stomach.

After all the plates have been cleared Bobby summons me to his office. I feel like I'm heading to the principal's office, much like the first time I met Justice Williams. Wyatt is beside me holding my hand.

"Have a seat," Bobby says from where he's seated behind his large wooden desk. Bobby's office has an old world feel to it. The bookshelves are built into the walls and are filled with tomes. His office is very organized and neatly kept. We sit down on leather chairs and Wyatt takes my hand in his rubbing his thumb across my knuckles in a calming gesture.

"Kendall, I know this may seem extremely sudden for you but I can assure you it's for the best. I spoke with Mary and she told me about some of your reservations." I feel Wyatt tense next to me. I haven't even gotten a chance to speak with him about everything.

"This family will welcome you with open arms and you'll never have to worry about that side of the business. It will never touch you."

Did she also talk to him about his son not ever being able to love me? That maybe I want to walk away? Mary said I could, but Bobby is acting as though this is all a done deal.

"Now, I've spoken with Justice about your reports and ideas. After reviewing your documents, I think you're going to be a huge asset to our legit companies. I like the way you think and I told Justice that he needed to get on board with it as well. You and he will work side by side on some of the restructuring of the company. Don't worry, he will not be giving you any grief. He and I had a conversation about the way he was treating you and it won't be a problem anymore."

I can't believe he spoke with Mr. Williams about me *and* that he likes my ideas.

"Thank you," is all I manage to get out.

"I think you're a dazzling young lady, Kendall. I think you can offer this business a lot as well as this family. I know I seem like I'm pushing things pretty fast, but I only want what is best for all of us. I also think after meeting with your aunt and uncle things will become clearer to you."

I nod because what is there to say really? *Will he take me off for a ride to the desert if I disagree?*

"Good Mary and I are excited to meet your family this weekend and once that happens, we can move forward." Bobby stands up, and it's clear this meeting is adjourned.

We rise from our seats and Wyatt kisses my temple. "Go ahead. I need to have a word with Dad."

I give him a quick kiss and leave the room. I make it halfway down the hallway next to the bathroom door where I first ran into Wyatt, when the yelling starts. I can't make out what is being said but I know from the tone that I don't want back in that room. I keep walking and find everyone still out on the patio having mimosas and other drinks. Harper sees me first and makes a break for me.

"Kendall, what in the hell is going on?" she whisper-yells.

Everyone notices and starts moving our way.

"I will tell you everything later, but not here," I plead.

She nods as Gabe places an arm around her waist and she snuggles into his side like it's the most natural thing. He nuzzles her neck, and that right there is what I want. In a moment of clarity, I realize that I want to be cherished. To be loved and held every day. Can Wyatt be that for me?

"Where are our men at?" Mary asks when she sees I'm the only one who came back from Bobby's office.

"Umm, they needed to discuss some things." I don't mention the yelling I heard once I left.

"Kendall, Gabe wants me to leave with him for the rest of the day unless you want me to go back with you to the apartment?" Harper asks as we all stand around. She narrows her eyes to let me know an inquisition is in my future.

"You and Gabe have fun. Kendall and I have plans for today and tomorrow," Wyatt answers Harper as he comes up behind me and nuzzles my neck, planting a kiss there.

I give Harper a smile then turn in Wyatt's arms to face him. I look at him wondering what the yelling with his father was about, but his face gives nothing away. I smile up at him and wrap my arms around his neck to bring him close to me.

"Babe, let's get out of here so I can have you all to myself," Wyatt says in my ear and I nod wanting to get some distance from the group too.

We say our goodbyes to everyone except Bobby, who hasn't come out of his office. Wyatt suggests handing over my keys to Harper so she and Gabe can take my car since he and Gabe drove here together.

"Don't dent or scratch my ride, got it?" I half-joke with her.

She is smiling from ear to ear. I don't normally let her drive because she's not the most aware driver on the road.

Gabe steps up and takes the keys from her. "I'll make sure it comes back to you in perfect condition," he says and Harper puts on her pouty face knowing she lost her chance at driving my car.

Wyatt and I walk out of the house and he helps me into his truck. We take off out of the gates and head east. Wyatt refuses to tell me where we're going so I play with the radio and sing along, trying to quiet the noise in my head about what's going to happen this week.

Forty-five minutes later, we're turning down a dirt road toward Lake Mead. You can tell hardly anyone comes this way because the road is unused. There is a large cactus right when you turn down the dirt-filled road.

"We're going to the lake!" I say excitedly and clap my hands.

Wyatt nods after putting the truck in park. He gets out and opens the back to grab a bag and cooler. He hands me the bag as he opens the tailgate and lifts an umbrella and large blanket out of the bed of the truck.

He planned this.

He planned this for me. For us.

I follow him down to a secluded area near the water. The day is perfect and I can't wait to see what else he has planned. After setting up the umbrella and blanket we lay down and take in the view.

"Wyatt, this is absolutely perfect. How did you find this place?" I ask.

"I found it after we buried Avery. I was so lost and mad at myself that I hopped in my truck and just drove. I saw the road and decided to see what was down here. It was so peaceful and secluded. I come here when I want to get away from everything and think. You're the first person I've ever brought here." He turns to me and cups my cheek. "Kendall, I know things are moving really fast, but I know deep down that you are the one I've been waiting for." He kisses me softly and then stands. "Want to go for a swim?"

I'm still tingling from his words as he pulls me up with him. How can he say those words and not feel love for me?

"I don't have a swimsuit and it's way too bright outside for us to go skinny dipping," I say playfully.

Wyatt starts taking his shirt off showing me his deliciously sculpted and tattooed body.

"The bag has our suits and towels in it." He points to the bag I carried from the truck.

I open it and pull out his trunks and a tiny green bikini that almost matches my eyes. Wyatt has already stripped naked waiting for me to hand him his trunks and makes no moves to hide himself. I toss them over and he locks his eyes with me waiting for a show of his own. I feel the heat in my cheeks spread throughout my entire body. I can't believe he's naked out in the open. I've never seen a more perfect body. And his…

"Are you going to change?" He breaks me from my naughty thoughts.

I know he's already seen me naked but thank god I got that wax at the spa the other day. I bend down and unhook my sandals before sliding them off. Since I'm in a romper I slowly pull down the silky material revealing my strapless bra and the tiniest thong I own. I turn my back to him and shimmy down the thong when I hear Wyatt groan. I reach to unhook my bra when Wyatt's hand is already there helping me. He starts kissing my bare shoulder and the feeling sends a shiver down my spine. He cups my bare breasts with his large hands and gives them a light squeeze. My breathing has become heavier as I feel his hard body against mine, and my needy little self wants him to bend me over and have his way with me. I give my butt a shake, brushing up against him and one of his hands leave a breast and moves to my hip.

"Babe, haven't you heard the saying *don't poke a bear?*" He thrusts himself against me causing me to gasp. "I suggest you get your swimsuit on now before I can't stop myself from ravaging you," he says but makes no move to step away or remove his hands.

I nod and bend over to pick up my suit. That makes him groan even louder. I quickly step into the bottoms and tie my top on.

"I think you're trying to put me in an early grave with your body," he comments tying his trunks and adjusting himself. "Come, let's go for a swim."

We walk down to the water and get in. The water is pleasantly cool and so refreshing. It truly is peaceful here. Wyatt and I swim and splash around a bit before we decide to get something to drink and lay out on the blanket under the umbrella. In the cooler, he packed waters and some fruit for us. We lay everything out and sit across from one another.

"Kendall, is there anything you want to ask me? About my lifestyle or about me?"

I put my bottle of water down. "Well, your Mom answered a lot of my concerns yesterday but I do have a few for you." I see him take a deep breath readying himself. "Are you going to tell me everything that happens? All the details of your day or are you going to tell me only what you want me to know?"

"I'll always be honest with you," he says and takes my hand. "If you want all the details then I'll give them to you. If you want me to only tell you the basics, then I will. Or if you don't want to know at all, I'll respect that as well. We can do this however you like and however you're comfortable with."

"Okay. I think I want to know but not the gory details of cutting off fingers or other body parts," I say, and after a pause, we both laugh. I'm pretty sure most couples never have a conversation like this.

"Does that mean you want to do this with me, babe?" Wyatt sounds so hopeful.

I look in his beautiful blue eyes and give a slight nod. This is it. No turning back now.

"You have to say it, Kendall, to make this real for me."

"Yes, Wyatt, I want you and I want to make this work if we can," I say aloud.

In a flash, Wyatt jumps across the plate of fruit and is all over me. He lays me back on the blanket and hovers above me looking into my eyes.

"You don't know how happy you've just made me, Kendall. I never thought I would find someone I wanted to spend the rest of my life with after everything that has happened to me. I lo… think we are going to be really happy together," he confesses.

And I think it's time to make a confession of my own.

"I think so too, Wyatt." Maybe we just need to take small steps and slowly find our way to love each other.

The shocked expression on his face quickly dissipates as he covers my mouth with his. I feel every emotion from Wyatt in this kiss. I break away and put my hand on his face cupping his cheek.

"Make love to me, Wyatt. Show me how much you want me."

CHAPTER THIRTEEN

"Are you sure? We don't have to do it now, I don't want you to feel like there's any pressure. We can wait until you are—" I place my finger up to his mouth.

"I'm ready Wyatt," I say.

"God, you are so beautiful." His eyes never leave mine but his hands are all over me, igniting a rapid fire in their wake.

Once we are completely naked Wyatt hovers over me between my legs still not breaking eye contact. He places his large warm hand on my sex and moans when he finds me soaking wet. Using his fingers, he plunges them into my hot core.

"Oh, Wyatt!"

Another moan escapes my lips as he adds another finger stretching me to prepare me for his massive size. He continues his delicious assault in and out of me bringing me to the edge. My hips start to move in sync with his movements as he hits that tender spot deep inside me.

Wyatt shifts his body down sucking my needy body on his way. He nips at my breasts leaving an electric current shooting through every nerve ending. Once his mouth finds my pelvic bone, he uses his perfect mouth and attacks clit. We've done this before but for some reason today feels like a different experience. More intense.

"Please," I beg, not recognizing my own voice.

My begging only makes Wyatt work harder. Just as I think I can't take it anymore he bears his teeth and lightly pinches my throbbing clit.

"Oh my God!" I rush out and white spots take up in my eyes. My body shakes as my muscles tighten and my orgasm floods out before Wyatt licks me clean.

"Beautiful," I hear Wyatt comment as he leaves a soft kiss on the top of my sensitive sex. I'm floating on cloud nine trying to bring my heart rate back to normal. "Babe, I know I should worship your body in every way, and I will, but I need to be inside of you right now," Wyatt says. "I need to show you that you're mine." He pauses for a split second, looking as though he's debating what he wants to say. "Kendall, I need to hear you say it one more time because once I enter you I'm never letting you go. Do you understand? We. Are. Forever."

I nod but I know he wants to hear my voice for his confirmation. I can only imagine he's praying I don't change my mind. "Wyatt, I want to be with you, I want this life with you. All of it."

I hear a growl leave his throat. "Eyes on me, babe. I want to see you as we become one."

I do as he asks and focus my green eyes on his deep blue ones. He reaches down again for a kiss and at the same time his lips meet mine, he enters me in one swift motion. I immediately tense at the intrusion and a small whimper escapes my throat. Shit, he's big. Wyatt plants soft kisses around my face staying still to give me a chance to grow accustomed to his size. After a few moments, I shift, needing him to move. Wyatt starts to rock his hips slowly at first and when I meet him thrust for thrust he picks up his pace. It feels amazing as we never break our contact.

"I'm sorry, babe, but with the way I'm feeling right now this is going to be quick. I promise to make it up to you."

Wyatt's speed increases in a rhythm that's beyond delicious. His hand slips down our sweaty bodies and finds its favorite spot.

Moving in a circular motion, petting my clit, my legs wedge his hips in a vice.

"Oh God, Kendall. I didn't think you could get any tighter," he grunts out. It's evident he's trying to hold off as long as possible. "I need you to come, babe. Jesus," just the need in his voice is enough for me to fall over the ledge of ecstasy. He roars my name and his hard body stills after light shockwaves jolt his muscles.

Wyatt lays on top of me trying to balance on his elbows as we calm our bodies. I can't believe we just did that. Not only that but out in broad daylight. He felt so good and…Shit, he didn't wear a condom!

"Wyatt!" I say in a panic and he lifts his head up off the valley of my breast. "We didn't use protection." I know I'm on the shot but who knows if he's clean. He's alluded to being with a lot of women before me and now I'm nervous and hate that I was so careless. What was I thinking? He still has made no move to remove himself from inside me, so I try and lift up but he holds me back down.

"Kendall, it's okay. I'd like nothing more than to put a baby in you."

"What?!" I almost scream. I just committed to him and now he wants a baby. This is moving way too fast. Yes, I want kids, but not right now. "Wyatt I'm on the shot but I am more concerned about being safe. We never talked about you and your flings. Are you clean? Do I need to worry about anything?"

His eyes narrow at me and for a split second something passes over his beautiful face. Outrage maybe?

"Kendall, I would *never* put you at risk. I was always careful with my past hookups. Never have I gone bare with anyone else. I was tested a month ago and was clean." He looks away as if I've hurt his feelings. We still have a lot to learn about each other, but I guess we have all the time in the world now. "You didn't seem to care when you were shoving my cock down your throat. But now you have a problem?"

I grab his chin and make him look at me. He is completely right and I need to stop panicking at every turn. "I'm sorry, I panicked. This is all still very new to me and a big leap of faith. I know you would never intentionally hurt me in any way, but I think we should table having children right now," I say and place a tender kiss on his cheek. We just had sex, the kid discussion can be way down the road. His tense body relaxes a bit and the lines across his forehead smooth out. "We still have so much to learn about each other. Maybe we're rushing things when in reality we should pump the brakes."

"We'll navigate through this together, okay? No rush and no pressure," he says and kisses my forehead with his soft lips.

"Deal."

"Now, I think I promised someone I would worship her body." Wyatt wiggles his eyebrows and starts sucking on my neck making his way down south again.

When we pull up to Wyatt's house after an exhilarating afternoon at the lake, the sun is almost setting. Wyatt wants us to have a lazy evening in the media room to relax after all the excitement of the day. His phone has been buzzing, but he made it clear that he isn't leaving my side. We settle in on the couch and watch an action movie before Wyatt draws us a hot bath and then we snuggle under the cool sheets until sleep catches up with us.

The next morning, we wake up early and both of us hit the gym in Wyatt's house to work out some of our sore muscles. All I can think about during our workout is how I'm going to tell Aunt Sarah and Uncle Liam about Vegas. I know I should've done this before I came here, but a part of me knew I wouldn't take the risk and agree to the internship if they had put their foot down. I don't really know why they hate this place so much. Yeah, the flashing lights and the gambling can be intimidating, not to mention the mafia connections here, but it really has a lot to offer business-wise.

After an extremely long and steamy shower, we dress and walk to the kitchen where Carmen is making breakfast. We attempted to make the shower a quick in and out but Wyatt, being a dirty sex machine, had other plans. He played my body like a finely tuned instrument and didn't stop till I begged for mercy.

"Wyatt, I'm going to step out on the patio and make the call to my aunt," I call over my shoulder and walk out of the room. I know this is not going to be a pleasant conversation and I don't want to answer to them in front of him. No one likes to be lectured in front of an audience.

The phone rings three times before Aunt Sarah picks up. Texas time is ahead by two hours so I know they've started their day already.

"Hello?" Aunt Sarah answers. There are sounds of drills in the background and I know she's at Uncle Liam's shop.

"Hey, Aunt Sarah. How are you?"

"Oh, Kendall it is so good to hear your voice. I was just telling Liam I needed to call and get an update on how your summer adventure with Harper is going."

"It's been thrilling. We are having a blast!" I tell her and try to build the excitement in my voice.

"That's good, honey. So, where have the two of you ended up so far?"

Here goes nothing.

"Well, that's what I wanted to call and talk to you about. Harper and I are in Las Vegas for the summer," I blurt out. Good job, Kendall. Couldn't you have made it sound better or something? I mentally slap myself.

The line goes silent and I think maybe she hung up on me. Glancing down at my phone, I see that we're still connected.

"Hello? Aunt Sarah? Are you there?"

"Ken..." She trails off. "How—why are you in Las Vegas? I thought you heard what Liam and I have tried to tell you the last few years. That is no place for you, Kendall," she snaps and I can hear the disappointment and ire in her voice.

Oh, s-h-i-t!

"I got offered an internship here and I didn't want to pass it up. I really thought it could be good for my career." A long drawn-out sigh leaves me and I try to rein in my attitude. "I'm sorry I kept this from you and Uncle Liam. I wanted to tell you but knew how much you hated this place."

"Kendall, Liam and I have our reasons for not wanting you to go to *that* place. We made it very clear that we wanted you to steer clear. I can't believe that you'd go behind our backs and totally disregard our wishes."

"I know, and I'm sorry for not being honest," I say solemnly.

We both sit there in silence for a few moments not knowing what else to say.

"I met someone," I say gently. Maybe changing the subject to guys will ease some of her anger when she tells Uncle Liam?

"You did?" I can almost hear a hint of excitement come back to her tone. Aunt Sarah always loved gossiping. She and Molly would get along great. She would always try and press me for information on my dates with guys in college.

"I did and his parents want to meet you and Liam this weekend."

"Kendall, Liam is going to flip his lid when I tell him what you've done. You really think he'll want to go to Las Vegas after firmly telling you to avoid that place after all these years? You don't understand the history we have there."

"Please, Aunt Sarah. I have fallen in love and want you to meet him and his family," I plead.

There's a pause before she speaks. "I'll speak to Liam and get back with you, but, Kendall, make no mistake I'm still very upset that you did this behind our backs." I can just picture her shaking her pointer finger at me through the phone. "We know you're an adult and can make your own decisions but there are things you have no idea about. Things that happened in Vegas with our family."

"I know, and again, I'm sorry."

"Okay. I love you and stay safe and keep Harper out of trouble. Lord knows what y'all been up to already."

"I will, Aunt Sarah. Let me know about coming and I'll send you all the details."

We say our goodbyes and hang up. My head finds its way into my hands. I can't believe I completely went behind their backs and came here. A hand on my shoulder pulls me from my thoughts.

Wyatt is standing there with a concerned expression. "How'd it go?" he asks and squats down in front of me.

"It could've gone better." I shrug. "I think I really screwed this up. She was so mad, Wyatt. I've never heard her take that tone with me before." I can feel the tears welling up in my eyes. This has to be the worst thing I've ever done to them. Worse than the time I drove home drunk and plowed over her flowerbed. I wasn't a bad kid growing up but I did push some limits in high school.

"Shhh, it'll be okay, babe. They'll come around once they meet me and my family. They only want what's best for you." He pulls me into a hug and kisses my forehead. "Come on. Carmen has breakfast ready." He stands and holds out his hand for me to take.

We walk back in the kitchen and sit down at the breakfast counter. Carmen serves up our food of ham and cheese omelets, hash browns, and toast. We eat in silence while I stew over the phone conversation with Aunt Sarah. What happened to make them so uptight about Las Vegas? Whatever it was had to be dreadful enough to warn me off of this place.

The sound of Wyatt's voice pulls me out of my thoughts. "Babe, I have to get going. I'll call you later today to check in."

"Okay, have a great day, honey," I say smiling at him as if we've been sending each other off to work for years. *I love you.*

Wyatt circles my waist and pulls me to his body flush. "I don't think I'll ever tire of hearing you say those words." He laughs and nuzzles the crook of my neck before releasing me and nipping at my bottom lip. He then heads to the garage to leave for work.

I thank Carmen for the meal and gather up my things to head into work.

Wyatt and I talked yesterday about me returning to work. I was reluctant at first because of how Mr. Williams was a complete ass to me, but Wyatt told me I have nothing to worry about and that Justice will be singing a different tune now. I agreed because if I plan on being a part of this family, I want to pull my weight and help out. Knowing I'm working on the legal side of the business makes me feel at ease. I still have some reservations about this entire situation, but I know deep down Wyatt would never put me in harm's way if he can help it.

Frankie and I pull up to our parking spots and kill the engines. Why am I so nervous? I feel like it's the first day at a new job and my nerves are shot. I exit my Camaro and nod to Frankie who is walking beside me.

"Kendall, I'll be here in the lobby if you need anything," he says as we approach the sidewalk. It's a little awkward since the last time I saw him I skipped out while he went to the bathroom.

"Thank you, Frankie. Sorry I skipped out on you the other day," I say because I have a feeling he got into trouble for not keeping a better eye on me.

"It's okay, but next time boss says he'll place a tracking device in your ass if you pull that again," Frankie says and I can't tell if he's joking or not. I return the laugh but have a feeling Wyatt would do just that to prove his point. "Let me know if you need to leave or want anything."

I nod and make my way up the elevator to the top floor.

"Good morning, Molly," I say as I approach the desk.

I must have startled her because she jumps slightly. "Oh, good morning, dear!" she greets with a warm smile. "You look to be feeling better."

"Yes, much better. Thank you for covering for me."

"No problem, dear. Us women need to stick together around here." She winks and continues to gather papers from the printer.

I walk around the desk and place my stuff in my cabinet and start to help Molly out but she stops me. "Kendall what are you doing? Mr. Williams and you have a meeting in two minutes."

"What? A meeting? For what?" I ask unsure what I could've possibly done this time.

"I'm not sure, but I do know he came in early this morning and proceeded to clear his morning for a meeting with you."

I gulp. What could we possibly meet all morning for?

"Okay. Thank you, Molly," I say barely above a whisper.

"You'll be fine, dear. Now go before you're late. Mr. Williams hates late." She pushes me towards the door and I feel like I'm walking down death row to meet my maker. It'd be hard for him to hide my dead body with the way Molly gossips so this might not be too bad.

I timidly knock on the wooden door and wait for his voice. Just when I think I didn't knock loud enough, the door swings open and Mr. Williams is there to greet me. I have to lift my head to see his face since he's so much taller than me despite the fact that I'm in heels.

"Good morning, Kendall. Please, come in and have a seat," he offers and steps aside.

I think I've officially entered a parallel universe. He is speaking to me in a completely different tone than before. I glance over my shoulder and see Molly wink before answering the ringing phone. Mr. Williams closes the door behind me as I walk to the leather chair in front of his large desk and I notice the desk is immaculate and organized, not like the last time I was here. Sitting down, I place my hands in my lap and wait for him to start this impromptu meeting. He bypasses his chair and sits in the leather wingback next to me.

"Kendall, first off I'd like to apologize for the abrupt way I've been towards you since you started working here. I was under the impression it was a temporary thing and that I was to keep you somewhat busy until the summer was over." *So, because this was a short gig it was okay to treat me like that?* "It is now my understanding you'll be here on a more permanent basis and will be a valuable asset to our team," he explains, although he's had all weekend to rehearse this, his tone is as if we are meeting for the first time. "You will be set up in the office next door and Mrs. Bowen will be there to assist you with anything you might need," Mr. Williams says of Molly. "As I was saying—"

"Excuse me, Mr. Williams—" I start but he interrupts me.

"Call me Justice. We're going to be working closely together from here on out and I think we should be on a first name basis."

This is crazy. What is happening right now?

"Mr. Will—Justice, I'm not sure what's happening. What exactly am I going to be doing now?" I ask giving him a questioning look.

"Kendall, you'll be working on improving our company similarly to you the proposal you made. Mr. Dawson and I had a lengthy meeting and went over your ideas on Friday. We both agreed you have some impressive ideas. We want you to manage that part of the business and save us as much money as possible. We also want to expand in other areas and would like your opinions there also."

I have died and been brought back to life. I want to make a snarky comment about how he treated me so poorly but have a feeling Bobby and Wyatt set him straight in their meeting. So, I take the high road since I'll be working so close with him in the future.

"Thank you, Justice, for this opportunity. I know working together will make your job a lot easier by taking some of this off your plate," I say swallowing what I really want to tell him.

"Good. Now let's get you set up in your office and we can go over your reports. I have a few suggestions that might be helpful and then I'll let you get to it," he says and stands.

We walk out of his office and to the right is a wooden door that's always been closed. I thought it might be a broom closet and never thought to peek in. Molly is right behind us with a huge bouquet of roses in the most beautiful vase. We enter and I see it's an office just like Justice has but on the smaller side. The view is the same and I'm sure at night the Las Vegas Strip is stunning with all its lights. I have a small leather sofa along with my own private bathroom. The desk is the same one Justice has but the walls are bare. I'll have to go shopping to personalize it once I settle in. Molly approaches and sets the flower arrangement down on the desk.

"Is there anything I can get you, Ms. Drake?" Molly says, her tone formal.

"Molly, don't you dare be so formal with me. Where did you get those beautiful flowers?" I ask as I smell them. I search for the card but there isn't one.

Molly reaches into her pocket and hands a card to me. No doubt she's already read it.

Kendall,
I hope you have a phenomenal day. I'm so happy you're choosing to take this journey with me. I promise you won't regret it. See you at home!
Yours,
Wyatt

It amazes me how sweet and touching he can be. It almost makes me forget he does horrible things to people for a living. I push those thoughts to the back of my mind and return my focus to Justice and Molly who are watching me.

"Thank you, Molly," I say moving over to the small conference table where Justice is now standing.

Over the next few hours, Justice and I work on my reports and make a plan on what I should start on first. He really is a brilliant businessman and I know I can learn a lot from just watching him. Once we have a plan in place, he tells me we should meet once a week to see my progress and if there is anything I might need. It's like he's had personality transplant and made a complete one-eighty from the first time we met.

I walk him out of my office and make my first phone call.

"Hello," the voice answers on the second ring.

"Why didn't you tell me what I was walking into this morning?" I chide.

"Babe, I thought you'd want to be surprised. Your proposal really caught my dad's interest, not to mention Justice was also very impressed," he explains. "I'm sorry, I thought you'd be happy." I can tell he is in the middle of something because I can hear yelling in the background.

"Wyatt is that someone yelling?"

"Oh, umm yeah. I'm on a job right now and stepped away to answer your call."

What kind of job involves people yelling and screaming?

"Well, I will let you get back. Oh, and thank you for the roses, they are absolutely gorgeous."

"You're welcome, I'll see you at home."

"Okay, honey!"

Wyatt lets out a small moan. "I love hearing you say that." The yelling seems to increase in the background and Wyatt lets out a sigh. "I gotta go."

We hang up and I head out to the breakroom to grab a coffee before I start my assignment. I see Molly jump up from her desk and rush over to me. "Can I get you anything Ms.…Kendall?" Molly asks. For a woman in her early sixties she sure can move around quickly.

"Oh no, Molly, I was just getting some coffee before I settle in but thank you."

"Well, let me know and I can get you anything."

"Thank you, but I'm more than capable of getting my own coffee. If I need anything I'll let you know, I promise." I'm sure Justice has her running ragged as it is.

Hours later a knock on the door alerts me that Molly is leaving for the day. I'm at a good stopping point, so I gather my things and place them in a folder to start right back up tomorrow, and place them in a locked drawer. I organize my desk and take one more whiff of my incredible display of roses before walking out of my office. *My office.* I don't think I'll ever get used to that!

Frankie and I walk out to the cars and head to Wyatt's house. I notice Wyatt's car parked in its spot so I know he's home. Carmen is in the kitchen and from the smell of it, I think we are having barbeque chicken.

"Hi, Carmen," I greet.

"Hello, Kendall. Wyatt just got home and dinner will be ready in thirty minutes," Carmen says.

"Thank you."

I make my way down the hall to the bedroom. The shower is going and I strip in the bedroom, before sneaking into the bathroom to surprise him with a thank you for the flowers today.

Steam fills the room and I see his clothes in a pile on the floor. Normally, I wouldn't care about clothes being on the floor except these clothes are covered in blood. I gasp thinking the blood is from Wyatt and tear open the shower door to see Wyatt in all his glory with blood running down his body and into the drain. His eyes are still closed as he has his head completely immersed under the water. I scan his body for any sign that he may be hurt but see nothing. No cuts or open wounds anywhere, which tells me the blood is not his. What was I thinking to agree to this lifestyle? I want to leave the room and pretend I never witnessed this.

"Kendall?" My eyes shoot up to Wyatt's face and see concern there. I try to take a step away from him, but Wyatt latches onto my wrist and pulls me into the shower. We aren't touching but we're close.

"Babe, look at me," he commands and I do as he asks. "I know what this might look like, but I need you to understand that this is part of the business. It was him or me," he tries to explain.

My eyes go wide. "What—what happened Wyatt?" I ask, trying to avoid the last small splatter of blood on the bottom of his throat.

"I was headed up to a safe house with the crew to unload a shipment and was ambushed. They took out one of our cars but we were able to neutralize the situation and finish the drop off." He has his hands on my shoulders giving them a light massage.

What if Wyatt and his crew hadn't been able to neutralize the bad guys and were the ones who ended up killed? My mind is racing at the possibilities but Wyatt just bends his knees so he is eye level with me.

"Babe, stop. I will always come back to you. I have people in place so I'm never in harm's way," he says as if reading my mind, but I still feel uneasy about all of this.

I place my hands over his as he gives me a soft peck on the lips. I reach over to the hook on the wall, grab for the sponge, and pour some bodywash onto it. Once the liquid turns to bubbles, I start to wash away any remaining traces of blood. He's watching me closely never letting his gaze roam over me. Once I finish the front and back of him he takes the sponge and tosses it out of the shower and onto the pile of bloody clothes.

"My turn," Wyatt says and grabs for my sponge on the hook. He lathers up my body wash and starts at my neck and works his way down my body. He pays special attention to certain areas that sets my core on fire. Next, he turns me around and starts all over again with my back.

Wyatt spends the next half hour reassuring me everything is okay with hot shower sex. We only stop when the water turns cold and we both start to prune. Stepping out, Wyatt gets a trash bag from under the sink and gathers the bloody clothes and sponge. We get dressed in loungewear and make our way to the kitchen where I watch Wyatt hand the trash bag over to Carmen.

"Please take care of this, Carmen. The usual place," he says to her.

She responds with a nod and heads out the back door with the bag.

Like it never happened.

CHAPTER FOURTEEN

WEDNESDAY NIGHT HAS ME STANDING AROUND THE circular breakfast table setting up for tonight's exciting event. The week has been full of stress and a little fun is in order. Not to mention I get to hang out with my favorite people. We've decided to double date tonight, and Harper and I have a little fun planned out for our men. Everything is just about set up and all I need is to pop the food in the oven before we're a go for the evening.

Wyatt and Gabe are coming straight from work and Harper is coming from shopping with Gracie. She's supposed to hit up a secret store before meeting up with Gracie and we're going to give our men a little show tonight if they're good.

I hear the rumble of a loud exhaust from outside and race to the window. I really hope Wyatt and Gabe don't beat Harper here. My shocked face is evident at what I see. Rushing out the door, I see Harper in a car that is definitely not hers.

"Where did you get this?" I ask as she climbs out of a Dodge Charger. We didn't bring her car from California, so I'm confused where it came from.

"Oh, it's one of Gabe's cars. He didn't want me to Uber or call a cab to get around town," she says as she pulls the shopping bags from the back seat.

In one of the hotels on the Strip, Harper and I saw servers wearing costumes to get the drinks for the people who gamble. We thought we'd have a poker night and dress up like them while we play. The boys know we're eating and hanging out but they don't know we're playing cards tonight, and they definitely don't know about the costumes.

After dressing we put on our five-inch platform heels and walk out to the kitchen in time for the timer on the oven to beep. The sound of the garage door opening alerts us that our men have arrived home. *I hope Wyatt likes the outfit!*

Harper grabs a plate of food and I grab two cold beers from the fridge and wait by the counter. We hear them talking and their voices get louder as they get closer but they stop dead in their tracks when they walk in and see us standing there.

"The fuck?" both boom.

We strut over to our guys and welcome them home from work. Shock is still present on their faces as they each take a beer from me. Gabe doesn't look my way; he only stares at Harper. Wyatt doesn't take his eyes away from me. I watch him lick his lips while appraising me in my playboy bunny outfit. Black stockings with little bows at mid-thigh, a bow-tie collar, wrist cuffs, and bunny ears.

"Welcome home, honey," I greet kissing his still open mouth. It doesn't take him long before he responds. Out of my peripheral view I see Gabe devouring Harper.

Wyatt has me pinned up against the counter sans beer and his hands are roaming every inch of my exposed skin. He finally pulls away and looks at me. "Welcome home, indeed! What are you doing dressed like this?" He puts himself between me and Gabe and Harper blocking their view.

"Well, Harper and I wanted to have a poker night with our men and thought we'd play the part. Do you like?" I give him a slow seductive twirl. He starts tracing his finger across the curve of my exposed breasts and wets his lips again as if they're dry.

"Oh, I love, babe."

He palms my breasts. As he is about to pull my top down Harper lets out a giggle reminding Wyatt that we aren't alone. We both peer over and see Gabe whispering in Harper's ear making her laugh.

Wanting to get the night started, we fill our plates with food and have a seat at the table. The cards are all set up at one side and the other has bottles of liquor and four shot glasses.

"Okay, so it's dealer's choice on the game and if you pull a drinking card then you must take a shot," I instruct.

"You do realize we have work tomorrow, right?" Gabe says and looks over at Wyatt.

"I already told Harper to bring some clothes for tomorrow if the drinking gets out of hand," I offer. "If you don't want to drink, Gabe, it's fine we can do something else."

Harper and I used to do this back during freshman year at our sorority house. Those were the good old days before loser Chad had to stalk Harper and ruin the rest of the year.

"Trust me, I don't back down. I just wanted to make sure you could handle your liquor," Gabe jokes.

"Maybe she can drink you under the table," Wyatt pipes up jabbing him in the side.

We play five card poker, blackjack, Texas Hold'em, Go Fish, and a few others. We've all pulled the drinking card several times and are pretty buzzed off of the shots and beers within the first hour. We tell the guys about our wild times in college and they let us know some of the crazy things they did growing up as kids. Overall, it's a good night of drinking and fun. At midnight we call it quits and go to our separate bedrooms.

In the hallway, Wyatt throws me over his shoulder and smacks my ass making me yelp. In our room, he tosses me on the bed and strips himself of his clothes before stalking towards me to remove mine. Wyatt loves taking his sweet time getting me naked. It's almost torture but this has been his nightly routine since Monday, and who am I to deny him his now proclaimed favorite nighttime chore?

I can smell the alcohol on his breath as he kisses up to my mouth after starting at my ankle. His body heat is a comfort against these cold sheets.

"Thank you for a fun night," he says. "I don't think I've done something like this in a long time. You seem to bring out this play-ful side I didn't even know I had."

"Get used to it, we'll be having more of those kinds of nights on a regular basis."

"Will you be in a different costume each time? Because I almost blew my load walking into the kitchen tonight." He nuzzles my neck peppering it with kisses that shoot straight to my wet core.

"Oh, you can count on it. Maybe a school girl outfit next time? You can be the headmaster."

He growls in my ear after licking the shell of it making me shiver. I throw my arms around his neck pulling him close to me. I can't seem to get enough of him. He's become an addictive drug in such a short amount of time.

"Hold tight, babe, I plan on us fucking like bunnies all night." And we do.

It's Friday morning and I'm only working for a few hours since Aunt Sarah and Uncle Liam are flying in this afternoon to visit me. After the wild Wednesday night poker party, my phone woke me up with Aunt Sarah calling. We talked for a long time and she finally explained a little more regarding my parents and their time here in Las Vegas. They had gotten involved with the wrong group of people and made some enemies, which is why they left. They agreed to come for a visit for the weekend since I was adamant on staying put. They were still disappointed I lied to them but under-stood why I did it. I hope after meeting Wyatt they'll see how happy I am and forgive me.

I bought them first class airline tickets instead of having Bobby send his plane. I didn't want my aunt and uncle feeling overwhelmed since they already had a problem coming out here. Wyatt understood and discussed this with Bobby and Mary to smooth things over. I think he's starting to understand how overwhelming his family can be at times.

Harper had to leave last night to head home for a few days because of her grandmother's birthday party celebration and without her I'm feel extra anxious as the minutes slowly tick by. I plan on picking my aunt and uncle up and taking them back to my apartment to show them my new digs even though I don't spend my time there. After, I'll let them get settled in the guestroom, and then we'll meet at the Venetian on the Strip where we'll eat at a restaurant called *CUT* in a private dining room. Mary planned everything and understands my reservations about being too flashy. She suggested catching a show afterward but after hearing about Aunt Sarah and Uncle Liam's history, I think it might not be a good idea. I wanted to meet at Wyatt's house for dinner but didn't want to overwork Carmen in any way. At least eating out at a restaurant gives them an option to go back to my apartment or escape if they don't like the Dawsons, though I hope they do.

After chugging three cups of coffee I'm bouncing off the walls in my office. I can't focus on anything in front of me and when I check the clock again, I only have an hour before they arrive. I really have missed them. I stare at the spreadsheet one more time and decide to call it a day. I'm no good to anyone here right now. Putting away all my papers in the locked drawer and grabbing my purse, I walk to the reception desk where Molly is seated.

"I can't work anymore. I think I'm going to head out for the weekend," I tell her leaning on the desk.

"You're that nervous?" I nod in answer. "Don't be, everything will work out just fine, dear," she says. Molly and I went out to lunch this week and I spilled everything to her. She may be the little gossip lady but she's also a good listener. If I had to choose a grandmother, she'd be my pick.

"I know, I just want everyone to get along and like each other. What if they don't?"

"I wouldn't worry about it. Not all families get along, you know, but still maintain a friendly relationship for the sake of their children. My in-laws hated me." She lets out a laugh.

"Really? Who could hate you?" I'm astonished anyone could not like Molly.

"I know, right!"

We both laugh and say goodbye for the weekend.

Frankie follows me to the airport but then heads back to my apartment. I spoke to Wyatt and after a mega argument he relented on not having Frankie tail me one I've picked up my aunt and uncle. Ever since I evaded Frankie, Wyatt and I have shared each other's location between the three of us. This way if something were to ever happen, we'd be able to locate the person immediately. I don't want Sarah and Liam to feel like they're being followed though. I haven't told Wyatt about Liam and Sarah's past. I'm worried he'll want to track down the group who was involved.

Once I pull up and park at the airport, I have about ten minutes until the plane arrives, so I make a call to Wyatt.

"Hey, babe, are you at the airport yet?" Wyatt says after it rings twice. He knows how nervous I've been about them coming here.

"I am. About to head in and wait for them at baggage claim. I just wanted to call you and tell you that can't wait to see you tonight."

"Wish I could've met them at the airport with you, but I'm finishing up a deal with the Falcones."

The Falcone Family, I've learned, is one of the Five Families in the mafia here in Las Vegas.

"It's fine. I'll see you at the restaurant in a few hours. It gives me some alone time with my family before we meet up."

"Kendall, I know you're worried but don't be. Everyone is going to get along just fine, I promise."

"Wyatt, listen, no matter what happens tonight I—" I pause. Why did I have to do this over the phone? But I've already opened my mouth so I might as well finish it. "I just wanted to tell you that I love you."

"Kendall—"

"I know you said you'd never be able to love me back but I just wanted you to know how I feel about you and tonight changes nothing for me."

There, I said it and it feels good to get it off my chest.

"Kendall, I—" He's hesitant in his words so I stop him.

"Listen, I'm not expecting you to declare it back. You've made it perfectly clear how you feel, but I wanted you to know that I'm all in. I'll see you tonight."

I hang up before he can respond and walk to baggage claim to wait. I need a few minutes of quiet before the weekend activities begin. Fifteen minutes later, I see them walking in my direction. Uncle Liam is scouting around everywhere and Aunt Sarah is playing with her phone. I yell out for her and she runs over to envelop me in one of the biggest hugs.

"Oh, Kendall, look at you." She holds me away at arm's length. "You've gotten some sun and you look stunning!"

"I've missed you so much." I wrap her back into another hug.

Until now, I guess I didn't realize how much I need them in my life. They love that I'm independent and give me my space, but I need to make more of an effort to physically see them.

"Hey, what am I, chopped liver?" I hear Uncle Liam say behind us and I pull away and launch myself at him.

"Uncle Liam! I missed you too!" I hug his neck. He always swings me around just like when I was a little girl.

"I swear you have grown three inches since I last saw you," he says just like he says every time I come for a visit.

"Have not and you just saw me a month ago."

We wait for their bags at the carousal and then walk out to my car. They tell me about the business back home and they've picked so many more customers that they've had to hire two more workers. Of course, the discussion turns to the upcoming football season for the *Dallas Cowboys* and their chances of winning this year. When I lived back home, Sundays were spent watching football and cheering on America's team. Aunt Sarah tells me all about the nosy neighbor who was snooping on the other neighbor and fell off a ladder, breaking her hip. That nosy neighbor was always spying on everyone in the neighborhood. *Sometimes karma's a real bitch.*

When we arrive at the apartment, I introduce them to the doorman and the concierge before entering the elevator. On the ride up Uncle Liam asks me something I never would have imagined.

"Kendall, do you still have the guns I got you before leaving for college at Stanford?" he asks. Their past must be a lot heavier than they let on if he needs a gun to carry with him.

"Yeah, I have the one in my Camaro in the hidden compartment and then the other two are in the apartment. Why?"

"I'd like to have one while I'm here. I'll give it back before our flight on Sunday."

"Sure, that won't be a problem," I offer because if that's what makes him feel safe during his stay here then I'll give it to him. I'm the one who brought him back to a place he's been avoiding.

We exit the elevator, and when I open the door to the apartment, Aunt Sarah loves the place right away. We still have a few hours before dinner, so I offer them some drinks and give them the grand tour before showing them their room and letting them settle in. I then go to my room and retrieve one of the guns from between the mattress and the box spring before going to the kitchen and pulling the other down from the top shelf in one of the cabinets. I check the safety and knock on my aunt and uncle's door. Uncle Liam opens it and I show him the guns.

"Thank you, Kendall, for letting me borrow one," he says as he tucks the 9mm into the back waistband of his jeans and pulls his shirt over it.

"Anything you need, it's yours," I say. "The other one will be up in the cabinet right next to the stove. Top shelf."

"Thanks, sweetheart. Listen, I know we were a little hard on you about not telling us about Las Vegas, but we are truly proud of you and all your accomplishments. Sarah and I are so blessed to have helped raise you. I know both of your parents would be over the moon about who you've become and who you're going to be." He kisses the top of my head and retreats into the bedroom.

I am touched at his words. I've always felt guilty about surviving the fire. The therapy I went through growing up helped ease my guilt but deep down I've always wondered why I lived and they didn't. I always wonder how different my life would be if they had. Would I have met Harper and decided to go into business? Probably not. Aunt Sarah and Uncle Liam have always said that everything happens for a reason and to live each day to the fullest to honor them the best I can.

I text Wyatt as I look through my closet to find something to wear this evening. He's left me several messages about our earlier phone conversation but I ignore them.

Me: The packages are secured!

Wyatt: Good to know. Did you have a nice reunion?

Me: Yes! It's great seeing them. They told me how proud they were and what I have become.

Wyatt: You should be! Can we talk about earlier?

Me: Let's get through this weekend and then we can talk okay?

Wyatt: If that's what you want. Are you sure you can't stay the night with me? The bed will be so cold without you.

Me: I'm sure but it is only for two nights. I think you'll survive.

Wyatt: Maybe I'll sneak over after they've gone to bed.

Me: I don't think my uncle would go for it.

Wyatt: It was worth a try. See you soon!

Me: Bye 😊

I find the perfect dress for the evening. It's a black and white silk sleeveless fit and flare paired it with black peep-toe red sole pumps. I do my makeup and put soft curls in my hair. Picking a white clutch, I make my way out to the living room to wait for the others.

Uncle Liam is wearing a dark suit with a white shirt and no tie. He looks as though he'd fit right in with Bobby and all their men. He's flipping channels on the TV when I sit down next to him and wait for Aunt Sarah to make an appearance. She and Harper are on the same clock when it comes to getting ready—late.

Twenty minutes later she comes out in an emerald shift dress looking absolutely stunning. Uncle Liam beats me to her, wrapping her into a hug and dips her into a kiss. Since I can remember, they've always been so affectionate towards one another. They have always been my 'couples goals.'

"Aunt Sarah, you look fantastic," I say.

Liam still hasn't let her go.

"Thank you, sweetheart. Shall we go? I know we're running late because of me."

I check my watch and see we should've already been there. I text Wyatt that we're leaving now and will be there shortly. The drive isn't long, and once inside the restaurant, I give our name and we're escorted through the dining area to the back where the private rooms are. I notice Frankie and some other guys who are usually around Mary, seated at a table close to the private door. Frankie nods to me acknowledging my presences then turns back to the other guys at his table.

I take a deep breath before our host opens it. This could go either way. The room is well lit and decorated very fancy. Bobby, Mary, and Wyatt are seated at the table and turn when the door opens. They stand to greet us and I notice about halfway to us both Bobby and Mary stop mid-step looking like they've seen a ghost. Mary lets out a small shriek causing Aunt Sarah to go stiff next to me. I turn to see her eyes widen and lips part just as Uncle Liam sees who we're meeting. He reaches for his gun and points it at the Dawsons. It all happens so fast I don't understand what's happening.

"Stay right where you are and don't come any closer," Uncle Liam says and pulls the hammer back on the gun.

CHAPTER FIFTEEN

Uncle Liam pushes Aunt Sarah and me behind him making me stumble. Thankfully Aunt Sarah catches me before I hit the ground. Wyatt pulls his gun from the back of his waistband.

"Easy. There's no reason for anyone to get hurt here. Let Kendall go or put the gun down and we can talk about this," Wyatt says and has his gun trained on Uncle Liam.

"Not a chance, boy. You lower yours then we'll walk out of here with no one hurt," Uncle Liam demands.

Bobby and Mary still haven't moved from their spots. Mary looks starstruck where Bobby just observes my uncle.

"What is going on here? Uncle Liam put your gun down, this is my boyfriend and his parents." I place a hand on his shoulder trying to get his attention and calm the situation. This definitely is not how I thought their first meeting would go.

"Kendall, please tell me it's not true," Liam says still keeping an eye on Wyatt and Bobby.

"How are you alive? They reported you dead in the fire; you both died in the fire," Bobby says. For some reason his entire demeanor is cool and calm, like having a gun pointed at him is an everyday occurrence.

"You're alive and have a daughter…wait that can't be right she's too old—" Mary says in the quiet room.

I have no idea what is going on but apparently, they know each other. Are these the enemies that made them flee to another state? This is turning into a nightmare.

"She couldn't be—no she died too—" Mary continues but now she's staring right at me as if seeing me for the first time. She goes to take a step to me but Uncle Liam pushes me back further against the wall behind him and Bobby stops Mary from coming forward.

Wyatt doesn't know what to do and keeps glancing from Liam to me. I know his first instinct is to shoot the threat but with it being my family he's torn.

"Liam, I think we need to sit down and have a discussion. Right. Now," Bobby says after more silence. Despite his even tone, it's clear he's pissed. This is the Bobby I'm used to seeing. "You'll never make it out of here with all of my guys out there." He nods towards the door.

"Will someone tell me what the fuck is going on!" Wyatt yells.

"We had to—" Aunt Sarah starts but can't finish. Her voice is as shaky as her body.

"Sarah, please tell me. She is all I have left of her," Mary pleads with her.

Just then the door opens and Bobby's men walk in to assess the situation. It doesn't take them long for them to take in the room. They all pull their guns and have them pointed at Uncle Liam. I step in front of them with my hands up in front of me not wanting him to get shot.

With at least seven guns pointed at me, my legs feel like giving out.

"Put your fucking guns down!" Wyatt screams and they follow his orders.

"I see the apple doesn't fall far from the tree, Bobby," Uncle Liam taunts.

"Let's sit down and talk Liam. We can't talk with guns in our faces," Bobby says. No one makes a move. This seems like the stand-off of the century. Bobby sighs, realizing Uncle Liam isn't budging, so he stays put and continues to talk. "Where have you been all this time? Why did you hide her from us?"

Hide? Who did they hide? Me? Are they talking about me or Sarah?

"Uncle Liam? What is going on?" I plead. Someone needs to start talking.

"Nothing, sweetheart. We need to go though," he states, but Sarah remains frozen in place.

"Did you hide me?" I step away from him. I need to get to Wyatt, so I can get him to put his gun down and then Uncle Liam will do the same.

"It's not what you think, Kendall. Bobby and I have history," he says and it confirms my question from earlier. "Sarah and I will tell you, but not here. Okay?"

"Tell her now, Liam. She deserves to know the truth about who she is and where she came from," Bobby continues to drop hints.

"Shut up, Bobby!" Liam yells and grips the gun tighter.

Wyatt has been taking small steps to me while Uncle Liam is focused on Bobby. He is about four steps away now.

"They were our best friends, Liam. You should have come to me. You have no idea what our family went through when we found out," Bobby argues.

"Come to you? Some of your guys were there that night! For all I knew it was your order to set the house on fire and kill every-one!" Liam spits back at him.

Fire? Are they talking about the one that killed my parents and brother? Is Bobby responsible? I turn just in time to see Wyatt reach out for me but a hand yanks me back away from him. I'm now in the arms of Uncle Liam and he has an arm around my waist.

"Kendall, I know this is confusing but I need you to trust me right now," Uncle Liam whispers.

"That's impossible! Nicholas and Rachel were our friends. I'd never do anything to hurt them. It almost killed me when I got the call," Bobby spews.

Mary is crying and shaking.

"Really? Then how do you explain Corbin or Eric or even Ivan being there? I saw them with my own eyes. I snapped Eric's neck with my own two hands before he could finish off Sarah and Kendall in the woods," Liam spits back.

The look on Bobby's face goes white as a sheet. I can tell he had no clue that happened.

"Kendall, look at me—" Uncle Liam says but is interrupted by Bobby.

"That's not even her real name, Liam. Tell her her real name."

I turn to face him and he tries to take a step towards the door that is blocked by Bobby's security. I see Frankie with his hand on his holstered gun. His eyes are darting back and forth between us and the Dawsons.

"Kendall, we need to walk out of here and then I'll tell you everything. Okay? But right now is not the time. We need to get away from these people," Liam repeats and takes another step toward the door with his arm still wrapped around me. He slowly moves Aunt Sarah who's clutching the back of his jacket as we go. His calm behavior and what Bobby is saying is confusing the hell out of me.

"Kendall is not going anywhere with you," Wyatt grits and cocks the hammer back on his gun.

"Sarah, please don't leave here with her again. She is all I have left of her," Mary begs. I can see how truly devastated she is and it makes me want to walk over there and give her a hug. "I knew the moment I saw her that she was theirs." Mary turns to Bobby. "I told you and you called me crazy! Wanted to call my doctor!" She punches Bobby on the shoulder.

Bobby is at a loss but tries to calm Mary down and console her.

I need to do something or someone is going to get hurt or die because Uncle Liam is feeling like a cornered animal. With the guards blocking the exit we have nowhere to go.

"Stop! Just everybody stop right now," I yell and look at Uncle Liam. "Tell me right now. If Bobby had wanted something to happen we all would be dead right now. Please, Uncle Liam, tell me."

I can see the look of defeat in his eyes but he's always been so stubborn.

"Tell her, Liam. It's time," Aunt Sarah says putting her hand on his forearm.

"Security out now!" Bobby yells and they file out quickly. "We need to put the past aside for now and figure this out. Something has happened and we need to get to the bottom of it. That starts with telling her the truth."

Liam puts the safety back on the gun and lowers it. I watch as Wyatt does the same when Bobby puts a hand on his shoulder. Liam releases his hold on me and I take a step back relieved all weapons have been lowered. Wyatt takes this as an opportunity to sweep in and tugs me to him, turning us away from Liam and Sarah. His hold on me is so tight I'm finding it hard to breathe. When he finally lets me go, he looks me over. I place a small peck on his lips to reassure him that I'm okay.

"Let's all have a seat so we can talk and figure this out," Bobby suggests and I notice Aunt Sarah and Mary are embracing as Uncle Liam sits down with his face buried in his hands. His gun is already set on the table in front of him.

Wyatt walks me over to a seat, pulls it out, sits down, and places me on his lap. One minute turns into five as the silence fills the room. No one seems to want to start, but I want answers.

"Uncle Liam?"

"You have to understand we didn't have a choice. What Sarah and I did was the only thing we knew to do. You have to believe me. We wanted to tell you but as the years flew by, I just thought we could leave the past behind us, so you could have a normal life."

"Uncle Liam, what is it? What are you hiding?" I beg.

"Kendall, our names aren't really Drake. Sarah and I are actually Liam and Sarah Martin. We were very close with your parents and when they died we took over as your guardians. Your father always had a backup plan for everything; he never left anything to chance. I was his righthand man and my wife was your nanny." He pauses to let my brain process what he just said.

"When the house was attacked and set on fire, we made a run for it hoping your father's plan was fail proof. And it was until you came here."

"I—I don't understand. Why did we have to run? Who was after us? Why did they kill my family?" I'm so confused and frustrated.

"I don't know for sure, but there were a handful of enemies your dad had. It could've been a deal gone south or a dispute over territory. I thought we could run to Mary and Bobby, but after seeing some of his men there I couldn't take the risk with your life or Sarah's. So we fled to Texas, got new identities, and started a life there."

"Wait, if Drake isn't my last name then what is it then?" I ask, my brain slowly processing the information and I feel like I'm on a two-minute delay.

"Kendall, your real name is Alexia Blaire Chapman."

Wyatt lets out a gasp and I feel his arms crush me tighter as if trying to keep me grounded. I push out of his grasp to stand and move around while I let everything sink in. I can't believe this. My entire identity has been a lie.

"Hold on. Chapman? I've heard that name before. Where have I heard it?" I say more to myself.

"Is she *my* Lexi?" The pained sound coming from Wyatt unsettles me and I turn to look his way.

"Yes, baby boy. She's your Lexi," Mary answers him with tears still streaming down her face. His Lexi? What?

And then it hits me like a ton of bricks. Wyatt told me the story about Lexi. He was supposed to protect her. He has the tattoo of her on his chest. *My Angel* with an LC under it.

I need some space to think this whole thing out. I must look ready to bolt because Liam is standing but at a safe distance to give me room to breathe. This is crazy. I'm the long lost Lexi, the one who was born here and was to be married to Wyatt. The one he gave his heart to. My world has just been blown into pieces.

"Uncle Liam, this is nuts! How could you not tell me? Wait?" There's something he said earlier that is just now registering. "You described our house was attacked and then burned. My nightmare! The nightmares I've been having for over a decade actually happened, didn't they?"

Liam nods and Aunt Sarah stands to make her way over to me. Her eyes are puffy from crying; her makeup is ruined and there are streaks down her cheeks. She reaches out to touch me but I take a step back. I don't want to be touched right now. I want answers.

"Kendall, we thought it was best not to tell you. We were scared. If anyone found out that you were still alive, they would've come and finished the job." She's weeping and holding her hands against her chest. "We have loved you since you were born and we thought we were doing the right thing."

"By not telling me!" I scream out. "I can understand it might be a lot for a kid to take, but I'm an adult. You should have told me! You made me believe I made it all up. That I was some kind of weirdo who imagines their parents being murdered. You have no idea what I've gone through over the years! And now to find out it was all true. You lied to me." I can feel my heart being ripped out of my chest right now. How could they not tell me? The only two people I've blindly trusted have been betraying me for years.

I back away from Aunt Sarah more and see her eyes widen, but I need space. This large room now feels like a tiny box. I look around the room and all eyes are on me. Bobby is watching my every move. Mary is patting her eyes with a napkin but has a soft smile playing across her lips. Wyatt has stood up and is about ten feet away looking me over from head to toe. I guess trying to rack his memory of the old Lexi and putting the pieces together. Liam and Sarah are the closest to me and both have their hands up, not moving, treating me as though I'm a wounded animal ready to bolt. Which sounds good right about now.

"I need some air. I am leaving to be alone," I announce.

"Lexi, you—"

"My name is Kendall!" I shout cutting my glare towards Mary. I know this isn't her fault but I can't control my emotions. My life has been one big cover up. "Fuck!"

Then I flee the room. I see security right outside the door and move past them quickly. Frankie takes off towards me and I know I need to come up with a plan. I head for the casino and weave through the crowds. I can't believe how well I'm doing in these killer heels. I get behind one of the *Wild Cherry* slot machines and pretend to be a player watching as Frankie runs right past me. I wait a few more minutes then make my way out to the valet to retrieve my car. Thank god I was still holding my purse. I tip the guy then jet out of there as fast as the wheels will take me.

I drive with no purpose or idea of where I'm heading. I'm reeling at the info from tonight. My mind tries to recreate my nightmare to give me some memory of that night years ago. Tears are flowing down my face making it almost impossible to drive. I try calling Harper but it goes to voicemail so I shut off the phone to think.

After what feels like hours I pull down a familiar dirt road with a large cactus and come to a stop by another car. I get out onto the unpaved road and walk over to the parked car.

"I knew you would come here," Wyatt remarks sitting on the hood of his car.

"I didn't know where I was going until I spotted the dirt road and the cactus. I'm actually surprised I noticed the turn off in the dark."

He stands and offers me his hand, which I take and he leads me down to the lake. He takes off his suit jacket and lays it down for me to sit on. I lean against him when he sits down beside me needing some comfort after having the rug pulled out from under me. He seems to have a calming effect on me whenever he's near.

My security blanket. I wonder if it's because we've been bonded since birth.

"Babe, you can't run away like that again. You almost gave me another heart attack when Frankie lost you in the crowd at the casino. It's not safe especially now that we know who you are."

Why does it matter who I am?

"I needed to breathe. The walls were closing in on me. I mean, my entire life has been one big lie and cover up by the people I trusted with everything. How could they not tell me, Wyatt? How?" My emotions are starting to flare up again. I hate crying.

"I guess they thought they were doing the right thing by keeping you safe. You know ignorance is bliss and all." His phone rings with Elvis echoing across the lake and I know Bobby is calling. "Hello…I have her…yes, she is fine…no…not tonight. We'll see you all in the morning…okay…bye."

"Sending out the search party?"

"Well, you're a very important person, Kendall, and I don't think you completely understand that right now." He holds me close to his side.

"How do *you* feel about me being Lexi Chapman?" I ask wanting to know how much this affects him. Will this change things between us?

"Christ, Kendall, I don't even know! I mean, I spent years with guilt and sadness over the loss of Lexi. I swore to never love another because of our bond, but then I met you and finally felt at peace and happy again. This entire time I've felt guilty being with you. Like I was tossing the promise aside because of these emotions you bring out in me. I was betraying her by falling for you. And now, to know you're the same person has me in a tailspin."

"Falling for me?" I try to keep the hope out of my voice. Before he can respond, I add, "I understand. I can't even imagine what a shock this must be for you."

Wyatt lifts me like I'm light as a feather so I'm straddling him. He pulls my chin down so we're at eye level.

"Kendall, everything has changed for me. I was going to wait until after this weekend to talk to you but everything went to shit tonight. I love you, Kendall. I think I've loved you from the moment we met. I buried Lexi the day I ran into you at Mom and Dad's house. I realized after meeting you I was a walking corpse just letting life pass me by. You bring me to life and give me a purpose. I was having a hard time letting Lexi go and letting you in my heart because she's been in my soul for so long. Yes, you may be the same person but Lexi is gone and has been since she was five. You are my forever, Kendall, right here right now. I don't care if you're a homeless college student or a hidden queen. I just know that you and I are meant to be together." His words fill the aching gap in my heart. He reaches for my hand and places it over his heart. "This belongs to you. I belong to you. We might have been lost for years but in the end, we found each other again."

I'm crying at his declaration. "Thank you, Wyatt." I kiss him long and hard.

When we finally break apart, I stare back into his blue eyes. "This belongs to you too." I take his hand and mimic what he did. "As long as we're honest with each other then nothing can come between us."

"I love you too much to let anything happen to us."

"I love you too, honey."

The stress of the evening is starting to set in and I feel bone-tired. Wyatt must sense it too.

"Come on. Let's get you home and to bed. Our families still have a lot of answering to do about the past tomorrow."

Wyatt stands with me still in his arms, and he carefully places me on the ground. He grabs his jacket and we walk to the cars. The passenger door to his car opens and Frankie gets out.

"I was hoping when I found you that you'd come back with me in my car. Frankie will drive yours back if you want."

"Yeah, I think it's a good idea right now." Exhaustion has taken over my body.

Wyatt nods to Frankie and he makes his way over to my car and leaves. Wyatt opens my door and helps me in before getting in on his side. He starts the car and we make our way back to the city. I take my phone out and turn it back on to see a ton of missed calls from Wyatt, Liam, Bobby, Sarah, and Frankie. I text Liam letting him know I'm okay and I'll see them tomorrow before placing it back in my purse.

Wyatt takes us back to his house and we walk to his bedroom in silence. The weight of the day finally hits me, but here with Wyatt, I feel safe and loved. I sit on the bed and slowly take off my heels, rubbing my aching feet. Wyatt comes over and works his magic by massaging them, working his way up my calves and thighs. I let out a low mewl loving the way my tight muscles relax under his touch.

"Babe, do you want me to relax you and take your mind off of everything?" Wyatt asks as he works his way to my upper thigh.

"Yes," I moan out. I don't think I'll ever be able to deny this man.

"Sit up."

I do as he asks and he lifts my dress over my head leaving me in just a bra and panties. He unhooks my bra and takes turns sucking each nipple into his mouth. My head falls back at the sensation and I plant both hands on the bed to steady me. Once he's devoured both of them he goes to my panties and rips them from my body in one swift tug. The fabric bites into my skin, but I welcome the pain. He lowers his head and the moment he makes contact with my dripping wet sex I fall back, unable to hold myself up any longer. The things he's able to do with his tongue should be against the law. It doesn't take long before I feel it in my lower stomach. With one last flick of his tongue my body lets go. My eyes roll closed and I'm panting when I feel him kiss his way up my body.

"Is this what you want, Kendall? You want me to devour your sweet pussy then fill you with my hard cock?" Wyatt presses himself against my hot core.

"Yes!" I reply breathless. He has such a dirty mouth and it turns me on even more.

He kisses me and with one swift thrust he's sheathed himself fully inside me. We both let out a moan at the magnificent feeling. He starts to move at a slow pace reveling in the feeling. Every thrust and every kiss I can feel the love he has for me and I try to pour just as much into every kiss and touch against his body. He reaches down and presses his thumb to my sensitive clit and it isn't much longer before I'm coming undone again. When I release my heavenly orgasm Wyatt comes long and strong coating my womb with his seed. He continues to thrust, making sure I take all he has to give and then collapses on top of me, burrowing his head in the crook of my neck. We both are trying to catch our breaths while he leaves open mouth kisses against my skin. I hope it will always be like this.

Finally, after what feels like forever, Wyatt pulls out and gives me one last kiss before standing.

"Do you want to shower now or in the morning?" he asks with his hands on my thighs. I'm still lying there limp and completely relaxed. The last few hours have been monstrous, but Wyatt knew exactly what I needed.

"In the morning. I don't think I can move after what you just did to me," I utter with a smirk.

I peek an eye open and see a smug look morph into the most beautiful smile before he turns to head into the bathroom. He comes back out with a washcloth to clean me up then scoots me over to the center of the bed and climbs in behind me. He places his large arm around me and pulls me into his chest.

"Babe, no matter what happens, I'm here for you. Anything you need, I'll give it to you."

"I know, Wyatt, thank you."

"Night, Kendall. I love you."

"I love you too, honey."

After a few minutes I hear his breathing even out and know he's fast asleep. I'm having a hard time finding it right now even though I'm exhausted. My mind is racing at the revelations that were unveiled today and wonder how life would be different if none of it had happened this way. What if I never accepted Mr. Slater's offer to come to Vegas? I'm starting to see his offer wasn't such a coincidence. Would Liam or Sarah ever have revealed my past to me or would they have kept going on as if that life never happened? They still have some hard questions to answer tomorrow and I expect them to be honest with me. They need to tell me everything that has to do with my family and their deaths. I'm not a child anymore and I don't need to be handled with kid gloves.

I turn in Wyatt's hold and face him. We have this pull to one another and growing up away from him couldn't separate us. It was like the universe knew we would end up here even if we didn't. I lightly kiss his soft lips and close my eyes. Tomorrow we'll get the answers I need. And tomorrow I'll make a plan about how I want my life to play out.

Tomorrow.

CHAPTER SIXTEEN

*S*ARAH AND I ARE RUNNING THROUGH THE YARD HEADED *for the wooded area behind our house. We finally make it to the tree line and stop to catch our breath. We look back to my home and see the entire house engulfed in flames. There are explosions throughout the house shattering windows. The men with guns all have masks and are dressed in all black outfits. It's still dark outside with the moon and stars high in the sky. Sarah has her hand covering my mouth and the other one is rubbing up and down my arm for comfort. I can hear one man bossing everyone around speak.*

"The boss said to leave no survivors. Make sure they're all dead!" he states to another man and into a radio.

Off in the distance, I see men lined up and a round of gunfire go off. I notice one man lifts his mask and turn towards the woods in our direction. I can almost see his face…It's…

A scream echoes through the room and I bolt up in bed. Wyatt, who was still sleeping beside me, jolts up out of the bed pulling my attention turn to him as he reaches for his gun on the nightstand. I'm breathing so fast I think I might pass out.

"Kendall, it's okay it was only a dream. I won't let anything happen to you."

I try and focus on him and his comforting words. I'm covered in sweat as if I just walked out of the shower.

"It was—someone like Liam this time."

Wyatt just stares and listens, holding me tight against his body.

"I was having *that* nightmare again and this time someone who was like Liam was the man who lifted his mask. He gave the orders to kill everyone." I put my face in my hands.

"It's okay. It was just a dream." He rubs my back in a soothing motion.

"I know. Liam was the one who found us in the woods. I know it couldn't have been him, but my nightmares feel so real sometimes." Well, now I know they're real.

I peer over at the clock on the nightstand and see it's still early. Given everything that happened earlier and now this nightmare, I know I won't be able to go back to sleep.

"I think I'll hit the gym. You go back to sleep and I'll wake you when I'm finished and we can shower together," I say not wanting to keep him from sleeping too.

"No, if you want to sweat it out then I'll be right there with you. I can't imagine what it feels like to have your world turned upside down, but you can lean on me. We can get through this together."

At breakfast Wyatt mentions Bobby's call. He says Liam and Sarah are at their house and they wants us to meet there to talk. We finish up our meal and make our way over to Bobby and Mary's house in complete silence. My nerves have come back full force, and if I'm honest, I'm a little scared at what I'm going to learn.

We're greeted at the front door by Mary and she practically knocks Wyatt over to get to me. After a few moments, she holds me at arm's length and stares at me, keeping a tight hold on me.

"I knew the moment I met you that you were related to Rachel. When I saw your emerald green eyes I was looking at my best friend again. I told Bobby you could be hers, but he kept saying you were dead and there was no way it could be you. But I knew." She takes my hand and leads me through the foyer and to the kitchen. Now our first encounter makes a little more sense.

Bobby, Liam, and Sarah are all seated in the living area off the kitchen drinking coffee. Mary offers us coffee and tells us to take a seat. Before we sit, Liam and Sarah both hug the life out of me and I return their hugs.

"I guess I'll start." Bobby speaks first as Wyatt holds my hand tight. "Kendall, you being alive and the last heir to the Chapman name puts a kink in our organizations here in Las Vegas. When you come out to the public the top of the food chain will be making a shift of power." Organization? Why would it matter?

"I don't understand. Coming out? Shift in power?" I ask.

"Yes, Kendall, you are now the Head of the Chapman Organization. The Boss. You'll be in charge just like I am. Like Arturo is over the Falcones and Ox is over the Bishop Family and Vic Slater over his. You make up one of the Five Families here in Las Vegas. You have an organization to run and deals to fulfill but everyone will want a piece of you. You'll need to surround yourself with people you can trust and who will be willing to get their hands dirty for you."

Is he saying what I think he is saying? Is he crazy?

"You mean my own mafia family?"

"Yes, that is exactly what I'm saying. Your father and I, along with Arturo Falcone, built our organizations together, but we also did our own thing. We created a wonderful life for our families here, but also gave back to the community as well. When your family was killed a man named Adam Wilson took over in his place and has been running it ever since. The four Family bosses here in Vegas got together and instead of distributing the Chapman territory we voted and allowed Adam to be the leader of the Family. He's been a nightmare to my organization over the years but he's untouchable because he is the head of the organization."

"So, this Adam guy is just going to stand aside and let me take over?" I don't see it happening. Most movies show a total flush out of all the men for the new owner to take over.

"No, Kendall. No one wants to give up that much power and money. Especially to a woman," Bobby says flippantly. Wow, talk about a slap in the face. I guess not everything has been brought into the twenty-first century.

"This is an awful idea, Bobby. You're putting a target on her back by asking her to do this. Adam was always a snake and he'll make her life a living hell," Liam says. "She isn't ruthless like us and will get eaten alive by our lifestyle."

"It needs to be done and you know it. If anyone finds out about her and she is not under the right protection, then she'll be taken out," Bobby says to Liam. The women are sitting there quietly listening to the conversation.

"Is that why Mr. Slater contacted me? Does he know about me?" I look up at Bobby.

"What do you mean Victor Slater contacted you?" Liam jumps to his feet like a bomb went off under him.

"That's why I came to Las Vegas," I tell Liam and spill everything that's happened from declining the internship to being almost kidnapped at the restaurant by his men.

"Kendall, we need to get you out of this city now!" Liam says pacing the length of the couch. "The longer you're here the more the likelihood of you being found out. It's too risky."

"Absolutely not. She is not going anywhere," Wyatt pipes up. He stands to his full height. The wildness in his eyes shows a man about to go to war. I've only ever seen him like this when I was cornered in the parking lot before Wyatt went to pound town on one of his men for touching me.

"Okay, everyone, just calm down. If Victor already knows about Kendall, then there is no hiding anywhere in the U.S. This is why we need her to take her seat at the table. To protect herself," Bobby interjects. "We'll need to bring Arturo in on this to help with protection and to secure her spot."

"What if I don't want to be head of a mafia family? What if I just want to be Wyatt's wife and help out at your business?" I say, finding my voice since everyone has decided to talk around me instead of including me.

"Then you can," Wyatt says and kisses me on the forehead.

"No, Wyatt, she can't. That's not how this works. There are only two ways out of this lifestyle. You either die from old age or you go out in a body bag. No one walks away," Bobby states with finality. "Especially, being a boss."

Holy shit! I don't get a say. I don't get a choice. My body starts to shake and Wyatt wraps his arms around me.

"I...I don't know the first thing about running an organization or a business for that matter. How am I supposed to be responsible for an entire criminal organization?" My butt finds the couch cushion as my legs become jelly.

"With the right people in place, you'll be just fine. I'll help you, so will Wyatt, and many of my men. You'll be okay, Kendall," Bobby tries to assure me.

"Uncle Liam..." I'm scared. Will he stay with me or leave me to fend for myself? This was the whole reason he fled from Las Vegas in the first place.

"Yes, sweetheart, I'll be there for you every step of the way. I was for your father and I will be for you as well." He comes over and drops to his knees in front of me taking my hands. "You will have my loyalty and guidance whenever you need it," he pledges to me.

I feel the tears in the corners of my eyes and lunge for him wrapping my arms around him. We may not be blood, but he is my family.

"I'm so sorry I didn't listen to you and Aunt Sarah. Please forgive me," I plead into his ear.

"There is nothing to forgive, sweetheart. We love you and we should have told you a long time ago," Liam says, Sarah is now by his side holding me too.

After a short while, we break up the family reunion and get back to business.

"After we prove Kendall is Lexi Chapman I'll present her to the other bosses and then it will only be a matter of time before the reins are turned over to you," Bobby informs us of his plan.

"How are we going to prove that I'm me?"

"A blood test will need to be run for DNA. All Family members give a sample by the age of three and they're stored at different labs across the state. This way when something happens to one of us or a Family member we can identify them," he says. "In the Chapman case, the bodies were burned too badly and were cremated before anyone could match them up. That's how you slipped through our fingers, young lady. Your father and I made a promise to each other that we'd look after our families if something should happen to one of us. I intend to keep that promise now."

I nod. I'm still in disbelief about all this and wonder if I'm going to wake up soon to find out this was only just a dream.

"You also know you're one wealthy woman now. Once you're declared Lexi Chapman all the accounts will be at your disposal, which means hundreds of millions of dollars, Kendall."

"I don't need any money, I've had a trust fund since I turned eighteen. Uncle Liam and Aunt Sarah showed me how to make my money last." Wait! Did he just say hundreds of millions? Ever so discreetly I pinch my arm to check if I'm still awake.

"Kendall, when you take over the business you can do whatever you like with the money. The fact is, you'll be one of the wealthiest women here in Las Vegas, which means the vultures will be coming out of the shadows. I'd suggest getting a large circle of the best security your new money can provide. I'm sure Liam will agree and together we'll make sure you're protected."

After we have lunch in the dining room we sit in the formal living room, the men pour amber-colored liquor into tumblers and the women drink fruity cocktails Mary made.

"Bobby, can you tell me about you and my father growing up

and building an empire here," I ask as we all sit down. I've heard Liam talk about my dad but I'd love to hear what Bobby has to say.

"Well, it starts way before Las Vegas. Our grandparents were from the same town. They lived in New York for several years before moving to Chicago then here to Las Vegas. They saw how the mafia was ran in New York and Chicago, so both families wanted to do better and be as superior as those mafia families. They settled on Las Vegas because it was an up and coming city. Both families changed their last names to make sure the men in Chicago and New York didn't recognize them and it worked out. Our fathers laid the groundwork and when Nicholas and I were of age we created a successful empire. We met Arturo along the way and we made it all work. The two other families in town came on slowly and we all had an agreement of sorts. Las Vegas was growing leaps and bounds and becoming too much for only three families to take on. So, we created our own five mafia families here in Las Vegas and tried to steer clear of anything to do with New York or Chicago. Many years later here we are." Bobby stares at his now empty tumbler.

"How did my parents meet?" I ask curiously because Sarah and Liam never could tell me.

"Oh, well, he met Rachel at a casino. She was a cocktail waitress at the time in the high-limits area. He was so smitten with her that he waited for her shift to end and they went for coffee. They were married two months later." He smiles as if it happened yesterday.

There's a pregnant pause in the room as if everyone is reminiscing but my focus is now on my future. "What does all this mean for Wyatt and me?"

"Well, when you were born your father and I wanted to keep our families close. We made a deal for Wyatt and Lexi—umm you, to wed after your eighteenth birthday. Obviously, that never happened because you were killed in the fire, or so we thought. I still have the contract we signed all those years ago."

"You signed a contract? Like an arranged marriage?" I'm

shocked. Do those things still exist these days? I thought it was just a hope Lexi and Wyatt would marry one day.

"Yes, it was the only way to secure our territory here," he explains.

"But you aren't going to enforce it are you, Bobby?" Liam speaks up and sets his tumbler down a little too hard on the glass table. "Things are a little different now. She didn't grow up in this environment."

Bobby looks at both Wyatt and me, his face is not giving anything away. I already know I want to marry Wyatt and not because of some contract but because I love him and he loves me. It will be our choice though, not some signed piece of paper.

"I don't think I'll be needing to. They seem like they're already heading that way." Bobby's smug look puts an irritated expression on Liam's face.

Wyatt grabs my hand and brings it to his lips. "I would marry her tomorrow if I could."

I flush beet red. Of course he would, and he'd knock me up by next week if I allowed it.

"Let's not get ahead of ourselves. We—"

"Okay!" I cut Liam off staring right at Wyatt, not really sure why I said it, but why wait? We both want this so why not? Both of our parents got married soon after meeting and they made it work and have been together for years. I've already decided to jump off the cliff and be with him in his world, so why not make it official? My father set this up and it would be like following through on one of his last wishes before he died.

"Really? You want to?" Wyatt's eyes widen.

"Why wait? We both know what we want, and I want to spend the rest of my life with you," I admit.

Our lips crash into one another after Wyatt tugs the back of my neck towards him. The celebration is short-lived when a booming voice startles us apart.

"WAIT! This is too fast. You don't know what you're saying!"

Liam's voice echoes from wall to wall shaking glass. "Kendall, this is all so overwhelming, and making a rash decision is not the best idea right now. Sure, if you want to marry him, then date for a while and see how it goes. You may not like him in a month or two. Just give it some time before you jump the gun and do something you might regret later. We still need to see how the other families accept you."

Wyatt's body goes rigid and I know he's transitioning into fight mode. He's extremely territorial with me and if he thinks someone is going to take me from him then God have mercy on their poor soul.

"If you think you're going to keep me from marrying her then you're sorely mistaken. What Kendall and I do is our business and no one else's." Wyatt is standing now his fists clenched, his knuckles turning white.

Bobby steps in front of Liam and I move in front of Wyatt. We walk over to the other side of the room, but Wyatt never takes his eyes off Liam. One little spark and this room will light up in flames.

"Kendall, please listen to reason," Liam continues.

"Liam, that's enough," Sarah says as she and Mary stand from the sofa. "We married two weeks after meeting and Mary and Bobby did the same after six weeks. If they want to marry it's their choice; we will not stand in their way. Besides, this is ultimately what Nick wanted for his baby girl, remember?" Sarah puts her foot down and I can see the defeat in Liam's face. "You were there when the contract was drawn up and signed."

"We need longer than a day to plan a wedding," Mary speaks out of the blue. The joy in her voice is contagious.

"Three weeks and that's all I'm willing to wait," Wyatt announces and covers my mouth with a kiss that should only ever be experienced in a bedroom behind closed doors. Is it weird in the midst of all this chaos that I feel giddy?

After a long and exhausting day, we go our separate ways for the evening. Liam and Sarah are flying back to Texas first thing in the morning on Bobby's jet. They need to get some things to make a permanent move out here to be with me. They were reluctant to leave me here alone in Vegas, but Bobby assured them that I'm well protected and that he is going to meet with Arturo and his son, Luca, to discuss their next move.

Wyatt's been distracted for the last hour. He even had me drive his car home so he could text or email whoever keeps blowing up his phone. I'm wondering if the magnitude of getting married is settling in and he's starting to have doubts.

"Is everything okay?" I finally ask after not being able to stand the silence anymore.

"Huh? Oh, yeah everything is fine," he responds, blowing me off and turning back to whatever he's typing.

"I really like the area around here. I think I'll see if anything is on the market and try to buy it," I say as we pass by the nearest gated community. It's on the outskirts of Vegas but secluded. It seems like a secure place to live.

"What? You don't like the house we live in? We aren't living separately. I'm not sure how people in Texas and California live, but we'll be under the same roof and in the same bed every night. End of discussion."

"Calm down before you have a stroke. I was just saying I like the area and I want to buy something for Liam and Sarah so they'll be close to me. That's all."

"Oh," he sounds relieved. "There's plenty of space if you want to build them a home on the property."

"I think having their own place will be good for all of us."

We pass through the next set of gates separating our property from the other community and drive up to the garage. I get out and start to walk into the house when Wyatt yells out. "Hey, I gotta run. I'll be back soon, okay?" He grabs the extra keys next to the door and takes off without another word.

I walk in kind of upset at being brushed off and dismissed. Is this how our marriage is going to be? Something must be wrong. He's never acted like this before towards me.

Setting my purse down on the counter, I grab my phone and

walk to the fridge for a bottled water then make my way to the movie room to watch crap TV. My phone rings and I hope it's Wyatt but it's Harper.

"Hey, Harp."

"Hey, girl, how are Aunt Sarah and Uncle Liam?"

"They're good. They hate that you weren't here. How was Grandmother Evelyn's birthday?"

"Boring as always. I can't wait to be back with people my own age," Harper whines, and I can hear the party going on in the background.

"Not enough alcohol to keep you busy?"

"No, grandmother is a recovering alcoholic so the party is dry."

"God, that sucks. How will you ever survive?"

"Don't laugh. You know how my family is. I did happen to sneak in a flask but Mom noticed it and drank the entire thing." She pouts. "Anything new at home going on?"

Should I tell her about Wyatt and I getting married? She is going to be my Maid of Honor. I think I should wait and tell her in person. She makes the best surprised face expressions. They are not to be missed.

"Not much, but I do want to tell you something in person when you get back. So, pencil me in for a girls' night."

I hear her name being called in the background and she lets out a drawn-out groan. "Oh crap, it's Aunt Becca. I've got to go. See you in a day or two."

She hangs up and I turn my attention back to the TV to channel surf. My phone goes off again and I see it's a text from Wyatt. He probably won't be coming home for a while.

> Wyatt: Sorry I left in a rush but I had to do something really important.
>
> Me: K

I give him a short answer because I really am upset he just left like that. I know I'm being a brat but I just thought we'd spend the evening together after the day we had. I need to learn to get used to this, I guess. We both will be busy soon once I'm in charge of my family's organization.

Wyatt: I promise to make it up to you!

Me: Sure

Wyatt: Babe don't be mad.

I can't even respond because the more he says the more I'm fuming. Get the hint I don't want to converse.

Wyatt: Kendall?

UGH!

Me: I'm busy right now

Wyatt: What are you doing?

Me: None of your business

Wyatt: I know you're watching crap TV

What? How would he know that? I quickly peep around the room expecting him to be hiding in the shadows but find the space empty.

Wyatt: Open the movie room door and follow the path

What in the hell? I jump up from the plush couch and rush to the closed movie room door to swing it open. Rose petals are scattered on the floor. Slowly I make my way down the hallway and with each step, the irritation I felt disappears. He really knows how to make it up to a girl! I continue on through the kitchen and out the back door, where I find a rose wonderland. Roses are everywhere; petals are on the ground, long stemmed ones are in beautiful vases. They all lead up to where Wyatt is standing under the arbor with twinkling lights hanging from it. Wyatt is holding a large bouquet with a huge smile on his face. I walk slowly to him and stand right in front of him returning his smile. He hands me the roses then kisses my cheek. When he clears his throat it's as if he's nervous about something.

"Kendall, the moment you ran into me I knew you would change my life forever. I was the biggest prick to you and yet you still stuck with me that night and stayed through my bullshit. I'm so glad you gave me a chance and hope you'll let me show you how much I love and appreciate you for the rest of our lives. There's no denying the pull we have to each other, and as fate would have it, we're meant to be together." Wyatt drops to one knee and pulls out a light blue Tiffany box. My empty hand covers my mouth and tears are threatening to fall. "Kendall, will you please do me the greatest honor and stand by my side through this life and be my wife? Will you marry me and make me the happiest man alive?"

I nod wildly. "YES! Yes, I will marry you Wyatt!"

He stands and swings me around before kissing me then sets my feet back on the ground. He takes the ring from the box and slips it on my ring finger. It is absolutely the most stunning ring I have ever seen. It has a four or five-carat solitary diamond and the band has diamonds all the way around it. I think Frankie might need another guy just to watch over the ring.

"Oh, Wyatt, it's absolutely gorgeous. I love you so much!" I cheer and pepper him with kisses.

"I love you too, babe! Here"—he hands me a flute full of champagne—"to us and a life full of love and happiness." He holds it up in the air for us to clink together.

"To us," I declare and we clink our glasses. "Is this what you were doing this entire time?"

"Yes, I thought you deserved a better proposal than the one at Mom and Dad's house. Our families helped make this happen." He waves his hand around the flowery backyard.

"I'll never forget this as long as I live. Thank you for being everything I could have ever wanted!"

"You're my whole life. I'd do anything for you!"

He lays me down on one of the lounge beds by the pool. Under the stars he shows me just what I mean to him. There is no doubt in my mind that Wyatt Dawson will love me until our final breaths.

CHAPTER SEVENTEEN

THE NEXT WEEK GOES BY IN A BLUR. BESIDES HAVING blood drawn for the DNA test, Mary, Harper, Gracie and Sarah have been bugging me about the wedding and I haven't had a chance to catch my breath. Harper was so excited to learn I was getting married and that she was going to help plan it.

The blood test came back this morning and I am 99.98% Alexia Blaire Chapman according to two different labs. Bobby made the decision to have me focus on the wedding and my big meeting with the other Families. So, my presence will not be needed as his intern since I'm about to take over my own entire organization. He elaborated saying I needed to be more confident and understand the illegal side of what they do. I've spent most of my days with him going over the types of trades they run underground.

The Dawsons' deal in drugs, prostitution, run guns, and fixed fights. Hearing this, I am completely shocked. They make an exuberant amount of money which they then launder through some of the legal businesses. He also informed me of each Family having safe houses and warehouses to store all their merchandise. They move the items regularly because the police, who are not on their payrolls, are always snooping around and would love to take down a big fish like him or any other member of the mafia. It also made me realize that I didn't stand a chance making a bet with Gracie. That little hooker knew she was going to win the MMA fight we bet on and Harper and I had to go on that blind date. It worked out in the end but now I know better than to underestimate Gracie.

My Family Organization, the Chapmans, which is run by Adam Wilson at the moment, deals in prostitution and bookies. The legal part for my Family is casinos, hotels, restaurants, construction, night clubs, real estate and we own most of the tourism companies here in Las Vegas. My father started going more legit towards the end, giving up a lot of illegal businesses and deals. Bobby told me that his and Arturo Falcone's organization had picked up most of the business because they didn't want anyone else to come in and sniff around. Bobby also mentioned my father wanted to go more legit which meant less money. A lot of people were up in arms and it caused a big stir. He thinks that's why my family was murdered but was never able to prove who did it.

The Slater Family, run by Victor Slater, is in chop shops, prostitution, stolen goods, and drugs—mainly the hard stuff like heroine. They also have casinos, auto shops, restaurants, tow truck companies, and salvage yards. Bobby reiterated that this Family has always been hard to deal with. Slater is trying to push more and more onto Bobby's turf, stealing shipments and causing discord amongst the other Families.

The Falcone Family, who is run by Arturo Falcone, only deals in drugs, guns, and prostitution on the illegal side. They own the trash business and real estate on the outskirts of town.

"Arturo, myself, and your father were best friends. We always promised to look after each other's families. He will be there for you. You call and he will answer and it's the same with me, Kendall," Bobby tells me as we go over each Family. "If you hear something or see something, you call, no matter the time or what it's about. It's how we've survived in power for so long."

Lastly, the Bishop Family, who is run by Maddox 'Ox' Bishop, handles laundering money. He owns most of the banks here in Las

Vegas and is into building shopping malls, casinos, and the new sports stadium. He has twin sisters and stays out of all the disputes that don't directly involve his money.

I write down pages and pages of information on each Family. I need to know about their wives and kids and their favorite liquor. Bobby tells me about each one's strengths and weaknesses. We also discuss the police department and who is trustworthy and on the payroll. He introduces me to several captains and men on the force who would stand with me when I take over my organization.

"Not everyone can be bought, Kendall. Those are the ones we have to look out for." Bobby says. "Carry a gun at all times. Just because you have security doesn't mean you shouldn't be able to protect yourself if something arises."

During a lunch break, Mary brings in a photobook, and we sit at the breakfast table looking through the album with pictures of my mom, dad, and brother Thomas. Wyatt, Gracie, and Avery are in some of the photos with us along with a boy named Luca who is Arturo's eldest child. I see many pictures of Bobby and Mary with my parents and they seemed so happy and in love.

"Can I have copies of these?"

"I have all the photos scanned and being put in a book for you. They said it'd be here sometime tomorrow."

The rest of the afternoon, Bobby and I are tucked away in his office going over what to expect in the meeting. He shows me how to greet each Don and the rules at the table. Women have never been allowed; only men run the businesses and my presence is going to ruffle some feathers. He reassures me he'll be there the entire time and would never allow anything to happen to me.

"Just show them you aren't a pushover. Stand tall and firm. There's no room for weakness in this line of work," Bobby instructs.

Liam and Sarah are flying in tomorrow morning so Liam can be there for the meeting. They've settled everything and have tied up most of the loose ends in Texas. They have a moving company that will pack them up over the weekend and should be at their new home, which is in the gated community I found next to Wyatt and me, by the middle of next week. I couldn't pass up the house I bought them. It was perfect and everything Aunt Sarah has always wanted in a home. I wasn't sure if I could make it happen so quickly but after and few phone calls from Wyatt and paying in cash, the deal was done late last night. I also have a surprise for them waiting in the garage with a big red bow on each new car.

With information overload, I go home and soak in the bathtub until dinner. Wyatt wants to go out tonight so he can show me off—his words, not mine. I dress in a short-sleeve black-crepe slit-cuff jumpsuit that fits my body like a glove with a black belt around the waist and a pair of Louboutin Leopard print red-sole pumps. I go with light makeup and do my hair in a side fishtail braid. The only accessories I have on is my engagement ring and my diamond studded earrings. I look ready to hit the town with my man tonight!

Wyatt came home while I was doing my makeup and hair to shower and change his clothes. I'm waiting in the kitchen for him to finish when I hear a low whistle. Turning, I see the most handsome man I've ever laid eyes on. He's wearing his classic black suit with a light blue shirt and no tie. He looks edible.

"You ready to be shown off like the Lombardi Trophy, babe?" Wyatt comes up to me and kisses my cheek, making sure not to smudge my makeup.

"I was born ready!" I grab for my clutch and his hand.

He leads me to the garage and helps me in his Bugatti Veyron. I've hardly seen him drive this car so tonight must really be special.

"Where are we going tonight?" I ask as we pull onto the road.

"I thought I'd take you to dinner and a show at the Bellagio. They have a spectacular French restaurant there called Picasso and the show is "O" by Cirque Du Soleil." I've wanted to see a show on the Strip since we moved here but haven't had the time. "We might meet up with my friend, Luca, and his wife, Gemma, if they can sneak away."

"That sounds exciting! How was your day?"

"Ugh, it was a nightmare. One of the new guys—" Wyatt starts to say but stops and glances in his rearview mirror. He swears under his breath and then turns to me. "Kendall, do as I tell you, do you understand? Don't react to anything they say to you or me, okay? These guys are pricks."

I turn and see red and blue lights behind our car as we roll to a stop on a side street. Wyatt pulls out his gun from the inside of his jacket and places it in the glove box then places his hands on the steering wheel. There's a tap on the window on Wyatt's side as a flashlight blinds us. Wyatt rolls the window down and a man with a terrible haircut and mustache stares into the car smacking gum.

"Well, well, well if it isn't the spawn of Satan out and about tonight. Where're you heading?" the officer asks. His name badge says A. Daniels.

"Just going out to dinner. Is there a problem Officer Daniels?" Wyatt spits.

"You better enjoy your little ride around town as much as you can. Chief Jones is on his way out and the new guy vows to clean up all the trash in town. And that starts with you and your father." He chuckles at his lame joke then bends down to rest his arm on the door and notices me in the passenger seat.

"Well, she appears much higher class than the whore's you usually run around with." He eyes me up and down making my skin crawl. "I guess Daddy must've given you a raise with the blood money you make. She must charge by the night and not by the hour like usual," Daniels implies. I can see Wyatt's knuckles turning white on the wheel. He's trying like crazy to maintain control but I sure as hell am not. How dare he!

"EXCUSE ME!" I practically shout. "How dare you speak about me in that way!"

"Listen, sugar—"

"I'm not your *sugar* and unless you have a real reason for stopping us I suggest you let us go. My attorney would love to slap a harassment suit against your department and have the local news here in no time."

"Step out of the car, Ma'am," Daniels orders.

I look at Wyatt, realizing I might have crossed a line, but he has no right to speak to us that way. Wyatt nods, and I open the door to step out and then walk to the front of the car, crossing my arms over my body. I see Officer Daniels is not alone and the other officer is now at the driver's side door talking with Wyatt.

"What's your name, honey?"

I roll my eyes at his condescending manner. "My name is Kendall Drake." I don't mention I'm also Lexi Chapman.

"Listen, Ms. Drake, you seem like a really young innocent girl and I think you should steer clear of Dawson. He's not who you think he is."

"Thank you for your concern, Officer Daniels, but I can judge for myself. Can we go now or do we need you to make a call to your supervisor?" I ask too sweetly.

He is about to say something but is interrupted by the other officer. "Let's go, Daniels, there's a call for a break in two streets over."

Daniels looks right into my eyes. "Get away while you still can," he says and walks away. He stops at Wyatt's window to exchange a few words as I walk back over to my door and carefully get in.

One he leaves, I could cut the tension with a knife. I chance a look over at Wyatt and he still has his hands on the steering wheel so tight it might pop off. "I told you not to react!" He raises his voice. "This is what those pigs thrive on and you played right into his hands."

"I—I—"

I'm shocked he would speak to me that way. He has always been so kind and gentle with his words. The only time he was like this was when we first met. "I was shocked he would say something like that to you—or me for that matter. I'm sorry." I twist my hands in my lap trying to stop the tears from falling down my face. I feel like a chastised kid.

"Well, next time listen to me," he snaps.

What am I doing? Why am I apologizing? This isn't my fault! I did nothing wrong. If he thinks I'm just going to sit by and let some pencil dick get his rocks off by belittling me or trying to intimidate me, then he's got another thing coming. Bobby spent the last week telling me that *I* now answer to no one if I'm going to be running a long and successful organization. He said letting someone believe I'm an equal to them is a sign of weakness. While I do consider Wyatt to by my partner and equal, he needs to treat me as one also.

"Well, fuck that! I didn't deserve to be treated that way by him and if you aren't going to stand up then I will. I don't care who is saying it." I match his fury.

"I couldn't do anything. That prick has been breathing down my neck waiting for me to step out of line to throw my ass in a jail cell. I knew he was going to get a rise out of me, that's why I put my gun in the glove box so I didn't shoot his damn head off!"

"Not everything has to end in violence, Wyatt. There are different ways to get your point across and yelling at me isn't one of them." I cross my arms over my body. I'm so mad I could spit bullets right now. "I'm not one of your *made men*, Wyatt! I'm your fiancée and the woman you bed every night. I won't be treated with such disrespect or spoken to this way."

I know from the look on his face he wants to punch a wall right now and I feel the same. Wyatt rights himself and starts the car. He pulls out towards the house and not the Strip.

"Where are we going?" I hiss.

"Home, we missed our reservations at the restaurant," he snaps.

"Well, I still want to see the show," I retort. "Just because you want to throw a fit and act childish doesn't mean you're going to ruin the entire night for me."

"Really, Kendall? That's how you want to be?"

"You take me to the show or you drop me off at my apartment. Your choice." I stare him down.

The rest of the car ride is so silent you could hear a pin drop.

Wyatt pulls up to the Bellagio valet and tosses his keys to the guy. He takes my hand in a tight grip and leads me through the hotel and casino area to the theatre. After being shown to our seats, which of course are the best in house, we wait for the show to start.

I hate that our night has been tainted by this. We haven't had a lot of dates as a couple and hate that what was going to be an amazing night has turned out where neither of us is talking.

"Wyatt, I love you but you can't be like this with me. This is all still so new to me. We are supposed to be a team and I don't want to fight with you," I say trying to mend our first real fight. I place my hand over his hoping he doesn't reject my touch.

"I'm sorry too, babe. I—I was mad the prick said those things about you and couldn't do anything about it. I'm not mad at you, and I'm sorry I took it out on you. This is all I've ever known and it's a huge adjustment for me. I'm truly sorry, do you forgive me?" We're almost nose to nose. "Protective over you doesn't even begin to describe how I feel and now that I've found my Lexi, I can't begin to explain how much your safety means to me."

His words melt the animosity building from the fight. He leans in and kisses my lips just as the lights flicker indicating the show is about to start.

The show is awe-inspiring. It's staggering how they are able to put on a show like this with so many people doing so many different things at once. Wyatt never stops touching me the whole time, and when the show ends we walk out of the theatre into the casino. The room is buzzing with machines going off and people talking. Wyatt leads me around the corner and we walk into a half open room with the words High Limits across them. I see some tables set up with dealers behind them and a few players at each table.

"What game do you want to start with? Poker? Blackjack?" he asks as we walk by the tables.

"Oh, I don't know. I didn't bring any cash, so I'll probably just watch you play."

"Babe, my money is your money. Come, let's start with

Blackjack. If memory serves me correctly you killed it at our private casino night in that bunny outfit."

He leads me over to the table and sits me in a chair. Nodding to the dealer, he walks over to the cashier and comes back with two trays full of chips. Upon inspection the smallest chip amount in the tray is five hundred dollars and there are a lot of them.

"Wyatt!" I call out, shocked.

"We came out tonight to have fun and that's what we're going to do."

"What if I lose all of this?"

"Then we know gambling is not the right occupation for you." He gives me a little wink and the dealer starts to shuffle a new deck.

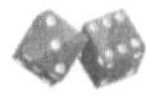

Today is D-Day.

I'm meeting the Dons of the other mafia families. Bobby wants us to be a few minutes late so everyone is seated and we'll have their full attention. According to him, the meetings are always at a different place so the FBI can't set up a sting. We're headed to a town called Pahrump, which is just under two hours away from Las Vegas. Liam and Wyatt are also coming, but not allowed in the actual room with us.

Bobby is wearing his black suit with a white shirt, no tie and an expensive pair of shoes. He looks very commanding and ready for this confrontation. Liam and Wyatt are dressed similarly and have their holsters occupied with steel. I'm in a fitted black classic suit with an ivory blouse paired with black leather booties. I feel and look powerful and need to keep this confidence walking into the lion's den. The meeting could go in a lot of different directions and I'm hoping it will be in our favor. Bobby mentioned we'd be checked before the meeting, so we're keeping our guns in the car. We have Liam, Wyatt, and whoever else is coming with us for protection, so we were covered.

The drive is long, which only makes my confidence drop the farther we get away from Las Vegas. Bobby and Liam, with two other security guys, drive in a SUV in front of us, while Wyatt and I drive with Frankie and some other guy named Benny. I've brought my notes I've been reviewing them like I'm studying for a final exam. Bobby had shown me pictures of each member to recognize who they are when I meet them for the first time. They won't see me coming, but I'll hopefully know everything I can about them to catch them off guard.

Wyatt has been on his phone the entire time and seems caught up on a situation back home. Finally, after what feels like an eternity, we approach the city but stay on the outside of it. We pass through the industrial section and drive to the far back lot of one of the properties. There are other SUVs and quite a few men, dressed similarly to our guys, standing around.

Bobby and Liam get out and straighten their suits.

It's go time Kendall!

"Are you ready for this, babe?" Wyatt asks me with his hand on the door handle.

"I think so."

"Just stay close to Dad and he'll take care of you. Liam and I will be right outside." He leans in for a kiss that leaves me breathless. "Remember no sign of weakness."

We get out of the SUV and walk over to where Bobby and Liam are talking.

"Alright, so Liam and Wyatt can't go in. They'll be waiting out here. Kendall, you and I will have to leave all phones and electronics with our men, so hand them over now so when we get patted down it won't be a problem. Also, if you have any guns on you leave them as well," Bobby instructs.

He gives me a little embrace then walks toward the rundown warehouse. Wyatt puts his arm around me and we slowly follow with our men close by.

"I love you, Kendall. You're going to knock them dead. They'll have to accept you. The only one who will be up in arms is Adam and that's because you're dethroning him. Stay strong and don't back down from any of them," Wyatt says.

At the sliding doors, Bobby turns around and faces me. He tells everyone to be on the lookout and to take their places, leaving just Bobby, Liam, and me.

"Kendall, I need you to stay calm and don't react in a big way to their reactions when the bomb is let out. These men can smell fear a mile away and that is one thing you never want to show," Bobby tells me.

"Sweetheart, you can do this. Don't take any shit from any of them. You deserve to be there just as much as they do. Your blood comes from one of the originals. This is your birth right. You are a Chapman and Chapmans bow to no one. They take what is theirs and don't apologize for it." Liam gives me a little more encouragement. He grabs me in a hug and then whispers, "Your father would be so proud. Stand tall and own the room."

Liam walks in the direction of Wyatt and our men, leaving me and Bobby, and I notice he has a large envelope in his hand as he looks at his watch.

"Okay, show time," Bobby states as we walk into the warehouse.

You can do this Kendall.

Stand tall.

Don't take shit from anyone.

You can do this.

Make your father proud.

The Chapmans don't bow to anyone.

CHAPTER EIGHTEEN

Across the warehouse, there appears to be an office. The warehouse is hot and the walk is long. It's completely empty and dark. The only light is coming from that office. As we approach the door I can smell the tobacco smoke coming from the room. Bobby reaches for the knob then turns his head in my direction. I let out a breath shaking all nerves away then nod to him.

Bobby opens the door and walks in blocking me from seeing the room. First thing to hit my nose is the rancid stench of cigars. The room has a smoky fog to it and then the smell of alcohol hits me. These men must be chain-smokers for it to already look like this in here. We're only twelve minutes late.

"It's about damn time, Bobby. You were the one who called this meeting and you've the nerve to show up late, asshole," I hear one of the men say.

I'm still blocked from their view behind him.

"Yeah Bobby, what gives?" another man questions.

"I have a surprise for you all and if you have a seat I'll tell you," Bobby says and I hear chairs scratch the floor.

Bobby moves over and I finally get a better view of the whole room. In the middle, is a large table with men sat around it. The rest of the room is set up just as an empty office. One of the desks in the corner has alcohol of every kind set up with stacked shot glasses and tumblers.

I lock my eyes with the men at the table and can't tell if they're eyeing me up like a piece of meat or a nuisance.

"What is the meaning of this, Bobby?"

"Is she here for our pleasure?"

"You know only the Heads are allowed to be here!"

They all start chiming in at the same time giving their opinions, but Bobby holds his hand up silencing them.

"She has the right to be here," he says and we walk closer to the table. He grabs another chair along the wall and sets it down next to the only other empty chair at the table.

"What do you think you're doing, Bobby?" one man says then stands. He's of average build with blond hair. He's the one who remarked if I was *there for their pleasure.*

"Sit down, Adam. I think *you* of all people will want to know who she is," Bobby commands. Now I remember him from the pictures Bobby provided for me.

"Well, don't keep us waiting any longer. Get on with it," another man comments. He is a built man with military style sandy blond hair. Maddox 'Ox' Bishop. The banker and money launderer.

I peer at the other men at the table and see Victor Slater staring at me. I remember him from my research when I was offered the internship. He's of medium build with dark hair and dark menacing eyes. I can tell he is looking me over as if memorizing every detail. The last man at the table is Arturo Falcone. We've met several times over the last few days along with his son Luca. He's going to play neutral until it gets down to the vote.

"I would like to introduce you to, Kendall Drake. She just moved here and will be staying a while," Bobby starts. I'm still as a statue not letting their intimidating glares affect me.

"Who the fuck cares. Why is she even here?" Adam pops off.

"Bobby, what is the meaning of all of this?" Maddox asks.

"Kendall has the right to sit at this table and I wanted this meeting with everyone so she's able to take her rightful place."

"Who is she? I've never heard anyone by the name of Drake before," Adam says, still eyeing me up and down.

Victor still hasn't spoken a word, which makes me think he's known who I was for a while.

"Drake is not her real surname. Meet Alexia Blaire Chapman. The only living member of the Chapman Family and the daughter of Nicholas and Rachel Chapman," Bobby drops the bomb.

All hell breaks loose.

Adam jumps to his feet sending the chair crashing back. Maddox looks bored out of his mind. Victor Slater is still stoic, showing no emotion what so ever. Arturo is watching all the reactions, taking it all in.

"That can't be true! They all died in the fire. You really think we'll believe she's a dead girl walking? What kind of powerplay are you trying to make here Bobby?" Adam yells.

"Sit the fuck down, Adam, and calm yourself before you have a heart attack. I want to hear the rest of this," Victor Slater finally speaks up.

I'm still standing next to Bobby not saying a word or moving. I need to stay cool, calm, and collected.

Bobby throws the folder in his hand on the table. "Look for yourself, it's all right there. Confirmation from two different labs across the state. She is Alexia Chapman and has been in hiding since the murder and fire. Liam Martin has kept her hidden all these years. She's here to reclaim her rightful place at this table being the last surviving member of the Chapman Family."

"Liam? He's alive?" Adam says with wide eyes. He looks as if he's seen a ghost.

The other members start looking through the folder at the documents and pass them around to each other. Adam seems to have recovered from his shock and is seething after each paper is placed in front of him. In a way, I feel sorry for him. He's been in charge for almost two decades, and now a vote will push him out of the comfort of being a Don and all the perks that come with it.

"I move to vote to have Alexia take her place at the table for her Family and for Adam to be removed," Bobby states and sits down in his chair.

I don't make a move to sit down. Bobby told me that until I was voted in that I didn't have the right to sit at their table. So, I stand and wait for the vote to begin. I won't speak unless I'm questioned by a Don.

"You want a woman to sit with us? Be a Boss? Does she even know anything about our organizations?" Maddox asks Bobby.

"She can hold her own. And yes, she knows about the organization; she has for a little while."

"This is absolutely fucking ridiculous," Adam rants as he takes his place at the table after picking up his chair from the floor. "What is a woman going to do in the organization? Women are emotional. They have no business in *this* business."

How dare he say women don't have a right to run a business like this? And emotional? Is anyone going to point out his little tantrum with a side of throwing a chair back? Doesn't he know it's the twenty-first century? Asshole. I know he can feel the glare I'm now giving him because he turns and the tops of his ears burn red. Yeah buddy, you've pissed me off. Not a good way to make an impression on your new boss.

"Well, it would be satisfying to have something delightful to look at rather than all of your ugly mugs," Arturo Falcone replies lighting another cigar. It's the first he's spoken since the meeting started, trying to play the neutral game.

"Let's get this vote over with, I've got plans," Maddox pipes up.

"Yes, let's get this over with. I vote to have Adam step down and have Alexia take her Family seat at the table and be the Head of her Family's Organization," Bobby votes and slams his hand on the table.

"I vote for Ms. Chapman to take her rightful place," Arturo agrees with Bobby.

"I vote no! No, she can't have my seat I've held it for almost two decades. I kept this name alive and the organization flowing with money. NO!" Adam screams and slams his hand down. "And another thing, I want the name of my organization to change after this. Instead of the Chapman Organization I want it to be the Wilson Organization."

I have two for me and one against me now. Victor Slater once again is being way too quiet as he's taking in everyone's reaction.

"I knew your family well, Alexia. I think it was a travesty what happened to them. You're awfully young to be in this life and I wonder if you shouldn't be out partying with your friends instead of running a criminal organization. This vote will change your life forever. There's only one way out of this lifestyle and it doesn't include breathing. I just don't think you really understand this decision you are making," Victor expresses and I think he is saying no.

"Just say yes or no Victor. We don't have all fucking day and she doesn't need a life lesson speech," Bobby says with an irritated growl.

"I just want her to understand what this means to take that seat." He points to Adam's chair. There's a smug look on Adam's face as he thinks Victor is going to vote with him. "Fine, my vote is no. I don't think she should take her Family's seat. Sorry, but Adam has been doing this for a while and I think he should stay." Victor pounds his hand on the table and my lips part in surprise.

Crap! It now comes down to Maddox Bishop. It's up to him now if I'll keep my Family's name alive. He rubs his chin and stares at me before draining his tumbler. The anticipation is high and I can tell everyone is waiting with bated breath.

"I vote yes. I think this is exactly what Nicholas would've wanted. I have two sisters and would want them to take over for me and keep my legacy alive," Maddox reveals and bangs his hand.

I can't believe it. I just got voted in and will take the seat with a bunch of men. I'm now part of the mafia.

Holy Shit!

"Un-fucking-believable! I can't believe you all did this to me. What are my guys going to do with a woman in charge?" Adam demands.

"You're still a member of the Chapman Organization, if Alexia wants it to be. The men will fall in line or they'll be dealt with accordingly. Consider it a demotion but it'd be in your best interest to help Alexia get familiar with the organization," Bobby warns Adam. His voice drops low and deep, threatening.

I think it's time to make myself known and that I'm not a push over. That I can hold my own with these men. I walk to where Adam is sitting, my boots echoing off the walls as I come to stand right next to the chair.

"Get up, Adam," I command, staring down at him.

He looks up at me in surprise. "What did you just say to me?" Adam spews venom behind every word. You can tell no one has challenged him in a long time.

"I said get the fuck out of *my* chair. Liam is waiting outside," I declare in a commanding voice I didn't really know I had.

Adam looks around the table for support, I guess, but finds none. He places both hands on the table and pushes up, helping his body to stand straight.

"All of you are going to regret your decision. Mark my words," Adam says before he walks to the office door and slams it behind him.

I exhale the breath I was holding and look around the table to see all eyes on me. I glance at Bobby and he gives a slight nod. I take my seat and wait for someone to start talking.

"Well, sweetheart, I hope you know what you just signed up for," Arturo warns. "Welcome to the boys' table."

"First, I'm not your sweetheart. My name is Kendall. Remember it, write it down if you need to. Second, I know exactly what I'm getting into," I respond not skipping a beat.

"I like her already," Maddox laughs. "I see a ring on your finger I take it you have a family now."

"I recently got engaged."

"Congratulations," Maddox announces. "Will we get to meet him or are you going to hide him away like Victor does his wife?" He thumbs over at Victor.

Victor has a wife? All the reports I've read from Bobby said he was single. I take a quick glance at Bobby and see that he and Arturo are both side eyeing each other.

"I imagine you already know him. Wyatt Dawson and I are getting married in a few weeks," I reveal.

"Really?" Victor challenges and doesn't look happy at all as he whips his head in Bobby's direction. "Wow, Bobby, you sure are trying to keep it all in the family aren't you?"

"Correction, this was arranged when I was born by both Bobby and my dad," I say in rebuttal.

All the men nod and stand. They walk over and one by one each kisses both of my cheeks and welcomes me into *The Family*. They also give their condolences for the deaths of my parents and brother. Bobby had prepared me for this greeting. Each member addressed me and spoke with respect before returning to their chair.

"So, you want to be called Kendall or Alexia or Lexi?" Maddox asks. "I remember your dad used to bring you to some of the meetings and have you play outside the room where all of us kids had to wait. You had every guy wrapped around your finger. It was hard to say no to you." He chuckles at the memory.

I wish I could remember those times. I have no real memories of my family and hate it.

"I'm Kendall since it's what I grew up with. Business wise I'll be going as Kendall Chapman. Legally, I'll be a Dawson in a few weeks," I inform them, as I have everyone's attention.

"Well, I think it's going to be one hell of a wedding! Can't wait to see how it all turns out. Just make sure you have our favorite liquor available," Arturo says with a wink.

I nod. Bobby seems to be taking in how welcoming everyone is as they speak to me.

"When this wedding happens, does it mean Wyatt will be leaving the Dawson Family and joining the Chapmans? Or will it be the other way around? We have certain rules that this might breach," Victor pries looking at Bobby.

"I'm aware of the rules, Victor, and we haven't even thought about the merger of the two Families yet. You know it will be brought to the table when we have a definitive answer," Bobby challenges him.

"If this is some kind of power move then you're calling for war," Victor warns.

War? Over our marriage?

"I'm not trying to start anything. This agreement was made almost twenty-two years ago by Nick and me. *I* would never disrespect *The Family* without bringing this before the group with a vote. Ultimately, it will be up to Wyatt and Kendall how they want to proceed, but Wyatt is my successor with the Dawsons," Bobby informs everyone at the table.

Sitting back, I take everything in listening to how each one speaks and interacts with the others. Bobby is really the main guy at the table. Arturo is a silent spectator. Maddox is there for the money, but I can see a 'gather all the info' type of guy in him. Victor Slater seems to be the most power hungry of them all. He pushes back at every turn.

"Is there anything else we need to discuss or is this it?" Maddox asks eyeing his watch.

"Yes, there is. The new supplier from Canada has not followed through on their shipments as promised. I say we cut our losses and find another supplier," Bobby offers.

I have no idea what they are talking about now. Canadian supplier?

"Yeah, I haven't been happy with them either. I don't like to wait for our product, especially if we're shelling out the big bucks up front," Arturo pipes up getting right to business.

Maddox must see the confused look on my face. "Kendall, we have our drugs shipped in from Canada. Up until recently they've been making us wait or not had the products at all," he explains.

"Why are we going up north when Mexico is within our reach?" I ask.

"Well, we hate working with the cartel and once you're associated with them they tend to be high maintenance. Their demands only get bigger and they expect favors from you. We wanted to go that route but have been waiting to use them as a last resort," Victor responds.

"Have you all thought about making the drugs yourself and cutting the middle man out. You would need to find a place off the grid and then have your own workers doing the dirty work. I think you'd see a lot more on the profit side if you do it that way. Plus, we wouldn't have to worry about owing anyone or waiting around for it to get here," I offer. "We could even have it done in another state but close enough to get it here within a day or two. There's plenty of desert land in Arizona."

I can't believe I'm actually helping break the law now. Every year at career day the school had dozens and dozens of categories spread across the lunch room for the students to explore. Never in all my years did I see someone stand at a booth labeled criminal organization. This is a far cry from the law enforcement recruiting Harper and I sat through during one of our last lectures before graduation.

"Well, fuck me. And here I thought you were only a pretty face to look at. Bobby?" Maddox says and continues puffing on his cigar. I can tell he's going to be the funny one in the group.

"It's not a bad idea. We will have to research it and pull a lot of strings to make sure it's left alone. Good job, Kendall. Way to think outside the box," Bobby answers with a smirk.

"Okay, I vote we finish out the month with the suppliers from Canada and then try and get our own system in place," Maddox proposes.

"I agree," Arturo votes.

"Same here. We'll need to meet again before the end of the month to discuss our options," Victor comments.

Bobby nods to me and I take it as my turn to have my first vote in the 'Family.'

"I think we cut all ties from Canada and work it ourselves," I state my vote.

"I'm with the consensus. Everyone get with your people and start looking into this new venture. Let's meet up before the wedding because the kids will be on a honeymoon at the end of the month," Bobby says and everyone nods.

With that, everyone stands to shakes hands. Maddox is the first to pull me aside. "Kendall, take this and use it when needed. I'll have my guy reach out in the next day or so." He hands over a business card but the only thing on the white matte square is a number. No name or anything.

"Thanks, Mr. Bishop," I say tilting my head up to meet his eyes. He's in his mid-thirties and keeps in very good shape. If I didn't already know he was part of a mafia organization I'd bet money on him being in the military with the way he carries himself.

"Call me Ox." His chin dips. "I've been where you are right now. Use that number if you need to talk or want money advice. Adam was a dipshit and I have a feeling your books are a trainwreck."

He gives my upper arm a pat then moves around me. We all file out of the office and walk toward the warehouse sliding door. I feel a hand on my back and turn to see Victor.

"Kendall, I'd like to have lunch with you to get to know you better. I knew your father and mother very well and would like to connect with you outside of these meetings. There's so much I'd love to tell you," he offers.

"Maybe this time we can meet up without your goons manhandling me," I chide and pull my arm away from him.

"Yes, of course. I must apologize for that. It was not my intention to scare you. I was concerned after you had turned down the internship and sent two amateurs to the restaurant that day," he explains but I'm not buying his apology. He is still up to something.

"Have your people call my people—" I say sarcastically but cut off my conversation with him when I hear a loud commotion.

One of the security guys slides the door to the side and I see who is causing all the ruckus.

Liam and Adam are standing nose to nose giving each other a verbal assault.

"How dare you accuse me! I did everything that man asked me to do. I couldn't help he made enemies everywhere he went," Adam yells at Liam.

"Why weren't you there that night?" Liam stands straighter towering over Adam. I see Wyatt is about two steps back with Luca, Arturo's son, watching the entire argument unfold. I imagine each family stays out of the others' disputes.

"I was out on an assignment for Nick. Not everything was run by you, Liam," Adam sneers.

"I'll find out what really happened that night, Adam, and when I do I plan on making *everyone* involved pay. Kendall is in charge now and I'll make sure nothing happens to her."

"Get ready for some push back. How do you think the guys are going to feel having to answer to a woman?" Adam grits out and Liam grabs his shirt pulling his feet off the ground. I make my way over to them but Bobby places a hand on my arm stopping me.

"I'll put a bullet between everyone's eyes if they so much as look at Kendall the wrong way. You better get everyone on board or I'll make an example out of you first!" Liam demands. Adam is trying to pry Liam's hand from his shirt but is having a hard time achieving it.

I don't think I've ever seen Liam this way before. It's like watching a different person inside the body of the man who raised me.

"Put me down, asshole!" Adam demands and Liam drops him to the ground. "Fine, I'll call a meeting and have everyone there to meet Kendall or Alexia, whoever the fuck she wants to be called," Adam says begrudgingly as he smooths down the wrinkles on his shirt.

"To you and everyone else she is Ms. Chapman. Set it up for

tomorrow at the usual place," Liam asserts with his neck vein strain-ing and his muscles tight. I think this is my cue to step in.

"Is everything okay here?" I ask approaching them.

I see Wyatt make his way over to me and stands right at my side but he doesn't touch me. Liam and Adam both take a step back from one another and look in my direction.

"Yes, Ms. Chapman. We were just catching up for old time sake. There will be a meeting tomorrow so you can meet all the captains and upper made men of our—your organization," Adam corrects himself as Liam pats him very sternly on his shoulder. He is like a completely different person than he was in the office.

"Terrific. Make sure to give all the details to Liam," I reply then walk past them toward the SUV with Wyatt right behind me.

Frankie opens my door and my butt slides onto the comfort-able leather seat. Wyatt opens the other door and enters beside me. "How was it?" he asks.

I let out a breath as the adrenaline starts to wear off. "Very overwhelming. I think it was the tensest situation I've ever been in."

"I'll bet."

The doors to the front of the car open and Frankie and Liam get in.

"Where's Benny?" I question.

"Kendall, now that you're a boss, I'll be by your side at every turn," Liam explains.

"Okay. So, what was with Adam back there?" I inquire as Frankie pulls out of the warehouse and we start our trip back to Las Vegas.

"A pissing contest. Adam always wanted to be your dad's lead man and hated that it was me. I've always thought he was a little weasel. Listen, I want you to be careful around him. I still don't trust him, but until I can find you proof to take him out, we'll have to be on alert."

"Liam, Frankie and I have been talking while you were in the meeting," Wyatt says, "and we think it would be best if Frankie stayed on and helped with your security. I know he comes from the Dawson

Family but we'll be married soon and I trust him with your life. He's only here to protect you, not to spy."

"I would like that. If everyone is in agreement. I like knowing that I have people I can trust around me."

"How was Vic?" Wyatt asks.

"He didn't seem surprised that I was Alexia Chapman. He was real quiet the entire time until it was time for the votes to be taken. I thought he was going to vote for me but he didn't. I would bet money he has known for a while and that is why he contacted me to come here."

"Interesting," Liam murmurs from the front seat.

"Yeah, I thought so too. He wants us to get together and bond, I think. He says he knew my parents well and wants to connect with me. He told me he has a lot to tell me."

"I wonder what he'd have to tell you?" Wyatt inquires. "Dad has never mentioned the Slaters and Chapmans ever being close."

"I agree, Wyatt. Nick never went out of his way with Victor. I would be interested to find out what he has to tell you, Kendall. Maybe if you're up to it we can have a lunch or dinner at a mutual place and find out what he wants. See what his angle is," Liam comments then turns to his phone and starts typing away.

I wonder what Victor Slater has up his sleeve. Something is going on with him. He wouldn't have sent those two men after me that day if it wasn't important.

I'm mentally exhausted after the meeting and I can only imagine what it is going to be like tomorrow when I face my crew. *My mafia men? Team? Shit, what are you supposed to call them?* Will they take to me being in charge? Is Wyatt going to be a part of this with me or do I have to go it alone until he takes over for Bobby? I also need to speak with Liam about the suppliers from Canada and making the drugs here under our watch.

CHAPTER NINETEEN

I CHECK MYSELF OUT IN THE MIRROR ONE MORE TIME. I've been a nervous wreck all morning. After breakfast, Wyatt had to take care of some business at one of their strip joints and said to call if I needed anything. Liam and Sarah arrived shortly after and we went over some of the business paperwork he was able to obtain from Adam. We think Adam is going to be a problem now that I've stepped up as the boss. I'm not sure if I can trust him to have my back and it poses a huge problem for me. How do I know he won't rat me out to the police or FBI? Or worse, turn my crew against me?

"Okay, Kendall, you can do this. You are confident, smart and you don't want to let your father down," I recite to the reflection staring back at me.

I'm wearing black pants with a blood-red shirt. I read somewhere that the color red shows strength and I'm going to need it to get through this meeting. I lace up my black boots and grab my black leather jacket. I know all the other Don's wear expensive suits, but I want to be on the same level, in some ways, so my crew will feel more open to accept me. I'm not a stuck-up kid who is given everything but someone who is willing to work hard alongside her people. I put my 9mm in the belt holster in the back waistband of my pants, then add a few clips in the inside pocket of my jacket and walk out to the kitchen where Liam and Sarah are waiting for me.

"You ready, sweetheart?" Liam asks after he looks up from his phone.

"I think so," I utter in an almost convincing tone.

Sarah comes over and gives me a big hug. "You'll be brilliant, Kendall. Just remember who you are and that your family helped build this town. You belong here. Don't let them see if you're feeling unsure of yourself; most can smell fear. Be firm and stand your ground," Sarah says.

"Thank you, Aunt Sarah."

"You have your gun and clips?" Liam asks as he picks up his leather jacket and kisses Sarah on the lips.

"Yes, got them. I'm ready."

We walk out and Frankie is there waiting for us by the SUV. Liam takes a seat in the front with Frankie and I get in the back alone.

"Liam, how's this going to work with Wyatt and me? Will he be involved in my business and I in his?"

"Sweetheart, that is something you and he will have to have a discussion about. If anything, look at it as he goes to work and so do you. You don't have to let the work and home collide if you don't want."

I peek back out the window and wonder if it's even possible. Could we separate our business life with our home life? How would it work? He makes it sound so easy. Could it be?

I shake off the dreadful feeling I get every time I think about keeping things from him and focus on the meeting we're headed to. I pull out the folder and scan some of the papers. After a twenty-minute car ride, we pull up to an abandoned building and Frankie scopes his surroundings. He steps out after a few moments then opens my door.

I step out into the Las Vegas mid-afternoon heat and follow

both Frankie and Liam through a metal door. The inside reminds me a little of the warehouse I met all the Dons at. Several men are standing around outside the office talking and joking with each other. They must not realize who I am because a few whistle at me and say stuff under their breaths. I walk with confidence to the door and open it to see Adam speaking with a few of the men. When he sees me, he nods in my direction, and the men turn and look over at me. I have Liam and Frankie flanking me and that helps with the nerves.

"Ms. Chapman, can I offer you a drink before we get started?" Adam says as he approaches me.

"No, I want to get this meeting going. I have quite a few questions for the men," I say as I breeze past him to the front of the room. I know he doesn't like my response but I don't give a rat's ass. "If I can have everyone's attention," I yell over the din of conversation in the room but the noise is a little too loud for some to hear. Placing two fingers in my mouth, I let out an ear piercing whistle. It bounces off the walls and startles the men, but it seems to have gotten everyone's attention. "Now if you don't mind, listen up," I start but am interrupted by a guy around my age.

"Listen, sweet cheeks, unless you're going to drop your clothes, I suggest you leave the meeting to the big boys here." The cocky little shit earns several snickers amongst the group.

Frankie leaves my side in a blur. In a matter of seconds, he disarms the guy and has his gun on the back of the guy's head. The room stills and others reach for their guns. I notice the smug look on Adam's face and can tell he is loving this. *Enjoy it while you can, buddy. It won't last for long.*

"Well, dude," I sass and motion for Frankie to bring him to me, "I'm not your sweet cheeks. My name is Kendall Chapman. Or some of you might know me as Alexia Blaire Chapman. The daughter of the late Nicholas Chapman."

I hear disgruntled murmuring from some of the older men.

Liam is now by my side in better view for the entire room to see him. Whispers bounce off the walls.

"As most of you know, the Chapman Family was murdered, but I was saved by Liam Martin and his wife Sarah. I've been in seclusion since that day and now am here to take over what is rightfully mine. Most of you also know that Liam was my dad's right hand man and he will stay that way for me. Adam Wilson is no longer the Head of the Chapman Organization and was voted out yesterday with the other Dons."

The talk is now overpowering the room and everyone is glancing back and forth between Adam and me.

"And what if we don't want to work or be associated with a woman in charge," the man who was speaking to Adam when we walked in says.

The room has gone silent again waiting for my response.

"What is your name?" Walking closer to him, I see him shift uncomfortably.

"Patrick Richards," he states boldly.

"Well, Patrick, when you joined this organization you pledged yourself to the Chapman name. It doesn't matter who runs it as long as you are loyal to the name. If me being a woman is a problem for you then there's the door. But I want to remind you and anyone else in this room. There are only two ways out of this organization. Dying of natural causes or being put in a body bag." I let that sink in. "The moment you turn your back on *ME* and *MY* organization, expect a bullet in the back of your head and a target on your families' backs."

I see him swallow hard. I can't believe I just said that. I just threatened someone's life.

Holy Shit, where did that come from!

He looks from me to Adam and back to me again.

"Ms. Chapman, you have my loyalty. Whatever you need, I'll be there," Patrick acknowledges, swallowing his pride.

"Good. Now, does anyone else have a question for me?" I

challenge scanning over the crowd. "Now is the time to say your piece."

I see Adam slip into the crowd away from the front but still close. I hope he understands I'm not going to take any shit from him or let myself be set up by any of his lackeys. I put my hand out to Liam for the folder he's holding and skim through it to see who I want to speak with first. Once I decide, I nod to Liam.

"Okay, I want to meet with each of you to talk about the areas you're working in our organization. I want to know how everything is run and who you answer to." I look down at the paperwork. "I need to see Brandon Jenson and Jason Stein first. The rest of you will need to get with Liam and exchange numbers for now." I dismiss them and walk over to Liam and Frankie who are off to the side.

"You did good, kid!" Liam whispers to me.

I give him a tight nod but inside I'm shaking like a leaf as two tall blond-haired men making their way over to us. I can only assume they're Brandon and Jason.

"Ms. Chapman," one of them says and offers his hand. I take it and feel a firm grip. "My name is Brandon Jenson and this guy is Jason Stein," Brandon says and Jason offers me his hand to shake.

"Nice to meet you both. Let's step into the other office and get started, shall we?" I walk over and open the door. As I'm entering, I see the room has pretty much cleared out, but Adam is lingering, talking with a few members.

Taking a seat behind a small desk, Frankie comes to stand behind me but off to the side. I see both Brandon and Jason sizing him up.

"Oh, this is Frankie. He'll be wherever I am so feel free to speak your mind without worry."

I look out the small window and see Liam being embraced by several people. They must have been with him back before the murder of my family.

"I see you two are the captains who run the prostitution

branch," I comment looking over the paperwork. They both nod. "So, if you will tell me a little bit about that. I want to know where the women come from, if they are tested regularly, the conditions they are housed in, are the cops up our ass; everything."

Brandon clears his throat. "We import the women from overseas and have them shipped here using Benson Shipping Company or some come from the strip clubs we own. They can make more money this way and decide to switch. As far as testing, we ask each woman to test every month or month and a half," he says. "You own a specific community that houses all the women. Like duplexes and a small apartment complex. Depending on the size of the place we have two to three women in each. The cops are not as involved in our side of this business except when a fight breaks out in one of the strip joints."

Benson Shipping? I wonder if they are any kin to Harper's family.

We spend the next thirty minutes discussing profit and loss. Brandon also gives me the names under him and Jason who help with the day to day affairs.

"I would like to visit the strip joints and see the conditions," I say as I finish writing down the last of my notes.

"You—want to go see?" Jason asks.

"Yes. Why? Is that a problem?" If I'm going to be involved I need to know what I'm dealing with, which means getting my hands dirty and learning from the ground up.

"No. It's not a problem. I just can't picture you entering a place like that, Ms. Chapman," Jason utters.

"Well, I'd like to see them and get an idea of what is going on and how they look."

"Yes, ma'am."

When we finish, I get their numbers and we plan on meeting up tomorrow sometime to have a walk through at a few of the clubs. I see Liam in deep discussion with a man who's around the same age as him. They both finish up their discussions as I approach and stand beside Liam.

"Kendall, I want you to meet Nathan Dennis. He and I came in around the same time to the Chapman Family," Liam says.

"Hello, Nathan, it's nice to meet you." I shake his hand.

"Ms. Chapman, you have grown into a beautiful woman. I think Nick would have been so proud to know how you turned out."

"Thank you."

Over the next few hours I meet with the captains over our drug branch, Lee Donovan and Harris Goldman. We briefly touch on the revenue and our main clients we push to. I tell them I'll be in touch and will have a meet up soon. They leave and Frankie gets the next two captains for me. The last branch is from the bookie section: David Brooks and Sal 'The Snake.' "I know for a fact my dad would never have those guys in charge of a business simply because I know neither Liam or Bobby would tolerate their ilk either." These two are the shadiest people I've ever met. They'll be the first to go when I restructure. I have a feeling Adam put them in place for a reason, and now I need to find out why. The meeting doesn't accomplish much since the two only want to tell stories of breaking kneecaps and busting heads. I make a few notes on my paper about overhauling this branch completely and then dismiss them.

Standing to stretch out my stiff back, Frankie and I walk out of the office and see Liam and Nathan saying goodbye. We head out of the warehouse and notice Adam waiting by our car.

"Ms. Chapman, I wanted to apologize for Patrick's comment. I've known him a long time and he's very loyal to me. He means no harm, I can assure you," Adam says, but I have a feeling he put him up to going nose to nose with me in front of everyone.

"No apologies necessary, Adam. Once I've done a thorough assessment of the organization I plan on restructuring and putting *my* team in place the way *I* see best benefits this Family. I want this organization to run like a well-oiled machine and any kinks will be ironed out or disposed of. But please do inform the others I won't allow any disrespect from here on out. Those who disregard that warning will be dealt with accordingly."

Frankie opens my door and I climb in, ending our conversation.

Adam is going to have to prove his loyalty to me. I don't like the things he has done and revealed the last few days. I want to weed out any problems before they explode into something bigger.

Once we are on the highway heading home a thought comes to mind. "Liam, have someone follow Adam. I don't trust him."

"I was thinking the same thing, especially after today," Liam says and Frankie nods in agreement.

"Also, have someone dig into the bookie division. The two captains are sketchy and I'm getting a really bad feeling about both of them."

"I agree with you, Kendall. I've been working for Mr. Dawson for a while and those two are bottom of the barrel," Frankie says.

After the short drive, we pull into the driveway of my home. My home.

This is where I'll be living the rest of my life. Where Wyatt and I will raise our family. All kinds of emotions are running through me right now. I don't know if the day is wearing on me or if 'Aunt Flow' is about to make a visit, but tears fill my eyes.

Carmen is in the kitchen and offers me a glass of wine. I thank her and gulp it down. Wyatt isn't anywhere so I guess he's still at *work*. Walking into the bedroom, I strip my clothes and start a hot bath with bubbles. Once I've sunk into the water, there's a knock on the door followed by Carmen's voice. "Kendall, I brought you another glass of wine and the rest of the unopened bottle," she says.

"Come in," I call back after checking to make sure I'm completely submerged under the bubbles.

Carmen walks over and places the glass and bottle on the side of the tub then leaves after I thank her. She is worth every penny Wyatt pays her. It isn't long before another glass is empty and I'm repeating the process. I hear the door open and see Wyatt standing there in the door way. He must see how upset I am because he strips his clothes and gets in the tub with me. I wrap my arms around his neck and my legs around his waist. Then the flood gates open. I cry and cry into his neck and he holds me tight rubbing circles on my back. I finally calm down and rest my head on his shoulder.

"It went that bad today?" Wyatt finally speaks.

I pull back to look at him. "No. I think it went okay."

"Then what's got you so upset?"

"What if I'm not cut out for this, Wyatt? What if I can't be like my dad? The thought of letting him down is killing me."

"You'll be just fine, Kendall. Just make sure to put the right people in place and everything will work itself out. You're one of the bravest women I know. You can do this."

"I threatened a guy today. And his family," I say sadly.

"Did he disrespect you?" Wyatt snaps.

"Kind of…" I pause.

"Kendall, sometimes you have to make an example out of people to show your power. You need to throw your weight around and show them who's boss. It's already tough that you're a woman coming into a man's world, but you're also being thrown into this life. You are going to have to earn everyone's respect. Some will be harder than others, but they'll all come around, and for those that don't, Liam and Frankie are there to take care of it."

Wyatt always knows the right things to say, and he's right. I need to put my big girl panties on and make a statement. I need my crew to trust me and show them that I belong here.

"Am I going to have to kill people?" I ask.

"Kendall, I think you already know the answer to the question. This is the life we live. Violence is a big part of our work.

Sometimes you have to get your hands dirty to clean up a bit. Do you understand what I'm trying to say?"

"Yes," I mumble in defeat.

Never in my wildest dreams did I think this was the life I would lead. Now to know that in the future I'll be taking another person's life is a lot of weight to carry. Do I even have it in me to pull the trigger?

"Wyatt, are you going to help me with my organization or are you going to stay with the Dawsons."

"What do you mean?"

"I mean, how do we do this? Working for two different organizations? Do we combine them or do we just not ask questions about our day? I don't know how all this works."

"I don't know either, Kendall. We need to do what's best for both of us. At the end of the day, we're the ones who decide our fate. I'm a Dawson and when my father steps down I'm the one who will take over. Our fathers wanted us to marry and join our Families and that is what we are doing. I'll be here for whatever it is you need and vice versa. We can make this work," he says.

"Okay, but what if our worlds collide and we are put into a war? What then?"

"As long as we communicate, then we'll be fine. I don't think there's anything that could tear us apart. If you want my help, I'll give it to you. I will be whatever you need."

I hug him tight. "I love you so much, Wyatt. Thank you for showing me what true happiness is."

"I love you too, babe. Let's get out of this cold tub and relax for the rest of the evening. You can tell me all about your day and I can give you some pointers if you want," Wyatt says as we get out and dry off.

The rest of the evening we devour the wonderful meal Carmen prepared for us and sit out on the patio in lounge chairs by the pool. I tell him all about the meeting and everything that happened. Wyatt is not happy about Patrick disrespecting me, and when I tell him about the bookie captains he's shocked Adam has such scum working for him. I also mention that Harper has the same last name as the shipping company we use and ask him if her family is involved with the mafia too.

Wyatt gives me a raised eyebrow. "I think it's a question you should just ask her if you really want to know."

Wyatt gives me some insightful advice on how to handle the men who work for me and also what to look for when I visit the businesses. We seem like a normal couple talking about each other's day. Our jobs are just a little different than most. We head to bed shortly after our talk. Tomorrow is a big day for me. Not only am I going to visit some strip clubs, but I'm also going wedding dress shopping in the morning. Mary, Aunt Sarah, Harper, and Gracie are all meeting me to find the perfect wedding dress.

CHAPTER TWENTY

THE NEXT MORNING BOTH WYATT AND I ARE BOMBARDED with the girls who got to the house at an ungodly hour to whisk me away to find a wedding dress. Carmen starts breakfast for everyone while we get dressed before heading out to greet everyone.

"Just so you know, we're changing the codes to the house once we're married," I grumble as I throw on a pair of tight leather pants, a blue blouse, and black booties. I place my gun in the back of my pants and grab the matching leather jacket that conceals the gun.

"Babe, I don't think it'll matter. I've already changed the code twice since you moved in and they still keep finding a way in," he jokes putting on his usual attire of a crisp suit and button-down shirt.

I laugh knowing he's probably telling the truth. "Honey, is there anything you want to have a say in as far as the wedding goes? Colors? Food? Flowers? I want this to be what you want too."

"I don't care about any of that. I just want to meet you down the aisle and vow before our friends and family that we are one. Everything else is a bonus. Just make sure the whiskey is top shelf."

Well, that doesn't really help.

"Oh, and make sure you buy the sexiest little outfit to wear under your dress. I want to be able to rip it right off you after taking your wedding dress off."

He is such a caveman.

We have breakfast with all the women and Wyatt gives me a kiss on the cheek before rushing out the door to go to work before he's asked one more detail about the wedding.

Piling into two different vehicles with Frankie driving mine, we head over to Mary's salon. They want me to have my hair and makeup done so I'll have a better idea of what the dress will look like on my wedding day. After two mimosas, my makeup is done and my hair is curled and pinned to the right side so the curls flow over my shoulder. I have side bangs and a small poof in the back to give it some volume.

After saying our goodbyes, we get back into our cars and make our way to Carolina Herrera. Mary made sure the store was shut down just for us. Janet, the store manager, is there to meet all of our needs.

I try on about a dozen dresses and am starting to get discouraged when Aunt Sarah comes to the door and hands me a dress she spied in the back of the store. I vow if this one doesn't work out for me, I'll have to look at dresses another day. I have so much to do today for business and the day is slowly slipping by. I gently pull on the dress and Janet is there to button up and tie the bow. I see her hand move to her mouth and wonder what she sees. I slowly turn to face the mirror and stare at the most beautiful dress I have ever seen. It is a part of the bridal line called Mary. It is a lace V-neck sheath gown with beautiful beading around the waist and it fits me like a glove. The only alterations that need to be made is the length. Tears well in my eyes and I know this is my dress! I walk out of the fitting room and Janet adjusts the dress as I make my way to my family to show it off. They're all chatting on the gray and cream-striped sofas when I stop in the middle of the room. Their reaction is the same as Janet's and I know they love it just as much as I do. Cheers and tears are shared.

"Kendall, I wanted you to have these when you found the right dress." Harper hands me a box. I open it and find a pair of blue-diamond high-heeled Louboutins.

"Harper!" I gasp.

"I know your favorite color is blue and you'll need something blue for your outfit, so I thought of these when I went shoe shopping a few days ago! Do you love them?"

"Yes, of course! They are perfect! Help me get them on," I exclaim with excitement.

Janet guides me over to the wrap-around mirrors and I can't believe what I'm seeing. I don't really recognize myself. Everyone has tissues in their hands, dabbing their eyes. I smile back in the mirror and then a flash of sadness washes over me. I wish my mom was here to see me.

"Kendall, I know what you are feeling and I wish the same thing." Mary wipes her eyes. "I wish more than anything that Rachel could be here to see you right now. Your mother would be so proud of the woman you've become." She grips my hands and then engulfs me in a hug only mothers can give.

"Thank you, Mary," I whisper in her ear. I think if I try to speak anymore I might let the dam open and there would be no stopping these tears.

We go back and forth over almost every little wedding detail, but in the end, I tell them all I want is the colors to be light blue, chocolate, and cream, top-shelf whiskey, and no fish. I leave everything else up to them, and Gracie and Harper jump in as if it's their wedding.

It's after lunch when I leave the girls and Liam and Frankie are both waiting for me outside the restaurant to make our way over to the first set of clubs. Liam hands me a folder of papers with all the details of each business, and we pull up to the most profitable club called Allure first. I have to say I'm impressed this is what a strip joint looks like. From the outside, it looks like a high-end restaurant. As we walk in, there is a dance club feel to it with the music and lights. The building is two stories and is laid out over fifteen thousand square feet. After walking through the foyer we're met with four different entries, all with a different line and person to help. The choices are to go into a sports bar, a topless area, an all-nude area, and a bachelor/bachelorette party area. Each person is carded and charged for entry to each area. Women and men are also walking around the foyer in skimpy outfits luring people to certain entries.

After going through each of the four areas and meeting the managers, I log a few things I think will help improve the club's profits. I also notice the back rooms where the dancers take people to do private dances. All in all, I don't think having strip clubs is a disgraceful thing here in Vegas.

After I've seen the next three strip clubs though, I think I might need to bleach my eyes. I cannot believe the difference between them compared to Allure. The clientele is sleazier and the buildings are completely run down. I talk with the manager, Drew, and find out that not a lot of money has ever been spent on renovations or the girls who dance there. I wonder where all the money is going if not back into the club? Is someone pocketing it?

I phone the captains, Brandon and Jason, who were supposed to meet me here, and tell them to get their asses here now. I hang up before hearing their responses. I think it's time for the men who work under me to know who the boss is around here.

Twenty-two minutes later they stroll into the back office and plop down in the chairs across from the desk. I've already spoken with Drew, Liam, and Frankie about what needs to happen.

"It's nice of you to finally join me today." I deadpan. "Can I see your phones?" I hold my hand out. Both men look at my hand and then at each other.

"Why do you need to see our phones?" Brandon asks defiantly.

In a split second, both Liam and Frankie have Brandon and Jason up against the wall, a hand around their throats. I really was hoping it wouldn't go this way.

"Ms. Chapman asked for your phones," Liam repeats in a menacing voice.

I sit there acting bored and unmoved. Brandon and Jason both reach into their pockets, digging for their phones, and hand them over to Drew who passes them to me. Looking through the call list, I notice right after I called them, Jason made a phone call to Adam.

"Why the call to Adam?"

Neither speaks a word. I give a glance at Frankie and Liam and they give a little compression on their throats.

"He…told us to report back to him after meetings and calls with you," Brandon wheezes.

"Really? So, you have no loyalty to me then?"

"Yes—yes, we do but—but Adam is a vile underhanded man. He goes after families if he doesn't get the results he wants. That's how he has always done business." Brandon chokes and looks over at Drew.

I follow his gaze and Drew nods his confirmation on how Adam conducts business. He obviously doesn't understand that he is no longer in charge.

"I'll handle Adam. As of now, you will pledge your loyalty to me or else the vultures will be picking your bones for a meal. Do I make myself clear?" I'm standing now with both palms flat on the desk leaning towards them.

"Yes, Ms. Chapman," they both recite in unison.

"And the next time I call, you will get your asses here faster than you did today. Don't ever mistake my kindness for weakness, because I have no problems throwing your dead bodies in a shallow grave in the desert." I sit back down in the office chair. "Now get out of my sight."

Liam and Frankie throw them out the door and take their seats. Drew makes himself scarce and heads out.

"Kendall, I think you're going to have to make a power move with Adam. He still has a tight hold on most of the captains and it trickles down from there," Frankie says to me, and I know he's right.

"What kind of power move are we talking about?" I ask wanting to hear their ideas.

Frankie peers over at Liam and gives him a grim look.

"I think Frankie is right." Liam sighs.

"What are we talking about exactly?" I ask again.

"You're going to have to kill Adam."

The next few days I work my butt off trying to get everything in order to make the improvements to the strip clubs and the prostitution branch. I've gotten the managers at Allure to take the other strip clubs under their wing to renovate them and bring them up to par.

Under Liam's advisement, I've reached out to Ox Bishop. He is, after all, the one who controls most of the banks here in Las Vegas. I asked him for names of financial advisors who I can trust with the organization's money since I don't trust anyone who Adam has chosen. He gave me a list of candidates and with Liam's help, I've found and switched everything over to this guy named Davis. He's a young guy in his late thirties who is also a computer genius and can hide money very well.

We've hit a few roadblocks on some of the shipments in our territory, but I have a feeling Adam has something to do with it. It always seems as if we're moving one step forward then two steps back. The conversation the other day with Frankie and Liam about killing Adam has been plaguing my mind. Can I take another person's life? Is this who I want to be? A killer? I keep pushing it to the back of my mind, hoping it'll work itself out and Adam will come to his senses and fall into step.

Wyatt and Gabe have some business up in Reno for the next few days, so it's just me and Harper at home hanging out until our men come home. She is staying with me at night but is at Mary's house during the day helping with wedding preparations along with Aunt Sarah, Gracie, and Mary.

I can tell Harper has become very attached to Gabe. They're always on the phone talking or texting. I wonder if it will turn out to be a long-term thing or if this is just a fling for them. I also wonder what Harper's parents are going to think about Gabe. I know she hasn't told them about him yet, so I think it'll be interesting to see how she tells them when they come for a visit.

Harper's parents, Doug and Jennifer Benson, are coming in a few days before the wedding. I really need to find out if Harper is aware her family works with the mafia. I've confirmed that their company is the one we use to ship our girls in for prostitution from overseas.

I sit down on the couch next to Harper and grab the remote to shut off the volume. Harper turns in her seat next to me giving me a raised eyebrow.

"I need to ask you something, and I don't know how you are going to feel about it." I take a large gulp of my wine.

"Okay, what's up?"

"The business your family owns and runs, do you know the type of things they are shipping in or who your father associates with?"

"Well, Dad always tried to keep it separate from the family, but I have an idea. Why?" Harper asks and shifts in her seat.

"I do business with your father apparently," I start to say.

"No! What do you mean you do business?" She grabs my hands.

I exhale trying to find the right words. I want her to know about my family. She is my best friend and sister and we don't keep secrets from each other.

"Harper, I'm the daughter of the former mafia boss, Nicholas Chapman. I just recently learned this and found out I'm the only heir to the Chapman Organization. Which in turn makes me the head of my Family."

I see her jaw go slack. Then she chugs the last of her wine down. "Wow." Harper's voice is barely above a whisper and she's avoiding looking at me.

"It turns out those nightmares I have are true memories of my family being murdered."

"Oh, Kendall, that's so horrible."

"Yeah, well, I'm inheriting a multimillion dollar business to run on top of that as well."

I go on and tell her everything. I hold nothing back and she listens intently to every word only asking questions intermittently. I feel like a huge weight has been lifted knowing I now have a confidant that isn't apart of all of this craziness.

Several minutes of silence pass as I let it all sink in for her. She hasn't moved and if her eyes weren't open I might've thought she fell asleep.

"Harper, say something," I finally say.

"Can I help run your legit businesses?" She asks with the biggest smile plastered on her face.

"What?"

Did I just hear her correctly?

"You know, the ones that are legal and all."

"Harper—"

"No, hear me out. You are going to need someone you trust to help with the legal side and have your back. I know you already have someone in place, but how do you know Adam isn't going to plant a mole to try and ruin everything now that he's been pushed out? I can be your eyes and ears. I know you think I only care about having fun, but I have a good business sense too. I can help grow and expand your legal side," Harper says.

She has done well for herself through college and we both graduated top of our class. Maybe this could work. I would love to have someone I could trust, but would it ruin our friendship if it didn't work out? I don't know how I would handle it.

"I know what you're thinking, Kendall. I promise you won't regret letting me help and our friendship will always be number one. If you don't like the way I run things, then I'll walk away. But I think we could take this city by storm!" I can see the wheels turning already in her pretty little head. "Plus, it takes a load off your plate to focus on the other side of business."

She makes a fair point and it'll give me more time to manage the illegal side and make it run smoother. "Fine, but let's start with a three-month trial first before we commit."

"Kendall, you won't regret this, I promise you!" She squeals and launches herself at me. Once she's pulled away she places her hands on my shoulder. "And yes, I do know my family is a part of the mafia. My dad does like to keep that part away from us, but I've always known."

"Really?"

"Yeah. I guess ignorance is bliss and all, but now my best friend is a 'Big Boss.' You and Dad are going to have quite a few meetings. It will be kind of hard to keep it from me. Honestly, I don't really care; a job is a job. You have stood by me through a really rough time in my life and that has bonded us for life. Where you go I go. I love you, Kendall, and I don't care who your family is or what they do or did."

"I love you too, Harper." I let out a long breath. "Let's get some sleep and then I'll set up a meeting with everyone so you can get started after the wedding."

"You won't regret this, Kendall, I promise! I'll make your life so much easier now, just you wait and see!" She looks so happy right now, and who am I to deny that? Then something washes over her face in an instant. "What are we going to do about school?"

"I really have no plans on going back right now. I have so much going on, and plus, I kind of already run an empire." I shrug.

"You're right. We don't need to have our master's degrees now. I bet my parents are going to be happy about this and all the money they're going to be saving," Harper jokes and we both laugh.

"Harper promise me no matter what happens you'll always be in my life."

She nods and a mischievous smiles plays across her face. "Do

I need to submit a resume for this job? If so, would you mind helping me with it?"

We stand from the couch and we fall into another round of giggles before heading to bed.

I hope I'm making the right choice in letting her in. Besides Liam and Sarah, I don't have anyone else I can trust. I know the Dawsons are going to be my family, but I still need to be able to separate them and my business for now. There needs to be a balance and I have to be able to stand on my own two feet first.

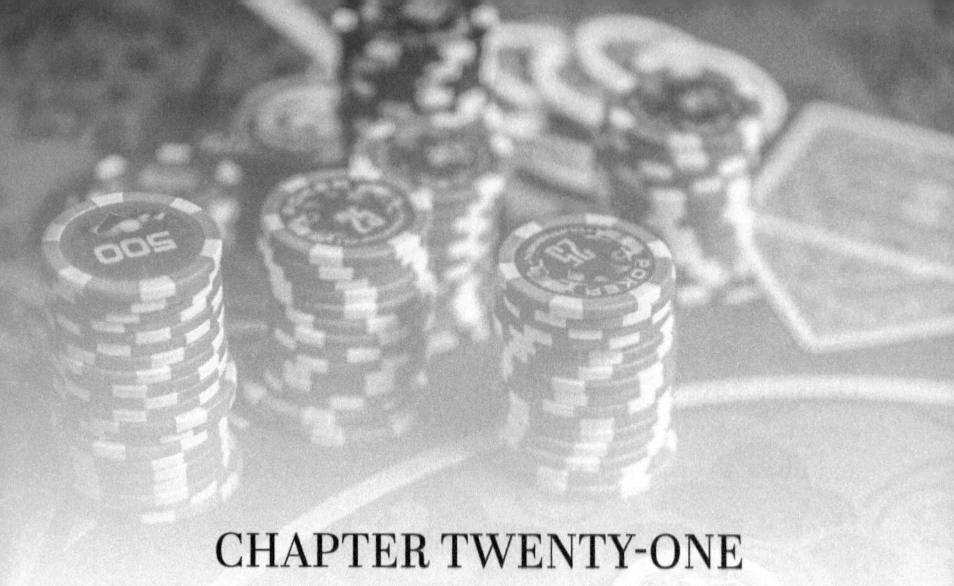

CHAPTER TWENTY-ONE

As the days start to mesh together I feel like I've run a marathon each night I come home. Wyatt and Gabe finally made it home a few nights ago and from the bruises and cuts on them it seemed like an intense meeting. Wyatt didn't go into every detail but let me know everything was settled on their part. He and Gabe needed to stay over at one of the safe houses for a night to make sure the blow back didn't follow them.

Safe houses, I have learned, are an important part of being in the mafia. If you need to hide out, that is where you go. If you need to interrogate someone for information, you take them out in the middle of nowhere so you can get your answers. Wyatt has told me the Dawsons have handfuls of them across Nevada and California. Per Liam, I have about the same, but only in Nevada.

Over the last several days Victor Slater has been blowing up my phone wanting a lunch meeting. I have been trying to put him off for as long as I can, but I know he'll eventually corner me. I finally agreed to meet today but haven't told Wyatt. I know if he were to find out all hell would break out. The Dawsons hate Victor, but I have to work with him, so I can suffer through this meeting for a few hours and then be done with it.

Wyatt left early this morning after breakfast, so I take my time getting ready. I blew off meeting up with the girls about wedding stuff even though it's less than a week away. I can't wait for our honeymoon to shut off my brain for a while. I think a break and some time off from this place is exactly what Wyatt and I need right now.

I put the finishing touches on what I'm wearing; diamond studs, my engagement ring, and a heart shaped necklace to go with my knee-length black skirt, white button-up blouse, and a pair of black heels with white polka-dots. I grab my Hermes purse and make my way out to the living room where Liam and Frankie are waiting for me.

Over the last week, both Liam and Frankie have been recruiting men who they trust and can align their loyalty with the Chapman Family. We now have over a dozen men who I can call on at any time to get things done. Most have military training and Liam seems happy we're slowly weeding out Adam's men. Frankie is trying to decide who will be his second in command when he is indisposed; he has really stepped up to help and has pledged himself to the Chapman Organization. Bobby and Wyatt were completely on board and support it.

We pull up to The Capital Grille. Liam and Frankie suggested we meet Victor in a public setting.

"Reservation for Chapman," Frankie says to the hostess.

The young woman looks over her book and gathers a stack of menus.

"Right this way," she says politely and turns to walk through the restaurant.

We're shown to a corner table and I notice even though it's busy the four closest tables are empty. After pulling my chair out for me, Liam and Frankie take the closest table and maneuver themselves so they have a clear view of their surroundings. Victor and his men show up five minutes later and he greets me with a kiss on each cheek.

"Thank you, Kendall, for meeting with me. I know you must be extremely busy getting in the swing of everything."

"Things are finally coming together, but I have an exemplary team in place to help this transition."

"Well, if there is anything I can do to help please don't hesitate to ask. I have been where you are and I think Nicholas and Rachel would be proud of you for stepping up."

"Thank you, Victor."

"The reason for my incessant calling is because I have a bit of information I would like to share with you. I think we could be excellent allies and help each other moving forward."

"What kind of information would that be?" I ask, curious.

The waiter makes his way over with waters and takes our lunch orders. I watch as Victor slides his hand into his jacket and pulls out a manila envelope and pushes it across the table. Out of my peripheral vision, I see both Liam and Frankie rise out of their seats slightly. I place my hand on the envelope and look up at Victor.

"What is this?" I ask.

"It's a show of good faith. I want what is best for you and your organization," Victor offers. "What you decide to do with it is your business. This business is very cutthroat and only the strong survive. I want you to succeed and have everything you could possibly want. I know I come across as an asshole and a hard man to get along with, but I make things happen. There's always someone who is wanting what you have and will do anything to get it."

I nod. I need to get a feel for this man. Can he be trusted? Can I believe a word he says? The Dawsons don't think so, but I need to make that decision for myself.

"Your father was a very closed off man. He, Arturo, and Bobby were the first to make their name here after their fathers passed. Nick and I were just starting to get close when they were attacked and the house was burned…" His voice trails off like he's remembering back to that time. "You look just like your mother. I knew when I spotted you in California a few months ago you were a Chapman."

"So, you knew who I was. Why did you wait so long?"

"I needed to make sure before I did anything. I wanted to get you here and somehow get your DNA and have it tested. I didn't want to upturn your life if there was a possibility that you may not be a Chapman. I would have painted a target on your back for no reason. Then you met the Dawsons and I couldn't get within twenty feet of you."

"Yes, this whole thing has been so surreal and in just a short amount of time."

The food is brought out and we tuck into it. Over the next thirty minutes, Victor tells me stories of what he remembers of my parents and brother. I notice he always mentions my mother. If I didn't know any better, I would say he had a thing for her, but I push those thoughts to the back of my mind. From the pictures I have seen from Mary, my mother was beautiful.

I've not touched the envelope on the table and it's in the same place it was when Victor slid it my way. I'll look at it when I'm alone with Liam and Frankie.

"Victor, thank you for this meeting and I look forward to working with you in the future," I say kindly. I need to wrap this meeting up and discuss a few things with Liam.

"Me too, Kendall, and remember if there is anything you need, please call. I have some other things I'm working on right now, but need to make sure I have all the facts correct before I share them with you. I hope when I do you'll be more at ease with me and know I do have your best interest at heart." He kisses me on the cheek and we walk out of the restaurant before heading in different directions.

Once in the car, Liam and Frankie turn from the front seat and glance back at me.

"What's in the envelope?" Liam asks impatiently.

I pull it out of my purse and open it. The contents are photos of Adam with a group of street gang members. The members have the same neck tattoos Bobby and Wyatt had shown me in photos from a previous stolen shipment of theirs. They're huddled together in an alley. Another picture shows him shaking hands and taking money from one of the members. They look like a pretty rough group.

"What do you think he's up to?" I ask after passing the photos to Frankie and Liam.

"I think he's doing some backdoor deals. These North Vegas gangs can be brutal. They don't live by any rules or codes; they take what they want. Wyatt and Gabe were always running into shipment being stolen or intercepted. Adam must be in their back pockets." Frankie looks over each person in the photos.

"This could get ugly, Kendall. We're going to need to shut this down now. We need to make a statement and an example of Adam and this gang," Liam comments.

"What are you suggesting?" I ask, but already know what is coming. I have been avoiding this subject for days now.

"It's time to take Adam out. He's a parasite; the longer we allow him to live the more he'll try to poison others against you," Liam proclaims.

"Okay," I know this has been coming since I took over. "Why do you think Victor gave me this?"

"Maybe to offer an olive branch or he could have a hidden agenda. We'll need to keep a watch out just in case," Frankie says. "Slater never does anything unless there's something in it for him."

"Why didn't our guy who's following Adam report this to us? Do you think Adam has more support and we don't know about?" I ask.

"Maybe. We will need to watch our backs a little closer. Frankie and I have some really good guys in place now, so once Adam is done, we'll be able to put people we trust in place there as well," Liam says as Frankie pulls the car out onto the road.

"Is this something we are going to be able to handle on our own or will we need to ask for help from Bobby? I know you've been gathering new men for us that we can trust. Do we have enough loyal guys to handle this?"

"I would like for us to handle this ourselves first, but if we need to bring in another Family, then Bobby would be our next call," Liam says.

"Okay, let's put one of our new guys on Adam from afar then go from there."

We drive back to the house and I notice Wyatt's car is in the driveway along with all the others from his family. Walking in, I'm bombarded with all the women.

"Kendall, I am so glad you are here! We need to go over which cake you want and finalize the rehearsal dinner," Gracie exclaims excitedly.

I look around needing some back up and see Wyatt and Bobby in the kitchen having a drink. Depositing my purse on the foyer table, I maneuver around everyone and hightail it to my security blanket. Wyatt sees me coming and opens his arms clearly anticipating that I need comfort.

"Hey babe, everything alright?" Wyatt embraces me, knowing I need his touch.

"Yeah, I met with Victor for lunch."

Wyatt puts me at arm's length. "What the hell do you mean, you had lunch with Vic?" he grits with so much rage.

"Wyatt," Bobby says in warning.

"He has been calling me for a while now wanting to meet up and talk. I finally gave in and heard what he wanted. It was no big deal," I say.

"Wyatt, Kendall is now in charge of an organization. She is going to have dealings with Victor," Bobby says trying to calm Wyatt down.

My man can be such a hothead.

"I don't like it. He has been nothing but a thorn in our side, and I don't want him tainting her with his poison," Wyatt says to his dad.

"Wyatt, I know you don't like him but I had Frankie and Liam there with me the entire time. He was completely polite and really only talked about my parents. He stated he wanted to extend an olive branch. I have my eyes wide open with him, trust me. He also told me he saw me in California months ago and had a hunch I was a Chapman, which is why he offered me an internship. He wanted to get close and confirm I was actually related," I recap.

"Well, next time I would like to be there with you. I think he has a hidden agenda and I don't want you to be alone with the bastard," Wyatt says.

I know he harbors a lot of hate for Victor and thinks he had something to do with his sister's death. This is where married life and business life gets complicated.

"No, Wyatt. I can't have you making a scene when I'm trying to conduct business, but if it will make you happy and give you peace of mind, I will inform you next time I meet him."

"Wyatt, this is business and you will need to understand this when it comes time for you to take over for me. You may not like him but at some point, you still must work with him. Kendall is just doing what she thinks is best for her organization," Bobby says.

"Hey, enough business talk! Come sit down at the table and decide on a cake for the wedding that's only a few days away," Mary interrupts and I'm thankful for it.

Wyatt kisses my forehead and leads us to the dining room table where there are over a dozen plates of different flavored cakes. How in the world are we going to decide on our favorite?

"How am I ever going to fit into my wedding dress after trying all these sweets?"

"Don't worry, I'll give you a workout after everyone leaves," Wyatt whispers in my ear from behind.

"I'll hold you to it, mister," I say and slap his ass when he walks around me.

Plate after plate is tried and passed around. When all is said and done we decide on a different flavor for each tier. The bottom will be chocolate with raspberry filling, then red velvet with cream cheese, then vanilla with buttercream. The top two we left up to the rest of the group to decide. I couldn't possibly pick after sampling every slice. Wyatt and I both agree the taste was starting to run together about halfway through.

Once everyone has left and all the plates and dishes have been put in the dishwasher, I grab a glass of wine and a glass of whiskey and make my way out on the patio where Wyatt is sitting. I offer him the glass and snuggle up next to him in the lounge chair.

"Sorry for earlier. I hate that guy and no one is ever going to change my mind," he huffs and takes a long draw from his glass.

"I know and I hate that I have to deal with him, but I don't really have a choice. I can assure you that I will always have someone from my crew with me at all times."

"I know." He exhales a defeated breath.

"Are you ready for this wedding?" I ask.

"Wild horses couldn't keep me away." He kisses my temple. "What about you? Any cold feet?" He runs his long finger up the pad of my foot making me almost spill my drink.

"No, I wish now we'd have Elvis marry us at The Little White Chapel." I laugh but am also completely serious.

"I think both our families would kill us if we did that. Plus I love all the faces you give when everyone freaks out about the cake or flowers or colors." He chuckles.

I let out a yawn and try to get closer to him.

"Let's get you to bed, babe. I need some lovin' before I let you sleep!" He picks me up and carries me into the house and towards our bedroom.

I hear my phone going off in the kitchen but ignore it. I'm sure Gracie or Harper want to talk about wedding stuff and I'm not in the mood. I hear it go off again as we enter the bedroom and then feel Wyatt's phone vibrate. He places me on the bed and starts to unbutton my blouse, ignoring his phone. He reaches the last button when it goes off again. With a long sigh, he gives me one last kiss and grabs his phone from his pocket.

"Hello!" Wyatt snaps. I see his eyes dart to me and then hands the phone to me. "It's for you. Liam is trying to get ahold of you."

I take the phone from his hand and put it up to my ear.

"Hey, Liam," I say as Wyatt starts to play with my breasts.

"Kendall, we have a problem. Our shipment was intercepted about thirty minutes ago. It was a pretty big load. We're talking about three hundred thousand dollars' worth."

I sit up abruptly forcing Wyatt to take a step back. "Really? Do we know what happened? Who it was?"

"The North Vegas gang, per one of our guys. He also mentioned he watched one of our men with them loading up our product in a delivery van."

"Who?"

"Adam."

CHAPTER TWENTY-TWO

"Adam?" I yell. "Are you sure?" I bolt off the bed and start to button my shirt back up.

"Yes, we have a guy following them right now. He is in the shadows keeping a watchful eye on the product and Adam. We need to dispatch men to reclaim it and make a statement to this gang," Liam says.

"Have Frankie come get me and I'll meet you where they end up. I want to be there."

"Okay, I'll call him now."

"Thanks, Uncle Liam."

We end our call and I see Wyatt sitting on the bed watching me. I walk over and stand between his legs. "I have to go and take care of some things. One of our shipments got taken and Adam helped them."

"Do you want my help?" He rubs my sides soothingly.

"No, I think I'm going to have to deal with this on my own this time. I've been avoiding this for long enough."

"The first one is always the hardest, Kendall. I'll be here waiting for you when you get back, okay?"

I know he's referring to killing someone and I need all the reassurance I can get right now.

"Go change out of this skirt and into something commanding. Let all those fuckers know who's the boss!" Wyatt swats me on my ass as I walk to the closet.

I change into black skinny jeans, a black T-shirt, and black boots. Grabbing my leather jacket, I walk into the bathroom and pull my hair up into a tight ponytail.

"Very badass, babe," Wyatt admires from the door.

I walk up to him and grab the back of his neck and plant a hard kiss on his lips. I need all the courage I can get at the moment for what I'm about to do.

"I love you. Call me if you need anything."

"Love you too."

We walk to the hidden room in his closet and I load up on my ammo and grab two 9mm guns from the wall. Wyatt hands me a pair of black leather gloves and I place them in my back pocket. Once I feel like I have everything, Wyatt walks me to the living room. Frankie is waiting for me and I nod to him as I grab my phone. We walk out to the car and Frankie gets in while Wyatt turns me to face him.

"You can and must do this. This is what your father left for you. Make him proud."

I nod, not trusting my voice. This is still all surreal to me.

"I love you, Kendall soon-to-be Dawson!"

I smile at his words. He takes advantage and kisses me one last time.

"I love you too, husband-to-be. Wish me luck."

"You don't need luck, you were born a Chapman. You make your own luck."

I nod once more and climb in the front seat of the car. Wyatt walks around to Frankie's side. "Not one scratch on her or I'll skin you alive," Wyatt threatens as Frankie opens his door.

"Yes, sir. I'll keep her safe."

"One call and I'll be there with hell at my side if you need backup."

He nods and they shake hands. Frankie climbs in and I watch Wyatt's figure get smaller and smaller in the side mirror as we drive away.

"Kendall, when we get to the warehouse I'll need you to stay in the car until the building is secure. Liam or I will come get you once it's time," Frankie says never taking is eyes off the road. I see him reach for something in the back seat. "Here, put this on just to be on the safe side." He hands me a bulletproof vest and places it on my lap.

We drive for what seems like forever and end up in a sleazy part of an abandoned old industrial area. He pulls the car off to the side of the road down from a building and makes a call.

"Hey, it's me…yeah…okay, is everyone in place…okay, let me know." He hangs up the phone and turns to me. "Everyone is in position and in a few minutes the attack will take place. Once we get Adam and the others rounded up they'll call us. You'll come through those doors over there." He points to a pair of doors on the warehouse. "This is your chance to take charge of *your* organization. To make your mark and show everyone who is in charge. This is your moment."

Just then the sound of gunfire commences off in the distance. I take my eyes away from Frankie and see brief bursts of light illuminate the windows. All of a sudden the gunfire stops and there is nothing but the noise of chirping crickets.

Frankie's phone buzzes and it's our signal.

"Are you ready, Kendall?" Frankie asks me.

I nod and pull on the door handle to get out but leave the vest on the seat and shut the car door. Walking to the back of the car, I stand there waiting for Frankie to put his jacket on.

"Do you have your weapon on you?" He adjusts his holster and checks the safety.

"Yes." I pull my 9mm guns from the back of my pants and check the clip, switch off the safety, and place it back in the holster before pulling down my shirt. Frankie helps me into my leather jacket then turns me to face him by putting both hands on my shoulders.

"Kendall, when you walk through those doors, you own the room. Not once can you show weakness. Weakness will get you killed. Weakness gives other people the upper hand. This is your meeting and you rule this territory. Show them that." Frankie gives my shoulders a tough squeeze.

We walk the short distance to the now open doors and I can see Liam waiting for us.

"Good evening, Ms. Chapman," Liam says motioning for me to follow.

We walk into the warehouse and everything is in piles. There is trash and large mounds of metal throughout the entire building. It reeks of body odor, metal, and dust. There's also a hint of gunpowder in the air along with a few men laying lifeless on the ground.

Walking further into the building, I see a line of men on their knees with my guys surrounding them, guns pointed at their heads. In the center of the men, I see the man who has forced me to do this.

Adam.

He sees me as soon as Frankie moves to my side and I notice the smirk on his face.

A cocky one.

I guess I better help wipe it off.

I walk over to Brent, one of the new guys Liam and Frankie brought on, and stand next to him taking a much-needed deep breath before exhaling slowly.

"Who's the ring leader here? Who stole from me?" I ask looking at the eight men lined up.

The warehouse is quiet. I guess no one wants to own up to it.

"Cat got your tongue?" I start, walking down the row of men who are on their knees.

I stop at the second to last one. He seems the most likely to squeal like a pig. He's sweating buckets and squirming.

"Are you the ring leader who stole from me?" I scowl at him and he looks everywhere but at me.

Sorry, buddy, this is not going to end well for you either way. I motion for Liam to come over. "Do you have the shears?"

"Yes, Ms. Chapman," Liam answers.

"Good. Hold him steady."

You got this, Kendall.

This is who you are.

No one will mess with your family again.

Liam and two of my other men hold him down. Taking the shears Liam has given me, I snip off the man's pinky finger. His screams echo off the metal walls as blood gushes from the small stump I left of his finger. I have to step to the side to miss getting sprayed and step over the man's finger.

"Last time," I warn. "Who is the leader who stole my drugs?"

The man is crying like a baby and shaking. "Leo—Leonard," I hear him mumble between bouts of crying and moaning.

I nod to one of my men who is holding him down and they release him to sit back up. As he makes it back to his knees, I walk away. Brent picks the guy up and takes him over to the other side so he's facing the seven men who were part of the heist.

My body wants to flinch and shake but I need to stand firm and confident. I can't show weakness. I walk back down towards the other end of the line and see a slimy little weasel. I know he couldn't possibly be Leonard, but I think I'll play a little with him.

"One down, seven to go," I sing and look at this slimy guy. "Are you Leonard?"

The man shakes his head and keeps staring at my boots.

"Then who is?" I demand once again.

He doesn't say anything and keeps his head down. I pull my gun from the back of my jeans and fire a shot at his knee cap. He cries out in agony and falls forward.

"This bitch is crazy!" I hear one of the men utter. Brent is on him in no time and busts the guy in the nose with the butt of his gun.

The man is next to Adam and if I was a betting girl I would say he was Leonard. I leave knee cap guy and walk over to stand right in front of who I assume is Leonard.

"Did you have something you wanted to say?" I ask sweetly.

Off in the distance, I hear another gunshot and know knee cap guy just met his fate. Everyone in line is now starting to fidget. It goes to show if I don't get the information I want then they will meet their maker a lot earlier than planned.

I place my gun at the man's forehead pushing his head back so he looks me in the eye. "Hello, Leonard," I greet. "Why did you steal my product? Think really hard before answering."

"It was just supposed to be an easy grab. He said you wouldn't even miss it," Leonard admits.

"Who told you that?" I already know the answer because the piece of shit is right next to him, but I want him to say it out loud. To see if we have a snitch on our hands.

Leonard tries to peer over at Adam but with a gun to his forehead it is almost impossible.

"Say it out loud!" I grit my teeth. "I don't have time to play games."

I apply more pressure to his forehead.

"ADAM!" he screams.

"Point him out to me."

He gives me a knowing look as he points directly at the guy beside him.

Adam Fucking Wilson.

"Thank you, Leonard," I praise then nod to Brent.

Brent grabs ahold of Leonard and shoves him down next to pinky finger guy.

I sidestep and come face to face with the rock in my boot. He looks a little nervous but is trying to put up a bored front.

"Well, Adam, I didn't think it would come to this, but you leave me no choice—" I start, but he interrupts me.

"You don't have what it takes to run an organization like this. Your father barely knew how to run it," he sneers.

How dare he mention my father.

I swing the hand that has my 9mm in it up against the side of his head, hard.

"Don't you ever mention my father's name out of your filthy mouth. You are nothing but a traitor," I erupt, balling up my other hand and punching him in the face. His head snaps back.

"I may be a traitor but you will soon be in bed with one and not even know it," Adam says spitting blood from his mouth, and it lands right by my boot.

"What is that supposed to mean?" My patience is running thin and my blood is boiling.

"Your father was weak! He—" Adam rants and before I let him get another word out, I shoot him in the chest. From the stain forming on his shirt he should bleed out in due time. He looks completely shocked.

"I was there the night he died," he pants holding his chest. "I stood over his body as he pleaded for the lives of his family. We both shot holes in his body before we spit on him."

My mind and body snap causing me to unload the rest of my clip in Adam's head and body. I continue pulling the trigger even after it has emptied and his body is slumped on the ground. So much for making him suffer.

The flash of the masked man from my dream plays in my head as he lifts the mask off his face and I finally see him. My five-year-old self now connects with who I saw from the woods that night. Adam Wilson. I stare at his lifeless body and can't believe I didn't see it until now. The man who has haunted my dreams for years is dead below me. The man who ended my family.

Off in the distance, someone is calling my name but I don't

register it as if I have on noise canceling headphones on. I feel like I'm in a fog. Adam was a part of my dad's team and he betrayed him.

"Kendall?"

I feel someone's hand on my shoulder. I turn, gripping their wrist and twisting it so I have it behind their back. My breathing is labored and that is when I notice Liam is in front of me. I release him and take a step back. Liam and Frankie both have their hands up in surrender. I lower my emptied weapon and stare at Liam.

"Did you hear him?" I ask Liam.

"I did and I hope he rots in hell," Liam spews then spits on his dead body.

I hear a throat being cleared from behind me. "Ms. Chapman? How would you like to handle the rest of the men here?" Brent asks.

I pour over the warehouse and see my men standing around waiting for my command and the North Vegas Gang is still on their knees waiting for punishment. One is already dead along with Adam so it leaves six left.

I reach into my leather jacket and replace my clip. I walk over to Leonard and pinky finger guy and stand behind them next to Brent, facing the others.

"This is what happens when you steal from me. You tell the rest of your gang that if they so much as sniff at my territory or make a move towards me, this is what is waiting."

I put my gun to the back of pinky finger guy's head, pull the trigger, and watch his body fall forward. I do the same with Leonard. I need to put the fear of God into this gang.

Snitches get stitches, bitches!

Harper and I used to joke and say it junior year when someone had stolen a copy of a test and the teacher was meeting with students one on one to find out who had done it.

"If our paths ever cross again, I will cut more than a finger off of you and I will deliver it to your gang." I turn to Brent and nod. He has the men gathered up and ushered out while the rest of my crew cleans up the mess.

"Make sure you put Adam's body in the vilest place you can find. Cut his head off and put it in a box. I think it's time to find out who is loyal to us. Grab his phone and let's find out who's more loyal to him than me."

I confidently walk out of the warehouse with Liam and Frankie flanking me. I get in the car and we pull out on the road. We're almost home and not a word has been spoken. My head is buzzing as I try to wrap my mind around the events of the night.

I killed Adam.

I killed three men total.

Adam killed my father.

And I don't have a single regret.

My door opens and I realize we're already in front of my house. I nod and thank both Liam and Frankie before walking to the front door. Liam must've let Wyatt know because he is waiting there for me. He leads me straight to the bathroom and turns the shower on. I still haven't said a word as he strips me and himself of our clothing. He washes me from head to toe before turning off the water and drying me off with a big fluffy towel. I avoid looking in the mirror, afraid of what I'll see in the reflection. My mind is racing with so many different thoughts of tonight's event. Wyatt helps me slide into some silk pajamas and climb into bed with him right behind me.

"I love you, Kendall. I'm here for you."

I snuggle closer to him and place my head on his chest. The rhythm of his heart and his breathing is calming but all I can think about is what Adam confessed to me.

"We both shot holes in his body before we spit on him."

We.

Meaning Adam had help killing my family and someone must have been in a powerful position to help take out a big boss.

Whoever it is, I plan on finding them and killing everyone who means something to them.

I won't rest until I do.

Vengeance is mine.

CHAPTER TWENTY-THREE

THE NEXT MORNING, I FIND MYSELF WRAPPED AROUND Wyatt. I didn't get much sleep last night thinking over everything that happened. I thought I'd feel remorse or be upset but I feel nothing. I killed three people last night and I feel nothing. Three lives have been removed from this world, all from the squeeze of my finger.

What does that say about me?

I shake my head and feel Wyatt stirring next to me.

"Morning, babe," he mumbles with a raspy voice. He gives me a small peck on the lips.

"Morning," I say.

"What are your plans for the day?" he asks.

"I have a meeting with my crew around lunch."

"Do you want to talk about last night?" he asks.

"No. I did what I had to do and now it's over. Thank you for the support, but I'm fine." I roll over on top of him completely done with this conversation.

"Okay, but just know I am here if you want to talk. I've been where you are and the first is always the hardest."

I can tell he is trying to be sympathetic to help ease my worry on my warring feelings.

Is it awful that I don't feel remorse for what I've done?

"Wyatt, I appreciate your words and sympathy but I truly am fine. Now shut up and kiss me."

We spend the next hour intertwined showing each other just how much we love one another. Wyatt really knows how to command my body to mold to his will. Afterwards, we shower and dress before heading out to the kitchen for breakfast.

Liam texts me that the meeting will be after lunch at one of our warehouses. It should be a full house and everyone from each department should be there. I want as many men there as possible because this meeting only needs to happen once.

After clearing our plates Wyatt comes over to kiss me. "Alright, babe, I'll be home late tonight. I'm trying to tie up some loose ends before our honeymoon."

"Okay, I'm meeting the girls tonight and tomorrow for spa treatments. Don't forget your mom wants us to spend the night before the wedding apart. Some tradition she says."

I watch him roll his eyes. "Whatever makes the woman happy, I guess," he chuckles.

Wyatt leaves and I head back into the bedroom to finish getting ready. I pick out a pair of leather pants and a long red silk blouse. I put on my heel bootie boots and pull my hair up off my neck. After lightly dabbing on makeup and lip gloss I head to my office. I find the pile of paperwork for my legit businesses and comb through them. I type out an email to Davis, my financial advisor and IT guy, and let him know Harper Benson will need to meet with him soon to go over numbers and the different businesses she'll oversee. I let him know she'll have full rein over them and to hire anyone she deems fit. I copy Harper to the emails so she'll be in the loop about everything. I bought her a new phone that is business only and set up an email account so we can message back and forth without the risk of being hacked.

Looking up to stretch my back, the clock shows it's almost time to leave for the meeting. I walk out into the hallway and the doorbell rings again. All morning long it has been going off constantly. I walk to the living room and see stacks of boxes covering most of the room.

"What is all of this?"

"Oh, Kendall," Carmen steps out from behind a stack and scares the living shit out of me. "These are just more of the same as yesterday's deliveries."

"Deliveries? For whom?"

"Your wedding, of course. People from all over have been sending you and Wyatt wedding gifts."

"How am I just now hearing about this? This is crazy!" I stare at the five stacks in front of me. "Where are we supposed to put all of them?"

"With the others in the guest room?" Carmen offers and motions for me to follow her.

We walk down the hall and open the door to the guest room. The room is stuffed with packages and baskets. There is only room for a few more boxes and then the room will be full.

"Mrs. Dawson called to inform me that one of their guest rooms is also full of gifts for the wedding. She will bring them over once you and Wyatt are on your honeymoon."

"Well, shit."

What are we going to do with all of this stuff? The thank you notes alone are going to take weeks to do.

"Carmen, can you do me a big favor?" She nods. "Can you start opening some of the packages and write down what they sent. I'll write the thank you notes but if we get double items can you donate them to a shelter or charity around here."

"Of course."

I walk back out just as the doorbell rings again and I know another package has arrived. Checking my phone, I see Frankie is waiting out by the garage. I send Wyatt a text about the crazy packages.

Me: I gave Carmen the go ahead to open the packages that

are piling up in the guest room and to donate the stuff we get double of.

Wyatt: I was going to tell you about them but you distracted me this morning. 😊 Sounds great. Whatever you want to do is fine with me.

Me: Thanks. I will see you later. Love you!!

Wyatt: Love you too

Grabbing my bag off the kitchen counter and making sure my gun is secure in its holster, I walk out as Carmen sets down another package. Frankie is holding the door for me and as I slide in I pull out my phone.

"Frankie, have you spoken to Liam today?"

"Just got off the phone about fifteen minutes ago."

"Good. Was everything cleaned up last night?"

"It was, and your delivery will be there on the table."

"Thank you."

We ride in silence for a while until a question pops into my head. "Frankie, Harper is going to be running the legit side of the business. Do you think we should assign someone to be her security?"

"I do. Anyone you are close to needs to have someone with them at all times. The best way to get to you is through the ones you love and care about."

"Okay. After this meeting let's put someone on her you trust. I'll speak to her about it tonight at the spa. Hopefully, she won't give too much push back and will do as she's told."

We finally pull up to a building on the out skirts of town and see a lot of different cars there. Hopefully this will go smoothly and in our favor. Frankie drives right up to the door, gets out, and comes over to my door. I step out and see Liam and a few other men from last night next to him. Brent is over by the door and is keeping a watch out towards the road we just came from.

"Good afternoon, Ms. Chapman," Liam greets me.

I hate that he doesn't call me Kendall, but I know he wants to show his respect. "Liam," I acknowledge.

"Everyone is accounted for and waiting. You have your weapon on you?" Liam whispers the last part close to my ear.

I nod and we walk into the building. I wonder why he asked me that. I have over a dozen new military trained men scattered across this building willing to take down a fly if it so much as gets in my way. But I guess I can never be too careful.

Brent clears his throat making my presence known and the chatter dies down as I walk to the front of the room. There is a small podium with a table and a silver tray with lid on top. I watch as Frankie and Liam take a stand at the front of the podium and look out at the group of men in front of us.

"I got a very disturbing call late last night," I start. "The caller informed me that one of our shipments had been intercepted by a local gang."

I scan the crowd to see the men's reaction and key in on a specific face.

Patrick Richards. The man who tried to call me out at the last meeting. One of Adam's lap dogs. I watch him as a smug grin crosses his face. He tries to hide it but fails miserably.

"It seems as though we have some *rats* amongst us. Some who think it is okay to be disloyal to our Family."

Everyone is now looking at different people throughout the room, unsure of who it might be.

"Three people lost their lives last night as I retrieved my product. Three people who stole from our Family. From me. Three who stole from *me*." I make a gesture to point at my chest.

Now everyone is looking around to see who is missing. I glance at Patrick Richards and see him not able to find Adam in the mix of men. The smug face has long left the building and beads of sweat have now formed on his forehead.

Yeah, I got you fucker. And your little bitch too.

"Patrick Richards, come here," I command.

The room turns to him and everyone watches as he slowly makes his way up to the podium. The sweat has now bubbled up on his skin and I see Brent talk into his sleeve. Patrick steps up to me and is watching my hands very carefully. I make sure I keep them in view. I know he thinks I'll pull a gun on him if I have the chance, and I will, but I want to toy with him for a bit first.

"Patrick, where were you last night when the shipment was taken?"

"I—I was at the drop point waiting for the truck to arrive. Which never happened," he answers. His nerves are getting the best of him.

"What did you do when the drop didn't happen and the truck never showed?" I already know the answer; I saw Adam's phone and all of the text messages between him and Patrick. They had this planned for days and seeing it on his phone and hearing Patrick spew lies is making my blood boil.

"I waited and then after a while I thought maybe there was a mix up and came to the wrong place so I went home and waited for a call," Patrick says in a rehearsed way.

"Really?! Because I have it under good authority that you never showed up for the drop to begin with." I pause and let him dig his grave a little deeper. "I saw Adam's text messages, Patrick."

"I…" He can't form a single sentence right now. I've got him on the ropes.

I watch him scout the room for the other guys who were supposed to be at the drop point with him. Patrick now sees his crew of three men are nowhere in the mix of men. *Get a good look because you'll never see them again and neither will their families.* Panic has now set in and Patrick makes the mistake of moving his hand into his jacket, going for his gun. Before he can pull his hand out from the jacket he is lit up like a Christmas tree from every direction. His body drops and is dead before it hits the floor.

I look out and see my trained military men all have their guns aimed at the dead man next to me. Once the noise settles down,

I address the room. Everyone looks panicked but doesn't try anything, knowing they're all surrounded.

"This is one of the men in a handful of traitors who spit on this Family."

I walk over to where the silver plate and lid are. I lift the lid and the room is filled with gasps, low chatter, and mumbles.

"Adam couldn't stand down for me to take my rightful place, and he stole from us. He aligned himself with the North Vegas Gang and has had back door deals going this entire time. I will not stand to have a rat in my Family and if there is anyone else who betrays this Family, your head will be on the same platter."

Gazing out at my men I can see the disbelief on their faces.

"I didn't hesitate to kill him and I won't with you. You are either with me or against me. It is your choice, but remember the target on your back. I plan on changing our structure so it'll benefit us as a whole and not just the top men."

I glance out again for a specific person and don't see them in the crowd. *Very interesting.* I'll have to ask Liam or Frankie about Sal 'The Snake' and his partner, the bookies. I think they have their hands just as dirty as Adam had and we need to trim some of this fat to get all of Adam's cronies out.

"Do any of you have any questions or are we going to have to weekly meetings like this?" I call out.

Not a word is spoken and I think my point has been made. I still have a few questionable people here, but once they're handled I think it will be smooth sailing.

I step away from the podium, ending this meeting, and go over to Liam. He has Nathan chatting in his ear so I wait for them to finish. Brent and Frankie both approach me while I'm waiting.

"Brent, can you get your men to dispose of Patrick and the rest of Adam? Make sure to dump them somewhere fit for rats," I say.

"Yes, Ms. Chapman," Brent answers then turns and speaks into his sleeve again.

I watch as a guy brings in a tarp and rolls Patrick's body onto it. They wrap him and Adam's head up before two guys carry them away like the garbage they were.

By the time I turn back to Liam, he and Nathan have finished. Nathan is already out the door in a hasty retreat. I watch a very tense Liam come over and I raise an eyebrow in question as to what that was about.

"Nathan heard some talk underground about some information, but before he tells me everything and we act he wants to make sure it's solid and not rumors. It is something he thinks will blow The Five Families apart," Liam says but I know he is holding something from me.

"Okay, just let me know what he has and we can move forward as soon as we have proof."

Liam only has my best interest at heart and he'll tell me if it's something I need to know.

"Well, I think the meet went good," Frankie jumps in changing the subject.

We all laugh. Yeah, it's not often someone tries to kill you. I guess this is what my life has come to.

"Do you think there will be pushback or retaliation for what happened here today or last night?" I ask.

"No. I think you made yourself known to everyone in the room. You are definitely not to be messed with. We'll still need to keep our eyes open just in case," Frankie suggests.

"Did you guys see Sal was missing from the group and his bookie guys?" I ask just as my phone goes off in my back pocket.

I grab it and read a text from Harper wondering when I will be finished so we can start our spa day. Rolling my eyes, I shove it back into my pocket, and return to my discussion with Liam and Frankie.

"Yeah, I was looking for him in the group. I wanted someone watching his every move during the meeting," Frankie answers and Liam nods.

"Let's get someone on Sal to keep to see who he interacts with. He might lead us to the others who were loyal to Adam," I say.

They both nod and we walk out of the building to the car. I was hoping we could get all of this resolved before the wedding, but it may have to wait until I return. Or I could just let Liam handle it while I'm gone. I trust Liam to get the job done. He was my dad's right-hand man and served him well for many years. I couldn't ask for a more perfect person to help me transition into my seat as the Head of Our Family.

Before I get in the car I give Liam a hug and tell him I'll see him later. Aunt Sarah is meeting us at the spa and he is planning to pick her up from there.

"I think we need to have a talk later tonight about what Nathan finds out. I'll fill you in and then we can proceed from there," Liam says. "I think we might have to bring in some of the others to resolve this issue."

"Whatever you think is best. I want to weed out all the bad apples in our organization. I think we won't have to watch our backs so closely once we do."

"What Nathan heard wasn't good, but we'll get through this, sweetheart."

Frankie drops me off at the Mandara Spa inside the Paris Hotel and Casino. The spa is elegant and very European. It has a calming and healing vibe when you enter it. I step out of the elevator and see all the women seated on luxurious sofas. They see me right away and come barreling over. After a round of hugs we're ushered into a room where robes are set out for each of us.

"Kendall, before we get started we wanted to give you something." Aunt Sarah picks up a gift bag from the pile of others on the coffee table.

Oh boy, more gifts.

We all have a seat and from the smiles on the girls' faces I know I'm in trouble.

"What is all of this?" I ask.

"Well, since you and Wyatt didn't want a bachelor or bachelorette party we still wanted to give you a lingerie party!" Mary announces as Gracie hands me the first bag.

"Oh."

I pull out the tissue paper and find a silver silk gown. It is really short and has a slit up one side. It looks beautiful and the lace at the top is delicate.

"Thank you!" I try to fold it so it doesn't wrinkle and place it back in the bag.

"This one next!" Gracie bounces in her seat.

The light blue bag is medium sized and feels a little heavy. I pull the tissue out and out comes a leather top with what looks like spikes over the breast. *What in the world?* I can feel my cheeks heat instantly. The girls are all giggling now and Mary and Sarah both say how they once had something like this.

"Keep going, there's more!" Gracie says and I'm afraid to put my hand in again.

Next, I pull out a pair of leather handcuffs, a mini flogger, body oil, and the matching leather panties. Apparently, there's a theme here.

"Gracie! I can't believe you bought something like this!" I say but all the girls are in fits of giggles as I hold up the items.

"It's just to help spice up your sex life," Gracie informs me.

I grab the next bag and find a beautiful white satin baby doll top with matching panties and kitten heels to match. I know this one will be put to good use. The next few bags are more gag gifts than anything. I have a few books on different positions, a pair of love dice, and a booklet of IOUs for a later date. There are over a dozen lingerie sets. I have a naughty nurse, French maid, cheerleader, and a school girl outfit on top of everything else.

"Oh, Kendall, I almost forgot. Here, this is from all of us. We thought you could use this while Wyatt has out of town meetings." Mary hands me a heavy pink box with a heart on the front of it.

The words *Pure Romance* are written across it. I slide the top off and happen to catch all the girls leaning in from their seats. I push the tissue paper to one side and see four sealed plastic bags. I can't really make out what is inside the bags but my gut is telling me not to touch them. I pick up the closest one first and turn it over to read the label. Immediately I want to drop it back in the box and put the cover back on.

"Which one is it?" Harper asks like she's familiar with these types of things.

I don't think the red on my face is going away anytime soon. My aunt and future mother-in-law are sitting directly in front of me, and according to Mary they all went in and got these for me. Deciding to just swallow my pride and go with it, I proudly hold up the first item and show the room, never making eye contact.

"Oh, I have one like and love it! Kendall, it'll be put to good use!" Gracie says cheerfully.

I face her then look back down at the pink three-speed clitoral vibrator and bite my bottom lip. The floor can open any time and swallow me whole.

This is so embarrassing.

The next bag is pink and clear. Basically, a large vibrating dildo. Aunt Sarah grabs for the bag and each girl insists on having a look. As they pass around the large dildo, I grab the next bag hoping to get this horrifying experience over with. The next one doesn't seem so outrageous as it looks like some kind of lubricant, but the more I inspect it I find myself dropping it back into the box. Anal soothing gel. *What in the world? I don't think so. They must be crazy! No way, no how!* And in the back of my head I already know what the next bag is going to be, I just don't want to admit it. Quickly, I grab the last one and turn it over only to find I should have stuck with my gut. There it is in all its glory. A purple vibrating buttplug.

"Oh, Kendall, you are going to love this one," Aunt Sarah says and I snap my head to her almost giving myself whiplash. She's speaking as if we are talking about our favorite coffee flavor.

"I know, right! Just remember to give it a try before you throw it in the drawer and never use it," Mary says. Gracie and Harper both chime in asking questions and I feel like we are in an episode of the Twilight Zone. *Who are these people?* By now my face is the shade of a coke can with no chance of changing anytime soon.

After Mary and Sarah give a few instructions, I'm still staring at everyone like they have three heads. How are we talking so openly about this? Aunt Sarah was barely able to have the sex talk with me when I was a teenager. Now she is giving me pointers on how to pleasure myself and Wyatt?

"Just wait, the fullness and thrilling feeling you have when you are double penetra—"

A knock on the door lets us know the spa is ready to take us all back for our treatments. And thank the lord for the interruption!

We are all getting waxed, pedicures, manicures, facials, full body massages, and our hair trimmed and colored. The full works. I know Mary and Sarah had them block off several rooms only for us to enjoy. Refreshments and drinks are gladly appreciated after what I just had to endure. It was a sweet gesture, but my god, I'm going to need some therapy after this little show and tell!

In the end, we laugh and have a good time. I love my new family and think we're all going to get along gloriously. Mary and Sarah have really hit it off and bonded over all the wedding planning. I'm glad Sarah has made a friend and is getting along with her. It'll make the holidays so much easier, but I think they could be longtime friends after all this is over. I could not have asked for a more relaxing time with the girls I love. Especially after the last few weeks I've had. I just hope things will start to settle down now that the wedding is almost here.

I instruct Frankie to leave all the packages in the trunk of the car. First, I don't want him to see what is in them. Second, I don't want Wyatt to snoop around and find them. I need to surprise him with some of the clothing. The toys, I'm going to have to pep myself up with to even try and use. I know Wyatt can be pretty kinky but this is a whole different ballgame for me.

It's after eight o'clock when I walk through my house and see most of the packages have been sorted. There's a note from Carmen letting me know our dinner is in the warmer on the stove. She also has pages of names and the wedding gifts written down.

I text Wyatt letting him know I made it home and to wake me when he gets home. I reheat my grilled chicken and all the fixings before heading to bed. Sleep can't reach me soon enough when my head hits the pillow, but just as I'm being pulled under, my phone fills the room with a loud ring.

"Hello," I answer not opening my eyes.

"Kendall, I'm coming over with Frankie," Liam says. "It's worse than we thought. Nathan is being picked up to come over. He got what we needed. I'm calling in for some help with this."

"Okay, I'll put on a pot of coffee."

This might be a long night. Hopefully, we can squash whatever this is before the wedding.

CHAPTER TWENTY-FOUR

Today is the ceremony!

I'm going to be announced in front of our entire community as Mrs. Kendall Dawson.

I wake up in a soft bed with a plush comforter and reach out to the spot next to me. The bed is cold and empty. Then I remember I'm not at my house but at Uncle Liam and Aunt Sarah's house in their guest room. Rolling over, I check the alarm clock on the nightstand and see it's eight in the morning. The wedding is not until two so I still have a while before I'm needed. I get out of bed, throw some workout gear on and make my way to Liam's gym on the other side of the house. There's a few jitters I need to work out and running is the best way to do it for me. I pass Aunt Sarah in the kitchen and see her still in her silk pajamas but she has her hair in rollers. She is swaying to the music blasting and retrieving something from the oven. It smells like muffins.

I walk into the gym and see Liam working the bench press. He must have the same idea and needed to blow off some steam. We nod to each another because we both have our earbuds in and continue about our workouts. I head straight for the treadmill and set my pace to run.

I haven't had a nightmare since I realized it was Adam who

was the masked man I saw, but I still have this lurking feeling of who was helping him bring my Family down. Liam and I have had a lot of conversations about who it could be but we don't have anything solid yet.

I shake my head and focus on my breathing. This is my big day and I want to think of nothing but starting my future after today. Forty-eight minutes later I'm a sweaty mess but feel loose. Liam seems to have finished up his workout but stays and helps spot me on a few machines.

"Sweetheart, are you ready for today?" Liam asks as I sit up from the bench press.

"More than ready. Thank you for being here. I don't know what I would have done if it wasn't for you and Aunt Sarah." I feel the tears well up in my eyes. I'm not even sure if there are words that can describe what and how I feel for the two of them.

"We wouldn't have been anywhere else," his voice breaks a little.

I know they wanted children but it was never in the cards for them. They tried everything and went to a lot of doctors. I was the closest thing to a daughter to them and they are the closest thing I have to parents.

"Thank you, Uncle Liam."

"For what?" he asks dumbfounded.

"For taking me in and hiding me. You could have left me there and took off but you didn't. I don't remember my mom and dad but you and Sarah made sure to keep their memories alive with stories about them. I'm sure most were modified now that I think about it." I laugh out. "But thank you."

Sarah walks in with a plate of muffins and coffee for us.

"Thought we could have one last meal as a family of three before we leave for the church," Sarah offers.

We sit down in the middle of the gym and start munching on the muffins.

"Kendall, I know today is a big day and one of the most important days for a girl. Today will also be a very hard day because most girls dream of sharing this day with their moms, but I hope I can help you and be there for you in whatever it is you need." Sarah grasps my hand. I can tell she is holding back tears.

"Aunt Sarah, I have always thought of you as a mother figure and Liam as a father figure. I know I don't call you mom and dad but I truly feel that you guys are my parents, and always have." Tears are now streaming down both our cheeks, and somehow the three of us have formed a group hug.

"We are so proud of the woman you've become, Kendall. You make us so happy," Sarah says between sobs. A look passes between them as Sarah pulls out a box from her pocket.

"Kendall, I know we aren't blood-related but we have something we want to give you to wear." She hands it to me and I open the beautiful box.

I gasp and stare at the most exquisite necklace made of white diamonds and smaller blue ones in between. My favorite shade of blue. I'm scared to touch it for fear it might break.

"Liam and I thought since you don't have any jewelry from your parents, you might want to have something to pass down to your little ones one day."

I sob and kiss them both before finally finding my voice. "I love you two so much and couldn't picture my life without you. Thank you. You have no idea how much this means to me. I love you both so much." Then I ask the question I've wanted to ask for so long. "Do you think it'd be okay if I call you Mom and Dad?" I pause. "I know we've never talked about it but—"

"Oh, sweetheart, nothing would make us prouder than that. We didn't want to ever try to replace your parents so we never pushed, but know you are ours and not sharing DNA will never change that."

We all sob and cherish this long-awaited moment. I'll never understand why I was so scared to ask them this. The last few days have really made me realize that life is so short and we can't live with regrets.

"Okay, girls, I think we have cried enough on this big day. Try and save some for the church," Liam jokes and we resume eating muffins and drinking coffee.

We finish up and Sarah sends me off to take a shower. I wash up and make sure every spot of me is shaven and hair-free. I know we went to the spa two days ago, but I want to make sure everything is ready for the wedding night and honeymoon. I dry off and hear a crowd chatting in the living room. I still have my robe on per Sarah's instructions and walk out to see the living room has been turned into Salon Grand Central.

Everyone is here. There are makeup artists and stylists everywhere yelling and commanding people where to go. I just stand back and watch the chaos. Mary, Sarah, Gracie, Harper, and Harper's Mom, Jennifer, are all going a mile a minute. It isn't long before some guy with a comb sees me and starts yelling for everyone to take their places. I'm rushed to a chair and three people hover over me. Orders are being given and I must look like a deer caught in the headlights. A loud whistle echoes off the walls and everyone freezes.

"HEY! Everyone stop and take a breath. Let's get Kendall situated and then the bridesmaids. After that, we can send them to the church to have pictures done before Sarah and I come. Chop chop!" Mary yells and everyone falls in line.

While the rollers are being put into my hair someone is touching up my manicure and pedicure to make sure there isn't a chip or crack in place. Someone comes around with champagne and everyone toasts to an unforgettable day. While being pampered, I catch up with Harper's mom and tell her more about Gabe. Harper told her parents she's seeing someone but didn't give a lot of details. They seem very impressed with Gabe after meeting him at the rehearsal dinner but didn't get to talk long with him.

Jennifer and Doug Benson, Harper's parents, flew in yesterday for the wedding and I was able to speak with Doug about business before the rehearsal dinner. We spoke on how everything happened, about being a Chapman, and Doug told me some good stories about some dealings with my dad. I also informed him about Harper wanting to run the legit side of my business and asked his thoughts on the subject. I know he tried to keep her away from his business and I didn't want to have any hard feelings between him and I. Doug was just happy Harper showed interest in something other than shopping. I told him my plans to keep her away from the illegal side and only focused on the legit businesses. He was grateful and told me if I ever needed anything business-wise, he would be there for me. We went over Harper's security and he agreed with us that she'd need someone up close. It was startling to learn he'd had protection on us since freshman year but they were always off in the shadows keeping an eye out. Doug and Liam got together after we talked and coordinated sometime after the wedding to sit down and talk about what needs to happen as far as some shipping business. Then football and baseball was mentioned and business was the farthest thing from the men's minds.

Now, my hair is done the same way I had it styled when I went dress shopping and last night for the rehearsal dinner. It's curled and pinned to the side with a little volume in the back and a strand curled on the opposite side by my exposed ear. Makeup artists are the next to zoom in. The team goes with foundation, blush, eye shadow, mascara, eyeliner, and a soft color lipstick.

When they twirl me around to face a mirror, I don't even recognize myself and I can't believe how I look. The few pictures I've seen of my mother is what is staring back at me. My eyes are popping and a light glow has set in. I feel and look like a princess. As tears start to form in the corners of my eyes one of my makeup artists hands me a tissue.

"None of that! We put on waterproof mascara but everything else will smudge."

I nod and try to swallow the lump in my throat. This seems so surreal, and after yesterday this is going to be a very big day if everything goes as planned.

"Kendall, you look absolutely stunning, dear!" Mary gushes as she approaches. "I know your mother would give anything to be here today but know her memory still lives in you. Here, Bobby and I wanted to get you something to welcome you to the family."

Mary holds out a box and places it in my hand. I slowly open the jewelry case and can't believe my eyes. Inside are a pair of large diamond teardrop earrings. In between the two large diamonds is a smaller light blue one that matches the necklace Sarah and Liam gave me this morning.

"Oh my gosh, Mary!" I start. "They are so lovely! Thank you."

Everyone is now gathered around me as Mary helps me put them on. I see flashes going off and the photographer is shouting for some people to get out of his light. Sarah comes over with her jewelry box from earlier and helps put on the matching necklace. We stand there and take a million pictures of the three of us and then with the wedding party.

"Alright, the girls need to get going to the church, and Mary and I need to get ready. Everyone's dresses are at the church in the bridal suite waiting for us. We are now on wedding countdown people!" Sarah says. "Two and a half hours. Let's move!"

With the command, everyone starts moving. Harper, Gracie, and I are ushered to a white limo waiting outside the front door. I pass Liam and Frankie in a whirlwind as I slide into the car.

"Are you nervous, Kendall?" Gracie asks as we pull out of the driveway.

I shake my head. "No, I'm anxious but not nervous. Wyatt is my home, my everything."

"Aww, that is so sweet, you just gave me a cavity!" Harper teases me.

"Careful, Harper, you and Gabe are getting awfully close. You might be next," I tease back.

She gapes at me, but surely, she's thought about this. I mean she and Gabe are hot and heavy right now. They can't keep their hands off each other.

"Kendall's right. I've never seen him this way with someone before," Gracie jumps in and elbows Harper.

After a short drive, the limo pulls up to Our Lady of Las Vegas Catholic Church. With the short notice of putting a wedding together, this church was the only one that could fit in as many people that are coming to the ceremony. The church is gorgeous with immaculate brickwork leading up to the entrance and covered parking. After pulling up and getting out, we walk in through the double doors with stained glass crosses. Inside is a flurry of people running around, some with vases and flowers, some with candles and bows.

I follow a woman who is walking swiftly towards an open entry and can't believe my eyes when I round the corner and take a few steps inside to look around at each detail. The sanctuary is decked out with white and baby blue-dipped roses. Lantern lights hang from the exposed wood of the ceiling and there are dozens and dozens of pews on each side of the large middle aisle decorated with giant clear vases with tall flower arrangements. The center aisle has a sheer baby blue runner leading to the bottom marble step of the pulpit. A lattice covered in greenery with white roses and flowers dipped in blue is the backdrop. Candles line the outer edges of the four marble steps that lead up to the podium, and the natural lighting gives it an intimate vibe.

This is truly a dream come true, straight out of a fairytale. Never in my wildest dreams could I have imagined something like this.

"Wow! Kendall, this looks magnificent." Harper is in awe as she intertwines our arms and gazes at the view in front of us.

"I know. Never thought it would be this grand," I say in amazement. "Y'all did an amazing job."

"Girls!" Gracie yells down the hall. "Come on, we need to get ready to have pictures done before the ceremony starts. Mom and Sarah have just arrived."

We pull ourselves from the sanctuary and walk down the hall towards Gracie. In the bridal suite, my wedding gown is hung on one of the walls along with the other dresses. Mary and Sarah are there gathering the dresses to put on. The photographer has joined us and is snapping away. I've been told to sit down on the sofa and wait until everyone is ready. Only then will they help me into my dress and shoes.

Once everyone is buttoned up and has touched up their makeup all attention turns to me. I never really understood why it took so many people to help dress a bride but now that we are trying to slip it on without messing up my hair and makeup, I completely understand. Somehow, we manage to get it on without any snags, and Sarah zips me up before buttoning the last few buttons on the dress. She ties the bow in the back as the photographer clicks away. Mary brings over the veil and gently places it in my hair. Harper brings over my blue diamond Louboutins and slides them on my feet.

I turn to look in the mirror and can't help the small sob that escapes my throat. Never in all of my almost twenty-two years have I ever dreamed my wedding day would turn out this way. It doesn't matter how many pins you put on a board to try and create your special day. Only being here and seeing it firsthand can make those images come to life. Trying to rein in my tears so as not to mess up my makeup, I turn to show the rest of the room. There are gasps and hands cover their mouths as tissues are passed around.

"Oh, Kendall, I've never seen such a beautiful bride before," Sarah says, choked up, and wipes a tear away.

"You are the most stunning bride, Kendall, and my son is the luckiest man on this earth," Mary says as she and Gracie hold hands looking at me with glassy eyes.

"Thank you," I say but it comes out hoarsely.

"Tradition time!" Harper yells out. "Since you guys seem to lack those lately."

"Yes, yes!" Gracie cheers. Tears are quickly forgotten.

"Okay, so the saying goes 'Something Old'..." Mary steps in and hands me a handkerchief. "This is what my mother-in-law gave me on my wedding day."

"Then there is 'Something New'..." Sarah steps up and Mary

steps back. She hands me another jewelry box. Inside is a matching anklet. It has the same teardrop light blue diamonds as my necklace and earrings. "I know the dress and shoes are new, but Mary and I wanted you to have something you could pass down from generation to generation." Sarah kisses me on the cheek and bends down to latch it around my ankle.

"Our turn!" Gracie squeals and both she and Harper step forward. "Then there is 'Something Borrowed'…" Gracie opens up her hand and shows me a hair pin with real diamonds across the length. "This is only on loan for now; I expect it back when I get married." She shakes her finger at me and then goes around with the help of Mary to place it in my hair.

"Now for 'Something Blue'…" Harper opens a box and reveals a baby blue garter. It has the same beading around it as the one around the waist of my wedding dress. Harper bends down and slides it up my leg to fit on my upper thigh.

"Thank you, you guys. I love you all so much and don't know how today would've gone if you hadn't been—" I start to say but am interrupted by the photographer.

"Ms. Chapman, we need to start the pre-wedding photos. The guest are starting to arrive. My assistant will keep them out of the sanctuary for a little while, but the wedding will be starting soon," he says.

I nod. It's almost showtime and my nerves are starting to fray. Everyone helps me as we move through the church to stay out of the guests' view. I notice Frankie is flanking us along with Brent. Both are in tuxedos and have earpieces in. It's still hard to believe this is my life now.

After a thousand and one pictures in every pose and with my bridesmaids and Sarah and Mary, we finally make our way back to the bridal room. Liam is there waiting, reading over his phone when we enter. Hearing the noise, he looks up and sees me walk in and sucks in a breath.

"Sweetheart, you are the most captivating bride I have ever

seen," Liam says and makes his way over to me. "There are no other words for me to say than that. Sarah and I thank our lucky stars to have had you in our lives." His thumb catches a tear that slips out.

"Thank you, Dad," I push past the lump in my throat.

"Is Wyatt here yet?" Gracie interrupts our moment.

"No, not yet. He should be here soon and when he does, he'll be on the other side of the church to get ready," Liam says and I feel a bit of tension that he's not here just yet. I know they were going to get ready at Bobby and Mary's house. He wanted to wait until the last minute to get here so he wouldn't pace like a wild animal knowing I was a few steps away and couldn't see me.

"Gracie, we better go and wait for him." Mary nudges Gracie and they leave closing the door behind them. She must have sensed we wanted some alone time.

The photographer takes more pictures of me and Liam and then of Liam, Sarah, and myself. Harper is in the corner snapping shots with her phone.

A pounding on the door startles us. Liam's hand immediately goes to the back of his waistband, where I assume he's carrying his weapon. He never goes without it now. The pounding starts again and Liam nods for us to go to the other side of the room. Once we're in place he swings the door wide open almost ripping it off the hinges.

"What are you doing here?" Liam yells.

"I need to see Kendall. I have something important I think she is going to want to see," I hear a familiar male's voice.

"This can wait until after the ceremony. We can set up a meeting and talk then," Liam urges and attempts to close the door.

"No, this needs to happen now! It can't wait and she will want to know," the man says again and I find myself moving towards them.

I sneak around the door and see Victor Slater in the doorway. He's looking dapper in a black tuxedo and is holding a large manila envelope. He sees me and tries to take a step into the room but is blocked by Liam.

"Kendall, I know today is your wedding but you need to see this now," Victor urges. His voice is desperate which is strange coming from him.

I take the envelope from him, reaching over Liam's broad shoulders but make no effort to open it.

"Remember at our lunch meeting I told you that I had other information for you but was wanting to make sure I had all the facts before I said anything?" I nod, vaguely remembering the conversation. "Well, I got the confirmation this morning and got here as fast as I could. I knew you needed to see this before the wedding. I told you I wanted our Families to become allies and I meant it. I could've brushed this under the rug but I didn't. I brought it to you. Another show of good faith to bridge a relationship between us."

I look at Liam and nod. He walks towards Victor which makes him back up out if the room and closes the door. I guess he wants to have a word with him.

I turn the envelope over and focus on the seal. Do I open it now or wait? I can see Sarah and Harper out of the corner of my eye still standing on the other side of the room. I think they're trying to give me a chance to make up my mind whether to open it or not. It feels slightly heavy with multiple items in there.

I tear the top open and pull out the papers from the inside. They aren't papers though but photos. Black and white photos. Some from afar and some close. As I keep turning photo after photo the horror floods my entire being. This can't be true. How is this possible? A cold sweat has now overtaken my body and I feel myself start to shake.

These photos are lies.

Wyatt wouldn't do this. He couldn't be a part of this. Does Mary know about this?

No! No! No!

"Kendall?" I hear a voice off in the distance and when I look up from the photos I see Sarah and Harper slowly walking toward me like they've cornered a wounded animal.

"I…I can't be here. I need to leave…NOW!" I scream. I shove the photos back into the envelope and swing the door open.

I see Liam and Victor still standing there in each other's faces.

"How long ago was this taken?" I ask Victor.

"Most are from last night but some have happened within the last few hours," he answers.

"Kendall, what is in the envelope?" Liam questions.

I shove them to his chest. He grabs them and tears it open.

"Do you know where this was taken?" I ask.

"Yes. I have the address my guy gave me," Victor says glancing at his phone.

"Give it to Frankie." I point to Frankie who is now walking up to us with a hand in his jacket. Brent is not far behind.

I see the wide-eyed shock on Liam's face and know we are on the same page.

I step on something and almost trip. I look down and see I'm in my wedding dress. A dress for my wedding. A wedding that was supposed to happen today. It's happening right now.

I walk back into the room where Harper and Sarah are still standing. "Get me out of this," I demand and start to reach for the zipper and buttons. My mind keeps going over the photos I just examined. Liam is barking orders in his phone and snapping at Frankie.

Sarah and Harper move fast to help me out of my wedding dress, shoes, and jewelry. Finally, after some work, I'm standing there in only a bra and panty set. Now what? I can't leave here in a robe. Shit!

"Here." Harper goes over to the corner of the room and grabs for a black bag. "I brought it with me because I'm going over to Gabe's house after this."

Inside, she has a pair of dark wash jeans, a blue T-shirt with some rock band on it, and a pair of converse shoes. I pull on every item then head for the door. I peer back at Sarah and Harper and give a sad smile, nod, then open the door.

"Let's go," I say and my men flank me and Victor as I walk out the side door of the church to avoid any guest.

"My men and I will follow you in case you need back up. We already have a few men in place around the area waiting for my command," Victor says as our cars are pull up.

"Thank you," is all I want to say at moment, but I know I need to say more to him especially since he is the reason I have this knowledge. I climb in the passenger side of the car as Frankie takes the driver's seat. Liam has settled in the back and is still on the phone.

Frankie has the address in his navigation and we hit the road with Victor on our tail. Once we hit the highway, Frankie floors it.

"How far out is it?" I ask and turn to Frankie.

"About twenty minutes outside the city," he says never taking his eyes off the road.

The silence in the car is deafening and my mind is reeling.

"Kendall?" I'm snapped back from my thoughts by Liam's voice.

"What?" I say harsher than I mean to.

"We have confirmation of the photos. They're real," he tells me. "Nathan was right about this part."

I feel my heart splinter then shatter into a million pieces.

After a bit, we pull down a dirt road. Trees block the view in every direction so I can't see into the property. This is a first-rate place to hide your dirty little secrets.

"Whose property is this?" I ask hoping for one last moment that this can't be true.

Wyatt loves me. He'd never do anything to hurt or cause me pain.

"The Dawsons own it." The final nail in the coffin. I place my head between my knees and focus on my breathing.

In your nose, out your mouth. In your nose, out your mouth. Get your shit together. You are the Head of your Family and you have people counting on you.

When the car comes to a stop, we get out and walk to the front of the car. In my gut something is not right about this. It feels off but there is no time to waste. Any moment now and the Dawsons will be alerted that I have left the church and will be out to find me. We need to get our plan in motion.

"I need a gun," I demand and Frankie pulls a 9mm out of one of his holsters. He hands it to me and I check the safety before turning to Liam and Frankie. Brent is jogging to us, bringing up the rear with a few other men. I can see Victor's car coming into view. I need to get this done and get out of here.

"What do we know?" I ask my men.

"There are two guys around the safe house. We aren't sure if there are any on the inside," Brent says.

"Can we take out the two silently and then case the inside?" I ask.

"Yes, I have the men in place. They are waiting on your call."

"Do it now."

Less than a minute later we are charging at the safe house and have the 'all clear' to enter. Frankie goes first and I see it is a two room cabin. It's dusty and has the décor of an office. Nothing warm and inviting. There is a small kitchen off in the corner, a TV from the nineties with rabbit ears on a round table, and a few chairs. Frankie goes to the first closed door, opening it to scans it. Bathroom. He slowly walks to the last door and swings it wide. He rushes inside and we all take steps toward it.

I walk into the room, and in the middle, is a bed with someone in it. The person is bound by hands and feet to the head and foot board. They have a cloth bag over their head but I can tell it's a woman. Her hair is the same as my natural color and the shirt she has on shows she has breasts, even with baggy clothes on. I approach the bed and see the bindings are rubbing her skin raw. She hasn't moved since we marched in but I know she's alive because her chest is rising and falling. I reach for the bag and lift it away.

I gasp at the woman in front of me. It is in this moment I know nothing will ever be the same again in my life. Gone is the naïve girl who fell head over heels in love with a boy. Gone is the girl with a bleeding heart who was always concerned for other's well-beings.

Replaced is a woman who has a heart of ice. Replaced is a woman who shows no mercy for anyone. I will be the one who has the last laugh. I will be the one who stands taller and commands a room. The Family responsible for this won't know what has hit them until after the floor crumples under their feet. I will be the last face they see before a bullet enters between their eyes. My blood is boiling and I am going to make them pay if it is the last thing I do.

Something must startle the woman awake because she opens her eyes in that moment, and once she does my world turns on its axis.

"MOM…"

CHAPTER TWENTY-FIVE

"Do you think it's weird that she didn't really react to seeing me?" I ask Liam and Frankie. "It was like she was only concerned about Victor."

I'm super confused about seeing her. I thought I'd have some sort of reaction or connection but there wasn't one. She looked right in the same green eyes I share with her and glossed over me.

"I feel like this entire situation is suspect," Liam offers. "Be vigilant with all of your surroundings."

"Why didn't Victor allow me to ride in the van with her?"

"Not sure, but it's something we need to look into."

The team pulls up to Victor's warehouse after a long drive out toward the desert. My mind is still reeling from seeing who I believe to be my mother. Victor had a doctor in one of the vans he brought and she's getting looked over on the way here.

"Do you think it's really her?" I ask Liam.

"It appears to be. She's older than when I last saw her obviously, but it looks as though she's kept good company with a doctor and hasn't let herself age too much."

"Definitely had some work done," Frankie throws his two cents in.

"Should we push for answers now or wait until she's ready to talk?"

If she's been traumatized over the years I want to make sure she's in the right state of mind.

"Let's see how she responds to a few questions before we throw the gambit at her. Watch her movements when answering and her eyes," Liam offers then turns to look at me. "Don't discredit your gut or think you're being paranoid. If something inside you tells you it's not right, listen to it, then plan accordingly."

I nod as the knot in my stomach tightens.

My phone rings again for the tenth time. It's been blowing up since I left the church. I know I'll have to speak with Wyatt soon, but right now I need to focus on what's happening in the next few minutes.

"Are you going to answer?" Frankie asks.

"I need more answers before we can talk. Right now my focus needs to be on my not-so-dead mother." He and Liam both nod as the car comes to a halt. "Do we have our guys ready?"

"Everyone is here and in place to protect you. Don't worry about the Dawsons or anyone else, just focus on Rachel. She's the one who might give us the answers we need to find out who else was behind the murder of your dad and brother."

"Then let's go get those answers."

We get out of the car and all of my men surround me as we walk toward the door to the warehouse Victor just entered. We have five full SUVs and four vans in our crew with men to support this venture.

We don't have to walk far before Victor greets us.

"Rachel seems to be in overall good health, just a few minor scratches. The doctor is patching her up right now."

"How did you get the info that the Dawsons were holding her?"

"I've had a guy watching them for a while now. It's always good to have an eye and ear on your closest *friends*," Victor says.

"Why would the Dawsons want to hurt someone from the

Family? I thought we all shared a common interest and work together?" I ask.

"You're new to this but the Dawsons and Falcones have been trying to wipe us out for a while now. Take Las Vegas for themselves. They are the most money hungry men I've ever met. They'll stop at nothing to get what they want. I'm shocked Adam lasted as long as he did."

"I killed Adam because he was a disloyal rat," I state.

"He never did like sharing his toys. Adam was difficult to work with and all the Families knew it. He knew his days were numbered when you were voted in." Victor shrugs, not seeming to care that a man who he worked with for two decades was killed.

The doctor comes out a few moments later pocketing a pair of gloves. "Her wrists and ankles were a little raw but I put some ointment and bandages over them. They'll need to be cleaned and changed daily to avoid infection. I've left some supplies on the desk in the room. She's alert and wants to speak with you," he says to Victor.

"Of course. Mitch will see you home." Victor gestures toward a man by the door.

The doctor nods to us and takes his leave.

"Rachel seems to know you very well," Liam says after the doctor is out of earshot.

"She came to me after the fire." He crosses his arms over his chest in a defensive manner. "I helped hide her all these years. Gave her a new identity and money. I've had someone watching her all this time to ensure her safety. What happened to Nick was tragic and I thought it was what he would've wanted. Had I known Lexi—Kendall was alive I'd have reunited them decades ago."

"Can we go see her?" I ask.

"Of course. She might struggle a bit seeing as she thought you were murdered. She was terrified for a long time after that horrifying night. It took a long time for her to recover."

Victor walks us down a hall with several doors. It's like a

bunker of rooms with beds and conference rooms. I'd probably say this is where he holds all his important meetings with his men. When we walk into the room where Rachel is we find her in new clothes lacing up her boots. Other than the bandages on her wrists you'd never be able to tell she'd been kidnapped.

"Rachel, the doctor says you have just a few minor scratches and you'll be fine in the next few days," Victor announces as we all walk in. His voice is different when he speaks with her. As if they're very familiar with each other.

"I'll be fine." She chances a look in my direction and the breath leaves my lungs.

We share so many similarities that someone might mistake us for sisters.

"Is it true you really are Lexi? I mean you like so much like me but I was told you were killed," Rachel says then looks over my shoulder. "Oh, Liam, you made it out alive too! Is there anyone else? Or just the two of you?"

"Sarah is alive. She and Liam raised me all these years."

I'm no expert, but if I'd just found out that my child, the only child that survived an arson-murder, was alive I'd be all over them wanting to embrace them and never let them go. Rachel seems so far removed it's almost like she wants to keep her distance from us.

"Rachel go and give your daughter a hug. I know you haven't seen her in almost two decades but I'm sure she'd love one," Victor pushes, seeming to read my mind.

"Yes, of course," Rachel obeys and makes her way over to me. "I'm sorry but the last few weeks have been a nightmare."

She opens her arms and I take one step into her embrace. It's cold and nothing like what Sarah or Mary give. I keep thinking some sort of feeling is going to burst out of me but my emotions seem to have shut off. The awkwardness drags on and I'm the one who steps back. I give a polite smile and stand back next to Liam.

"Maybe we can catch up later after we get through with business," I say. Maybe we just need some time to get to know each other.

"That would be nice." She smiles back but it doesn't meet her eyes.

"Rachel, go to the room across the hall and get some rest. We've got some things to discuss and then we can get some food," Victor instructs.

Rachel nods and walks right past us out of the room.

"Fucking weird," Frankie mumbles under his breath.

"Kendall, have a seat and lets discuss our next moves. Liam and your other guy can wait out in the hall." He waves his hand toward the door as he takes a seat behind the desk in the room.

"I'd prefer Liam stay but Frankie do you mind rounding up the crew and letting them know our plans for later?"

"Yes, Ms. Chapman," Frankie replies then exits the office. Brent is right outside the door waiting for instruction and will stay there until Frankie gets back.

I take the seat opposite Victor but Liam remains standing behind my chair.

"So, what do you suggest our next move should be?" I ask.

"I'd think it's obvious that we'll need to band together and take out the Dawson Family," he states matter of factly.

"You can't take out an entire Family without a majority vote of the other Families." Liam speaks before I can.

"I know that," Victor snaps. "You have my vote, all we need is for Bishop to side with us but I think after he hears all the evidence he'll have to vote our way."

"Exactly what evidence are you talking about?" Liam asks. "Right now all we have is Rachel found in an abandoned house."

The look on Victor's face is murderous. His patience has left the building when he looks from Liam to me. "I thought you'd want to get revenge for your family," he snaps.

"Oh, I plan on getting revenge but I'm not going to just jump into to something without a plan in place." I interlock my fingers over my crossed legs. "Those involved will wish to never have been born."

"As you should."

"What else do you have to incriminate the Dawsons in murdering my family?"

"Rachel has a lot on Bobby and his dealings with Nick. I'll have her come tell you more in a little bit, but from the conversations I've heard, quite a few guys from his family were involved that fateful day." According to my many conversations with Liam, I know this to be the truth. There were at least three of Bobby's men there that night. "There was also some talk about Nick and Mary having an affair and that is what ultimately pushed Bobby over the edge to take out your family."

Mary was sleeping with my dad? Her best friend's husband? I'm not sure I can believe that.

"You have no proof of this. It all seems like speculation and a bunch of locker room gossip," Liam says.

I reach back and place a hand on his to try to calm him. The last thing we need is for us to fight while trying to sort all this out.

"Bobby also tried to set me up for the murder of his oldest daughter a few years ago."

This catches my attention. Liam has always told me that if you sit back and listen long enough, the more comfortable a person feels the more they will reveal.

"What do you mean? You're saying Avery's murder was by his own hand and he set you up to take the fall?

"I'm saying there have been rumors that the oldest wasn't his and he made it look as though it was done by one of the other Families. If you speak with Rachel she'll tell you all about the history between your family and the Dawsons."

"And what do you think is Bobby's ultimate goal?"

"I believe he wants to wipe out all the Families and rule Las Vegas by himself. You've been around him for a while now. Haven't you seen the way he demands to be the one in charge of things? Even bringing you into the fold was a power move for him. I was trying to quietly find out if you were Lexi but he bulldozed the entire situation. Things might've went a little more smoothly with the transition if Bobby didn't try to exert his power by pushing Adam out of the way. He has an agenda. Look how you and Wyatt were thrown together. Did you really get a choice? Think about it. You even have one of his men as your guard. He probably reports back to Bobby twice a day."

He's got me on that last one for sure.

"I think I'd like to speak with Rachel before we make any moves going forward," I say. "She seems to play a large role in all the conversations."

"I think you're wise for you age, Kendall. I absolutely agree to you speaking with your mom. I've got food being delivered. Why don't we all sit down and chat with a bite to eat."

We walk out of the office and head down the hall to a conference room that is set up for a feast while Victor leaves to retrieve Rachel.

Liam looks skeptical. "Be on alert. Something is off."

I nod but don't get the chance to reply as Rachel and Victor walk in.

"Let's eat and talk," Victor says.

Over the next several minutes we gather our plates of food and sit down at a table. Liam stays by the door to let us talk.

"Where have you been all these years?" I ask Rachel.

She wipes her mouth with her napkin and smiles. She seems more relaxed now.

"I've been all over, never stayed at one place for too long. Vic gave me a new identity with each move. The most recent was California before I was apprehended by Bobby."

"Really? And you never remarried or had any more kids?" I ask.

She peeks a glance at Victor before answering. "No, moving around always made it difficult to have long lasting relationships. It was just better to keep things casual."

After a while I lean back in my chair and focus on Victor. "What are your plans to draw and take Bobby out? You have to know he's not going down without a fight. Like you've said he's a powerful man and I can't see him not bringing in Arturo with his family to help in this battle."

"I've got just the thing that is going to serve Bobby up on a silver platter to me," Victor smugly states. "You'll see soon. As far as Arturo is concerned, he'll fall right into line when the entire Dawson Family is wiped out. He'll have no choice but to stand by us or meet the same fate as his best friend."

Does this include Gracie? Surely they wouldn't harm innocent women and the children.

"Rachel—"

"Mother…call me mother, Lexi." Her voice sounds stern almost chastising.

Before I can respond a few of Victor's men come barging in with someone bound and gagged with a bag over their head. My heart sinks to my stomach when the bag is pulled off and Mary cowers away from the men in a sobbing mess.

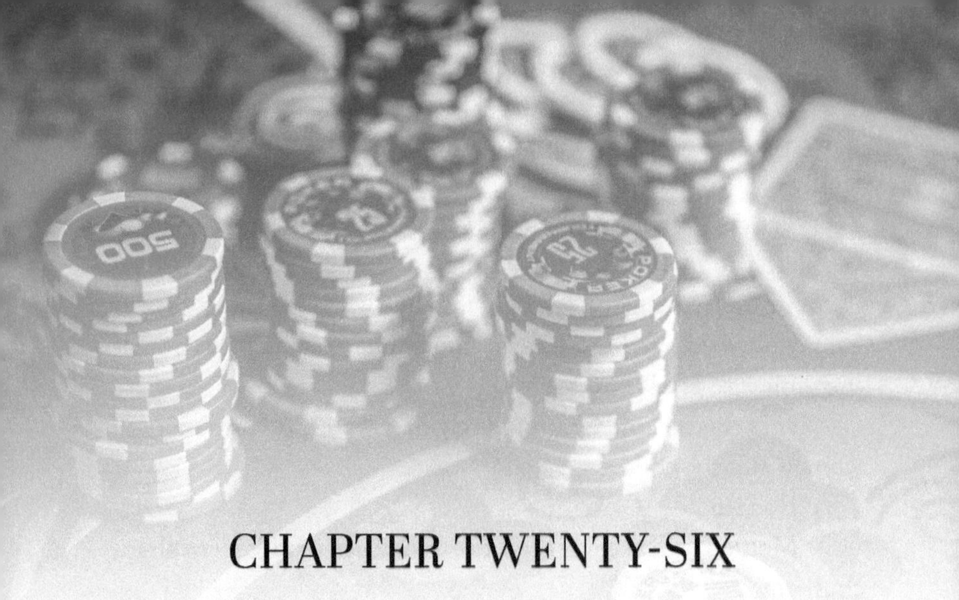

CHAPTER TWENTY-SIX

MY HAND IMMEDIATELY GOES TO THE BACK OF MY waistband for my gun.

"What is the meaning of this?" I raise my voice and move over to where she is on the floor.

Liam has his hand tucked in his jacket, most likely on his gun, and in a stance ready to take out the two guys who brought Mary in. I start untying her wrists as her body shakes with fear.

"Don't worry, Mary. Everything will be fine," I say trying to calm her.

"Bring her over to the chair and let her sit down," Victor instructs as I loosen the last bindings on her feet.

Walking her over to the chair I make sure she's steady before turning to Victor. "What the hell is she doing here?" I demand.

"You asked what I had to lure Bobby out and here she is. My guys were able to grab her easily in the church as everyone was scrambling."

"We don't use innocent women and children," I lash out and block Mary from his sight. This is going to get out of hand if someone doesn't stop this right now. Mary should never have been a part of any of this.

"Hello, little homewrecker," I hear a mocking voice and turn to find Rachel staring daggers at Mary.

What the hell?

"Ra—Rachel? Is it really you?" Mary stutters in disbelief. Her expression is as if she's looking at a ghost.

"Oh, it's me alright in the living flesh. Bet you didn't think you'd ever see me again, huh?" Rachel has turned into a completely different person now. Gone is the timid, terrified woman who was taken to an abandoned safehouse.

"But how? They said you were shot with Nick and Thomas and left in the burning house. What is going on?" Mary is in a tailspin trying to wrap her head around seeing my mother alive.

"Yeah, I bet you were just so happy when you got the news, weren't you?"

"What? Never. We were best friends, like sisters. How can you say that? I was devastated when Bobby told me what happened to you, Nick, and the kids."

Rachel looks over at the two guys who brought her in. "Tie her to the chair and put some tape over her mouth. I'm tired of listening to her annoying voice." The guys jump at the command to do as they're told.

I'm shocked because Rachel isn't Victor but they follow her orders. When try to get around me to Mary, I stand tall daring them to come closer. They both stop and look over at Victor as how to proceed.

"Rachel, go splash some water on your face and calm down. You've had a rough couple days," Victor orders. Rachel gives him a death glare but does as she's told. Once she walks out of the room, Victor turns to me and lets out a huff, as if exhausted.

"It's just a precaution, Kendall. This way she won't get hurt or in the way of things. She'll be fine." He waves his hand around dismissively.

"Not one person is going to lay a hand on her or tie her up. She'll stay right in this chair and not speak another word unless she's spoken to," I reply and pray to God Mary complies because I won't let these men treat her this way. "Right, Mary?" I turn my head and plead with my eyes for her to understand the situation we are in right now.

She gives a nod and Victor waves at the men to stand down.

I turn to Victor. "What the fuck is going on? We haven't even agreed to take on the Dawsons and you kidnap Mary? What really is your plan?" I ask.

"I want us to merge our Families together and rule Las Vegas. We can cut the others out and this will be our town."

"Merge our Families? How would that even work? We don't even peddle in the same areas. You deal with the hard drugs and we work in more legit dealings." Liam has moved further into the room towards me and Mary and I can see Frankie and Brent standing just outside the door ready to come in at a moment's notice. "Merge how?" I demand again.

Victor places both hands on the desk and leans forward. "By marrying the two Families together. Just like you and Bobby's spawn were going to do."

"Wait, you think you and I should marry? And merge our Families?" My first reaction is to vomit all of the food we just ate. The second is that maybe I heard him wrong. The guy is in his mid to late fifties for god's sake.

"What the fuck?" Liam shouts as a loud shriek echoes off the walls from Rachel.

Frankie and Brent blocking the door after allowing her back in, barring anyone else from entering or exiting.

"How could you do this to me?" Rachel runs over to Victor and starts hitting him. "I gave you everything! You said after this summer we'd finally marry and be able to go out in public like a couple and be a family."

"Sit down and shut up." Victor shoves her into a seat. "You don't get a say. This has been the goal ever since I found Kendall."

"You said we'd rule this town together if I helped you. You

said I could come back after being in hiding and things would be as they were but better." She looks over at me and Mary. "It's all your fault!" She points at Mary. *"Why can't you get along with everyone like Mary does? Why can't you be more inviting? Why aren't you helpful and supportive like Mary? Mary, Mary, Mary* that's all I ever heard Nick say. I got so sick of trying to live up to the great and wonderful Mary. Then he wanted to get into more of the legit companies and leave the illegal side for the other Families to pick up but that meant a lot less money. He was a fool." It's like my mother is unhinged. "It was stupid, and of course *Bobby* was there to help like everything else in our lives. So I decided to make a plan of my own."

"RACHEL!" Victor tries to grab for her but she dodges his hands. "Rachel sit the fuck down and shut your mouth right now!" Victor grits his teeth.

Rachel is so in her head she doesn't even notice Frankie and Brent overpowering Victor's men or that Liam now has Victor on the ground, subdued. This is what I've been wanting to hear the whole time.

"I wanted to be part of a powerful Family, not one that was hanging up their coat. Victor was making moves and I knew he was going to start taking more of Las Vegas block by block. So I floated a few ideas to him and he ate them up. We started seeing each other in secret and I'd give all the inside information I could get to him and his guys. Once we had everything in place we waited for the right time to burn that house to the ground and kill everyone in it." She looks menacingly over at me. "Almost everyone."

"You're the one who killed my dad and brother?" I ask even though she just admitted as much.

Rachel clams up for a moment then pushes both hands through her hair and holds them on top of her head. "I wanted to be the queen of the city. I came from nothing until I met Nick in that casino. He promised me the world but after two kids he wanted to slow down and be more present at home. He was ruining everything I wanted and so I took care of him. I got rid of everything that was stopping me."

"You're a monster!" Mary says, horrified.

Rachel snaps her neck toward Mary, scrunching her face. Her eyes land on the desk and I realize what she's about to do. In a flash, Rachel grabs the letter opener and rushes across the short distance to where we are. I don't even have to think about my next move when I pull my gun from behind my back and fire two quick rounds into her chest. The impact from the bullets jolts her back and knocks her off her feet. She's lying on the floor in shock as she holds her bloody hand up to her face in disbelief.

Chaos ensues as the sound of gunfire erupts from all directions of the warehouse, but my focus is solely on the waste of space lying in front of me. "Those were for my dad and brother," I say looking into her eyes. "And this one is for me, you soulless bitch. I'm the only queen in this city." I force the trigger one more time hitting her right between the eyes and ending the life of a horrible, selfish person.

A hand touches my arm, startling me.

"Oh darling, I'm so sorry." Mary pulls me to her and holds me tight.

I don't feel anything right now. I'm completely numb.

"Kendall!" I hear shouted over gunshots. "Mary!"

Just as the sound of bullets cease Wyatt and Bobby barrel their way into the room. Both have a gun in each hand. Relief is evident on their faces when they see us untouched. As they rush over to us, Liam, Frankie, and Brent pull Victor up from the ground and bind his hands behind his back.

"You are never doing something like this again. Ever!" Wyatt declares.

"I'm so glad to see you," is all I say.

We both holster our weapons and embrace.

"Are you okay, honey? Do you need me to call the doc?" Bobby asks Mary as he checks her over.

"Seems like you got yourself in a pickle, Victor," Arturo says as he and his son Luca come into the room.

"I should've taken you out when I had the chance," Victor grits out.

"Maybe, but you didn't, and look where it's landed you." Arturo shrugs and pulls a chair up to sit down. "You've got a lot to answer for Victor, and I think we all are going to enjoy taking our time with you."

"Fuck you!"

"Who's the chick?" Luca asks of the dead body on the floor.

"That's Rachel Chapman, the woman who gave birth to me," I offer.

"What happened in here?" Ox Bishop strolls in looking like he's headed to a baseball game.

"Aren't bankers required to wear suits and ties to work?" Wyatt jokes at Ox's attire. He's wearing ripped jeans with a Las Vegas baseball jersey and a matching hat.

"And how do you not have a single drop of blood on you from the ambush outside?" Luca questions.

"First, I've got a hot date tonight, and second, you boys need to learn to work smarter not harder."

They both roll their eyes. Ox is just a few years older than them.

"Is it the woman you brought as your date to the fake wedding today?" Luca asks. "Gemma loved her but didn't get a chance to get her number."

"Yeah, probably not the best first date but I'm hoping the game tonight will make up for it."

These men act as though we don't have a warehouse full of dead bodies.

"So how are we going to play this?" Ox points over to Victor as he pulls up a seat next to Arturo.

"Let me get Mary settled first." Bobby ushers Mary out but not before grabbing me and thanking me for saving her.

"I'm so sorry you had to choose, my sweet girl," Mary cries while cupping my cheek with her hand.

"It was never a choice, Mary. I was never going to let something happen to you. You were always safe with me." She engulfs me in the biggest hug and kisses my cheek before leaving with Bobby.

Wyatt has me sit down and brings me a bottle of water to sip while we wait for Bobby to come back.

A few minutes later, when he returns, he pulls a chair up next to me and grasps my chin in his fingers making me look into his eyes. "I will forever be grateful to you for keeping my love safe. If there ever comes a time when you need a favor I will make everyone at my disposal available to you. I'm so happy my son married you."

"Married?" Victor interrupts, shocked. "You're already married?"

Both Bobby and I smile at each other before he gives my hand a pat and turns to Victor.

"About that, sorry your invitation was lost in the mail, Vic, but yes. These two crazy kids got married two nights ago.

~ TWO NIGHTS AGO ~

We all gather in Wyatt's living room going over the evidence Nathan was able to get for Liam. We knew Victor was behind a lot of the shipments being stolen and now we have the proof. It wasn't enough to wipe the entire organization out with so we needed something more. Something that would nail him to either Avery's murder or something to do with my parents being killed.

"I don't think he'll let the wedding happen. It's his last ditch effort to make a move on one of us," Wyatt says as we talk things over. "I think he'll do something to stop it."

"That'd be the perfect place to upend our family and leave us spiraling. It'll certainly make us look like fools," Bobby suggests.

"Nathan said Victor plans to approach Kendall right before the wedding starts," Liam tells us. "Everyone will be at the church and not realize until it's too late that she left Wyatt at the altar."

"But then the kids won't get married and all our planning and preparations will have been for nothing," Mary chimes in.

"These kids deserve to be happy and have their moment," Sarah agrees.

"We could always take ourselves down to the Little White Chapel tonight and get married." I giggle and wag my eyebrows at Wyatt. We'd already joked about eloping earlier in the week.

The room gets so quiet you could hear the clock on the wall ticking.

"It's not ideal but…" Mary is the first to speak up.

"Why not? Let's do it." Wyatt hops up from the couch. "Marry me tonight, babe."

Thinking it over it doesn't seem like a bad idea.

"Sounds good to me."

"We can video the wedding tonight and play it at the church. Have Harper and Gracie announce the happy couple already left for the honeymoon or something and to enjoy the reception. It's a perfect distraction to get everyone in place."

Everyone looks over to Wyatt and me for confirmation.

"I like it. Let's gather our people and make our way to Elvis!"

"I'm pretty sure if this mafia gig doesn't pan out Liam and I will have a career in Hollywood. Don't ya think, Victor?" I give him my sweetest smile.

"It was a nice wedding, although I think Elvis went a little long with the ceremony," Ox jokes. All the Dons were present at the wedding sans Victor, of course.

"You won't get away with this. I have contingency plans in place that will expose everyone if something happens to me,"

Victor argues. He tries to lift up out of his seat but Liam and Frankie shove him back down.

"Oh we will, Victor. I'm sure about it," Bobby says.

"Let's get the ball rolling shall we?" Arturo calls out. "I vote for the removal of Victor Slater and his organization from the Family. Total wipe out."

"I vote for removal and wipe out," Ox agrees.

"I vote for removal," Bobby states. "And total wipe out."

The room turns to me for my vote even though it's not needed.

"I vote for the removal also."

Arturo bangs his hand on the table like a gavel in a courtroom.

Judge.

Jury.

Executioner.

"Well, my time is up. You guys have a nice night since this is a personal matter," Ox says as he goes to stand. "Make sure to make the bastard suffer." He shakes all our hands then heads out the door and out of sight.

"Should we do this here or back at our place?" Luca asks.

"Let's take him to ours. We've got the room prepped and ready," Bobby says as our men gather Victor up and push him out to a waiting van.

Two hours later Arturo and Luca are finishing up with their session with Victor. Bobby and Arturo flipped a coin to see who started Victor's torture and who was going to end it. Victor is strung up on a meat hook that's attached to a beam from the ceiling.

During Arturo's one on one time we learned Victor had brought in a man named Lorenzo 'Enzo' Perez and a gang to intercept shipments and cause havoc to a lot of businesses he owned.

Victor also paid Enzo to go after Luca's wife by blowing up their plane.

"He's all yours, Bobby," Luca says wiping his bloody hands with a towel as Arturo does the same. "Wish we were the ones to finish the job."

Victor looks like he belongs in a meat locker. He's stained in blood as it drips down on the floor towards the drain. They really worked him over good.

"Have the doctor pump him full of adrenaline," Wyatt says as he cracks his fingers and neck. His sleeves are rolled up and he looks ready to fight.

I'm seated in a chair positioned far enough away from getting splattered with blood but close enough to hear what Victor confesses. The doctor has been on hand since we arrived and has made sure Victor stays alive to feel every bit of pain.

"Tell me, Vic, did you know growing up I was known in my neighborhood as 'Bobby the Butcher?' Everyone knew not to steal from our block because I would find them and cut their hands off." Bobby circles Victor. "You stole a lot from me, didn't you?" He waits for a response but Victor just hangs there.

Wyatt is over by a tray off to the side and picks up two knives.

"You're the one who was intercepting our shipments and blocking our vendors from delivering our goods. You thought we'd fold but we didn't. You tried to turn me against my best friend. Then you helped killed my other best friend and murder his innocent child."

Victor remains silent, but when Wyatt walks over, he wastes no time stabbing him in the shoulder with one of the knives then follows up with a matching stab on the other shoulder. Victor lets out a cry like a wounded animal and it bounces off the walls.

"Please—"

"Did my best friend Nick beg for his life you piece of shit?!" Bobby yells as he punches him in the stomach.

Bruises have already started to form from the beating Arturo and Luca gave him so I know he must be sensitive in those areas.

"I—I—"

"You what?"

Wyatt has another two knives in his hands, and he doesn't wait for Bobby as he plants those in Victor's back jolting him forward on the hook.

"You're lucky Ox isn't here; he's an expert with knives," Wyatt says from behind Victor.

Bobby pulls out his gun from his waistband as Wyatt walks over to the mini stove in the corner. He turns to me and nods.

"The most important and devastating thing you did was murder my baby girl, Avery," Bobby says. "Did you give the order or did you pull the trigger?"

Victor hasn't lifted his head and continues to moan. A shot rings out and I resist the urge to cover my ears as the sound echoes in the room. When I look at Victor he has a hole in his thigh.

"She was shot three times," Bobby says louder as Victor begins to scream and shake. "Once in the thigh. Once in the stomach. And once in the chest."

Wyatt comes over with a poker in his hand and places it over the hole in the front and back of Victor's gaping thigh wound cauterizing the blood flow. He steps back as Bobby shoots him next in the stomach then the chest. Wyatt does the same routine and jabs Victor with the hot poker to staunch the blood. Bobby shoots him again three more times but on the other side of his body while Wyatt continues to seal the holes. Victor is a mess and his body hangs heavy on the hook.

Bobby walks over to the tray and picks up a jagged looking knife then returns to stand right in front of Victor.

He stops and turns to me. "Sweetheart, did you want some time with Vic before I put the last blow on him?" Bobby has been so calm during this entire process I almost don't know how to respond. He speaks as if we're out ordering a meal.

I shake my head and find my voice. "I got the person responsible for my dad and brother." Adam and Rachel are both dead and will never be able to harm another innocent life.

"Okay, darling." He nods and turns back around.

I stand when Wyatt approaches me. We watch as Bobby shoves the jagged knife in the center of Victor's stomach beside the bullet wound and twists. Victor, who was passed out, gasps in agony. Bobby motions for the doctor and he comes over and injects Victor with a clear syringe.

"He'll bleed out slowly now and the pain will be excruciating," Wyatt inform me. "Let's go get cleaned up and head home."

"Okay."

Wyatt takes me by the hand and we leave the room and the last bit of the past behind.

Now we can focus on our future.

EPILOGUE

"Thanks, Frankie. Let me know if everything goes smoothly with the shipment coming in tonight," I say as I exit the vehicle.

"Yes, ma'am. Enjoy your evening," Frankie says from the front seat next to my driver.

Over the last few years, Frankie has become integral to the organization. He and Liam now work side by side on everything. It's been a big help to delegate and have them each tackle a different area and keep it all running like a well-oiled machine.

Just as I'm about to open the door to the house my phone rings. Seeing who it is puts a smile on my face. "Hey."

"Girl, how do you feel about getting into the car business?" Harper asks as her greeting.

"Uh—I'm not sure." I lean back against the wall by the front door. "Are we talking new or used cars?"

"I got an inside tip that a very large vehicle manufacturer is shutting down and we could possibly buy it up for pennies on the dollar, not to mention we could use Dad's company to ship the product over for little to nothing for us. This could put us over the billion-dollar mark as a company."

"Is it going to be profitable long term?"

"The numbers say yes but before I deep dive into it I wanted to run it by you first," she responds. "I've got a few other things in the works but this is at the top right now."

Harper has been absolutely fantastic running the legit side of the business the past few years. She's really come into her own and has stepped up her work ethic.

"Put pen to pad and I'll stop by the office when it's ready and we can decide if it's the right move for the company," I offer. "Are we talking about selling only in Nevada or nationally?"

"I thought we'd stay in Nevada at first then branch out, but that might change once we run the numbers."

"Let me know when you've got it ready and we'll talk it out."

"Good. Are we still on for tomorrow night?"

"Yes, ma'am! It'll be nice to have all the girls out for a night of fun while the guys play poker at Ox's place."

"See you tomorrow."

"Okay, bye."

As I open the door, I'm met with the smell of delicious pasta. Carmen is a heaven-send to our family and we are so lucky to have her with us. I'm also assaulted by the noise of squealing as my one-year-old twins—who refuse to walk because their grandparents never let their feet hit the ground—crawl at lightning speed toward me.

"Mommy's home!" I hear Wyatt announce as I bend down to scoop the little munchkins up and kiss them all over.

"How are my babies today, huh? Were y'all good for Mimi?" I ask. We refer to Mary as Mimi and Sarah as Nana.

Wyatt looks so casual in shorts and a T-shirt as he comes over and leans in for a long kiss only to be pushed away by our son, Nicholas. Our daughter, who is much smaller than her brother snuggles close to me as her brother hugs us both to him. He doesn't like for anyone other than his sister to have my attention. Wyatt didn't like it at first but loves how protective he is with me and Zara Avery. Zara was born four minutes after her brother. Nick weighed in at six pounds five ounces, but Zara was barely five pounds. She's been catching up over the months but she's still tiny.

"Let me take your bag and piece to the bedroom," Wyatt offers retrieving my purse from my shoulder and my gun from the waistband at my back, making sure to cop a feel as he relieves me of my steel.

"Thanks, honey."

I walk the kids to the living room where we sit down and start playing with blocks and toys as we wait for dinner to be ready. Wyatt rolls the soft squishy ball with Nick as Zara and I press the buttons on the musical stand that lights up.

The front door opens and Mom and Dad come in with bags of things. The kids lose interest in Wyatt and me and crawl over to Sarah and Liam as they sit on the floor with us.

"What are you guys doing here? Not that I'm unhappy to see y'all but I thought you had plans tonight."

"We do and it's taking care of our babies," Mom says as she opens her bag full of toys and clothes. The babies cheer.

"Tonight?"

"I've got something for us to do." Wyatt stands and holds out his hand for me to take.

"Should I change?"

"Shorts and a shirt are fine."

After I change we kiss the spaghetti-faced babies and head out. Wyatt takes the back roads to our spot out on the lake. He pulls out a large towel and blanket with a picnic basket of Carmen's pasta and bread.

"How was the meeting with the Canadians?" I ask between bites.

"It went like we thought. They know better than to try and run guns in our territory but needed to be reminded of who they're dealing with. Dad made it very clear that next time we won't stop at just the seven body bags we delivered to them."

"Hopefully they'll listen now."

"Time will tell." He shrugs.

After we eat we snuggle up with the blanket as the sun has already set and the stars have come out.

"It's really beautiful out here at night," I say as Wyatt lays me down on the towel and hovers over me.

"Not as beautiful as you are," he says and plays with my heart-shaped necklace. Inside is a picture of the twins on one side and a picture of us on our wedding day on the other.

When I was moving all of my stuff from the apartment to our house I found my box of keepsakes from when I was little. Inside, I found the two items that choked Wyatt up. I'd never seen Wyatt show his emotional side but when I pulled out this necklace he lost it. He couldn't believe I'd kept it all those years. It was the last gift he'd ever given me before the fire happened. Then I pulled out the sandy brown bear named Xander I'd stolen from his house and slept with most nights. He cried and hugged me so tight.

The phone rings in Wyatt's pocket.

"Hey, is everything okay?" Wyatt asks. He listens for a moment then holds the phone away from his ear. "Xander's not in the crib. The twins won't lay down without him."

"Oh, he's in the dryer. He stunk to high heaven, so I washed him before your mom got there this morning."

We planned to give the teddy bear to our first baby but having twins meant they had to share him. They both love him as much as I did and don't fight over him. We tried to put them in separate cribs when they became mobile but Nick always found a way over into his sissy's bed during the night. We finally gave up and let them sleep in the same crib. Most mornings, when we go into their room, they each have a hand holding onto the teddy bear while they sleep.

Once Wyatt hangs up we lay there holding each other.

"Did you ever think this would be your life? Married with a wife and a dad to twin babies?"

He tightens his arms around me. "Never thought happiness or love was ever in my future until you surfaced again and brought me back to life."

"You always say the sweetest things." I kiss his lips.

"Only for you."

THE END

Thank you for reading Hidden Queen! I hope you loved it and will leave a review. I wrote this book in 2016 when I first started to dabble in the writing world. At the time I had no intention of ever releasing it or letting anyone read it. Originally this was going to be a duet and I was going to leave it on a major cliffhanger but changed my mind. When I started thinking and writing The Prince I knew Hidden Queen would make a great second book and decided to make my Las Vegas world into a series.

Follow me along this journey for updates on the current and next project.

Goodreads
www.goodreads.com/author/show/48624101.Amber_Allee

Facebook Page
www.facebook.com/AmberAlleeAuthor

Facebook Group
www.facebook.com/groups/655580198616583

Instagram
www.instagram.com/author.amberallee

ALSO BY AMBER ALLEE

Las Vegas Mafia Series

THE PRINCE

HIDDEN QUEEN

BISHOP (Coming Soon!)

ACKNOWLEDGMENTS

Kevin, your support has no bounds and I love you more every day. Thank you for taking on the workload with the kids so I could get this done. You are the glue that holds us together! Love you so much.

Mom and Dad, you guys have been with me on every journey I've ever done supporting me. Romance books might not be your thing but you are still there as my biggest cheerleaders the entire time. Thank you.

Sharlyn, thank you for always listening and supporting me. We have gotten into some wild adventures and I can't thank you enough for being there for me.

Erica Marselas, girl, you have been the best navigator through the entire publishing process. Thank you for all your comments, notes, calls, text, and emails. Your feedback has been a tremendous help finding the missing links and pulling the story together.

Kristen Portillo, I think I will continue to say this every time because it's true: you are a miracle worker! Thank you for always being a Beta and Editor for me. I'd be lost without you and my books would suffer if it weren't for your feedback.

Stacey Blake, thank you for making the inside of the books beautiful. You amaze me with your creativity.

To the Readers, thank you so much for continuing to support me through this journey. Your reviews and kind messages fuel me to be a better writer.

To the Promoters and Influencers, thank you for getting my book out there and seen by the readers. You guys make such a difference for indie authors like me and I am so thankful for each and every one of you.

ABOUT THE AUTHOR

 Amber Allee is a brand-new author with her debut novel *The Prince* released in early 2024 and *Hidden Queen* in June 2024. She started writing in 2015 but finally pulled the trigger to publish recently. Amber loves to write about romance, drama, and suspense along with hot alpha heroes.

She lives in the great state of Texas in the same town she grew up in. She lives there with her husband and two kids. When she isn't writing, Amber can be found under blankets reading or playing games with her family. She loves to travel and shop. She is the lover of wearing animal print and everything bling!